THE COLOR
OF GREED

EREBUS TALES: Book II

Norman Westhoff

IGUANA

Copyright © 2021 Norman Westhoff
Published by Iguana Books
720 Bathurst Street, Suite 303
Toronto, ON M5S 2R4

Publisher: Meghan Behse
Front cover design: Ruth Dwight, designplayground.ca

ISBN 978-1-77180-490-5 (paperback)
ISBN 978-1-77180-491-2 (epub)

This is an original print edition of *The Color of Greed*.

For my children and their loving partners:
Ben and Anna Westhoff
Alex Westhoff and Sean McCormick
Julia Westhoff and Jay Senter

CONTENTS

CHARITABLE DONATION

Fay Del Campo knew she was stepping into a trap. It might be fanged or it might be fur-lined, but when Sir Oscar Bailey summoned her, she guessed his intentions immediately and mustered her high cards.

She remembered this place oh-so-well. Two years past, at this very suite in the Matterhorn Hotel, she'd laid a trap of her own, bluffing Oscar into letting her be part of the first — and so far, only — mission he dispatched to Antarctica. It took a bit of cajoling — some called it blackmail — before he agreed to let her join his crew, to be his liaison for locals who might otherwise object to an alien race invading their land to haul away minerals.

After so long without contact, his phone call surprised her. In his masterly and disarmingly casual tone, he mentioned that he was in Zürich on business and felt like they needed to catch up. Would she care to renew their acquaintance? No hard feelings, etc., etc.

Fay checked her hand mirror, tucking a sprout of gray hair into the still-plentiful dark-red curls. She was not about to tint the gray. Not yet, anyway. She knocked.

Oscar opened the door and stood at attention, not one feature changed in the past fifteen months. The same piercing steel-gray eyes, pug nose, thin-set lips and prominent chin, offset by glossy white hair and clear smooth facial skin. His pores emitted the male scent of verbena. How sweet it would be to have Oscar's team working on her own body, forestalling the whole aging process.

His figure always reminded her of a bowling pin, solid but balanced. His casual uniform had not changed a bit: signature velvet robe, solid crimson except for a discreet white cross emblem sewn onto the left breast, cream-colored sash and matching scarf, anchored by a gold pin in the shape of a ring.

"Fay," beamed Sir Oscar. "So glad you could make it."

"Oscar. Thank you for the invitation. I was hoping that we could reconnect sometime."

"Of course. Let bygones be bygones." He drew back and gestured for her to sit, then glided across the room and opened a decanter. "A bit of Yukon Sherry?"

He still had a flair for the exotic. "Don't mind if I do. We hardly ever get Canadian imports in Switzerland anymore."

"A shame. I'll have to look into that. Do you think there's a market?"

"Among certain oenophiles, yes. Those who aren't troubled by their enlarged carbon footprint from consuming imported luxuries." She took a sip of the sherry and immediately regretted her judgmental display. This really was good stuff.

Oscar chuckled. "Just like the Orfea Del Campo we have come to know and love." He eyed her over the rim of his glass as he sipped. "One can hardly turn on the telly these days without encountering your charming persona. I was afraid you would be too busy for a chat."

If you only knew. All those public appearances, she was the person most qualified to make them. Yet they had come to serve another purpose: warding off the single-middle-aged-woman blues. She had become adept at dealing with velvet-sheathed daggers. "Never too busy to meet with you, Oscar."

"Excellent." He put the glass aside. "Look. I know you're still concerned that I might have designs on iridium rights in Antarctica."

"I should have been able to figure it from the get-go, but it was the Onwei tribe's old witch, Yoka Sutu, who put two and two together. The main reason you're so enthralled with big deposits of iridium is to put them to their main use."

"That use being…?" The bushy eyebrows rose.

"Coating ever-larger airships to navigate the caustic skies of the Earth's middle latitudes. This only makes sense if you wanted to ferry large quantities of something to, not from, Antarctica."

"I'm all ears."

"People, Oscar, farm families to till virgin soil that's been buried under ice for eons. Everyone knows that Canadian farmland is being swallowed up by rising sea levels. Another generation, you'll need to import food. The only country exporting meat or grain these days is China. Clearly this is a matter of national security." Fay felt the flush rising in her cheeks.

"Hear, hear," said Oscar.

She reached for her glass. "It won't hurt that you can turn a few bucks in the process."

Now Oscar turned mum, just a coy smile upon his lips.

Fay was quite sure that he had deliberated the whole scheme, and only refrained from a public announcement until he could line all of his ducks in a row. She aimed to flush him out. She tilted her head to study him. "Am I being overly alarmist?"

"I was naïve in my previous calculations. It seemed to make good business sense at the time. Now I realize that I need to factor in other variables."

"Such as?"

"Such as, number one: Is the stuff from down there really radioactive?" Oscar fixed his gimlet eyes on Fay as he posed the question.

"That was Keltyn SparrowHawk's conclusion," said Fay, hoping this would suffice. The truth wanted to surge out of her chest, but she was not inclined to break the bond of trust that the critically wounded geologist had forged with her. The radioactivity ploy that so upset the Onwei tribe was a desperate attempt to safeguard the iris stone from being used to coat more airships, or any other industrial use that Oscar's engineers might think of.

Fay was the only person in the developed world who knew the truth of the Erebus stone, that it was the finest and purest iridium to be found anywhere, that its industrial potential was unmatched. She aimed to keep it that way, to protect the Onwei from Oscar's designs.

He shut his eyes briefly. "So it was, and I don't wish to disparage her judgment, especially if she is not alive to defend it."

Fay shut her eyes too, squeezing them to blot the tears that were sure to follow. No one on this end knew Keltyn's fate, but the odds were way against her surviving a gunshot wound to the chest. The memory haunted Fay daily: she, Harry and Buck, threatened by hostile gauchos, had been forced to abandon Keltyn to the mercy of those few Onwei who cared anything for her.

She opened her eyes to search Oscar's as he probed hers for the truth. She needed to meet his gaze unflinchingly. "And the other variables?"

He blinked. "Competition. We can't let the Chinese get ahead of us in iridium technology. They could dominate global air transportation."

"They must have their own sources."

Oscar leaned back and twirled the stem of the sherry glass between his palms. "Here's what we know. Savant SparrowHawk spent time with their geologists as a graduate student. Her reports from China and Antarctica indicate that the ore from meteorite craters is less pure than that from volcanoes. The Chinese have their own craters in Siberia, but likely haven't been able to tap any volcanic sites yet." His fingers beat a staccato rhythm on the arm of the chair.

"But if they could . . .?"

"A big if. There are several on Kamchatka Peninsula, but that's one of the most remote places on earth."

Where there was a will... Fay's gaze locked into Oscar's. There might be a downside from her acting pushy, but so far, he had been surprisingly frank. "Any other factors holding you back?"

"Finding another qualified geologist, but I'm working on that."

Fay waited. She knew there was more.

The color rose in Oscar's cheeks. "There is one other impedance, Savant Del Campo, which is why I thought we should have a chat."

Uh-oh. Brow raised, she pictured the dagger being drawn from its velvet sheath.

"This NPU league that you founded. Perhaps you could edify me on its purpose."

"Native Peoples United? It's simply a cross-cultural consciousness-raising group. So many of the world's Indigenous tribes are threatened with extinction from environmental degradation. As an anthropologist who happens to have a media presence, leading such an effort fell to me."

"How noble an endeavor." Oscar's sarcasm dripped as thick as honey. "This all sounds quite straightforward as you describe it, so imagine my dismay to see recent advertisements threatening to boycott the Bailey line of consumer products."

Aha. The cat was out of the bag. She had suspected as much when he phoned. "Naturally, we hope it won't come to any measure so drastic."

"Indeed. Wouldn't you term it drastic to threaten a boycott for an act that hasn't happened yet?"

"You realize it would be too late for a boycott if we were to wait until you colonized Antarctica."

"Oh, here we go again. Savant Del Campo, you are the epitome of conjecture."

"Deny it, then," said Fay, her voice rising. "Go public and repudiate the whole idea once and for all."

"The idea may have crossed my mind, but it's a long way from clear. And if you know anything about Oscar Bailey, Savant, it's that he doesn't care to be bullied into making a decision."

She felt the blood pounding her temples. "So, this grand scheme could very well be put into play. I knew it."

"You imagine a lot, Savant, but you know nothing. I'm a cautious man, despite your reckless image of me. 'There's many a slip twixt cup and lip.' Which brings up another unpleasant matter."

Another one? Fay was sure that Oscar had already dealt all his cards.

"Bailey Enterprises has suffered a spate of unexplained accidents over the last few months."

Fay sat up. She had heard rumors from her own people.

"A boiler explosion here, a train derailment there. Broken windows, vehicles vandalized. Cyber-hacking activity has picked up significantly." Oscar's gimlet eyes pierced hers in the recounting. "None of these acts unique or even unusual, just more of them. Any idea why that might be, Savant?"

"How should I know, Oscar? Maybe your security needs beefing up."

"It certainly does now, although it's never been lax in the past. Actually, my people are pretty sure we're dealing with eco-terrorists. The only question is whether they are isolated or organized. No one has taken responsibility for the incidents. Yet."

"I see," said Fay. "That does put you in a predicament of how to respond."

"For now, but not for long. I've got an elite security detail analyzing the pattern of these 'accidents.' So." Oscar cocked his head to study Fay from a different angle. "You weren't aware of any of this?"

Fay jolted back. "Me? What makes you think that?"

"Just a wild guess, Savant." He set down his glass and clasped his hands. "Some of your group's ads have been rather inflammatory toward Bailey Enterprises. It occurred to me that perhaps certain segments of your membership might be less principled than yourself in achieving your goals."

Fay's mouth gaped open, but she recovered immediately. "Now, that *is* a wild guess, if I ever heard one."

Oscar smiled. "I'm glad to know that my conjecture is far-fetched." He tented his pudgy fingers. "On a more certain note, I happen to know that your group has fallen far short of its fund-raising goals."

"Don't you worry." Her heart skipped a beat. How was he privy to their proprietary data? "We have enough to keep running the ads, and our members are committed to implementing a boycott, if it comes to that."

"Perhaps yes, perhaps no. But you'll never reach your ambitious main goal. It's just a pipe dream."

"You mean relocating threatened Indigenous Peoples to safety. Yes, that will be a huge project. What concern is that of yours?"

"Perhaps we can reach another détente, Fay. Something you want for something I want." A gleam sparkled in those gimlet eyes.

Yes! He just took the bait. Fay could barely keep herself from gloating. The substantial time and effort that she had directed into threatening a boycott was about to pay off. Oscar was offering hush money. She tried to act shocked. "Are you trying to buy me off?"

"Goodness gracious." Wrists flipped up; head arched back. "Attempted bribery. Where could I ever have gotten such an idea? Is it so different from blackmail, Fay? Think about it. Just another business proposition."

Oscar had a point. Who was she to judge him, when she had resorted to the same tactics at their first meeting? She gathered herself. "What amount of a donation are we talking about?"

"Substantial, shall we say. It will have to come from one of my foundations, so as not to arouse suspicion. Let your people talk to mine. I'm sure we can work out something to everyone's satisfaction."

"I'm sure," said Fay. So, this is what being bought off felt like. Not nearly as shameful as she had imagined. She raised her empty glass and he rose to fill it.

Oscar handed her the glass back and raised his own. He flashed a full but closed-lipped smile. "To collaboration."

"Collaboration," said Fay. As the sherry tingled down her throat, she recalled the old saying – Machiavelli, was it? "Hold your friends close and your enemies closer."

I

BRIXA

Red, white, black and pale, four chariots race across the angry sky, pulled by steeds of matching color. They strain at their bridles and gasp for breath, eyes bulging with effort. Their masters, four ghostly wraiths, brandish whips. Crack, crack, crack, crack. In their eye sockets glow orange coals. Each phantom trails a cape flying behind in the wind. The chariots' wheels spew green fire.

Below these deathly winged messengers, the earth too is enraged. Grass fires billow mountains of acrid smoke. Two- and four-footed shapes flee in a futile effort to elude the flames, their wild screams drowned in the inferno's roar. Behind the advancing wall of fire, the bleak charred landscape is littered with corpses: cattle, horse, human and a multitude of smaller creatures unable to escape the conflagration. The stench of burnt flesh is visceral, overpowering.

Towering in the background, a great cone rises high above the flat terrain. The cone's point is severed, replaced by a gaping hole. Mirroring the destruction below, the great cauldron spews its own dark orange bile. It spills over the hole's rim and slides down the cone's edges like so many winding serpents, unhurried but unstoppable.

My eyes snapped open. I sat bolt upright, bathed in a cold sweat.

***

"Come in." A croaky rasp greeted my knock. I opened the door with one hand, a pot of yesterday's stew cradled against my chest. The fetid twin odors of urine and decay wafted toward me. Labored breathing wheezed from the far corner of the hut's single room. By the light of a flickering candle, I could barely make out the shrunken figure of Yoka Sutu, propped on a stack of pillows. She was failing fast.

My heart, already laden with worry and self-doubt, sank at the sight of how much the crone had slipped in just two days since my last visit. I desperately needed Yoka's wise counsel. For weeks I'd been biding my time, hoping the crone would regain the strength to hear me out properly. Instead, her end seemed ever nearer. Best to speak up before it was too late.

The old woman was too weak to stand on her own anymore. On my last visit, she admitted to conversing with voices in her head. I didn't know whether to believe that, yet surely, she still kept a supply of her hallucinatory Venga nuggets handy. Perhaps the voices were tribal ancestors, channeled to console her.

"How are you feeling, *abela*?" I used the Onwei term for grandmother.

In response, Yoka lapsed into a spasm of coughs and gurgles, ending by spitting a large glob of mucus into a bucket by her bed. She lay panting and wiped her shriveled mouth. "I have been better." She turned toward me and nudged her head toward the pail. "Be so good as to empty this thing. It seems like my bodily wastes are all erupting from the wrong end."

Wincing, I held the pail at arm's length and took it to the larger water bucket to rinse out. I felt a twinge of resentment for having to deal with the excretions of this shriveled old woman. How easy it would be to nudge her that last step into the grave and be done with it.

With a shiver, the bitter feeling passed as quickly as it came. I could never do anything to hurt the person who nursed me around the clock for five days when I, myself, lay at death's door after a bullet ripped through my chest. Was it only a year and a half ago? Now the tables were turned.

I dished out the stew and pulled up a stool to feed Yoka. The crone puckered her shriveled grin and reached for my arm. "You are a sweet girl to look after a sick old woman, Keltyn. You are patient. Luz always seems in a hurry when it's her turn."

"She has lots on her mind these days," I responded. The truth, I knew, was that Luz Hogarth longed to be emancipated from her mother. She was ready to elope if Trieste did not acquiesce soon, and that would mean trouble for me. I doubted I could handle the role of Trieste's surrogate daughter. "Mama" could be demanding, fussy, self-pitying, overwrought or hypochondriacal, sometimes all at once. At other times she was the salt of the earth.

I watched Yoka dutifully slurp the stew broth and gum the vegetables. After five minutes, she lay her head back and waved off the spoon. "Done. All I need is enough fluid to keep up with this cursed phlegm." She stared at the ceiling. "Who would have thought that you could end by drowning in your own discharges?" She coughed up another gob and pulled the pail up to her mouth, eyeing me as she spat. "How can you bear to watch this? Disgusting." She used two fingers to wipe her mouth.

Good question, I wondered. After my time on the mountain with Luz, I was no rookie at caring for another person's bodily functions, but experience didn't make the task any easier.

"Abela, I need to ask you something."

Yoka raised her formerly bushy eyebrows, now wispy strands.

"Do you believe in premonitions?"

"Ha," she barked. "You seem to forget my job, girl. For years, I alone guided this tribe's fortunes, through the gift of prophecy."

True enough, though the way she wielded this power gained her an ample share of skeptics and outright enemies. I focused on a spot on the wall behind Yoka. "No, I mean, should the average person put stock into their intuition?"

"Of course." Yoka eyed me closely. "If your powers of reason can't give you an answer, then you must listen to the quiet voice within."

"The voice isn't quiet, and it's telling me something I really don't want to hear." I took a deep breath. As if dreams weren't enough, badgering me on and off for almost the whole seventeen months I had lived among the Onwei, lately the visions appeared in front of my eyes during broad daylight.

I pressed a hand to my temple, caught in the memory of yesterday. I went to visit Efrain. We sat on the rug facing each other. He tried to purr a melancholy love song — his stock in trade — while strumming his guitar. He halted in its midst, staring at me. I saw herself in his eyes, pale and shaking. At that moment, I decided to seek help from Yoka, ill or not.

"Tell me," said the crone.

"They're coming back. Sir Oscar Bailey is plotting a return."

Yoka's watery eyes studied me. "I thought you managed to convince him that the stone is radioactive."

"He didn't buy it. He could see right through me. I was too nervous to carry off the bluff."

"Ha." The crone glowered now, struggling to sit up straight. "If your crazy plan brought all that chaos to our people with no benefit at all on your end, well then, you must be cursed."

I must be. Yoka wasn't acting as sympathetic as I hoped. "There's more."

"More conflict? I hope I'm gone before it hits us." Yoka humphed and plopped her head back.

"Do you remember Buck Kranepool?"

"Your pilot? Oh, yes. He stuck out like a sore thumb at Aldo's funeral, quite ill at ease."

"When I first voiced an inclination to stay, Buck predicted I should help the Onwei negotiate mining rights. I accepted that, but now this forewarning raises the stakes. In these dreams, I am the one who leads the Onwei to resist an invasion."

Yoka gaped as she turned to face me again. "Aha. A regular Joan of Arc. Say this for you, girl. You dream big. An invasion."

"No, Yoka. I don't want any of this. I'd rather leave things as they are. Sometimes I wish I were still a junior geologist in Ontario. But I fell for Bailey's promise. When I returned, he was going to give me the cushiest gig that any scientist could ever get."

"He cast his spell over you," said Yoka.

"Exactly. It was the ambition of every researcher, too good to be true for a twenty-five-year-old nerd, especially for a Cree person, the first in her family ever to attend college."

"'Too good to be true' means there is a catch," she observed.

"I thought I had found the best outcome." My jaw clenched. "I could be dead. I could be in prison in Canada. I could have been exiled to Chinese Siberia. But now, these premonitions tell me I need to prepare for another showdown. I can feel it, deep in my bones. Sir Oscar will send another mission to find iridium here, and this one will have higher stakes than the last." My head rattled. "The only mystery is why he hasn't moved yet."

"So." Yoka slumped back on her pillow. "Why do you disturb an old woman's peace with these malicious hunches of yours?"

I chewed my lip. Yoka could be gratingly distant. "I…I hoped you could tell me whether there is any truth to them."

She sniffled. "Truth? Truth is like history, defined by the winners. You won't know it's the truth until afterward. If you would act, you must do so before the truth becomes clear." She lapsed into another coughing fit, managing only to croak, "Go now. Leave me."

By the time I cleared the dishes, lit a fresh candle, and filled the water bucket from the rain barrel outside, the old woman had stopped coughing and pulled the blankets over her head.

The crone hadn't offered consolation for my troubled musings. Indeed, she had only compounded them, but I knew Yoka better than to expect sympathy. It was not in her nature.

What I really craved was daylight to help me feel alive again, but that would be several weeks in coming. If, two years ago, someone had told me I was destined to live the rest of my life in Antarctica, I would have never been able to imagine such a scenario.

I desperately wished this cup would pass from me, knowing all the while it was not to be. My fate was sealed the moment four Onwei rode into our camp, the morning after Bailey Voyager crash-landed in a crater.

"Joan of Arc!" If Yoka's analogy was correct, I would need a thick suit of armor.

***

I stumbled forth into the dark, into the series of ruts and mud-holes that passed for a lane. The storm gave no sign of letting up, the endless Antarctic winter's night as dark and furious as ever. Trieste had bid me stop at Nomidar's community vegetable bin on my way home. Now, hurrying back with my arms full, I stumbled and almost lost my balance. The driving rain whipped my face as I stopped to feel my ankle through the boot. I tested my full weight on the foot and winced before limping on.

From the sheaf of carrots atop the bag of produce, a ghost scolded me, braying Trieste's admonition: "Eat more carrots. They will help your night vision, Brixa." That, I now realized, proved essential to survival in a part of the world where darkness reigned supreme for three months a year.

I needed to escape the spray of water relentlessly pummeling my face. Out of the corner of my eye I caught the outline of a man some thirty feet behind. This wasn't the first time I'd been stalked during the Nomidar winter, but my shadow was becoming bolder and more frequent.

I'd gotten half a mind to wait it out, to call the man's bluff by standing my ground. Yet, between my bum ankle, my burden of vegetables, and the storm, I was in no mood for a face-off.

Hurrying around the last corner toward home, I pivoted too fast and felt a stronger stab of pain in the ankle. I jarred to a halt again. The sinister figure advanced closer.

I limped hurriedly down the lane, wincing with each step. At the lane's end, a light beckoned, a candle shining from the front window of the small stone cottage I shared with Trieste and Luz. Somehow, with the remainder of the path pitch black, the single candle pierced the driving rain. I measured the distance in my head. How much longer until I was safe? Suppose the stalker had a weapon?

Hobbling, grunting with each step, I spied an anxious face peering through the hut's candlelit window. The next moment the door swung open and a small but surprisingly strong hand grabbed me. I almost fell into Trieste, whose petite wiry figure was so much like my own.

My unlikely savior's face contorted into its default expression: frown, squint, knitted brow. "Yuk. I shouldn't have sent you out into this stuff. We could have gotten by until tomorrow." Trieste whisked the bag onto the table.

I plopped down onto a stool and struggled out of my soaking poncho, trying not to shake too much water onto the hut floor. "What would it matter?" I muttered. "The weather's been the same every day — rain and wind." I decided to keep mum about the stalker, yet now he knew where I lived.

Trieste, blissfully unaware of my dilemma, pawed busily through the bunch of mostly root vegetables. Culinary etiquette, it seemed to me, was one of many social graces dispelled by the endless dark Antarctic winter. Not that the long bright summers in dusty cattle camps called for white gloves and tablecloths either. Yet, if you were stuck indoors for long stretches, you expected more amenities than when hoofing it on the trail.

"And dark. Did I mention dark?" I peeked at Trieste, hoping my black humor would register as intended.

Trieste's eyes shot up to glare at me. "Take it or leave it, Brixa. No one is keeping you here." She grabbed a sweet potato, still recognizable in shape, and vigorously scrubbed the dirt off in a bucket of water. "Go back to where everything is bright and shiny all the time. See if I…Ow!" She held up a bruised finger and sucked on it.

I turned to my throbbing ankle and tried to wrestle my boot off. So much for levity. The woman had never addressed me as Keltyn, not once. But "Brixa" was at least better than what I and my crewmates were tagged when first ushered into the Onwei camp: "Sky-Bornes," like we were some kind of celestial aliens.

There! The boot finally gave way and slid off with a "thwop," confronting me with a purple goose egg.

Was it a coincidence that the sound of "Brixa" called up *"bruxa,"* or "witch," for those in this tribe — certain gauchos, mostly — who might still harbor resentment for an ex-Sky-Borne? If I had to guess, my stalker buddy was one of these.

Trieste finally looked up from scrubbing vegetables. "What happened to you?"

"I stepped in a hole down by the corner." I felt like a rookie. It wasn't the first time I'd injured myself in the dark.

Trieste huffed through pursed lips. "You need a poultice to take down that swelling, and where is my daughter when we need her? Off at a barn dance."

"If you'll bring me the curandero kit, I can take care of it," I said. "She has shown me how to mix this kind before."

Trieste lit another candle and stepped into the next room. I heard her rifle through scattered trinkets and accessories. She returned and dropped the kit into my lap, set the extra candle down, and held up a three-pronged carrot to scrub next. "This one is just for you and your mishaps in the dark, Brixa."

"You got it, Mama," I said. Trieste liked to be called "Mama." Once she forgave me that disastrous attempt to hoodwink the tribe, she thawed. I figured that my own reticence and small physique made it easy for Trieste to regard me as family.

I unwrapped the burnished leather healer's kit and studied its multiple pouches, each containing a unique ingredient. They never failed to fascinate me. Some were tiny gourds, sealed with beeswax. Others were bone needles and horsehair thread, ready to sew a wound, packed neatly next to coca leaf to numb the pain and stanch the bleeding. Opposite were sewn pockets with hemp-wrapped dollops of salves. I was amused to learn that, even without labels in this illiterate culture but thanks to Aldo's tutoring via séance, Luz had learned to identify most of them by smell.

Now I took out a fresh piece of hemp gauze. Using a tiny spatula, the size of my little finger, I scooped out a thimbleful from each of three different wraps, blending aromas of mint, loam, and rotten eggs. I stirred them carefully and then slapped the gauze on my throbbing ankle. Within minutes came cool relief.

Trieste glanced back from her cooking. "Better? Good. I can't afford to have you laid up at home."

I tensed. Was I not earning my keep? "Why not?"

"You know. We discussed this. You must pay a visit to all the women who make tortillas, so we can finally put to rest those bad feelings from last year."

I sighed. Who would have guessed that the most pressing issue among these people had to do with tortillas? Being dragged into the ongoing petty squabbles that stemmed from banishing the khokri wasting disease made me wish I had never cracked its secret. It was like they were hazing me a second time around for my troubles. Yet, if I wished to become accepted into this tribe, I knew I must act the part.

"Yes, Mama."

Trieste removed the lid from the cook-pot simmering on the wood stove and began slicing in her vegetables. The smells of the poultice were drowned out by those of herbs, stew beef and bone marrow. The cooking odors swaddled me, transporting me back to my childhood home, to a time when my family was still intact, before I left for boarding school on a scholarship, before my father died of TB and my mother hit the sauce.

Now, my only home and family were here, on the other side of the world, but, if I believed these visions, all signs pointed toward another upheaval.

2

THE APPRENTICE

When it came to a barn dance, Joaquin Beltran was always the first one there. Not just the first musician but the first person, period. It was wonderful, and scored him sincere thanks from the older folks, instead of those patronizing smiles that used to make him feel like a mascot.

He began by lighting the dozens of vanilla-scented candles that graced the cavernous walls of the old barn. Then he swept the musty, warped wooden floor and set out folding chairs for older folks. The dancers would need them too, after working up a sweat. He filled the water pitchers from the rain barrel, and when the abelas showed up with spiced hooch and orange juice, they let him mix the punch.

It was good business to cultivate the old ladies, he discovered, as they would often invite him to visit their huts the next week to conduct a Venga session. For some, it became almost a sacrament to channel a departed spouse, or perhaps a long-lost lover. Now that Joaquin had, under Yoka Sutu's coaching, become reasonably adept in baking the nuggets and arranging the desired mood for séances, he had begun to earn a small but steady income.

Maybe this could become his full-time calling. It might have to. He had not tried to approach Ysidro, guessing that the new jeaf would have no spot for him to join the cattle migration with his band of gauchos. No matter. He knew that Ysidro had neither the interest nor the patience to mentor Joaquin as Aldo had. Besides, now with two gimpy limbs on his still-scrawny frame, Joaquin had come to accept what was long obvious to everyone else: he could never make it as a gaucho.

Perhaps the Venga gigs could become a sustainable trade, especially if he could develop a word-of-mouth business at the annual summer Rendezvous. Trieste had successfully cultivated her joya clientele and other Nomidar artisans had done the same. Still, even if he could pull that off, there was something mildly distasteful about taking advantage of lonely old women.

By contrast, the chance to play in the barn dance band thrilled him. Tonight would be his first chance to prove himself before the entire audience, and he intended to make the most of it. He alone would comprise the rhythm section. Matin, the tanner, had played percussion forever, but his gnarled hands could no longer keep up and he graciously ceded his drumsticks to Joaquin. He had practiced on a variety of

Matin's percussion devices, everything from tambourine to booran to a cymbal activated by pedal and discovered he could make it work.

Dario, the butcher, who played fiddle for these dances, seemed convinced Joaquin could carry the beat. So did Efrain, who played guitar. Only Soriante, who played panpipes in between singing, yodeling and generally carousing, was skeptical. "You'll need more than two paws to carry your weight, gimp."

Behind the stage, Joaquin unlocked the chest that held his collection of noisemakers. Dario usually liked to start the first set with something up-tempo. Joaquin picked out the booran with its accompanying peg-like drumstick. Holding the large flat drum vertically, with his left hand splayed out behind the playing surface, he practiced a few riffs of the rat-a-tat beat using the peg, snub-nosed on each end.

Next, he pulled out the cymbal and its elaborate rigging. Matin had invented the contraption, including the foot pedal, and Joaquin admired how the man banged the cymbal for emphasis while his hands simultaneously drummed. Joaquin would just as soon leave the cymbal in storage, but that would only work if he came up with some other signature noisemaker to take its place. It would take inspiration, as well as Matin's help to build. All in good time. The idle thought flitted through his mind: was there some way he could ever make a living from playing music?

Efrain wandered in. He removed his guitar from its beat-up case and began tuning the strings by ear.

Joaquin eyed him. "How do you know when it's in tune, charro?"

The big gaucho winked at Joaquin. "My ear tells me."

"What about the fiddle and the pipes?"

"The pipes stay in tune by themselves, but you know Soriante. We'll be lucky if he makes it up here on time. It will be too noisy to depend on him."

Indeed, people were already gathering. Other charros — he spied Gabino and wild-eyed Onofre — collected by the far wall, near the punch bowl. The wanton sisters Carmen and Pilar sidled in between the gauchos, ready, Joaquin knew, to ply their trade later in the evening. There at the refreshment table, with his back to the stage, stood Soriante, pouring a stiff shot. He already tapped his feet in time.

Older couples drifted in as well. Hortensio, the smith, who served as caller, ushered in his addled wife Char. Teenage girls and a few unattached young women drifted in as well, mostly in groups of three or four. Joaquin watched them out of the corner of his eye as he finished his preparations.

At one time, he expected just showing up for such an event would be enough to attract a girl's attention, that he could stand around, minding his own business, and a pretty young thing would come ask him to dance. Later he figured out that, with his clubfoot and splinted wrist, he could never impress a girl with his dancing. Anyway, girls expected boys to notice them and make the first move, not vice versa, and he had yet to get up the nerve.

In the meantime, so long as he could beat time, he could have fun with the musicians and share in some of their reflected glory. More than once at previous *bailas* he noticed a *chica bonita* steal a glance his way as she applauded.

Speaking of pretty girls, here came Luz, alone as usual. She flashed her bright smile at Joaquin. "Ooh, there's my little drummer boy."

"Yup, here I am." Joaquin gave her the once over. Unlike most of her mates, Luz sprouted form-fitting black breeches tucked into lattice-stitched boots. "Where's your dancing shoes, baby?"

Luz scanned the hall. "You know, I didn't really come to dance, Joaquin. I just wanted to see who shows up and, honestly, to get out of the house for a while."

Joaquin nodded. Claustrophobia was the Onwei's winter nemesis. The rain and the ultra-long nights combined with the only show in town — you had to be too old to move, or too grouchy, to stay home tonight.

"Besides," Luz continued, examining her freshly painted nails, "a lot of these girls I may not see again." She lifted her eyes. "This is probably my last winter in Nomidar."

"You mentioned that." Now was not the moment to get sentimental, but he would miss her. Each of them was an only child. She never knew who her father was, while he still lived. He never knew either of his parents, period. Perhaps that explained the soft spot she had for him. She was like the older sister in the family he never had.

Dario jumped up on stage and began his warmup. He and Efrain faced each other. Dario barked something and they riffed through the first eight bars of a polka.

"Guess I better get ready," said Joaquin. He felt vaguely annoyed in having to cut short the chat with Luz. Was she serious about leaving Nomidar? Despite the confidence she now radiated, Joaquin wondered if she was bluffing. He knew that her mother was still opposed.

"Don't let your eyes wander," laughed Luz. "Stay focused on the beat." She waved and headed toward Marisol, another tall eighteen-year-old.

When he finished his warmup, Dario dropped his arms to his sides, fiddle in one hand, bow in the other. Joaquin watched him glower at Soriante, who blithely chatted up Carmen by the punch bowl and showed no inclination to make music. Finally, Dario turned to Hortensio. "Start us up a mixer."

Hortensio's strident voice announced the protocol for the first dance. Soriante gulped down the rest of his drink and elbowed his way through the crowd toward the stage. He looked shocked to see Joaquin sitting in Matin's spot as drummer, and a sneer spread across his usually light-hearted face. "Oh, Lord. We must be scraping the bottom of the barrel." Joaquin tried to ignore him and focused on adjusting his seat.

Soriante ducked behind to retrieve his instruments and pulled out three different sets of pipes, ranging between them over four octaves in pitch. He jumped onto the stage just as the first bars of the reel began.

Joaquin watched Efrain finger the chords to pick up his beat: steady but not fast. Hortensio pattered his instructions, nonstop at first, then dropping to a reminder phrase at the beginning of each new round of partners.

As he settled into his rhythm, Joaquin could observe the dance line form into thirty-some pairs of hands in a circle. The women wore white blouses, bright flouncy skirts and dancing slippers. Some of the men dressed up, others wore a cleaner version of the hemp tunic and breeches one might spy during the cattle drive. All the men wore boots, however, and the boots stomped the beat together, louder than anything Joaquin could muster on his drums. No matter, he knew his time would come later.

The women and men took turns weaving in and out, one group toward the center of the circle, the other away from it. They met again midway, where each man would pair off and swing the woman next to him. Then he would guide her down the line to her next partner, turn and meet a new partner of his own. A mixer meant that each man would get to dance at least once with each woman. Joaquin tried to picture himself in this line. The steps didn't look too hard. He could swing any number of chicas bonitas, but he'd have to take turns with the ugly ones too.

By the time they returned to their original partners, most dancers worked up a sweat. The hall was warming up quickly, no less so Joaquin. Starting with the tambourine, to be on the safe side, he chose to use the cymbal only for emphasis, at the end of each time through the tune, to signal a change of partners. It had all gone as well as could be expected, and Joaquin basked in hearty applause for the band.

Burly Hortensio barely had time to announce the next dance before Dario launched into a wild tune. Joaquin grabbed the booran and dove into the rhythm as if his life depended on it. Couples paired off and flung themselves counterclockwise, trying to stay in the dance floor's orbit, but whirling at such a speed as to threaten a launch out the door at any moment.

Both of Joaquin's wrists began to ache, the right from continuous rotation, the gimpy left one cramping from holding the booran steady. His arms were definitely not in shape. He had practiced polka and all of the other tempos on the drum before, but not for five minutes nonstop, and not in front of dozens of people. He gritted his teeth and soldiered on.

Dario and Soriante alternated taking the melody lead, which meant that each got a bit of rest. Efrain strummed like a madman while stomping his boot, but his three-chord progression was simple. He looked like he could keep doing this in his sleep; indeed, his eyes had closed.

Joaquin glanced up at Dario, hoping the fiddler would give some signal to end it, but one peek at the dancers told a different story. They were having altogether too much fun, the kind of thrill that small children get when swung in a circle by their outstretched arms.

He flashed back to the time he helped Aldo sew up Heriberto Paz's mare, gored by a crazy bull. Even sewing that wound, as painstaking as it had been, allowed him to rest for a moment now and then. Now, if Dario did not finish off the tune soon, Joaquin felt sure that he would faint from exhaustion.

Perhaps he could rest for just a moment. He tried again to catch Dario's eye, Hortensio's, anybody's, but each was enthralled in the same trance. Somehow, Joaquin had the premonition that, if he were to quit before the others, the spell would shatter into pieces, its magic charm broken.

A blister ached on the inside of his thumb, but he'd be damned if he would quit now. An extra shot of adrenaline surged through him. The muscles in his hands seemed to take over the operation of the booran; his brain no longer needed to will them to perform.

And then, finally, Dario stuck his foot out, the signal for the last round. At the very end, he flourished his bow, Efrain riffed the last chord, Soriante tweeted the last note, and Joaquin banged the cymbal. The dancers hooted and whistled with what little breath they had left and retreated toward the punch bowl.

Sweat dripping from his brow, Joaquin raised his water mug and took a deep swallow. He wished he had brought salve for the cursed blister on his palm, now the size of a grape. Reaching for his bandana, he tore off a strip and wound it around the base of his thumb as a cushion. That would need to get him through the rest of the evening. In time, though none too soon, his hands would become calloused. No pain, no gain.

When Joaquin scanned the audience once more, he spotted a late arrival. There was Ysidro, decked out in fringed leather. The gaucho chief caught Joaquin's eye and raised his mug in salute. Wow. That was a first. A flush of pride coursed through his exhausted body. He lifted his chin, squared his shoulders, and nodded to meet the jeaf's gaze. Perhaps, just perhaps, Ysidro's opinion of him might be softening, and that could pay off in the next few months.

3

ROOTS AND WINGS

Luz Hogarth stood at the edge of the crowd of dancers, one knee bent, the sole of her boot propped against the wall of the barn. Drumming her fingers on her thigh, she tapped the rhythm of the reel the band now played. In her other hand, she balanced a cup of punch, diluted with juice. No buzz needed tonight.

These dances were the high point of social life in Nomidar, really the only organized fun for people her age, luring anyone with a social bone in their body. This would be the memory of her hometown she took with her. Better some excitement than the stagnation of her mother's hut.

One of the young town boys — Faustino, a carpenter's apprentice, polite and well-scrubbed, but clueless — had, in a charming gesture, asked her for this dance. Her heart belonged to another boy, on the opposite side of the continent. Still, it felt good to be noticed. She had to flash her promise ring at him before he backed off and turned his attention to Marisol, who was, after all, more his match in looks and temperament.

Marisol, though every bit as tall as Luz, was lighter on her feet. Luz watched the two of them stumble and twist through the caller's elaborate figures. They could make a couple. Both were physically awkward but easily laughed off their missteps, whereas Luz knew that she herself would chafe at each blunder.

The reel ended with a sustained bout of swing-your-partner, round and round at least eight times. Big Hortensio announced a waltz, to be followed by a break for the band. A good share of the dancers, still catching their breath, already had enough. Marisol grinned, curtsied to Faustino and turned away before he had a chance to ask her to waltz. She staggered back toward her friend, grabbed Luz's cup of punch and took a deep draught. Her cheeks were flushed.

"Thanks." Marisol handed the near-empty cup back.

"Looks like you had a good workout," said Luz.

The other girl glanced down and wiggled her toes. "I guess he didn't crack any little piggies. Faustino's a sweet boy, but he's got two left feet." They both giggled. "It's not fair for the guys to wear boots and we don't." She inspected Luz's footwear. "Except you."

"I already told you, I didn't come here to meet boys."

"Doesn't mean you couldn't dance."

Not much point in dancing except to meet a boy, Luz wanted to say.

Marisol inched closer with a conspiratorial look. "Is it true what I heard about you?"

"What did you hear?" She tensed. How much had gossip twisted the truth?

"That you're going off with a boy from a different tribe?"

"Partly true." Luz gazed at the ceiling. "Going off" made it sound like they planned to just wander about.

"Come on. Don't be coy. What's his name?"

"Ian Campbell."

"Campbell. Sounds like a Perth name."

"Good guess."

"What does his family do?"

"They raise horses."

"Ooh. Now I get it." Marisol jutted her lower lip and nodded.

Luz pictured Ian's wavy blond hair, the ocean-blue eyes that hypnotized her whenever they were close. There was more to it than horses, but best not rub it in, especially for someone like Marisol who might well end up hitched to a carpenter's apprentice with two left feet. She decided to play along with the horse angle. "I suppose I'll never get over losing Quintara."

Too late, she regretted the remark. Marisol, whose family struggled with a small dairy operation on the outskirts of town, never had the luxury of owning a horse. "Oh, you poor dear," she sniffed. "I'm sure Ian Campbell can lessen the pain."

Luz frowned. "What is that supposed to mean?"

Marisol shrugged and checked the sheen on her fingernails. "Forget it." She looked up and cast a concerned sideways glance. "What about your poor mother?"

Just like the Nomidar matrons. This was their standard guilt trip: what decent girl would think of abandoning her fragile widowed mother to live hundreds of miles away on some other corner of the continent? Trieste used this tactic so often that Luz had become immune to her pleas. She simply could not stomach the thought of living out her days in this dull village.

Besides, her mother now had Keltyn to help her. The Brixa had taken a sincere interest in learning Trieste's methods to smith the *piedra de yris*, something that Luz had not the patience for. The bond that developed between Keltyn and Trieste had not come easy — Trieste was superstitious and harbored grudges, the Brixa was beset with misgivings — but Luz hoped that it was now strong enough to support her planned exit.

"She will be well provided for." Luz fixed Marisol with a stare.

"Oh, really?" A sneer broke out on the girl's face. "Think about what you're doing." She spotted another friend and skipped off.

A twinge of jealousy coursed through Luz as she watched Marisol effortlessly break into giggles with her companion. Luz knew that, by spending summers away, she long ago forfeited any chance to find a confidante among her stay-at-home friends and neighbors. In six weeks or so, as soon as the cattle drive started, it would be goodbye to everyone in Nomidar. That part was no different than every other spring since she was a toddler, but this time there would be no coming back, not for a long time.

The matronly guilt trip had some effect, though. Luz frequently asked herself how she could sweeten the deal with her mother. The only enticement she could think of was to supply Trieste with the high-grade piedra de yris from Mt. Erebus. The ore was now there in plain sight and easy pickings, thanks to the previous eruption that felled Quintara and almost took her own life.

A grandchild would also appease Trieste, but Luz wasn't ready for that yet. Ian's parents gave her a thorough once-over appraisal when he introduced her last summer, and registered an approving look, or so it seemed to Luz. Unlike her frail mother, she had a full figure, inherited from Aldo no doubt. Yoka, in one of her prophetic moods, promised that Luz would bear many children. All in good time. She was in no hurry.

Luz peered at the onyx on her finger. Ian, not yet brave or foolish enough to ask Trieste for her daughter's hand, had meant it only as a promise ring. Luz knew she needed her mother's consent to marry. Either that or be prepared to elope. She still had six months before the Rendezvous, six months to work on her.

She eyed the other matrons, mostly sitting along the sidelines and clapping time to the music. Many were friends of Trieste, and some had wayward children, but she could spot no one whose child had slammed the door shut on Nomidar as she proposed to do.

Rows of sparkling candles lining the four walls of the barn made the old hall appear festive. She wondered where Perth held their line dances. How could she win approval from her new Perth neighbors? Being an accomplished horsewoman in a village that boasted many would impress no one.

Another girl joined Marisol and her friend across the hall. They jabbered away, eyes rolling, occasionally sneaking a glance at Luz. Their giggles left no doubt: Marisol was mining Luz's revelations about Ian for all they were worth. What a fool I was to confide in her. Luz tried to hold her chin high, but at the moment she was on the verge of bolting from this dumb party. The co-mingled sweat of dozens of dancers was getting to her.

The band warmed up for their second set. Hortensio barked out for everyone to find a partner. Luz finished her drink and turned to leave. Then she heard Hortensio call her name. He stood beaming, his arm stretched out toward her. "Our own saddle princess, Luz Hogarth. Wouldn't it be wonderful to watch her kick up her heels again, ladies and gents? It's good to see you back, sweetheart."

He led a brief round of applause while Luz flushed and ducked her chin. Hortensio ambled over to her. "Luz, help me demonstrate the moves for this next piece."

She let out an expression of mock horror as the big smith took her hand, then glanced over at Char, who sat in a corner watching her husband. The feebleminded woman nodded in approval.

Hortensio's lead was strong and sure. The manly scent he had slapped on reminded her of Aldo. After several go-rounds to exhibit the new steps to the other dancers, he signaled for the music to start. In all the previous dances of the evening, he moved back toward the stage and resorted to calling. This time, beaming down at Luz like a proud father, he continued to sashay her around the hall.

Within seconds, Luz felt herself transported. Even her boots, designed by her Uncle Ariel for a slow, stable gait, could not disguise the smooth, flowing steps. She relaxed and let herself sink into the milieu, oblivious to the curious gaze of other dancers.

Her feet found the right steps without any need to guide them. The twirls, the out-and-backs, the over-the-shoulder eye contact, all the moves seemed to spring with a life of their own. She felt scores of eyes fixed upon her, suddenly at the center of the limelight, and the feeling thrilled her, as if the onlookers were paying her homage.

How long was it since she had last partaken? At least five years, it must be. She reached her tall mature figure early on as a teen, but found her early attempts hampered by underdeveloped juvenile male age-mates or by older aspiring gauchos given to macho posturing. By contrast, Ian, despite his reticence, was polite and attentive. They had never danced, but she now imagined herself gliding effortlessly in his arms.

What had happened with her resolve to just stand and watch? Still, it was only a dance, and, partnering with a middle-aged man whose wife sat nearby, she could hardly be accused of cheating on her betrothed. Just before spinning herself into a giddy trance, one other question flitted through her mind. What if Marisol was right? Could she really leave all these people forever and start over again?

4

HATCHET MAN

Helmut Ganz forced himself to sit up straight on the divan. He watched his boss a few feet away, leaning back in a plush leather recliner, looking uncharacteristically somber as he flipped through pages of Ganz's report.

Sir Oscar's big, polished walnut desk, sprawled across the other side of the room, seemed empty without his presence. Over the last year the two men had developed an informal relationship on Ganz's frequent jaunts from Zürich to Bailey HQ in Alberta. When Sir Oscar put his feet on the desk, it meant Ganz had a chance to stretch out his long legs.

Not today. This was not a normal meeting. Incidents — they were still officially "accidents" — throughout the Bailey empire were escalating, and the boss had summoned his division chiefs to HQ, one at a time. Now it was Ganz's turn to be grilled, and he already felt the sweat inching down his armpits. His safest bet was to keep stroking the Chief's ego.

He finished Ganz's brief and tossed it aside. "Lots of speculation here, but not much for facts. I need names, contacts."

"Whoever they are, sir, they don't operate by any standard pattern."

Oscar's head slumped. "What did you nail down on that mine explosion?"

"It looks like someone shut the ventilation shaft damper."

"What? That's way deep inside. How could a saboteur sneak past, unless…?" His head shot up.

His boss paused, so Ganz completed the unwelcome deduction. "Unless it was an inside job."

Sir Oscar stared at the wall, his lips curling into a snarl. "Inside job. I hate to admit it, but that's the pattern emerging from our transportation and factory mishaps too. Our safety record slips, this could have all kinds of repercussions."

When he turned back to face him, Ganz detected an uncharacteristic gloom.

"Someone has it in for me."

In the thirteen years that Ganz had worked for Sir Oscar, he had never before sensed the least hint of paranoia or self-pity. He leaned forward to rest arms on knees. "What makes you say that, sir?"

"Someone who thinks I'm Satan for building an industrial empire. Someone who's determined, connected and organized."

Ganz felt a shiver. He could think of no single mortal capable of pulling off this score of incidents, scattered throughout Europe and Canada, all of which, if they were sabotage, required exquisite planning and technical expertise. "You have a person in mind, sir?"

Sir Oscar flashed a withering smile, of the type he favored when confronted by foolish questions, and Ganz immediately realized his faux pas.

"Not a person, Ganz, a ring, a gang."

This was all too mysterious. "Do they have a name?"

"They go by the charming tag of Native Peoples United."

Ganz made a note on his pad. He would have to study up on this group. "At least you have a suspect, sir. That's always the first step." He took the liberty of leaning back on the divan.

"Not to worry, we'll bring them down in due course. First, my security boys have to recruit spies to infiltrate the group. Meanwhile," Sir Oscar slapped his palm on the armrest, "let's talk about something more upbeat. Are you ready to visit Antarctica, Ganz?"

"Absolutely, sir."

Ganz allowed his legs to stretch out, but their length seemed to take Sir Oscar aback. "I didn't factor in your height. How tall are you, anyway?"

"One point nine three meters, sir." He involuntarily sat up straight again.

"You're going to have a tight squeeze fitting into the back seat of Bailey Voyager."

"On most trips other passengers defer to my need for extra leg room."

"Sorry, Ganz. This isn't 'most trips.' The pilot obviously needs one front seat, and Harry Ladou, who's still the nominal chief of this mission, will need the other. The lines of authority have already been diluted too much. If I tell him he's got to sit in back, he may just drop out altogether."

Ganz clasped his hands snugly. "And what, if I may be so bold, would be so wrong with that?"

Oscar stared at him. "I detect a note of self-importance, Ganz. That's the kind of mindset that could blunt your effectiveness."

Ganz stiffened.

Oscar continued. "I still need Harry. He proved that on the last mission by keeping his head."

Ganz raised his brows to inquire.

Oscar held up one finger. "First, despite a gear malfunction that forced them to put down way off target, and despite the pilot sustaining a concussion during a crash landing, Harry kept morale intact until Buck recovered sufficiently to fix the gear."

Up came the second finger. "Next, despite meeting the local tribe under adverse conditions, he went out of his way to promote a cordial relationship, one that we should be able to build on this time." Third finger. "Most importantly, he did everything possible to get the crew out alive. If Savant SparrowHawk was the exception, which we won't know until we get back there, it was her own damn fault." He slapped his hand on the armrest again.

The slapping noise jerked Ganz. He had not heard so many firsthand details before.

"I know what you're thinking," said Oscar. "If Harry Ladou is so competent and trustworthy, why do I need you along? God knows there are any number of important deals in Europe that may fall through during your absence."

Ganz nodded. He wondered the same thing.

"The problem with Harry, as I see it, and this is in strict confidence between us two, understand?"

"Yes, sir."

Sir Oscar gazed out the picture window across from Ganz. Outside, midsummer sunlight lit up the boreal forest. "The problem is that he shows signs of getting soft. I noticed it first when he tried to intercede on the side of Fay Del Campo toward the end of the previous mission. I'm keeping an eye out for his comings and goings, and I want you to do the same."

He whirled back to face Ganz, who nodded curtly.

"Harry already knows that your job is to seal the deal. And you hold the trump card in that respect. How are your Onwei studies going, Ganz?"

Ganz cleared his throat. "The lang-synch has proved very helpful, sir." It was true that he had a facility for languages, yet learning a completely foreign tongue with only the aid of a machine that translated simple phrases was like studying history by memorizing a bunch of dates. Context and nuance were everything. Still, he would have a leg up on the rest of the crew, and he intended to use it. "With whom will I be negotiating, sir?"

"Good question. Harry can fill you in about the tribe they encountered last time. I expect it will be with their new gaucho leader. Ha. The one who led the failed attempt to raid our camp."

"Won't this man still be hostile toward us?"

"Possible, entirely possible." Oscar drummed his fingers. "Don't worry. We're not going unarmed. And it may well be that we don't encounter anyone at this time of year in the Erebus region. The last mission took place in our spring, their fall; this time it will be just the opposite. These people are nomads, graze their herds over the same route each season." He stopped the drumming and flashed a thumbs-up sign. "So much the better if we don't run into them. We land right on target, harvest a big stash of the best ore, then goodbye, mission accomplished."

"So, my skills may not come into play at all," ventured Ganz.

"'Better safe than sorry' is my motto," said Oscar. "Plus, there is one other situation where you may be needed."

Ganz waited. A lot of 'ifs' were piling up.

"If there is any sign of Keltyn SparrowHawk still alive, I want her back." Oscar's lower lip jutted out in defiance. "She not only sabotaged the first mission, she tried to make a fool out of me. She needs to pay the price."

"What if she refuses to return willingly?"

"Ha! She would be more of a fool than I thought if she agreed to come willingly, but you certainly can make her any kind of offer that you think would entice her to do so, anything short of a promise of immunity from prosecution."

"So, if she refuses?"

"First you need to determine if she is involved in fomenting opposition to our ambitions. That would be my guess."

Ganz was still unclear on this part of his mission. "So if the tribal Chief is opposed to negotiations, and if I find that she is behind that opposition…"

"Then you are authorized to arrest and return her to Canada."

Ganz cleared his throat. "Suppose the tribe tries to shield her?"

"If worse comes to worse," Oscar said, gazing away once more, "you will need to neutralize her. I will leave the method to your discretion."

Rising, he went over to his desk, pulled out some stationery, scribbled a few lines, and signed the note with a flourish. He sealed the note in an envelope and handed it to Ganz. "There, Herr Ganz. You have it on my personal authority. One more thing."

"Yes?" It occurred to Ganz that he should still be taking notes. Sir Oscar's shopping list was lengthening by the minute.

"You'll be refueling at Chimera Space Station, an unavoidable detour, I'm afraid, thanks to the Hurricane Belt. I want you to interview a Chinese staffer who works there, name of Hunany Lin."

"Does he know something?"

"Walt McAfee seems to think so." Sir Oscar dug around in his files, pulled out a memo, and handed it to Ganz.

> To: Chief of Security, Bailey Enterprises
> From: Walter McAfee, Communications Technician First Class, Chimera Space Station
> Date: 10 March 2315
> Priority: SECRET
>
> After today's media briefing by three crew members of the Bailey Voyager mission to Antarctica, clandestine information passed between Chimera Systems Engineer Hunany 'Huey' Lin and Savant Keltyn SparrowHawk.
>
> Despite a partition that separated me from the two of them, I am sure of their identities. I am familiar with Huey's voice from daily collaboration on board Chimera, and I listened to Savant SparrowHawk's comments at the press briefing just concluded.
>
> The conversation in question lasted less than a minute, but several things about it struck me as odd. First, both participants spoke in Chinese, which was particularly surprising with regard to Savant SparrowHawk. Second, during the course of the conversation, it sounded like a message changed hands; one of the participants folded up a paper as he or she put it away. Lastly, the

hushed tone of both speakers suggested caution about being associated together, as well they might. Chimera protocol frowns on any such informal fraternization between Chinese and Western nationals.

I draw no conclusions from the above observations, but I believe they need to reach the proper levels of authority.

Ganz looked up. "Sounds like a smoking gun."

Sir Oscar smiled. "It does indeed."

Ganz checked the date on the memo. "Of course, this happened almost a year and a half ago."

"Granted, but we need to know what was in that message. It could become evidence in Savant SparrowHawk's prosecution."

"Can I have a copy of this?"

"Better commit it to memory, Ganz. I don't want Huey to guess the source. He and McAfee still share duties every day on Chimera."

"Right." Ganz stood. "Anything else, sir?"

Sir Oscar sprang to his feet as well, rather gracefully for someone his age. "Your role on this mission will be the most delicate one of the four crew members, Ganz. All of your mates, but Harry Ladou in particular, will think that you're there as my informant. That's true to a degree, but you'll also be investigator, businessman and corporate security agent. If I didn't think you could handle it, I would never have called on you."

"I'll try to reward your confidence, sir."

As they shook hands, Ganz did as was taught in school when done being dismissed. He bowed his head and clicked his heels. Then he turned smartly and exited, fully aware of Sir Oscar's gaze following him.

***

Ganz had barely walked out the front door of Bailey HQ when a giant blast from behind sent him sprawling forward. He fell onto his face, stunned. His nose throbbed and dripped blood.

His dialups were gone. He groped blindly with both hands until he found them, still intact, thank God. Pulling out a handkerchief, he squeezed it tight on his nose and tried to sit up. His knee gave out a shot of pain.

Smoke billowed from the lobby, and along with it the almond odor of plastique explosive. Scores of people around him fled the building, shouting and screaming. A big husky young fellow staggered by, pale as a ghost, one arm propped by an escort. Most of his other arm was missing, a tourniquet knotted below the shoulder. The first fire truck pulled up, followed by ambulances. Strange to have flashing lights without sirens, he thought, at which point he became aware of the deafening roar in his ears.

Ganz limped away until he found a spot on the grass, a safe distance from the rush of panicked humanity. He slumped down and watched the scene unfold. Then it hit him: but for ten seconds longer in the company of Sir Oscar — time enough to chat about the weather in Zürich, say — his own mangled body would be among those the medics now loaded. A deep shudder escaped him.

The rest of the building was still intact. Sir Oscar's corner office, on the far wing of the tenth floor, appeared pristine. Ganz wondered if his boss had even felt a tremor.

Who was behind this? He knew whom the Chief would finger with the blame, that Native Peoples United. Whoever these terrorists were, they had just upped the ante, striking the core of the Bailey empire. Now there could be no denying what the previous incidents had been — not accidents but sabotage.

Would this latest disaster change Sir Oscar's plans to launch the second Antarctic mission? If he postponed or cancelled, it wouldn't hurt Ganz's feelings one bit. Yet, bowing to any such pressure was not in the Chief 's nature. More likely, he would expect Ganz to perform double duty, instituting greater surveillance for Bailey Europe operations, while still engaged in this cross-world rendezvous with Antarctic cowboys. Go figure.

Sitting on the grass, Ganz checked his legs ruefully. He could still click his heels. He slowly pushed himself up and limped back toward the building. He needed to find out Sir Oscar's new game plan, likely already reformulated in the brief moments since the explosion. Every crisis was an opportunity in disguise.

5

RUMOR MILL

I'd had to swallow my pride many times since embedding with the Nomidar tribe, but that didn't make each new time any easier.

Trieste sensed the need for me to show my face and found me no shortage of errands. Scouring the community vegetable bin was one thing, a menial task. Today's chore once again involved tortillas, which meant delving into the village's factions and gossip.

When Trieste first broached her plan, I pictured the futility of trying to confront the wagging tongues, my youth sucked away in the process. "I wish I had never stumbled upon the cause of the khokri," I sulked.

"Then your stock in Nomidar would be even lower, if that is possible," humphed Trieste. "As is, just the women who had to change their tortilla recipe resent you, the bringer of bad tidings. Truth be told, they resent me too, for harboring an alien. My joya sales have suffered." She sighed. "I need to restore my good name among these embittered women."

"How can you do that, Mama?"

"The obvious way is to start buying our tortillas from each of them in turn. That will add up, since my household now has three mouths to feed. And I'm afraid you're the one who needs to make the rounds, Brixa."

Trieste needed not say more. It was part of my continued penance for disrupting the tribe's routine so profoundly last year. The wound from being spit at by the tribeswomen still festered, and not even saving future generations from the scourge of the khokri would exempt me from bearing this cross.

The week before, I'd gone to the home of Clara Hidalgo, who hastened to rub fresh salt in the wound. She met me with a frosty reception, standing in her doorway for at least half a minute and staring, as if in shock. Only the sight of a coin purse kept Seira Hidalgo from slamming the door in my face. The transaction was soon over; the woman did not even invite me to step in out of the rain while she fetched a bundle of tortillas.

On this day, Trieste readied me for a second attempt at neighborliness. "You must visit Alma Pastorius, the wife of Matin the tanner. His hands have become so arthritic that he must soon give up his trade. Alma's tortillas will become their sole income. She can hardly afford to turn up her nose at new prospects."

I shivered inside my poncho as I ventured forth. The sun was still nowhere to be seen, but at least the driving rain had quit. I felt a chill coming on. Glancing upward, I could make out nothing of a moon, but a myriad of stars shone across the heavens in every direction.

I was no astronomer, but since Canadian winters were likewise long and dark, I had a passing familiarity with constellations. Since living in Antarctica, I'd come to recognize not only the Southern Cross, but also Sagittarius and Scorpio. Yet, the most startling heavenly body of the southern winter sky was not a constellation at all. The thick star clouds of the Milky Way ran north to south nearly overhead, now in mid-August. Earth's home galaxy shone a signpost so bright that, so long as the day-nights were as cloudless as this, the Onwei could use it as their compass.

I approached the door of the Pastorius home. Despite my resolve, an evil voice whispered in my ear: If this woman was as mean as that Clara, forget it. Let Trieste shop for tortillas herself.

I was about to knock when a great sneeze shook me. I reached for my hankie as steps approached the door. I blew my nose hurriedly, but the door opened before I was able to remove the rag from my face. Matin stared at my awkwardness. His face made him out to be no older than fifty, but his stoop and gnarled fingers were those of an ancient.

He nodded almost imperceptibly, then turned his head and said to someone behind him, "It's the Brixa."

"Who?" came a sound from within.

"Brixa," shouted Matin. "The Sky-Borne."

"Oh," said the voice. "Well, don't just stand there, man. Invite her in."

I breathed a sigh of relief.

Matin stepped aside, dipped his chin, and pointed into the house. I nodded and scraped my boots before stepping across the threshold. The primal scent of fresh baking diffused through the small space.

A short, stout woman sat at a bench by the kitchen table. She wore a bright patterned apron that I guessed was one of Yoka's creations. She used the back of her hand to brush aside wisps of graying blonde hair that fell across her face, then wiped the corn mash from her hands onto the apron. She motioned for me to sit in a straight chair.

I sneezed again, despite myself.

"Pull the chair closer to the fire, girl. Matin, make us some maté." Despite being paralyzed from the waist down, Alma was clearly in charge of this household. Trieste said she was thrown off a horse some years ago, when a clap of thunder spooked the animal. Now she never left home.

In the meager candlelight, Alma squinted at me. I wondered if the woman's vision was also impaired.

"Brixa, our people call you. But among your own tribe, to what do you answer?"

"Keltyn."

"Killton," intoned Alma. She had the same trouble enunciating the "el" sound as everyone else. "I expect Trieste has sent you to stock up on my tortillas. To what do I deserve this honor?"

I cleared my throat. I had no idea how to respond. I expected a simple wordless transaction like that with Clara.

"Never mind." Alma snorted. "Poor simple girl. You don't deserve to be snubbed forever over that fiasco from last year. Sure, I had to adapt my methods, as did all of us who follow this trade. There's a learning curve to using cal." She held up the backs of her arms, now pockmarked with burn scars, some of them still glistening fresh.

I slapped my hand over my mouth. "I'm sorry."

"Can't be helped. If not you, someone else would have figured out the cal connection sooner or later. Meantime, many more would have died from the khokri. Me, I'd rather have a few scars, given the choice." Alma dropped her arms to her lap. "You know, I've told Matin, instead of slighting you, we should thank you."

I was taken aback. Was the woman serious? If so, this was a first.

As Matin handed Alma her drink, her gaze invited him to confirm this wisdom, but he only tilted his head back and forth. She took a sip of the strong brew and gave the bombilla back to Matin, who passed it on to me.

I wanted to say I didn't deserve any thanks, not with all the havoc my actions had brought to the tribe. Yet I sensed the best course was to stay mum. I sucked in the bitter maté and soon felt its bracing effects.

Alma moved her fingers in a constant kneading motion, as if leading up to something else. Finally, she said, "There are rumors about you, Brixa. Has Trieste ever shared these?"

I rubbed the back of my neck. Here it came.

"Ah, you have heard. It is said that you fell out with your mates, even before you were wounded, and they were forced to leave without you. That you wished to use our tribe as a refuge from troubles waiting for you at home."

"That is true." I hung my head.

"Is it?" There was an edge in Alma's voice. "As you can tell, I don't get around much, but when people told me those tales about you, another explanation occurred to me."

"Explanation for what?"

"For why a young woman would wish to take her chances with a tribe of hostile strangers instead of returning home. You would at least know the odds facing you there. Tell me, what is the worst that could have happened to you, had you gone back with your mates?"

I'd pondered this, many times. "If convicted of treason, I might have been thrown into prison, or exiled to another land."

"We have no prisons here. If someone commits a heinous crime like murder, they will be stoned to death. A lesser villain like yourself, despised by all for the bad fortune you brought with you, how do you think you would fare?"

I'd considered this possibility as well. I took another sip of maté before answering. "Banished?"

"Exactly. Sent off on foot, no food, no water, just the clothes on your back. How long do you think you would last out there?"

I gulped. "Not long."

"You deduced this beforehand, I'm sure." Alma pointed a finger at me. "The risks of staying here were greater than the risks of returning home, but you agreed to stay because your superiors made you an offer that you couldn't refuse."

My head swam. I didn't recall much from the days before I was shot and left in a coma. Could I have made such a deal and not remembered it? "What kind of offer?"

"Ha," snorted Alma. "During these long winters, I never leave the house, so my imagination boils over. Matin here is just the opposite." She nodded toward her husband, perched on a stool in the corner, his head leaning against the wall and his eyes half closed. "No imagination at all.

"What kind of offer, you ask? Simple. They drop these charges against you if you agree to embed yourself with the Onwei, gain our trust."

A choking sensation invaded my throat. "What good would that do for my superiors? They're up and gone."

Alma said nothing for a moment. I could barely tell the outlines of the woman's cloudy eyes in the dim candlelight, but they were clearly fixed right on me.

"The villagers who have met you say you seem intelligent. After our encounter today, I must report I'm not so sure about that. Are you trying to tell me your leader has no wish to return? With a whole mountainside full of his precious piedra de yris awaiting?"

I gasped. Alma's charge was the same as the visions, the dreams that had plagued me for months. But how could I admit that to Alma without sounding foolish? Could this idea have entered my conscious mind from some forgotten promise, some deal I had made with Harry? A plea bargain to avoid prosecution for allegedly spying on behalf of the Chinese?

Right now, I was sorely confused. I needed desperately to find out Sir Oscar's intentions. If he really planned another mission, I needed to know. More than that, I needed to figure out my own role. Should I rouse the Onwei to resist at all costs, or should I advise them to hold out for the best deal?

Whose advice could I trust? If only Fay were around, but Fay was somewhere in the Northern Hemisphere. She might as well live on another planet.

I squinted in the candlelight, focusing again on the cloudy eyes of Alma Pastorius. Suddenly it occurred to me: there might be a way to contact Fay. It would involve Joaquin, but would he cooperate?

I stumbled in getting up. "I hope to have an answer for your query soon, Seira Pastorius. Thank you for the maté." I pulled out my purse. "And two dozen fresh tortillas, if you please."

Alma opened her mouth to say something, but, apparently thinking better of it, reached across the table to wrap her wares and hand them to me. "See if Trieste can taste the difference between Char's and mine now."

I bowed to Alma and Matin, then hurried away from the home of this canny woman. Using deduction instead of intuition, Alma had validated my own dark vision.

***

I sat hunched forward on a stool, arms resting on lap, hands clasped, thumbs twirling. I faced Joaquin, who perched cross-legged on the small bed in his room of his Uncle Fermin's house. The air smelled stale. Joaquin must never have opened the door or windows. Soiled clothing lay scattered on the floor. What this household sorely lacked was a female presence.

Joaquin seemed none too happy with my proposal. "Tio Hector hasn't showed his face since last year. His advice always left me puzzled. He probably found someone else to haunt. Good riddance."

"You've got to summon him back, Joaquin. He's our only link to Fay, and she's the only way I can find out if and when Sir Oscar is planning another mission."

Joaquin shut his eyes and shivered. "Hector gives me the creeps. Sorry I ever mentioned him at Aldo's funeral. That was just the excuse Orfea needed to suck me into her plans." He looked up. "We parted on bad terms, you know. She probably don't want nothing to do with me after last year."

I sighed. "Quit feeling sorry for yourself. This isn't about you. It's about the future of your people. Fay is on our side. I guarantee she has made it her business to discover what Sir Oscar's intentions are."

Joaquin held his frown and looked away. "Okay, okay, but there's another problem."

"What?"

"When Tio Hector shown up last year, I never beckoned him, never even thought about him. He just shown up."

I considered this. "How about using Venga to summon him? This guy says he's your ancestor, after all."

Joaquin looked away and said nothing.

I studied him. "You've never used Venga by yourself, have you, scout?"

He addressed the floor. "Nope."

I arose and laid my hands on his shoulders. "My grandpa repaired and sold automobiles, machines that could move you from one place to another. They cost a lot of money, and people were skeptical. He used to say, 'Can't sell 'em if you don't drive 'em.' He made sure people in town saw him and his car out on the street every day."

Joaquin continued to study the floor. "So, I need to get buzzed?" He stuck out his tongue.

"Now and then wouldn't hurt, especially if you plan to peddle the stuff. You've got to understand the experience if you're gonna hawk it." I squeezed on his shoulders until he lifted his face. "I'll expect a report in the next few days."

***

"Brixita glances here" — twang — "and there" — twang — "and everywhere" — twang. Efrain contorted the fingers on his left hand to form the weird chords of the ballad he was composing on the fly. He eyed me while singing each phrase, then quickly glanced to see if his fingers were in the correct position for the next chord. I'm no musician, but I could tell the chords comprised a minor or perhaps a modal key. Huh? Was that supposed to reflect my personality? But then, it seemed all of his songs breathed melancholy.

His lyrics were equally quirky. The rhymes were a stretch — "stone" and "moan" seemed especially flagrant — making me smile despite myself. How did the big gaucho manage to keep a straight face?

I waited patiently for my chance to enlist him in my newly hatched crusade. Normally he would have come up for air by now. Had enough worry shown on my face that he felt obliged to take my mind off my troubles? Efrain styled himself good at this sort of thing. I hadn't the heart to interrupt him.

Each time I visited Efrain, now ensconced in jeaf Aldo's former home, I had to pinch myself. I still felt like a trespasser. The plush merino wool rug, heavy with lanolin, seemed more intimate than all those armchairs and cushions. And the big guy himself? One of the most eligible bachelors in Nomidar, he'd fallen for little old Brixita, oblivious to wisecracks from other charros about such an odd couple. How did I rate?

He finished and put down his instrument, then moved closer and draped his bear paw around my shoulder. I rested my head on his barrel chest, relieved that his minstrel efforts were spent.

Couldn't the two of us just hold each other close, without the need to say a word or sing some dumb song? Someday, hopefully not too long, that would come. For now, though, there were more pressing issues, so I began, with little success, trying to express the feelings and hunches that had weighed on me for months. Efrain remained silent as I rambled.

Finally, I turned to him. "You haven't said a word. What do you think I should do?"

He rested his free hand on his knee, tapping the thumb. "It is not my opinion that counts, Brixita."

It touched me how he turned the epithet into a term of endearment, yet his studied calm irritated me. I shrugged off his hand and sat up to face him. "But you know how the gauchos will react. That's the key. Are they more likely to oppose the next group of Sky-Bornes outright, or will they be enticed to strike a bargain?"

Efrain sighed. "It is my uncle Ysidro whom you must consider. He is the jeaf now, and more opinionated than was Aldo. Greedier too, I expect. Ysidro has made it more difficult for our charros to earn a bonus, where Aldo was always generous in rewarding extra work."

"So, you think he would allow the Sky-Bornes to hunt for treasure?" I considered this. "What a turnaround that would be. Last year, it was under his orders that I was captured, held hostage, and almost killed, all in an effort to drive us away." Just the memory of this would have made me shudder not so long ago. Now, I merely huffed a breath.

Efrain nodded slowly. "That was last year, when Ysidro needed to prove to everyone that he was bold enough to fill Aldo's shoes. And you must remember the state of chaos the whole tribe was in. Now," he chuckled, "I expect he will jump at any chance to line his own pockets."

"It won't end there," I insisted. "First it will just be a few Sky-Bornes come to collect however much of the iris stone they can cram into the plane. Oscar's metalsmiths will use that to build more and bigger planes. Before long, Canadian farmers, lots of them, will move here to till the soil, raise cattle, whatever." I locked eyes with him. "Is that what you want?"

"Of course not."

I raised my fists and thumped them on his chest. "Then you must help me to persuade Ysidro." Thumped again. "Trying to negotiate with Oscar's people will be suicide for the Onwei." My voice rose, and I began to choke.

Efrain grabbed both of my wrists in one of his great mitts and reached to draw me closer with the other. "Shush, shush, my little Brixita. You mustn't lose your calm. It's your finest trait." He bent down to kiss me on the forehead and wiped the tears gathering on my cheeks.

I gazed up at the rough-hewn countenance, the square jaw, high cheekbones, prematurely sun-creased skin and bristling roguish mustache, all so at odds with those sympathetic brown eyes. "Then you'll help me?"

He raised his shaggy brows and shrugged. "I am your humble servant."

I wiggled my hands free and locked them behind Efrain's neck. I lay back on the plush rug, bringing his head down slowly with me. Our lips met, briefly at first, then in a deeper kiss that sent another tremor through me. He kissed my neck, my ear, my mouth again. The bristle of stubble on his jaw rubbed my cheek. I caught the pungent scent of the trail, still exuding through his pores even after these many months in town.

I pulled my tunic over my head and worked to loosen the toggle clasps on Efrain's shirt. He lay on his back, his hands on my hips as I straddled him. I slid backward to wrestle the big gaucho out of his breeches.

We'd made love before, but always in the dark, furtively. Now, the crackling fire and my own desperation released something. Our eyes locked as I mounted him. His great paws encircled my small breasts, and I began to ride him. Soon, he transported me far away.

When it was over, I collapsed onto his chest. We lay with our eyes closed, his hand stroking my back, our breathing slowed. The flames danced near our feet and, still flushed, I nodded off, at peace for the first time in months. Mine was no longer a sole crazed voice. The big guy, and the respect he embodied, were now on my side.

6

QUEBEC STRATEGY

"You must try the dechets, Fay." Harry Ladou reached over and pointed to an item on the aperitif column of her menu.

Fay studied the list closely. She considered herself fluent in French, yet somehow had never encountered dechets before. She gazed into Harry's bemused face. "Oh? Why must I try these dechets?"

"It's a rite of passage for gourmands in Quebec." Harry eyed the tall young waiter standing poised to take their order. "Don't you agree, garçon?"

"*Mais oui*, monsieur. *C'est magnifique*, madame."

The boy's expression was more zipped than Harry's, but Fay detected a scheming air between them. "All right. I'm game. Dechets it is."

"*Tres bien*, madame." The waiter disappeared and Harry lapsed back to studying the list of entrees.

Fay took a sip of her Cointreau and glanced around their booth, ringed with plush leather upholstery. Antique burnished rosewood wall panels alternated with mirrors, lit only by table candles and muted light from high chandeliers. She could barely see around the corner to the backlit bar on the other end of the large room. Soft piano-like tones mixed with the occasional clink of silver on china. The perfect venue, she mused, to launch a seduction or, in her case, a campaign to unravel Harry from his decades-long allegiance to Sir Oscar Bailey.

Harry had suggested dinner here at Chez Boulay Bistro Boreal in Old Town, the ancient heart of Quebec City dating from the seventeenth century. The furnishings suggested that Boulay must be at least half that age, yet it still managed to shine in genteel splendor. If Harry was trying to make an impression, he certainly picked the right spot. Did he have his own agenda?

He snapped his leather-bound menu closed and appeared surprised that she had not yet studied hers. He lifted his own glass of wine. "What's on your mind, Fay?"

She shrugged with a smile. "I don't know. Just soaking in the ambience, I guess. Snobby cosmopolitan dame from Europe comes slumming to Canada, instead finds herself overwhelmed by elegance. Good pick, Harry, and don't tell me there are dozens of places like this in Quebec."

He puckered his lips and rolled his eyes. "I wouldn't say dozens, exactly..."

"You know what I mean."

"Actually, I don't." Harry suddenly turned serious. "You gave me no clue what's up when you called, Fay.

From the strain when last we parted, I guessed more likely business than personal. You have this telly appearance tomorrow. We can discuss how that may affect business at Bailey Enterprises, which means I can put dinner on the Bailey expense account."

Fay shook her head slowly and reached across the table to put her hand over his. "Dear Harry, you're entirely too suspicious. Can't a girl mix business and personal?"

He started to open his mouth, but before he could answer, the waiter brought their appetizers. Harry's was escargot. Though familiar with snails, they weren't something Fay would order for herself; she had tried them once and lived to tell the tale. She peered uncertainly at the dish the waiter set in front of her now. The various pieces appeared to be of animal origin, but nothing she was used to.

The waiter held his notepad at the ready. "Have we decided on an entrée?"

Fay signaled for Harry to order while she made a quick survey of the choices. When the waiter turned back to her, she asked, "What was the fish special you mentioned?"

"Le poisson du jour? Morue, madame, cod in creamy roasted red pepper sauce."

"All right, poison it is."

The waiter left, and Fay eyed her aperitif warily. She speared a dense, deep-fried nugget with the form and texture of blood sausage. The taste was intense and earthly. She reached for her water glass.

"Sweetbreads?" she asked Harry. "Is that what dechets means?"

"The English word would be 'offal'," said Harry, smiling.

"Well, it almost lives up to its name." Fay wiped her mouth and took sip of Cointreau. "I do love the foie gras, even though I feel sorry for the poor geese."

"Still the bleeding heart, I see."

From the set of Harry's mouth, Fay couldn't tell whether he meant to rebuke her or tease her. "That's how I'll always be known, I guess." She set her lips.

This time, Harry reached his hand across the table. "Sorry, Fay. That was a cheap shot."

She said nothing for a long minute. "Apology accepted."

"You know, I've been doing a lot of thinking since that trip."

"Oh?" She perked up. Speak, Harry. Show me a dent in your armor. They hadn't talked — had any communication whatsoever — since debriefing from their disastrous mission after Bailey Voyager returned to Canada fifteen months ago.

Harry plunged onward, staring at the wall behind Fay. "I wonder if Keltyn might have survived, of course. But I also wonder what has become of that tribe, after all of the trauma we put them through."

"Wonder enough to pay them a return visit?" Fay tried to catch his gaze.

"Oscar is floating another mission and wants me to lead it again." Harry sighed. "Not sure I care to. Don't think I could deal with that amount of drama again."

"But you would go if he asked you."

"Yes, I suppose so. Curiosity would get the best of me."

Good. That's step one.

Their entrées and wine arrived. Fay dug into her cod. It melted in her mouth. It took several minutes before she felt brave enough to ask the next question. "Have you figured out how to negotiate with the Onwei if you run into them again?"

"No. I haven't given that a thought, Fay. Somehow I just guessed that would be your job."

"Ha. Guess again. No way Oscar will allow me on board this time, blackmail or no."

Harry rested his knife and fork and stared at her. "That explains it."

Uh-oh. Fay stared back at him. "What?"

"Oscar had me search for one of those gadgets you used to translate on the last mission."

"The lang-synch?"

"Right. He had me send it to our Bailey Europe chief, fellow name of Helmut Ganz. I couldn't figure out why. Ganz is quite fluent in all the languages he needs for international business. But now..."

"You think Oscar wants Ganz to be part of a next mission?"

"He hasn't told me that, which bothers me even more. Still, I admit that foreign languages aren't *my* forte." Harry settled back into his meal.

Fay glanced up. "Speaking of which, tomorrow, after my telly appearance, I'm going to meet with the local chapter of NPU, part of our outreach program. You're Quebecois, right?"

"Hundred percent."

"I hear they have some very interesting stories to tell, but I'm not really up on the local dialect. Think you could come along and fill me in?"

"And get a free dose of brainwashing in the process. Is that the gist?"

"You can read me like a book, Harry." Fay lifted her glass and they clinked.

After dinner, they took their leave of the ancient bistro and strolled, arm in arm, down Rue Saint-Jean. They browsed in shop windows displaying the latest in Canadian fashions, carved wooden knick-knacks, and a travel agency promising a quick getaway to a beach in Norway.

"How do you spend your vacations, Harry? We never talked about that," said Fay.

"I don't take much time off, truth be told. Twice a year I go visit Monique in Alaska. I'll be a grandpa one of these days."

"Congratulations." Fay squeezed his arm. "When is she due?"

"December."

She remembered hearing that Harry's wife divorced him over ten years ago, both too busy with their careers. As Oscar's right-hand man, Harry was constantly on the road. The extra weight he put on, the gray curls in his receding hairline, the slump in his shoulders, the crow's feet around his eyes that gold-rimmed dialups did little to conceal, all testified to the toll he paid to reach the number two position in the world's largest corporation.

Fay wondered if Sir Oscar had ever offered Harry the services of his fountain-of-youth squad. Even if he had, she guessed Harry would decline. He breathed not a trace of vanity.

They strolled in silence until reaching Fay's hotel. She turned to Harry. "Thanks for a delightful evening," she said, and leaned over to kiss him on the cheek. "See you tomorrow."

Stunned for a moment, Harry recovered quickly. "*Bon soir, ma chère.*"

Fay flashed Harry her most seductive smile and headed toward the door. Once safely inside, she grasped an imaginary Harry in her arms and whirled in a waltz around the empty lobby. The evening had gone swimmingly.

Notably, he had not clammed up when she mentioned NPU. That meant Oscar was still keeping his suspicions to himself. So much the better for her plan to wrangle Harry free from the suffocating orbit of his boss.

***

Fay and Harry sat on folding chairs on one side of a large circle. The other chairs were empty, as was the rest of the large community center. Smells of stale coffee and cigarette smoke hung in the air from previous meetings.

Pipes clanged softly behind the far wall. The early evening sun shone through the windows on one side, illuminating a haze of fine dust throughout the room, and provided a fuzzy view of the working-class Quebec City neighborhood.

Harry fidgeted, crossing and re-crossing his legs and arms. He wore a black leather jacket, black chenille pants, and black boots. Fay knew he served as Sir Oscar's liaison for plant closings and various labor negotiations. On those occasions he must be used to cold and often hostile encounters, but here, with no one to talk with or even to size up, he looked out of his element.

"I wanted to arrive early," Fay explained, "rather than show up my hosts by playing guest of honor. Thanks for humoring me."

"Here comes someone." Harry lifted his chin toward the door at the opposite end of the hall.

Two women entered, one weighty and middle-aged, the other young enough to be her daughter. Both advertised their presence with small bells around their ankles, each step tinkling. They both wore bright print tunic tops and denim pants, supplemented with numerous necklaces and bracelets. The mother's hair was graying and hung to her shoulders. The daughter had her jet-black hair in pigtails.

Algonquian Cree perhaps, thought Fay, same as Keltyn's stock. She and Harry arose as the women approached. The two couples bowed to each other. Fay caught the scent of patchouli. She introduced herself, using her given name of Orfea, then pointed to Harry. "*Mon interprete*," she laughed.

"Amalie," said the mother.

"Daphne," said her daughter.

Amalie launched into an effusive greeting with a multitude of gestures, trying, so far as Fay could tell, to explain the difficulties of organizing these meetings. Fay kept watching Harry for clues, but Amalie would not pause long enough for the poor man to get a word out.

Fay invited them to sit as Amalie rambled on. Meanwhile, more people entered the hall in twos and threes. A few others sported print tunics, but most wore nondescript baggy clothing in faded grays and beiges. Some of the men carried canes. All were at least middle aged. What happened to the youth, wondered Fay? They, of all people, should be most concerned with threats to the future of their homeland.

By fifteen minutes past the appointed hour, the seats had filled. Amalie rose to introduce the group's guests and lifted her hand for Fay to join her.

"Madame Orfea Del Campo, famous anthropologist from Switzerland, the international director of PAU," she said, using the French initials of the group.

Fay saw a few knowing nods, but mostly blank faces. She wondered if any of them had watched her broadcast appearance earlier. Surely, they must have tellies. The thinly scattered clapping gave her pause.

Then Amelie signaled Harry to rise. "Monsieur Harry…"

"Ladou."

"Très bien. Un nom Québécois." Amalie appraised Harry's casual but expensive wardrobe. "And what, may I ask, is your position, Monsieur Harry, besides serving as Madame's interprete?" Her smiling face invited a show-and-tell response from her guest, something to amuse this docile audience.

Harry glanced at Fay as if he had walked into a trap. "I...I am the managing director of Bailey Enterprises."

At the mention of Bailey, Amalie's smile froze in its tracks. The room turned quiet enough to hear a pin drop. A sea of hostile faces confronted Harry.

"I'm sorry. Did I say something wrong?" He fell back into his chair.

"The name Bailey does not curry any favor in these parts," said Amalie. "Surely you must know that."

"Actually not." Harry pushed up the nosepiece of his dialups. "I had no idea."

"Mining rights, Monsieur Ladou." A man's guttural voice rose from the other side of the circle. He leaned on a cane as his bent frame struggled to rise. "Your company used the courts to rob our tribe of its land, paying but a fraction of its worth." His fist shook. "Now our people labor for slave wages in your nickel mills, while our former homeland lies ravaged by strip mines, ore for the mills scraped from its raw hillsides."

Spittle flew from the man's mouth. He tried to point the cane at Harry but lost his balance. A younger man beside him jumped in to keep him from falling, then eased him back to his chair.

"Thank you, brother Gaston," said Amalie. She eyed Harry, who was mopping his brow, his face nearly as pale as his handkerchief. "This story seems to come as a shock to you, Monsieur Harry."

Harry tried to clear his throat while Fay hovered beside him. Several times, he started to respond but each time ended in a choking sound. He made no effort to arise again.

Fay turned to Amalie. "He could use a drink of water."

The matron signaled to Daphne, who jingled toward a sink by the far wall.

Fay wasn't feeling that great herself. She wanted Harry to hear the dislocated workers' point of view, but their deep hostility made her cringe. She flashed back on reports of recent ugly incidents at Bailey Mines. Could an NPU splinter group have fomented those? She scanned the audience for clandestine saboteurs, then just as quickly shook off her paranoia. What could they do here, take Harry hostage?

She forced herself to sit up to face the group. "I must apologize on both of our behalves. Please tell us more details of this tragic story." She accepted the water from Daphne and held it front of Harry's mouth with one hand, resting the other hand on his back. He took several sips before waving Fay off.

Earlier, she had noticed a bowed giant, his gray hair braided in a queue, his arms folded across his chest, sitting near the rear of the room. Now he rose. Despite his heft, he spoke in a hoarse whisper, and everyone hushed at once, straining to hear him. Fay turned one ear, trying to catch his meaning, but decided that the problem must be his dialect rather than his pitch. She stole a peek at Harry, hoping he could translate, but he simply closed his eyes and shook his head. He appeared exhausted.

When the giant finished, he sat and again folded his arms, as one person after another arose to give his or her own testimony. Just like a revival meeting. Despite the dialect, Fay was able to piece it together; these people were the displaced victims of industrial "progress," thrown off land that had been their home for millennia, now relegated to dead-end jobs in mills, retail, and domestic service.

She peeked at Harry, who still sat with his head slumped, but occasionally glanced up at the speaker. She knew he was getting a full dose and then some and could only hope that he wouldn't resent her conniving to lure him here.

When everyone had their say, a good two hours later, he and Fay stood in the center of the hall to greet those few who ventured forward. Old Gaston, whose outpouring of wrath had almost done him in earlier, again waved his cane in silent rebuke as he shuffled past, clinging for support to his young friend.

Fay noticed that even Amalie seemed to have lost her earlier vitality. From the time Harry revealed his connection with the Bailey empire, her expression turned hard, and remained severe as Fay and Harry took their leave. No hug, no handshake, not even a bow this time, she gave only the slightest of nods. As they left, it was obvious to Fay that no bonds had been forged, no sense of hope. They had simply gone through the motions.

Deep doubts surfaced as she headed out. What kind of monumental task had she undertaken? Organizing one displaced tribe could take years; she knew that from her field studies. Of all the audacity, to imagine that she, that anyone, could somehow unite dozens of isolated tribes around the globe in common cause. What had she been thinking?

***

Driving back to her hotel, Harry seemed as somber as Fay. "Sorry I lost it back there. Thanks for stepping in. Took the heat off me, you did."

"Totally my fault." Fay chewed her lip. "I should have anticipated their pent-up resentment." She didn't want Harry to dwell on potential motives, though. "How about a drink when we get back? I'd say you earned one."

"Beyond the call of duty, eh?" said Harry. "I agree." He reached out a hand. Fay took it and squeezed.

When they walked into the hotel lobby, Harry cast his gaze around. "A nice place like this must have a bar."

Fay grabbed his arm and steered him toward the elevator. "My room has a more than adequate mini-bar, thank you." Middle-aged woman invites casual male acquaintance to her room for a drink. The story sounded familiar, but she sensed that somehow, this time there was more on the line.

Harry lifted his brow ever so slightly but said nothing. They moved arm-in-arm up to the doorstep of Fay's room. She unlocked the door and he held it open. She motioned to the fridge. "I haven't checked yet. This chain usually has a decent selection."

Light from inside the fridge illuminated Harry's face as he inspected the contents. "What'll it be, Signora Del Campo?"

"Oh, something on the rocks, I'm not picky." Fay settled on the couch.

Harry mixed the drinks and headed toward her. "Scotch seemed like a safe bet." He sat down beside her and they clinked glasses.

"Safer than pulce beer," said Fay. They both laughed.

"Don't remind me." Harry took a sip. "I was sick as a dog for more than a day after that barbecue. Didn't seem to faze you a bit. How do you come by such a robust constitution?"

Fay tilted her chin down and batted her lashes. "Even anthropologists have professional secrets."

"Is that so?" Harry slid his arm to rest on top of the sofa behind Fay's neck. "Ever share any?"

"Give away, never. Trade, maybe." She kicked her shoes off and pulled her feet up onto the couch.

"Fay, Fay," said Harry. "What do you want from me? Oscar's ten-year business plan?"

She laughed. "That would be a good start."

"Well, no dice, lady."

Fay struck a pout. "Not one secret?"

Harry thought for a moment. "Not unless you count a tattoo."

"Ah ha. Show and tell."

"It's in a delicate spot. I don't show it to just anyone." He inched closer.

"I'm not just anyone, am I, Harry?" Faces almost touching, she closed her eyes and felt Harry's lips meet hers.

Like a small bomb igniting a larger one, this first brush of their lips unleashed in her a torrent of pent-up desire. With the second kiss, deeper and much longer, Fay felt a convulsion course through her body. This is going to get complicated, she thought as she surrendered.

7

JOURNEYMAN

Returning from the stable after grooming Cisco, Joaquin stopped to brush the horsehair off his clothes on the porch of his uncle's block house. Uncle Fermin was fussy about keeping the dirt outdoors.

As soon as he stepped inside, Fermin whistled him over. "An urgent message for you, boy." One corner of his mouth twisted up as he swayed in his squeaky rocking chair. His breath smelled of rotgut whiskey from a near-empty flask at his feet. "That old hag Yoka wishes to see you. It is im*por*tant." He emphasized "por" with a sneer.

Joaquin grimaced. His uncle's cynicism had only worsened with age, and he longed for the chance to cut his ties with the old man altogether, before his scornful attitude could infect Joaquin as well.

What was so important for Yoka? He stopped to visit her three days ago, and the crone had very little to say. Reluctantly, he set off through the dark to her hut.

A month ago, she offered to take him in. He considered the proposal, though the thought of cleaning up the copious secretions oozing from her every orifice made him gag. Bless Luz and the Brixa for doing their part. He could not. In fact, he found it hard to show his face as her condition kept slipping.

Even worse than her physical ailments, she had lately taken to ranting about prophecy. It was not enough for him to simply learn the mechanics of Venga preparation and invite clients to partake. The *brux* — he hated that term — was more than a medium for channeling lost souls. He must grow into his greater role, the spiritual guide of his tribe. This meant keeping his mind and heart open to any new visions that might affect the tribe's welfare.

Thus far, Joaquin had shrugged off Yoka's charge. Since her days were clearly numbered, he meant to use the Venga art in its most obvious form, among single paying customers, perhaps a gathering of family members. He had no intention of styling himself a prophet. Look where that had gotten Yoka, mostly mocked by scornful laughter behind her back.

As Joaquin approached her hut, he noticed a multitude of lights and many voices from inside. Yoka must have summoned others. Perhaps she wished to throw a farewell party. Now, that was something he could savor.

He knocked, and the voices immediately fell silent. He waited a minute and was about to push on the door, when instead it opened from inside. He stepped into a sea of familiar faces, all smiling and shouting his name. Luz, her mother and her uncle Ariel, Efrain and Keltyn, Dario, Hortensio and Char, the charros Gabino and Soriante and their uncle Ysidro, all were here. Even Carmelo, Torme, and Gustavo showed up. Those three were his age-mates, but, with their bragging and bullying ways, he kept them at arm's length.

Strands of gaily-colored fabric spanned the room, wall to wall. Candles blazed throughout, their holders hastily fastened to the beams. He caught the smells of roast pig, herbed potatoes, cooked beans, fresh pies. Yoka's kitchen table groaned under the weight of all these, plus pastries, juices, milk, pulce. A jug of Ysidro's home brew made the rounds.

In the far corner, Yoka sat propped up in bed with extra pillows to witness the festivities. Joaquin could barely glimpse her behind the crowd of guests, but her wizened grin when she spotted him left no doubt whose idea this party had been.

All of this Joaquin took in at a glance, but even as everyone shouted his name, he did not grasp the significance of the event until Trieste led him to another table. There lay a glazed sponge cake with sixteen tiny candles sticking up. He had totally forgotten about his birthday; as far back as he could remember, no one had ever made a fuss over it. A lump formed in his throat.

Luz lit the candles with a frond from the fire. All the guests gathered round and sang the Onwei birthday toast: "*Felix complanos a ti.*"

"You must make a wish, Joaquin," said Trieste.

His eyes rolled upwards in deep thought. I wish that I could see my future. With that, he huffed and puffed and blew out the candles to hearty applause.

Luz moved to slice up the cake. She handed him the first plate and kissed him on the cheek. She sported some kind of floral perfume. "Happy Birthday, Joaquin. A big sixteen now. I can't call you twerp anymore."

"This is crazy," said Joaquin. "Whose idea was this? I don't even know if today is my birthday."

"Yoka's idea, actually. I gather she has something to say, and she wants everyone to hear it."

Luz cut a small piece of the cake and took it over to the crone's bedside. Joaquin watched as Yoka took a tiny bite, then waved off the rest. She made a drinking motion, and Luz went off to fetch her favorite sun tea.

Yoka beckoned Joaquin near. Her gnarled hands grasped his. "Surprised?" she asked. "You needn't be. You have done well by me this past year. Pull up a chair." When he did so, she pulled him toward her and croaked in his ear, "I wish to make you my heir."

Joaquin recoiled and stared back at her.

Yoka plopped her head back onto the pillow. "Why do you act so shocked? You know I have no natural successor, not since my Addys died from the khokri years ago. No other young person in the tribe has your combination of patience and curiosity. You have been a worthy pupil."

He gulped hard and tried to still his pounding heart. "Thank you, seira." He wondered what hidden obligations befell the heir.

"Well, pull yourself together," she croaked. "I am about to announce the fact for all to hear."

She signaled to Luz once again. The girl lifted the glass of sun tea to Yoka's lips, and she took several swallows. Then she whispered something in Luz's ear. The girl grabbed a spoon and banged it on the cup until voices dropped. The guests turned to face the frail old woman, propped up at the head of her bed.

"Friends," she began. The single syllable rang with some of her voice's past timbre. "You make my heart glad with your presence. I am afraid I do not have long for this world…"

She was interrupted with cries of "Say not so." and "No, no."

"…and this could be my last chance to address you in this lifetime." A few mock groans echoed, as Yoka's word choice suggested she might haunt them from her grave. "Joaquin is now sixteen. Maybe the true date is not until next week, or maybe he turned last week. I have consulted with others," she nodded toward Trieste, "and all we can agree upon is that the baby Joaquin was born near the end of the dark season. Since neither of his parents is around to set the record straight, let today be the anniversary."

Yoka broke into a coughing fit and flailed her arm until Luz eased more sun tea to her lips. After several minutes, she continued. "As you all know, this young man has apprenticed himself to me for well over a year now and immersed himself in the Venga arts. He still has much to learn but has the tools and the desire to refine his knowledge. So, I wish now, with no fear of embarrassment after my departure, to declare that Joaquin Beltran shall be our tribe's new *guia*."

Joaquin caught his breath. Guia — guide — implied more than "heir." She wished for him to lead Venga rituals and extol visions for the whole tribe. Worse, she saddled him with this burden in public. Even worse, he would need to pronounce these visions to an audience of skeptical neighbors who had known him since infancy, and who mostly still treated him as the town mascot. At this moment he would give anything to vanish altogether; he had no desire to become the leader of religious ceremonies, not now, not ever.

Yet, if he refused her call while surrounded by everyone he knew, his shame would be unbearable. He might have to abandon the village altogether. The crone knew all this when she planned the party, he decided. He would have no choice but to accept.

He bowed his head to another scattering of applause, but this time it seemed more tentative. Was it that guia seemed more genteel than bruxa, what everyone called Yoka behind her back? Better a guide than a witch. Still, if Yoka was right about her own imminent passing, it would fall to Joaquin, the new guia, to lead the mourning for her. How could he?

Yoka spelled out to all assembled that Joaquin would become her heir in full, the recipient of all she owned. If he wished to sell, trade or donate her looms to others who might find more use for them, that would be up to him. Her hut, her sparse furniture, her mule and cart, even her ailing setter dog Mugabe, all would be his to do with as he pleased.

She coughed numerous times through this portion, and it was clear, even with frequent stops to refresh herself, that her strength was being taxed to its utmost. When she finished, she collapsed back onto the bed. A pained smile and hand wave signaled for the party to continue.

Dazed, Joaquin felt someone put a plate of food into his hands. Well-wishers mouthed his name. Ariel, Soriante, Gabino and even Ysidro slapped him on the back.

Torme sidled up next to him. "Hey, Joaquin. I was wondering, like, how's about letting me try that Venga stuff sometime? My grandma, see, I wanna say hi to her."

Joaquin smiled at him and slid away, saying only "We'll see." He would need to contend with these inane requests, and he would also need to guard his stash of Venga from prying eyes and would-be guia charlatans.

***

Much later, Joaquin lay in bed at Uncle Fermin's home, the same bed in which he spent every winter's night as long as he could remember. Soon, much too soon at this rate, he would have his own home and be responsible for his own livelihood. All of those people who came to wish him well today would be there to support him, and that assurance gave him comfort.

Even Fermin, his "uncle" of no blood relation, made overtures that the two of them should come to better terms. This same Fermin had disdained Joaquin ever since the boy showed no interest in the man's trade of masonry. Funny how a sudden turn in one's fortunes brought with it so many new bosom buddies.

He had delayed long enough. It was time to heed Keltyn's charge to get in touch with Tio Hector. This other "uncle," in turn, could tap into whatever information Joaquin's "cousin," Seira Orfea, might have about another imminent visit from the Sky-Bornes. He had delayed his personal Venga baptism until now, fearing what? Loss of control, he supposed. It seemed unnatural, even profane, for a solitary person to engage in Venga without a guia.

Joaquin rested his teeth on his tongue before biting into a single nugget. The mealy morsels had an astringent flavor, like the skin of certain fruits. He tried to wash the taste away with a swallow of water, then lay back and waited. And waited.

Nothing happened for a good ten minutes. Then the telltale tingling began on the hairs of his neck.

"Not to worry, boy. Here I am." The form of Tio Hector appeared in the darkened room, sitting on the side of the bed. "Your favorite uncle – admit it, you like me better than that swine Fermin – must also have the chance to congratulate you, no?"

"Go for it. Everyone else wants a piece of me," rued Joaquin. "Them who sneered a few weeks ago now wanna be my best friend."

"Fame and wealth will turn people's heads. You must discern those few whom you can trust."

"And who might those be? You, I bet you'll say."

"Of course, and to prove it I bring a message from someone on the other side of the world."

Joaquin scurried to sit up in bed. "Orfea Del Campo? But, how could you read my mind?" Despite his excitement, he forced himself to whisper, so as not to disturb the sleeping Fermin next door.

"What good would your favorite uncle be if he didn't anticipate your desires? She is a very busy lady, I must say. Running hither and yon, and now in a romantic entanglement."

"How did you reach her?"

"It took a while to find the right moment. You can't rush these things, not when it comes to women."

Joaquin spread his palms in the dark. "Well? What she tell you?"

"Patience, my boy. I am coming to that. The Sky-Borne lord Sir Oscar Bailey is indeed making plans for another voyage to your land." Tio Hector nodded gravely.

So, Keltyn's intuition was correct. "How soon?"

"'Soon,' was all she could say."

"I'll tell the Brixa," said Joaquin.

Tio Hector nodded again. "See to it."

Joaquin felt a squeeze on his leg. Then the apparition vanished as abruptly as it arrived. He was left staring into the dark. What was that all about? No different, really, from all the previous times Tio Hector showed up unbidden. Except for one small detail. This time he, Joaquin, had summoned the ghost to appear, and it did. That must be the true power of Venga, he decided. Instead of losing control, the user gained it.

***

Two weeks later, during a single hour of daylight, Joaquin presided over Yoka's funeral in Nomidar's modest cemetery, a plot of land near a cliff overlooking the ocean. Some might claim that Yoka's spirit presided. In the brief time left to her after designating Joaquin as her heir, she specified just what lessons she wished to leave with the tribe upon her departure. But now she was gone, and Joaquin already had different ideas. The time had come to leave his own imprint.

He stood before the coffin and freshly dug grave. A salty wind whipped in from the ocean at his back and, facing away from the precipice, he had to brace himself to keep from being blown forward. Opposite him, hands clasped below their waists, the small crowd fanned out around the pit.

"We're here to bid Yoka Sutu farewell," he began. Lest the wind and roaring waves below drown him out, he made his voice as strident as he could muster without breaking into a scream. In a way, speaking loudly felt like a relief. Had the service been indoors, he might have choked on tears trying to get the words out.

"Yoka wished me to hand out Venga nuggets and have you all join in her musings. Someday, at the right time, I may do that. For now, I'm a rookie with Venga, though I 'spect to learn more. Plus, this windswept hill isn't the best for musing."

He paused to survey his audience, relieved to see they were still with him. Some were gauging his performance closely; Ysidro and Dario seemed to pay particular attention to his every move. He willed his breathing to slow.

"Most everyone here knew Yoka Sutu longer than me. You loved her or feared her, often at the same time. She could be snooty at one moment, charming the next, but, least around me, never boring. She was canny and narrow-minded. If you didn't agree with her, it was your tough luck. And always she proved right.

"Though I'm pretty sure that Yoka, even as a young woman, never won any beauty contests," a burst of laughter, "she had a nose for fashion. Under your coats, many you ladies wear a bright dress or skirt that come off her loom. As you can tell," Joaquin held open his plain brown hemp jacket to expose an even plainer beige tunic, "I haven't yet sprouted any fashion sense, but Yoka, she was a self-taught expert.

"There you have it. Her spirit, her craft, what she could do with Venga. What else shall we remember

Yoka for?" Joaquin's mood darkened with the painful memory of Yoka's hectoring over her final weeks. His inheritance of her estate and her gifts had come with strings attached. He must agree to act as her mouthpiece after she had passed on.

"The most important thing in her latter days, what she wishes no one to forget, is her prophecies. Some of her forecasts seem obvious now; the danger of climbing Mt. Erebus to search for piedra de yris." He watched Keltyn and Luz and Trieste all wince at this recollection.

"Later, quizzing the Sky-Borne Orfea, she figured out what Orfea couldn't. The Sky-Borne lord wishes to gather as much of the piedra de yris as possible. Why? To build more and bigger flying machines. For what?" Again, he scanned his audience. No one ventured a response. "To bring lots and lots of farmers from their land to 'settle' ours." He paused. "That means 'invade.'"

His voice grew hoarse. He wished he'd brought some water. As he paused again, he heard other voices raised, angry words shouted.

Despite the clamor, he still felt on sure footing. Even a few months ago, any challenge would have silenced him. Now he raised his hand for quiet. "I don't have to tell you, Yoka would push us to do everything to keep our homeland safe and secure. May we honor her wish and may her soul rest in peace."

Exhausted, he nodded. Dario, Soriante, Gabino and Efrain moved to grab the ends of ropes and lower the coffin into the earth. Ysidro alone stood stock still, his hard stare directed at Joaquin. Before he could decipher the meaning of the jeaf's gaze, several mourners crowded around Joaquin with more questions. He truly felt hoarse, almost to the point of choking. He put a hand to his throat and pointed in Keltyn's direction. She would need to lead whatever resistance their people could muster. The prophet's duties, he hoped, extended only to conveying the message, not acting upon it.

He stole a glance at the Brixa, now surrounded by eager questioners. Though he once cringed at Yoka's harsh rhetoric, he had just felt the power of her speaking gifts course through his veins. It was a heady sensation; words conveying thoughts could be as powerful as actions. Wow.

8

EMANCIPATION PROCLAMATION

Luz and Keltyn sat across from each other at the modest kitchen table. Trieste dished out fragrant polenta patties spiced with roasted peppers and caramelized onion, topped with a dollop of goat cheese. She dropped into her chair and they fell silent, the only sound the clacking of knife and fork on clay plates.

Glancing at Keltyn, Luz noted that the Brixa, who had seemed troubled for weeks, now appeared calmer, more focused. Her appetite, previously sporadic, was now positively ravenous. She reached for a second patty while Luz and her mother still daintily picked apart their first.

Luz felt a twinge of jealousy. She knew that Keltyn and Efrain were spending more time together. Though the Brixa was not one to betray her feelings, Luz decided she must be in love. How else to explain this change in her behavior? All the more reason for Luz to stake her own claim.

She put down her knife and fork. "Ahem." She waited for her mother and Keltyn to glance up from their plates, then stood. Dramatically holding up both hands for all to see, she removed Ian's promise ring from her right hand, then slipped it on her left ring finger. "It's staying here from now on," she announced.

Trieste gasped. "How dare you, girl?"

"It's done, Mama. I'm going to marry Ian this summer, with or without your blessing."

"You'll do no such thing. I'll not permit it." The veins in Trieste's temples bulged.

"I am eighteen, Mama, more than old enough to decide for myself. I don't need your permission anymore." Luz was pretty sure about this, but not positive. Honestly, all the girls her age who married had done so with their parents' consent.

Her hands clenched the side of the table as she stole a glance at the Brixa, who diplomatically kept silent, knowing that Trieste respected her judgment. "Ask Keltyn."

Trieste scoffed. "What would the Brixa know about our marriage customs?"

"Not much." Keltyn put down her knife and fork to answer. "But I agree with Luz that she is old enough to make up her own mind."

Luz smiled broadly and ducked her chin in affirmation.

"Still," Keltyn continued, "what only child would willingly abandon her single mother in favor of running off to marry someone in a distant village?" She turned to face Luz head on. "If Ian truly loves you, he should respect the needs of your family."

Luz couldn't believe her ears. Keltyn was siding with Trieste. Standing up to her full height, her fists balled at her sides, she glared at the Brixa. "What are you saying? Respect how?"

"Why couldn't he move here? Join the Nomidar tribe?"

"His father needs him," Luz sputtered. "He's the only boy in the family."

"You told me his sisters are married. How far away do they live?"

Luz's jaw dropped. There was no use arguing this. In fact, Keltyn was right. Ian's brothers-in-law all lived near his parents' home and could certainly provide help.

The truth, Luz had to admit, was that if she and Ian made their home in Nomidar instead of Perth Village, it would squelch her dream of joining the Campbell family horse ranch business, to say nothing of prolonging her terminal boredom with sleepy Nomidar.

Trieste watched this heated exchange with barely concealed glee. "The Brixa is right. You must persuade this Ian to come live in Nomidar."

Luz's heart pounded in her chest. "But he's never even been here."

"So?" said Trieste. "You yourself have never been to Perth Village, yet your head has been turned by blind love."

Keltyn leaned forward. "You could invite him to come spend time here after the next Rendezvous. He could stay a month and still make it back to Perth before winter."

Luz considered how that scenario would play out. On the one hand, she would have plenty of time alone with Ian. Her mother would likely wish to continue with other artisans who followed the route of seasonal cattle migration. Yet what kind of impression would Ian get of Nomidar, with all of its able-bodied residents gone? Not just a sleepy village, but a dead one.

More confused than ever, Luz could offer only one last objection. "The family horse ranch…" She couldn't even put the whole idea into words.

Trieste and Keltyn glanced at each other and nodded in unison. "A worthy enterprise, girl," said Trieste. "One that Nomidar could also use."

Luz snapped to attention. "What do you mean? How?"

"Surely this Ian can persuade his father to start another breeding operation here. A good horse is a gaucho's stock-in-trade. For now, he can only procure a new one during his short week at the Rendezvous. Little time to make a selection, and there are never enough to satisfy demand, yet he must still pay top price." Trieste paused, raised one eyebrow. "Imagine what a fine living the two of you could make here."

Luz stared at her mother's face across the small table. Was there merit in this scheme of hers or was it just a subterfuge aimed at keeping her daughter under her thumb? And what about Keltyn? Her friend had never before taken sides in a family dispute, yet now she boldly sided with Trieste. Why? Clearly, she wished to curry her favor, but for what?

Trieste eyed her daughter. "You must think on this, Lucita. Now, if you will be so kind as to clean up, I wish to show the Brixa a new technique for pendant-style earrings, one that I just stumbled upon today."

"Yes, Mama." Luz felt too battered to argue further.

Trieste and Keltyn retreated to the studio. The walls were thin enough so that Luz could hear their conversation as she washed the dishes.

"See how the stone stretches and curls on this set?" came Trieste's voice.

"Oh, wow," said Keltyn. "How did you ever manage that without cracking?"

"With this." Her mother must be pointing toward something on her workbench. "I mix just a smidgen with the molten ore. Gives the compound elasticity."

"Incredible," said Keltyn. "Who would have imagined you could get so many shapes and patterns?"

Trieste laughed. "Remember, I have been working with this substance since Luz was but a babe in arms. In every trait you can imagine, it is unlike any other mineral. Yet it gives up its secrets only to those who are patient enough to coax them."

"I bet no other artisan has ever spent as much time with the stone as you."

"True. The only source was that elusive trader, and I paid him well to divert his best findings to me."

"You must be relieved, now that you will have a steady supply of your own." Keltyn's voice dropped. Luz put the dishes down and strained to listen.

"And will you continue to gather it?" asked Trieste, her tones also hushed.

Luz bristled. She and Keltyn both collected a stash last fall, their saddlebags stuffed to overflowing. Ever since, Luz imagined this would be her ongoing job, perhaps along with Ian. They would harvest a quantity of stone from the slopes of Erebus each fall, enough for her mother's needs until the following year.

Now Trieste was soliciting Keltyn. Was she hedging her bets, worried that Luz would consider this task mundane, unworthy? Did Trieste know Luz's mind better than she herself did? The exciting part, finding the source of the stone, had almost cost her life, but now that she knew the spot, the rest was easy.

Still, the prospect of breeding and trading horses with Ian's family had appeal too. Now her vexing mother raised the stakes, forcing Luz to choose between her love of horses and supporting her mother's livelihood. It was all she could do to refrain from charging into the studio, to confront these two women. They were trying to force her into a win-or-lose decision.

Meanwhile, the two of them murmured on, oblivious to the feelings tearing Luz apart. "Of course, you can count on me," said Keltyn. "But listen. You are the only artisan who uses this mineral, yet there are other forces who still wish to exploit it."

"Your cursed Sky-Bornes," muttered Trieste. "I thought we had driven them out."

"I'm afraid they will return," said Keltyn, "and my hunch tells me sooner rather than later. The best farmland of Canada, where I come from, will be underwater in a few more generations. You heard Joaquin at Yoka's funeral. Canadian farm families will flock here to colonize your land."

Luz heard the sound of Trieste sucking air, then a thud as she dropped onto the workbench. The ominous prospect must have just now hit her.

"We must not let that happen," she managed to say.

"It will happen, unless we organize to stop them," said Keltyn. "I need your help to explain this threat to the other artisans."

"Yes, of course." Trieste's voice was almost a whisper.

Luz tried to picture the return of the flying machine to the Erebus region. Presumably the pilot, Buck or whoever might replace him, would be able to land the craft safely this time, and on target, closer to the volcano.

Would the Sky-Bornes come in peace, or would they anticipate a hostile reception? Perhaps they would not expect any welcome; indeed, it was only by mere chance that she and Joaquin had stumbled upon them, and then only because their landing came at the same time that the cattle migration took the herd through the Erebus region.

Keltyn had too much at stake to greet the next landing of the flying machine, whenever that should come. She was still a wanted woman in her homeland,

and Luz was sure that she had no wish to return. This might present an opportunity.

Luz finished the dishes, whistled for her mutt Flaco, gathered her coat, and opened the front door. As she strode along in the dark, the dog scurrying in front of her, she conceived the seed of a plan, one that might involve her instead of the Brixa as the go-between for the Onwei and the Sky-Bornes.

If her mother needed a supply of the iris stone, and so did the Sky-Bornes, who better than she to broker the exchange? She knew exactly where to look, and, if she played her cards right, might well be able to set the price. If that idea bothered Keltyn, too bad. She should have thought twice before siding with Trieste.

9

SHUTTLE DIPLOMACY

A summons to the Chinese consulate in Zürich: Fay had no idea what to expect. She had sent a note of sympathy to Savant Wan Xiang about the loss of their mutual friend, Keltyn SparrowHawk. She had half surmised this kind of a response, rather than a personal one, but that begged the question. Had her overture put herself or him in some kind of danger?

She willed herself to stay calm. After all, she had dueled Sir Oscar Bailey to a draw on several occasions. Surely emissaries of the Chinese Empire could be no more devious than he.

Fay approached the wrought-iron gate, the only break in a ten-foot stone wall that ringed an entire city block. In the cold war that pitted Chinese Siberia versus the West, neutral Switzerland provided a buffer zone for China in the heart of Europe. Fay wondered how, or if, the Chinese authorities would have contacted her, had she lived anywhere other than Switzerland.

At the gate, she showed her ID to the guard. He checked his list and made a quick call. Within minutes, a young man wearing thick, black-rimmed dialups and Chinese business attire — gray tunic buttoned at the left shoulder — arrived at the gate. With a slight bow, he led Fay wordlessly down fifty meters of shrub-lined pavement toward the three-story brick and stone fortress. Mounted cameras and motion sensors guarded the entrance hall like so many gargoyles. Her escort led Fay up the stairs to a second-floor reception room, deposited her in a leather armchair, bowed once again and departed.

She tried to use the detached perspective of her anthropology background to compare this welcome with those from other strange tribes she had encountered. "Hurry up and wait" had a familiar ring. She crossed her legs and rocked her foot.

The faint scent of sandalwood wafted through the oversized room. Not far from where she sat stood an officious-looking teak desk and chair. Beyond that, the art on the walls caught her eye. A series of small but superbly executed hangings depicted mountain and river scenes of the Chinese landscape, several of them accented with calligraphy. Though she had never visited China — Western tourism was virtually nonexistent, and anthropologists were about as welcome as missionaries — Fay was drawn to its ancient culture and had added several jade carvings to her small art collection over the years.

Just as she stood to examine the wall hangings, a door on the far wall opened. Another man appeared, also with thick, black-rimmed dialups and shoulder-buttoned gray tunic, but this man was shorter, older, pudgier. He seemed surprised to find Fay arising from her chair and greeted her by patting both palms downward.

"Please not trouble stand on my account, Savant Del Campo." The man executed a stiff full bow at the waist. "Consul First Secretary Teng Zhou at your service." He made no move to approach her, instead continuing on toward the chair behind the desk. He opened a drawer, pulled out a folder, opened it and scanned the first document.

Fay straightened her skirt and re-crossed her legs.

Consul Teng raised his eyes to meet hers. "You must wonder why we summon you to Chinese consulate." The tiny mouth opened, exposing a row of yellow teeth like kernels on a shrunken corncob.

"I assumed it must have something to do with my attempt to contact Savant Wan Xiang at the Siberian Academy of Earth Science."

"Savant Wan assistant courteous enough forward your note to Ministry Science and Technology." Consul Teng bowed his head slightly in approval, as he fished for a page in his files.

Fay tried not to act surprised. She had been warned that nothing of interest circulated in China without knowledge of the regime, and so was pretty sure the cybercensors on both ends would parse her message. She had carefully chosen the words that Consul Teng now read aloud.

"Dear Savant Wan Xiang, you do not know me, but I was a friend and colleague of your student, Savant Keltyn SparrowHawk. I say 'was', though we have no proof that she is deceased. She told me that she kept you up to date in advance of the mission. I am sure that you have heard the reports of what happened to her in Antarctica. She may have survived but would have no way to contact us if she did.

"Although the media did not report this, you should know that Keltyn and I both took a special interest in the Onwei people we encountered during our mission. Since my return, I have taken it upon myself to lobby on their behalf. Perhaps you have heard of our organization: Native Peoples United. It calls public attention to the interests of threatened Indigenous tribes.

"In any case, I wished to extend my sympathies to you, as Keltyn spoke highly of you and your instruction. If it should please you, I would be delighted if you could share some of your own recollections of working with her."

As Consul Teng recited in his heavy accent, Fay reflected. Had Wan passed on her note after reading it, which is what she expected to happen? Or had it been intercepted by the assistant and never read by Wan? That possibility would jeopardize his position. She felt an immediate pang of guilt. Still, she knew enough not to ask.

Consul Teng closed his file and watched Fay inscrutably. Somehow, she surmised, the next move was hers.

"Does my summons here have to do with your government's position on exploitation of iridium?"

"You may well ask, Savant. Indeed, you deduce reason for our attempt reach out to you."

"I am flattered, of course." Fay batted her eyes. "Yet I am at a loss as to why you would choose me."

"Come, come, Savant." Consul Teng slapped the folder closed. "Surely you must realize what qualities make you ideal envoy this sort of negotiation."

"Of course, I understand Switzerland's strategic position vis-à-vis China and the Western powers, but surely you could use Swiss government diplomats."

Teng betrayed the thinnest of smiles. "If only Western governments in position as strong as China's to control their half of this race. But no, we have determined main proponent to develop iridium technology is one man, Sir Oscar Bailey. He answer to no one. Pardon observation, but Canadian government sham rubber stamp."

Fay noticed a subtle trembling of Teng's lower lip and sat back in her chair.

"Nor will any European powers stand up to him," he continued.

She swallowed hard. She could see what was coming, and she was not at all prepared for the role Consul Teng was about to suggest. "So, your government wishes to negotiate directly with Sir Oscar Bailey? About some kind of iridium moratorium?"

"Quite astute, Savant Del Campo. Personal negotiation is key. Based on your outreach to Savant Wan, my government believe you ideally suited this role."

She gasped. Me? You've got to be kidding. "What makes you think that I have any interest in personal diplomacy?"

"Come now, Savant." Teng slapped her file with the back of his hand. "You already spell out your role: form lobby for threatened Indigenous tribes."

She studied him. "What of it?"

Consul Teng removed his dialups, held them to the light, pulled out a handkerchief to wipe them, and returned them to his nose. "Your reputation embrace liberal causes extend even my country. And we know your organization cut deal with Sir Oscar Bailey."

Fay gasped. How could the Chinese government know about that? Oscar's contribution to Native Peoples United, his hush money to fend off a boycott, hadn't even cleared yet. They must have spies in high places. It was all she could do to stay calm. "With all due respect, Consul Teng, that is no business of the Chinese government."

Teng flashed his corn kernels once more. "Please, Savant. These matters no stay secret long, but surely you not wish news of this donation make public just yet."

She felt a lump in her throat. A croaking sound came out of what used to be her voice. "What is it that you wish me to do?"

"Ah, Savant Del Campo. The question is, what position you and my government share, and how we best communicate that to Sir Oscar Bailey?"

"I see," said Fay, though she did not see at all.

Consul Teng tilted his head, waiting for Fay to spell out her position. After several silent moments, he suggested, "As I understand, your concern to protect integrity of Indigenous people of Antarctica. True?"

"Yes, of course." She grasped her throat. The raspy feeling wouldn't leave. "Could I trouble you for a glass of water?"

"Of course, Savant. My apologies." He reached inside a drawer of the desk for a small bell and shook it vigorously. Within ten seconds, the young man appeared who had ushered Fay in. Teng said a few words as he tilted his head toward Fay. The young man left and returned a moment later with water, which he presented to Fay with a full bow.

She took a deep swallow and coughed several times before regaining her voice. "Thank you. You must forgive me. Your proposition is, you might say, hard for me to swallow."

Teng gave a small bow of his head. "Quite understandable."

"But you are correct in assuming that I am opposed to having the people of Antarctica exploited in any way."

"And my government interest in this matter similar. We must keep Antarctica neutral territory, like has been since men first set feet on icy shores four centuries ago."

"Sir Oscar Bailey wishes to settle Canadian farmers there. I would think that your people must also face a shortage of arable land."

"Less of problem than expected." The corn kernels flashed once more. "Our agronomists make amazing leaps forward."

This was news she needed to file somewhere. "So why would your government care if Antarctica is invaded — excuse me, settled — by Canadians?"

"Would you believe we also oppose principle of crushing native cultures?" Consul Teng lifted his chin.

Fay did a quick mental survey of the past four centuries of Chinese history, touching on the former sovereignty of Tibet, East Turkestan, Indochina, the Philippines, Korea and eastern Siberia. She shook her head slowly.

Teng smiled. "Of course not. The truth is technological potential of iridium. For now, mainly to coat aircraft, fly safely through toxic vapors of tropical atmosphere. As Bailey himself point out, unique physical and chemical properties, iridium countless uses scarcely imagine."

"I remember him saying that its potential was similar to that of cold fusion," said Fay.

"Just so." The kernels shone once more. Consul Teng was in a jolly mood. "Bailey pay great royalties for Chinese companies license fees. His scientists try hard to make first cold fusion engine. Our scientists complete this long ago."

"And Sir Oscar wishes to get a head start in iridium technology so that he can have the same kind of commercial edge over China," said Fay.

Consul Teng nodded.

The geopolitical jigsaw puzzle was locking into place for her, piece by piece. And now she was being courted to join the game's players. The thought made her feel giddy. Yet something did not quite add up. She tried to recall Oscar's take on China's deposits of high-grade iridium ore. It was that remote peninsula in Siberia, ringed with volcanoes. "But you may be able to catch up when you begin to exploit your own reserves," she ventured.

Consul Teng turned his head quickly, breaking their eye contact. "Anything possible," was all he said.

Aha. She wasn't supposed to know about their reserves. She craned her head toward the ceiling. What was the name of that remote place? Kamchatka. Did his reticence imply that China was on the verge of breaking through at Kamchatka?

When she glanced at Consul Teng, Fay found him again studying her. "I suppose you wish to know if I will convey a message to Sir Oscar Bailey," she said.

"This is hope of my government, yes."

"And that message would be?"

"Moratorium. No develop high-grade iridium ore."

"'High-grade' meaning the kind used to coat aircraft?"

Consul Teng opened his folder and pulled out a page for Fay. "Sixty percent purity is rough cutoff, I believe. Metallurgic definition spelled out this sheet."

Fay glanced at the scientific jargon. "Why should Sir Oscar buy into this moratorium?"

One more display of those corn kernels, as Consul Teng stood to end the interview. "How you say, if push come shove, not even Sir Oscar Bailey in position to challenge Chinese Empire."

Fay stood slowly, her mouth agape. How could she convey such a threat to Sir Oscar without triggering his competitive juices?

Consul Teng approached, took her hand and bowed once more. "But please not transmit message in that way. Chinese conduct diplomacy like American President Theodore Roosevelt, four hundred years ago, 'Speak softly, carry big stick.'"

The analogy left Fay cold. She was being recruited as Teng's dog, to carry this big stick to a different master, who would no doubt toss it out for her to fetch again. Her only consolation was that she, as messenger dog, could nuance the message, bend the stick, so to speak. She intended to do just that.

***

Fay glared at the blank screen, lips razored, as she waited for the arrival of Sir Oscar on the other end. It was not hard to arrange the linkup, once she managed to pass security at the main gate of Bailey Europe HQ. She showed up without an appointment, believing that, with her name recognition, none was necessary. She told the guard that she carried an important message from the Chinese government.

He had stared at her vacantly for a long moment, clearly not a fan of the telly talk show circuit on which she appeared so often. Then he picked up the phone and relayed her message to someone inside, listened for a long while, and hung up. After informing Fay that she would need a photo security pass, he volunteered to provide one on the spot. She stood against a black panel and tried to smile as a red light came on.

A minute later, she had her laminated ID, with the admonition that she should keep it for future visits to any Bailey facility. If her new calling was to be shuttle diplomat, she would need this.

Helmut Ganz met her upstairs. Tall and thin, with hooded eyelids, a hawk nose, lantern jaw and thick curly brown hair, Bailey's Director of Transnational Operations looked every inch a man of business in his navy pinstriped neosilk suit. She asked whether Oscar's next visit to Zürich was imminent. If so, she would just as soon wait to see him in person. Ganz regretfully informed her that his boss might not return for months; he had just departed three days prior.

So here she sat in front of the screen, waiting for The Man to appear.

Finally, out of nowhere, Oscar's artificially smooth face lit the screen. In this medium, unless he were to don makeup, his skin, especially the nose, seemed too shiny. The thin-set lips seemed too severe, expressionless. The only feature to make a good transition onto the telly, his piercing blue eyes, seemed as sharp and penetrating on the screen as in person. His gimlet gaze immediately made Fay feel utterly incapable of deceit, had she been so inclined. But no, she intended to deliver Consul Teng's message straight up.

"Savant Del Campo. A pleasure to hear from you again. I trust our arrangement is moving along smoothly."

"It is, absolutely." She had to give that to Oscar. He fulfilled his promises, and the amount of his foundation's gift to NPU had been more than she could have hoped. Which made it all the harder to deliver this message.

"Ah, then this must be a social call." He beamed in anticipation.

"Not exactly. I have been enlisted for some personal diplomacy by a foreign government." She swallowed hard.

"Let me guess." Oscar shut his eyes and rested his chin on his thumb. A second later, the eyes snapped open. "Our friends in the Far East."

Fay smiled. There was no sense beating around the bush. "They have a consulate in Zürich."

"Of course. Herr Ganz has frequent contact with them." Oscar frowned. "License contracts for cold fusion, that sort of thing." He stared straight at Fay. "Why did they pick you for a conduit? What might you and the government of China have in common? Hmm…" His lower lip jutted out.

"You don't need to guess, Oscar. It's no secret. They want a moratorium on iridium mining."

"Do they now? How handy that would be. Antarctica is our only proven reserve so far. If we are to believe Savant SparrowHawk, the whole gob is polluted by radiation anyway, so no great loss. In return, the Chinese want what, exactly?"

"Sounded like they would likewise defer any mining."

"Ha. Unless they made you privy to some new intelligence…" Oscar searched Fay's face.

She immediately shook her head.

"Their only reserves are on that remote Kamchatka peninsula. No, if the Chinese had discovered some other source of the high-grade stuff, believe you me, they wouldn't be trying to push through a moratorium.

"One thing Savant SparrowHawk's research did confirm, for which I am grateful, is that the only high-grade ore comes from volcanic eruptions. The good stuff doesn't lie around in craters. Among Chinese volcanoes in accessible latitudes, Kamchatka is the whole ball game. Unless…did your contact give any hint that they might, you know, shoot the moon?"

"Shoot the moon?"

"It just occurred to me, dear Fay, that the Chinese government might be bluffing. Stalling, to keep me from another probe of Erebus while they get ready to fire one of their own."

Her neck stiffened. She really had no concept of global politics, less even than Yoka Sutu, who had deduced Oscar Bailey's long-term plans in a flash. Now Oscar read

China's intentions in much the same way. In both cases, Fay had been the conduit of the message, and in both cases, she had failed to parse them. Embarrassing, to be sure, but as a novice to this game, she was still learning.

"Ha. You seem surprised, Savant. True, I could be overreading their capacity. My metallurgists had to play with the low-grade ore for two years before they found a way to get the coating we needed for Bailey Voyager. I'm pretty sure the Chinese aren't close to that stage, using whatever ore they've salvaged from Siberian craters. But the longer I wait, the shorter the gap."

"So, you're willing to risk another mission?" Fay heartbeat quickened. She had hoped Oscar would bite at the idea of a moratorium. She really, really did not want to deliver Consul Teng's thinly veiled threat.

"I may be at that. I'll need to factor in your message, and how the Chinese government chose to contact me." His lower lip twitched slowly, before once more directing his attention to Fay. "Shall I let you in on a little secret, Savant Del Campo? Something brand new, hot off the press?"

Fay blushed. "I can't guarantee it will stay secret."

"No matter. I've been in touch with Savant Russell McCoy, our dear Keltyn's geology mentor. He works for me, you know. Bailey Science Fellow."

"The same position you promised Keltyn."

Oscar shook his head slowly. "What a shame she couldn't claim it. Anyway, McCoy has come to his own conclusion about whether iridium ore can be radioactive."

"Oh?" This was a twist. As Keltyn lay at death's door last year, she had confessed the ploy to Fay alone, but before that, she had planted enough seeds of doubt to scuttle the mission's purpose.

"You know what? It's chemically impossible. McCoy did the calculations, a lit search, the works. He even got some of my particle physics boys to bombard an ore sample with gamma rays. No radioactive products. Zero." Oscar's eyes gleamed.

"Wow," was all that Fay could think of to say.

"That's what I said. Then I made him an offer."

"What kind of offer?" This did not sound good.

"Asked him if he'd like to be the geologist on our next trip to Antarctica." Oscar beamed the smile of the cat that swallowed the canary.

"And did he accept?"

"He's giving it due consideration." Oscar nodded as if the deal was already set.

"Oh, my." It was all that Fay could do to keep her gaze fixed on Oscar's enigmatic visage. His effect was hypnotic. The screen seemed to flash different colors at her. She felt faint.

"Savant? Oh dear, I've said something to upset you." Oscar's head tilted sideways, his brows knit.

Fay rubbed her palm across her forehead and tried slow, deep breaths, but it was not enough. That dry lump formed in her throat again. "Excuse me just a moment, Sir Oscar." She wobbled to her feet and cast about for something to drink. Fortunately, Helmut Ganz stood a short distance behind her. She wondered if he had been privy to her whole conversation with Oscar. She made a motion of tilting a cup to her mouth, and he whisked off to find her a glass of water.

She scowled from having lost it a second time. When, finally, she dared face Oscar's image on the screen again, his visage of mock concern was unchanged.

"There, there. Feeling better, are we?"

Fay swallowed another gulp of water before answering. "It's just that, well, I assumed we had an understanding."

"Oh, that we do. The understanding was not sending Canadians to colonize Antarctica."

"But, but, sending Bailey Voyager on another mission, that's tantamount to the same thing."

"Ha. Bailey Voyager may hold up to five people, and that's if we install a jump seat. Hardly enough to start any kind of a colony."

"You know what I mean, Oscar. It's the first step."

"The second step, actually. You were part of the first step, and before you ask, no, I don't think we need an anthropologist along this time around. But it's still a long way from colonizing."

Damn you to hell, you and your mission both. Her temples throbbed, her chin quivered, but of course that was the reaction he wanted, the cat-and-mouse game he was playing with her. She had to stay calm. "Then why go back at all?"

"It's so simple as to be ridiculous, Savant. I'll bet that Chinese consul told you the same thing in so many words. Iridium has mega-potential for industrial breakthroughs. It's going to be as big as cold fusion. Only this time, Bailey Enterprises, not China, is going to be the one out in front. China will have to come to terms with us, instead of vice-versa."

Oscar's face remained impassive, but Fay saw the slightest hardening in his eyes. She remained silent. There was no use trying to rein in his ambition. Their deal from a month ago had been sealed only with a glass of sherry. Even if she tried to force the issue in the court of public opinion, Oscar could rightfully argue that another exploratory mission was a far cry from displacing the local population of Antarctica.

She pasted a vapid smile on her face. "Well, keep me posted."

"That I shall, Savant. That I shall." With that, the screen went blank.

Fay fumed at the empty monitor for several minutes before gathering her things. Pulling off the clip with her newly minted Bailey photo ID, she looked around for a trash can. To hell with shuttle diplomacy. Let some other flunkey feed the egos of megalomaniacs.

Then she caught Ganz's eye. He remained standing, ten paces behind her, his hands clasped behind his back. Best not to act in haste. Fay held up the badge for him to see before stashing it in her bag with other ID cards. He in turn made a slight bow.

She had not risen to Oscar's bait. Now she needed to stay poised and marshal her own forces.

***

Fay stared at the dimly lit ceiling above the bed. She pulled up sheets to cover her naked body, suddenly chilled. A cold feeling, beyond disappointment and verging on betrayal, crept over her like a wave of surf toppling a sand castle.

"I am so sorry, ma chère." Harry lay beside her. He, too, seemed to address the ceiling.

Truth be told, she had been lucky in the sack, until now. Paul Buchschreiber, her husband of seventeen years, had satisfied her needs, though she always initiated their lovemaking. Since Paul's untimely death eleven years ago, her occasional trysts never seemed to lead to long-term romance — if pressed, she would admit that she preferred it that way — but were nonetheless exhilarating sparks in the otherwise mundane arc of middle age. At the moment, she couldn't help but wonder if the sparks were gone forever.

As if reading her mind, Harry said, "It has nothing to do with you, my sweet. I promise." He reached for her hand and kissed it.

Fay used her other hand to pull the tip of the bed sheet up and wipe her eyes. "What, then?" But before he could answer, it hit her. She turned to face him. "It's something with Oscar, isn't it?"

A long sigh. "Who else? He says jump. I ask, how high?"

"If it will ease your mind, I already know he has committed to another Bailey Voyager mission."

Harry continued his confession toward the ceiling. "I knew it was a matter of when, not if. And I knew he would tap me to lead it again." He reached for the half-filled glass of cognac sitting on the bedside table.

Fay pulled another pillow behind her back, sat up in bed, and found her own glass.

"I'm losing my edge, and not just in bed," said Harry. "Oscar can sense it."

"What? How?"

He chewed his lip. "Maybe a guy my age shouldn't be flying reconnaissance missions to remote parts of the world. I admit, the first time was a thrill, perhaps too much so. This time, there's no fire in the belly." He flicked his fingers apart.

Another cold wave washed over Fay. She set the cognac down. Her plan to stall Oscar's ambitions depended heavily on Harry.

He turned and faced her. "Still, I can't very well deny him. He's already made it clear that iridium exploration is our new top priority, and that he needs me to make sure it gets done right from the get-go."

What a juicy conundrum. Fay felt caught between her relief that Harry would be on the mission after all and their shared misgivings about being coerced.

Harry turned back to stare at the ceiling.

Uncertainty made her tingle. "There's something else, isn't there?"

He flashed a tight smile. "You don't make it to the top of the food chain without a healthy dose of paranoia. Oscar doesn't have what you would call a trusting nature."

Fay tensed. When Harry phoned a week ago that he would soon be in Geneva on business and had booked a suite for them, she dropped a planned telly appearance in order to meet him. "You don't think he knows about us? Here?"

"I wouldn't put it past him to suspect something like that. But he hasn't given me any reason to believe he knows, and I haven't given him any cause for suspicion."

Fay exhaled. "So, what then?"

"Number one, he recruited Russell McCoy to be the geologist on this mission."

"He told me that McCoy proved that iridium has no radioactive isotopes."

"Right, but that was just the warmup. Once McCoy went on record as debunking Keltyn's claim, Oscar figured that whatever loyalty McCoy might have felt toward his former protégé disappeared. Now he can be trusted to assay the Erebus ore samples onsite, which is a lucky break for Oscar because Keltyn and McCoy are the only ones who know how to do that."

"Aha. I wondered how Oscar was going to pull that part off without Keltyn," said Fay.

Harry's jaw clenched. "Number two, this fellow Ganz, who he assigned to come along. Along with translating, he's supposed to keep tabs on me."

She narrowed her eyes. "What do you mean?"

"Helmut Ganz, the rising star of Bailey Enterprises." The name escaped Harry's lips with a sneer. "Maybe it's unfounded suspicion, but I see Oscar grooming him for my post. The boss, of course, will never retire so long as medical science keeps pumping him full of wonder drugs."

Fay huffed a breath of disbelief. The tall thin executive at Bailey Europe HQ was on the fast track to succeed Harry. "What exactly is Herr Ganz's official role, or does that matter?"

"Sure, it matters for appearances," said Harry. "All of us get presented to the media. You recall the big charade last time around."

Fay rolled her eyes. "Do I ever."

"Ganz has become Bailey's by-the-book guy, the compliance honcho who makes sure all the rules are followed. One of his assignments is to track down Keltyn, if she happened to survive, and bring her back to face charges. Remember the spying allegation?"

"That Chinese meter."

"Exactly. And now Oscar can throw in fraud charges for the radiation hoax."

"Oh my. Poor dear." Fay pictured the naïve, willful sprite whom the rest of the crew abandoned as she lay near death. "If she survived the gunshot wound, now her goose will be cooked."

"Ganz has another assignment, too," said Harry. "He's supposed to draw up a contract with the Onwei to get future mining rights for iridium. The primary negotiation is still my job, but Ganz has made his reputation in the company as a hatchet man. He'll be peering over my shoulder every step of the way, with Oscar's blessing. You can see how this limits my room to maneuver. Plus, I have no idea what to offer the Onwei in return for mining rights."

"Oh," Fay brightened, "I could think of a few things."

Harry turned back to face her, with the hint of a smile. "You know, you and I could make a great team, ma chère. What kind of things?"

She reached over to stroke the graying curls of his chest hair. "Like all-weather fabric, spices, sugar, antibiotics, to name a few. Those dialups I brought along last time were a big hit."

Harry considered that, then shook his head slowly. "I feel like my French fur-trading ancestors, trying to bargain with the Algonquin while avoiding getting scalped."

"Sounds like your heart isn't in it, Monsieur Ladou."

"*Au contraire.* That evening you introduced me to your NPU chapter in Quebec has left quite an impression. It's just…"

She slid toward him. "What?"

"I dunno," said Harry. "This is something I still need to work out."

Fay stroked his cheek with the back of her hand. "No pressure, dear." She pecked his lips, pulled back to her side of the bed, and doused the reading lamp. She huddled on her side, keeping her back toward Harry lest, even in the dark, he might sense the anxiety that now infected her as well.

Adding Helmut Ganz and Russell McCoy to the mission would mean a significant change in personnel dynamics. Would Harry, even if his heart were so inclined, still have enough influence to make sure that the Onwei got a fair shake?

Otherwise, the only forces left to counter Oscar's megalomania were dicey: the Chinese government and a bunch of eco-terrorists who, if she believed his allegations, were fringe elements of NPU. Though she was in no position to influence the behavior of either of these powers, now that she was linked to them in Oscar's mind, she knew he would hold her responsible for their actions. Like it or not, she was riding a whirlwind.

IO

HORSE RACE

It was late enough into August for me to savor nine hours of daylight as the sun crept along the northern horizon and teased me with premonitions of spring. Today, Efrain had coaxed me into a horse race along the beach, to test my mare, he said.

Yet I knew good and well that he was simply trying to distract me from my obsessions. Meanwhile, he still had not delivered on his promise to enlist Ysidro in my cause. He was waiting for the right moment, he said, but I knew time was running short. Soon the herd would be on the move. I needed to instill in Efrain the same urgency that was driving me.

"Ready, Brixita?" he hollered. The deafening breakers nearly drowned out his voice, even when raised. His gelding pranced on the wet sand as the surf slid in and out.

The salt spray tickled my nostrils. "I want a head start," I yelled. "Say 'go' and then count to ten slowly."

Efrain raised his arm. "On your mark."

I whipped the reins to face the length of the beach.

"Go!" He chopped his arm downward, and I kicked my heels into Tinto's flank. The small mare responded with a lurch forward that had me hanging on for dear life. Who would have guessed she had this much spark in her?

I leaned partway forward, grasping the back of the mare's neck. The spray of salt air blowing in my face, the pounding hooves beneath my stirrups, the roar of crashing waves to my right, the stark shadows on the sand cast by a bright strip of light on the northern horizon, all conspired to make me feel more here, more now, than I had in months.

For fifteen seconds, Tinto and I flew forward as one being. The mare took deeper breaths, but instead of slowing, she seemed to catch a second wind and galloped all the faster. I'd eased up heeling the mare's flanks and could hardly guess what spurred her to pick up the pace.

At this moment, an extra pulse vibrated through the packed sand and, a second later, a magnificent centaur drew up on my left flank.

The sight left me in awe. Just as Efrain easily outweighed me by double, his gelding massed perhaps half again as much as Tinto. The big guy rode bolt upright, holding the reins slack with one hand, while using the other to lightly whip his horse's flanks back and forth with the loose ends. Efrain's mount started to pull ahead.

The gelding was certainly more powerful than Tinto, but I had a hunch. I might have a chance to win the race yet. The steady ocean breeze blew in at an angle, almost a headwind. I meant to use it in my favor. When we'd advanced about half the length of the beach, I set my jaw and lowered my head so that it rested fully on Tinto's neck, at the same time digging my heels into the mare's flank. Now was the time to show us what you've got, girl.

Tinto picked up the pace yet more. I felt the rapid rise and fall of the mare's chest between my legs, the high-pitched sucking noise of air in her nostrils, a heavy rasp as it hailed out of her mouth. Her hide was wet and slick with lather.

The pace tightened as the two horses pulled neck and neck. Only a hundred yards of sand remained. We hadn't really picked a landmark to call the finish line, but with the race this close, I needed to pull up pretty soon or we would crash into the rocky crags that lined the beach. I wanted to pull half a length ahead and then rein in, but Efrain's mount, his competitive instincts aroused, showed no signs of slowing.

With but a few seconds to avert calamity, I pulled the reins hard, while at the same time trying to steer Tinto toward the water to hasten a stop. The mare lurched to the right and buckled, and I toppled off her back into the surf. Temporarily blinded by the salt water and dazed by the fall, I thrashed about to catch my balance. Before I could recover, Efrain hoisted me to a standing position.

"What was that all about, Brixita? It's only sport," he scowled. "Another few yards, you would have crippled your mount, and who knows how hard you would have hit. Don't you remember what happened to Luz and her horse?"

The girl's wail as she flies backwards. The dull thud as her spine rams into a boulder. The screams of pain that follow. Her awful grimace upon finding her legs paralyzed. All of these were etched into my memory as vividly as if I myself were the victim. "I'm sorry." I shook my head, as much to clear it of salt water as to get my thoughts in order. "Guess my competitive instincts got the best of me."

Efrain stood with his boots immersed in the surf. His frown softened and his eyes glistened. He pulled me close, hugged me in a bear's embrace, then bent down to kiss my hair. "I, I…"

I raised my head. A solitary tear rested on his cheek. I reached to brush it away. "What?"

He shook his head. "I don't know what I would do if anything happened to you."

I pulled back. For all of his sweetness, his caring, this was the first time Efrain had professed anything resembling a declaration of love. The big guy was a softie at the core. I felt long-standing knots around my own heart slacken.

We traipsed out of the water, arm in arm, and sat on the sand to dry out. The miserly sun was already beginning to fade. I hunched forward, suddenly cold, and Efrain reached his big arm around to draw me closer.

"It sounds like this is getting serious," I managed to say.

"Must be." Efrain stared out toward the ocean. "Who knew?"

I searched his face. "You sure this is a good idea? I'm kinda damaged goods, if you haven't already figured that out."

"I don't care about your past, Brixita, and I don't care about whatever dispute you may have with the Sky-Borne lord. You are brave, almost foolhardy, which is something I worry about. You have innate curiosity, and despite your tough talk, you are compassionate." Now he turned to face me and took both my hands in his. "I wish to make a life with you."

Wow. No one had ever made me an offer like that. I brushed away my own tears starting to form and stared at Efrain in earnest. He looked dead serious. I flashed back on the origins of this romance, back on the slopes of Erebus, when he first sang his melancholy love songs to me around a campfire, the night Aldo died in his sleep while Luz lay paralyzed. Somehow, I never pictured it would lead to this. Actually, I had, on multiple occasions, but each time I banished the idea. A long-term relationship among the Onwei involved marriage and family, and those weren't in my game plan.

Then again, why could they not be? I pictured what domestic life with Efrain would be like. If I were to abide with the Onwei for the remainder of my mortal days, being Seira Correon would carry both standing and wealth. By contrast, my current status, the stray dog that Trieste Hogarth brought in from the cold, led to a sure dead end.

"I…I don't know. There is so much to consider."

"What's to consider?" Efrain removed his arm from my shoulder and reached around to take both hands in his. "You. Me. What else?" He searched my eyes. "Are you afraid of childbirth? Motherhood?"

My lower lip jutted. "No, not really. Haven't given it much thought."

"The midwives in Nomidar are superb," said Efrain. "Ask around at the Rendezvous this year. None better."

"I'm sure you're right." I kept my gaze averted.

"What then?"

"It's just that this may not be the right time for me to settle down."

Efrain studied me. "It's about another Sky-Borne landing, isn't it?"

I nodded. I couldn't possibly accept Efrain's offer until that was dealt with. It wouldn't be fair to either of us.

"I should have guessed. I hoped that you would gradually dismiss your intuition."

"Ha. Wish I could. Soon we'll be into the grazing season. This is when it will happen."

"And what makes you so sure?"

"I told you about that message."

Efrain scoffed. "The one from Joaquin? Supposedly sent from Orfea via his imaginary uncle? Don't tell me you took that seriously."

"Perhaps by itself, no. But together with those dreams that have haunted me for months…" I hunched forward, my eyes on the sand.

Efrain reached around, squeezing me close and rubbing my arm. "It's okay, Brixita, it's okay."

I peeked up. "You're sure?"

"Sure."

"Then how about you help bring Ysidro around?"

Efrain let go of my arm and stared forward. "I have tried to avoid getting mixed up in this."

I waited. Here's your chance, dude. Show me how much you care.

"But it's no use." He lumbered to his feet and held out his hands to hoist me up. "I should know by now. When you set your mind to something…"

Now on my feet, I pulled down Efrain's head and gave him a peck on the cheek. "Might as well do it as dread it."

Yet even as I said this, dread filled my mind. If Ysidro agreed to resist the Sky-Bornes' next search, more violence was sure to follow. If he declined, who else could stop them?

***

The off-season allowed the jeaf to rise late. It was early afternoon when Efrain led me into his uncle's house. Several empty corn liquor earthenware jugs and half a dozen mugs, plus a pair of dice, lay scattered on the large low-slung table that made up the centerpiece of the hearth. Stale smoky air permeated the room. I crinkled my nose. He was probably hung over. Not the best time to broach a delicate topic.

Ysidro stood at the far end with a pan of water in front of a shiny metal slab that passed for a mirror, busy shaving his lathered chin whiskers with a straight razor. His throat and his strong chin were the only clean-shaven parts of his coarse mug, the rest of it was covered with salt-and-pepper whiskers that formed a shallow "U" on each side of the jaw, meeting above the lip.

He caught our reflection. Without turning to greet us, he waved in the general direction of several chairs on the side of the room and continued his trim. Finished with the razor, he splashed water on his face, grabbed a towel to pat it down, and checked his profile on both sides. Satisfied, he grabbed a small bottle next to the sink, shook some of its contents into his palm, then patted his throat, cheeks, and behind the ears. When he turned to face his visitors, I noticed his eyes were bloodshot.

He flashed a sheepish smile and moved to join his guests. His hands clapped together. "Hot date tonight."

"I figured as much," laughed Efrain, brushing his hand in front of his nose. "That aftershave is potent stuff, tio. Rich old farts like you shouldn't overdo it. Ladies expect you to be more subtle."

Ysidro, now sitting across from us, drew back in mock offense. "What does a twerp like you know?" He turned toward me. "Let us ask the Brixa. What is your opinion? Should a man smell good when trying to impress a lady?"

I crossed my arms and smiled. "If you put it that way, of course a man must be presentable, it's just…"

Ysidro butted in, pointing his finger at Efrain. "See, I told you, Seir Big Shot." He turned back to me. "My nephew thinks he knows all about women. I'll let you in on a little secret." He leaned forward, while shooting a quick glance at Efrain. "You're the first one he's taken any serious interest in. A big strapping boy of twenty-three, you'd think by now he'd settle down."

Efrain frowned. "Let not the pot call the kettle black, tio. Anyway, we have come on more important matters."

Ysidro harrumphed. "What then?"

Efrain gestured to me. I cleared my throat and explained my fears of an imminent Sky-Borne return. I left out my own premonitions, citing as evidence only the third-hand message from Orfea.

The jeaf listened in silence, his countenance growing steadily darker. When I finished, he sat fuming for several minutes, his gaze fixed upon the wall. When he faced me once more, his lip sported an ugly sneer. "I wish we had finished off all of your cursed mates when we had the chance. Nothing personal, Brixa. You have proved yourself worthy, and I regret having taken you hostage. Tell me, do your people have any way to know that you are still alive?"

I shook my head. "No. Orfea sent her message only for Joaquin's benefit, to pass on to whomever among the Onwei that he saw fit."

"And their great jeaf, was he not led to believe that the piedra de yris is poisoned?"

"Of course, that was my intent, but he is very shrewd and may have seen through my ploy."

Ysidro grimaced. "The Sky-Borne lord's greed is great indeed." He stared at me. "So, what would you advise now?"

I swallowed again. "My information is that he will send the same flying machine, which holds no more than four people. Even if you were to encounter them, there is no way they could overwhelm the number of gauchos in your command."

Ysidro raised his bushy brows. "So? Shall we try to avoid them?"

I shook my head. "That may seem like the easiest course now, but it would likely backfire in the long run." I explained Yoka's suspicions of Sir Oscar Bailey's long-term plans to settle Canadian farmers on Onwei lands. "You must find some way to scare them off and keep them from returning." I hoped the jeaf could strategize a plan that did not involve more killing.

Ysidro scratched the back of his neck and squinted at me. "I cannot think of any way to accomplish that without wiping them out altogether." He watched me squirm, then flashed a wicked smile and turned to Efrain. "How about you, nephew? Any ideas?"

"We must avoid more bloodshed." Efrain looked glum as he spoke.

Ysidro rocked his head to and fro. Abruptly, he brightened. "I say, let them come, and let us bargain with them."

I gasped. "You can't be serious."

"No? Why should our tribe not profit from their greed? Especially when we have you to advise us on the true worth of the stone for their uses." He watched my reaction intently.

I could only clamp my lips tight. What a fool I'd been to open this Pandora's Box. Better to have simply avoided getting close to Erebus for the next six months, ducking any contact at all, than to be drawn into a bargaining contest between Ysidro and Harry Ladou. Yet, having begged Ysidro to become involved, how could I now refuse his call?

No question, I needed to avoid being arrested and deported at all costs. There was absolutely no reason for me to ever return to Canada. I nodded to Ysidro and held out my hand. "I will advise you in negotiating with the Sky-Bornes, but I must stay in the background for there is a price on my head."

Ysidro grasped my hand in his iron grip. "Deal, Brixa. Not to worry." He nodded at Efrain. "You will have all the protection you need."

Yet, protection wasn't my main concern. I might never again show my face to my former countrymen, but it was now my job to set a price on the commodity they all so desperately craved. For all I knew, Savant Wan Xiang and his colleagues might well be poised to leap into the iridium race by now. The Chinese might end up sending their own probe to scout the Erebus region. How would I react to that?

Was I really savvy enough to get involved in such a highstakes game? Did I have the stomach for it? It was one thing to find the stuff, quite another to exploit it, or in this case, stand in the way of someone else who wishes to profit from it.

Rather suddenly, the game had changed. I needed a thorough primer on the rules. If Yoka were still around, she would be the one to ask. With the crone gone, I was desperate for other wise counsel.

"How much longer before you move the herd out?" I asked Ysidro.

"I still need to hire three more charros," he said. "Everything else is set." His gaze moved between Efrain and me. "You plan to accompany my nephew? These boys are a smelly and vulgar lot."

I smiled as I took Efrain's arm. "I shall be close, but not too close, bunking in Trieste's yurt again." Despite my new role as trade negotiator, I would still need to earn my keep.

II

EYES AND EARS

With equal hours of light and dark, the grazing season was about to begin. Despite his newfound financial security, Joaquin could not fathom another whole summer in Nomidar, stuck with those too young, too old or too infirm to travel. Whatever time he needed to practice the Venga arts with his townspeople, it could wait until the next dark season.

Even before Yoka's death, he had set his sights on the Rendezvous. There, among artisans like Trieste, food vendors, musicians and storytellers, he envisioned setting up his own booth, enticing a clientele of lost souls with the prospect of reconnecting with their departed loved ones.

But he needed to get there, and he sure couldn't travel that many hundreds of miles alone. The only way was with the gaucho band. For that, he needed to earn the jeaf's confidence, and soon. But how?

Ysidro had not spoken even a word of greeting since Yoka's funeral. Joaquin guessed it must have something to do with his call to be wary of the Sky-Bornes, but if the jeaf thought otherwise, it was certainly a far cry from how he treated them at their last appearance.

This morning, Joaquin climbed upon the fence that staked out the horse pens adjacent to Ysidro's house. Flies buzzed over each pile of fresh steaming manure, sucked in by its heady aroma. A filly and her colt tugged on new shoots of clover.

Joaquin needed to get the jeaf's attention without making a pest of himself. Within earshot, Ysidro interviewed a line of gaucho wannabees. Torme, big for his age, bigger even than the older Joaquin, tried to impress the jeaf with his bolo technique. He flung it toward a calf, trying to trap its feet, but the calf just scampered away.

Ysidro stroked his whiskers. "Keep practicing, kid. Maybe next year."

Torme glowered at the jeaf before stalking off. Joaquin breathed a sigh of relief. Ysidro likely did not wish to risk the ire of the boy's mother for nabbing her fourteen-year-old son. Joaquin's own chances to join the gaucho band would have been hampered with Torme on board.

Torme's buddy Gustavo waited next in line. He managed to snare the calf's legs with his bolo, but when he ran to secure it, the animal shrugged itself free in seconds.

Next came Carmelo, also big enough to ride a horse, but likewise too green to handle the tools of the gaucho trade. The bolo sailed away without landing anywhere near the calf.

The poor fortunes of Joaquin's age-mates meant good fortune for him. He smiled as he pictured his booth at the Rendezvous. Even though it lasted only a week, he expected lots of traffic. Fairgoers always flocked to a novelty. If he was organized, he could earn as much there as he could while festering in Nomidar all summer. He would need some word-of-mouth advertising, but he was sure that Trieste and other artisan camp followers who partook of Venga would oblige.

A whistle made Joaquin glance up from his daydreaming. Ysidro spied him sitting on the fence railing and waved him over.

"Boy, you have been watching for an hour. Probably hoping I could find no one better and summon you in desperation."

Joaquin laughed. "Oh no, jeaf. Took me awhile, but I finally figured out I wasn't made to be a gaucho. Still, I miss the open range." Best not to mention the Rendezvous. The charros tended to go berserk after months in the saddle, much to the jeaf's annoyance. He would have to pull them together at week's end and move on.

"I'll bet you do." Ysidro surveyed him head to toe.

Joaquin's gimpy left wrist no longer hurt, it simply hung half bent, like a withered leaf. The clubfoot was cleverly concealed in a special boot designed for him by Ariel Hogarth. Only when he tried to run was the deformity apparent. His previously scrawny figure had begun to fill out, thanks to platters of beef empanadas and *dulce de leche* teacakes that clients bartered for their Venga encounters. Yet he was still painfully aware that, though he could steer his pony Cisco, he would never be strong enough to handle a calf.

"Listen," said Ysidro, stroking his side-whiskers. "I may have a job for you." He glanced around and motioned for Joaquin to come closer. "I need someone to be my eyes and ears." He pointed to his own with two spread fingers. It was the same phrase with which Aldo recruited him some four years ago.

"What's up?" asked Joaquin.

"The Sky-Bornes." A sneer crossed the jeaf's lips. "They are planning to return, according to this prediction you have voiced."

Joaquin's heart leapt. He nodded.

Ysidro's lower lip jutted out. "I suppose they will aim for the Erebus region again."

Joaquin nodded again. "For sure. There lies the piedra de yris."

"When can we expect them?" Ysidro eyed him sideways.

He pondered this for a moment. The jeaf was testing him. "Likely again when day and night are of equal length." He did not understand why this was important, though Orfea tried to explain it. Something about less jet lag, whatever that meant.

Ysidro seemed to grasp this logic. "Before the next full moon. We have little time to prepare."

Now Joaquin was all ears. This was beginning to sound more and more like a plot, with Ysidro a co-conspirator.

The jeaf drew his big frame up to its full height. "To mine the piedra de yris, they will first need to negotiate with me. Our tribe uses the Erebus region for grazing. If they wish to enrich themselves from this land, they must compensate us."

Joaquin recoiled. This sounded farfetched, even pompous. Worse, it sounded like the jeaf wished to make a deal with them. Yoka would never have sanctioned that.

Ysidro laughed heartily. "Don't worry, boy. The Brixa has agreed to advise me in this matter. In fact, it was her idea." He read the shock on Joaquin's face. "Surprised? Look. This isn't kids' stuff." He pointed to his head. "I have considered all the angles. Believe me, this is the best course. Understand?" He stared at Joaquin until receiving a nod of assent. Then he pointed his beefy finger. "And you will be my lookout for when they arrive."

"You wish me to camp at that crater?" This did not seem to Joaquin to be the best plan. The flying machine had landed there only by accident last time.

"Camp near where they are most likely to land. Consult with the Brixa." Ysidro brushed his hand backward, as if this detail was beneath him. "The important thing is that you must know how to reach the herd and find me, as soon as they turn up."

Was this part of the test? He knew the herd always followed the same route. For the two seasons he served as Aldo's eyes and ears, Joaquin had become familiar with the terrain: hills, valleys and all-too-few streams. The route that led them from Nomidar to Lake Tal in the spring was almost parallel to that which brought them home by way of the Erebus region in the fall, separated by no more than a few days ride at any point. Still, he had never had occasion to travel directly between these two.

"How shall I find your camp?"

Ysidro lifted a finger. "We shall have a drill before we head our separate ways. You will learn all the important landmarks."

Joaquin nodded slowly, not wishing to seem too eager.

The jeaf leaned forward. "Well? How about it?"

Joaquin shifted his gaze, tilted his head. "Perhaps."

Ysidro spread his arms akimbo. "Uppity kid. You're looking for something to sweeten the deal."

"What happens to me after this business is done? Am I supposed to head back to Nomidar?" Ysidro likely had not given this aspect any thought.

The jeaf threw his arms into the air. "Hell if I care. You want to spend your summer with a bunch of stinking cattle and stinkier charros, be my guest."

Joaquin smiled. "You got it, boss. I'm your man."

***

That afternoon, Joaquin had a surprising new client, one with different needs than his usual customers. He had never been called upon to provide what she asked for now, but he tried to act business as usual. He prepared sun tea, the first step in the ritual of guiding the Brixa through her very own Venga session. She sat on the step, in front of Yoka's hut, her head cupped in her hands, her elbows resting on her drawn up knees. Now that the time had come, she appeared beset by fears.

"Maybe I should just stick with pulce beer."

Frowning, Joaquin glanced up and ceased stirring the tea. "That's what you want, hey, it's your party." Women! Just like Tio Hector said, they were forever changing their minds.

He tried to project more confidence than he actually felt. In fact, the whole prospect of sending the Brixa off on this quest of hers left him cold. Guiding elderly widows in trying to reconnect with the spirit of a dead spouse or sibling was one thing. What the Brixa seemed to want now was akin to Yoka's invocation at Aldo's funeral, and what a fiasco that had turned into. Still, she had come to him expecting to summon her ancient forebears for guidance. He could not simply toss her a bunch of Venga nuggets and wish her luck.

"I know what I want," she said. "I just don't know if Venga can help me find it."

Joaquin handed her a mug. She took a sip and cradled it in both hands. "The last time I took a solo Venga trip was in the company of Luz, up on the mountain when she lay paralyzed. I swallowed a couple of nuggets in desperation."

"Did you find what you wished for?"

"Yes and no, in retrospect," said Keltyn. "It reopened memories but didn't give me clear answers. What it did give me was courage. God knows I needed that later, when the shit hit the fan."

"If you wish for clear answers, you must first find someone who has them," said Joaquin. Yoka had drilled this into him, the fundamental principle of the Venga experience.

"I found that out later, on a second Venga séance. I sought out my Cree ancestors, who confirmed the proper way to prepare maize and prevent the khokri."

Joaquin picked up the pouch containing Venga nuggets and shook them. They rattled like small stones. "So, what is your quest today? Answers to certain questions, or great wisdom?" This give and take with the Brixa was taxing him, but he sensed there was a lesson here. Being a guia involved more than handing out hallucinogenic cookies to lonely old widows. It also meant helping them clarify their wants and needs.

"Hard to say, when you put it that way." Keltyn sighed. "Wisdom, of course, but particular points of strategy may come up along the way. I figured I could simply call on one of my own tribal ancestors for advice: can the Onwei remain intact if invaded? Yet my own forebears would be either aghast or ashamed at this question, for their culture has been decimated by the white man."

Joaquin said nothing, only mirrored the Brixa's bitter stare.

She went on. "It seems like I really need to talk to someone from the future, someone who can tell me how all this is going to turn out."

She said this in a fanciful way, as if, mused Joaquin, she wished to skip the coming conflict altogether. He chewed his lip and nodded. Perhaps fortunetelling would become part of his own future. Was that not simply a personal version of Yoka's prophetic calling?

Keltyn held her hands out. "C'mon, scout. You did a nice job at Yoka's funeral, and she clearly meant for you to learn this stuff."

"Yep, she did lay this extra burden on me." He pouted. "But even if I plunge in, it will take years to develop such a gift."

"Can't wait that long. I need it now."

Joaquin smiled. "Don't worry. The Venga will supply its own guide." He picked up the pouch of nuggets and rattled it once more.

Keltyn snorted softly. "Okay, but you need to stick close by, Seir Guia."

"As you wish." He removed four Venga nuggets from the pouch.

She eyed the morsels in her palm. "Why four?"

"Your people go back much farther than mine." The Brixa's First Peoples, in Canada, had been there for thousands of years. That much he had gleaned from Yoka's teaching. After a brief foray to pick up smatterings of the Cree language, he, Keltyn and even Yoka had given up. It was too different from the more recent tongues like Spanish and English.

The Brixa shrugged, picked up her nuggets in one hand, sun tea in the other, and eyed Joaquin.

"Go for it," he said.

Still sitting on the step, she consumed her allotment, while Joaquin remained cross-legged on a mat. Crows cawed in the distance; a gentle breeze wafted behind him. The setter Mugabe emitted a soft groan as he dozed some distance away.

After ten minutes that, for Joaquin, always seemed like an hour, the Brixa reached for her mug and took a swallow. She must sense the tingling, the nausea, the salty taste that came with a rush of saliva, thought Joaquin. Her complexion seemed to pale. None of his regular patrons complained of any side effects. He supposed that was from consuming only the standard single nugget, two at the most if they craved adventure.

Even after taking her long draught of sun tea, though, the Brixa seemed restless. She still appeared clammy, beads of sweat glistening on her forehead. Eyes closed, she wobbled on the step. Joaquin clambered up to grab her as she started to tip sideways. Panting, she retched several times.

He moved behind her, reached under her armpits, dragged her over to the mat, and laid her down gently. Her breathing gradually slowed, and her color returned. Her eyes stayed closed.

Joaquin wondered whether to try to rouse her or simply let her rest. He decided to give her a few minutes and see. He refilled the mug and knelt beside her prostate body. She appeared so much different from the short-haired flat-chested girl that he and Luz had mistaken for a young man on their first encounter. The Brixa had allowed her straight black hair to grow to shoulder length, with bangs across her forehead. She still preferred men's clothes — gaucho tunic, hemp leggings and boots — but that only added to her tomboy charm. He could see why Efrain was smitten.

Still no sign of revival. He began to panic. She should be waking by now. Were four nuggets too many? She'd ingested six while on the mountain with the crippled Luz, with no ill bodily effects that time. Were Yoka's nuggets somehow different from his own? She had not changed her recipe for the eighteen months of his apprenticeship, and he had not altered it one pinch since she passed on.

Frightened, he couldn't resist the urge to rouse Keltyn. Wait. Maybe he could glean advice from Tio Hector. Yet there was not time to ingest his own Venga nugget and wait another precious ten minutes. He closed his eyes, concentrating with all his might, willing his "uncle" to appear. Now.

"Let her be a while longer, boy." Here was the jolly festooned gaucho, resting one foot on the step.

Thank God. "I am afraid I gave her too much," gasped Joaquin.

"She will get over it, and next time, you will be more cautious."

"She said she needed to see into the future. I wanted to make sure she had a solid vantage point."

"Well-intentioned I'm sure you were, boy."

Joaquin huffed. "You must answer a vexing question. What will happen to our tribe when the Sky-Bornes come in greater numbers?"

"Those with superior technology are generally the victors."

"What does that mean? Better weapons?"

"Weapons, but also other knowledge they have mastered, like your cousin Orfea's language translating box. Their flying machine. Even reading and writing."

Joaquin frowned. "Then the Onwei are lost."

Tio Hector wagged his finger. "Not so fast, boy. In some circumstances, nature favors the rough-edged side."

"Meaning what?"

"Those who can best adapt to their environment will win. In this land, the Onwei have a three-hundred-year head start over the Sky-Bornes. You must use what few advantages you have been given."

Joaquin's mind was a blank. What advantages? Horseback riding? He debated whether to plead for more specifics.

"Ponder it, boy," said Tio Hector. Leaving Joaquin with inscrutable advice as usual, he was off.

***

The intense nausea subsided. My breathing slowed to normal. My heart no longer pummeled like a jackhammer; the seawater taste in my mouth had settled. During this stretch, I'd flown through the sky, but not of my own volition, more like a magnet whisked northward at warp speed.

In the first moments, I passed Erebus from above. A constant plume of smoke wafted from the cone of the volcano, its sulfurous stench rekindling frightful memories from last year's eruption. As I gained altitude, the whole Antarctic continent spread out below, mostly swaths of brown, with patches of green and yellow. Mountains, plateaus, shortgrass prairie, the waterways few and far between, like the eastern slope of the Canadian Rockies. How different from the pictures of Antarctica I had seen in school, the images left over from texts of the twentieth century.

I spied a deep-blue oval jewel in the distance. It could only be the magnificent Lake Tal, site of the Rendezvous. Though I might wish to tarry on that scene, I might as well wish a planet to stop in its orbit. By ingesting four Venga nuggets, I'd ceded all control of this trip.

Next came soaring cliffs, breaking down to crashing waves below, and I found myself pulled high above the ocean, straight across it. Only now, in these few moments whizzing across the Pacific, did I feel surer of my body. Seeing nothing but blue below had a calming effect.

This peaceful sensation dissipated in a flash, as the next moment I was immersed in a giant cauldron of hissing and bubbles. This mixture of chemicals run amok was even more frightening than the volcano, clearly not a natural phenomenon. It was as if some mad scientist in a wild experiment threw together everything he could find in the laboratory.

I was buffeted back and forth, like a ricocheting billiard ball. The nausea and clammy feeling returned, yet this time it soon eased, as the cauldron once again gave way to blue above and below. Only then did it strike me: I'd just passed through the Hurricane Belt of Earth's middle latitudes.

A minute later, I was blasted by a wave of cold and found myself surrounded by a giant landmass, covered with white stretching beyond the horizon. I hovered a hundred feet up, watching people, whole families, clad in furs. Dogs pulled sleds across the ice. In the distance ran giant herds of caribou, their hoofed, antlered heads six foot high. A handful lay felled by hunters' spears.

The panorama narrowed in front of me as I came to rest on the ground. I caught my breath. My unseen guide must have placed me somewhere in Ice Age Siberia, or perhaps ancient Alaska.

Fifty yards away stood a huge, lumbering, long-tusked mammoth, unmoving except its head, its eyes fixed on a large-fanged cat, stalking in circles, waiting for the right moment to attack. In a flash, the saber-toothed tiger sprang, and I nearly jumped out of my skin. The beast's fangs ripped into the hamstring of the mammoth's rear leg. The behemoth sagged a moment later, falling on its side and bleeding into the snow. Now the cat made a lunge for the mammoth's neck. It sank its fangs deep, held tight and waited as its victim thrashed in mortal agony.

Long seconds went by, until the mammoth struggled no more. The great cat sat down by the carcass and began to rip out chunks of flesh. Riveted in place, I shivered, wishing to be transported elsewhere, but whatever supernatural force had set me here now forced me to witness the grisly scene in its entirety.

The tiger's movements slowed, its appetite sated. Then I spied six hunters exiting a nearby wood and cautiously approach, flint spears and round wooden shields poised. Skins covered their feet as well as their torsos. They crept up behind the cat. Gorging on its kill, it perceived no danger. I tensed again.

Running up to within ten feet of the tiger, they heaved their spears and scattered. Streaks of red ran down the beast's flanks. It pushed itself up and eyed its foes, spread some twenty feet apart. It sprang forward to pursue the closest hunter, but the band had already readied its next step. The would-be target curled up under his shield to fend off the tiger.

Meanwhile, the other five crept up behind with more spears and flung them at close range. The great cat thrashed, but it had not the strength left to mount another attack. It fell on its side, savage eyes and gaping jaws wide open as if to challenge, even in death, any who might approach.

The hunters raised their arms, fists clenched, then pulled out shorter flints in the shape of knives to finish the job. The one who volunteered as bait took his reward, carving out the tiger's ears and saber-toothed fangs as trophy. The others busied themselves with stripping the hide, slicing the beast's belly open and tossing out its innards for the crows.

I tried to cry out to the hunters, sensing some distant kinship, but no sound escaped my lips. I could only bear mute witness as they packed the beast's hide and meat for transport back to their village. Likely they would return later to do the same with the mammoth. Perhaps I could tail behind them and visit the village itself, their women and children, their homes and fires. Perhaps I could somehow even find a way to communicate with these people, who could be none other than my own ancestors. They should have been able to tell me a thing or two about dealing with a powerful adversary.

Then, in a flash, before I could reflect any further, I was unceremoniously plucked away again. I clenched, trying to shake my body free. I felt like a rag doll.

Seconds later, my unseen puppet-master dumped me in a forest of evergreens, an open spot beside a crystal-clear lake. A canoe lay on its side at water's edge.

Three men stood in the clearing. Two of them were Cree. I recognized their markings from powwows my father took me to long ago. One of them wore a fringed moose-hide shoulder bag adorned with beads in a red, blue, and white diamond pattern. The other spouted Wampum bracelets on each wrist and a matching necklace, all fashioned from the purple-tinged mussel shells found in my sub-Arctic homeland.

I stifled a strong desire to call out to these two. Even if I had the voice to hail them, we had nothing in common besides facial features. My Nation's language went extinct some centuries ago.

Bare-chested in their hide leggings, these two watched the third person intently. He was white, a trader from the looks of it, bearded, with cloth breeches and a checker-patterned shirt like the kind I was fond of. His rifle sat on the ground. Beside it lay a stack of wool blankets. He pointed at a pile of furs lying at the others' feet, as if to bargain. They stood by with arms crossed, indifferent to his proposed deal.

The white man held up a finger and retreated to the canoe. He returned, dragging a heavy box, then pried it open and removed a bottle. He popped the cork, sniffed the contents, and passed it to Wampum. This man stuck his nose in and took a sip.

I knew what would come next. "Oh, no, no, no," I groaned. I would have given anything to grab that bottle and smash it on the rocks, to shatter all the flasks in that white devil's stash. Those brightly patterned blankets, just as alluring and just as lethal: they carried smallpox.

Wampum's eyes lit up, his head jerked back, and he passed the bottle to Fringe Bag, whose reaction was likewise animated. They both nodded to the white man, who smiled and rubbed his hands together. A sinking feeling pervaded my stomach, followed by a deep sadness, as I recalled all my people who had succumbed to liquor, not least my mother.

I wiped a tear as my guide once again pulled me away. Now I hovered high above the earth, floating up above the blue lakes and green forests, aware that this was what Canada must have been like hundreds of years ago.

An insistent voice behind my ear whispered that white men like this pernicious trader were to blame for my country's now barren state.

Soon, I was perched hundreds of miles above the earth's surface, once more bound southward. I felt stationary as the globe rotated beneath me. The ocean's blue stayed constant until I once again hurtled into a brief but frenzied encounter with the Hurricane Belt, skirting high above the Earth's surface into the stratosphere. That soon morphed into more blue, until, at last, I glided toward my new home, the brown Antarctic continent.

I expected to be carried back to Yoka's hut. Instead, my mind's eye whirled around the cone of Erebus. Now, the plume of smoke, which had always before seemed as constant as a chimney's, wafted up in discrete puffs. The reek of sulfur persisted, yet somehow the smell seemed tolerable, as if my nostrils had come to terms with it.

What seized me now, from this gaping hole, this ur-mouth, were plaintive groans. Some were long, some short, in synchrony with the puffs of smoke. The sounds were far removed from speech, yet somehow, I could comprehend their meaning. The soul of the mountain was beseeching me. The two of us, me and Erebus, had become kindred spirits, each dependent upon the other for sustenance.

I felt my arms reach out of their own volition, signaling to Erebus I understood and accepted this connection. A moment to savor my newly sealed bond with the mountain, before my unseen guide whisked me away. Within minutes, I felt myself descend as gently as a feather until, without so much as a bump, I alit once more in front of Yoka's hut.

I opened my eyes slowly and blinked several times. I turned to Joaquin, squatting beside me, and grinned. "I'm back."

Joaquin managed a relieved smile. "You had me worried."

"Why? Afraid I wouldn't make it?" I sat up and dusted myself off.

"Sort of. What did you discover?"

"A learned man once said, 'those who do not remember the past are condemned to repeat it.' I had some lessons in ancient history: a lesson in courage and a lesson in caution. My forebears made their share of mistakes and those cost them dearly. They also managed to survive, despite much tougher odds than I'm facing now, but had to make awful sacrifices.

"I also had an up-close-and-personal encounter with Mt. Erebus. We're buddies now." Despite my glib speech, my hand shook as I reached out. "Hand me the sun tea, would you?"

He did so, waiting expectantly as I sipped. When I wasn't forthcoming, he twirled his finger. "Well?"

I laughed. "You want to know what my new game plan is, Scout? Don't know that's changed at all, just my attitude. Whatever may happen, bring it on."

12

SEEK AND HIDE

"I wish that the Brixa would marry Efrain," mused Trieste. "Then she would move into his splendid yurt — it was Aldo's, you know — and you and I would have more room." She and Luz had just hitched up the two-wheeled frame that would carry their own folded yurt between campsites through the summer months. The herd, the gauchos, the camp followers, all were due to leave the day after next.

Luz recalled how cramped the yurt had been for the three of them last summer, especially on a rainy day when there was hardly space enough in which to turn around. Taking a deep breath, she announced, "You and the Brixa shall have more space for yourselves."

Trieste whipped around to face her daughter. "What are you saying? Surely you do not wish to remain here."

Luz snorted. No, she would sooner spend the summer lying on a bed of nails than in Nomidar. "I shall take a detour from your route, so that I may be the one to greet the Sky-Bornes," she proclaimed. In the last several weeks, she had mulled over this plan at some length.

Trieste drew her head back. "Oh, really. What gave you such a crazy notion?"

"Who better to welcome them?" Luz held her chin high. "After all, it was I who discovered their presence last year."

"And remember where that landed you. Paralyzed. Your fine steed wiped out." Trieste's fists clenched. She began to shake. "This fool idea is even worse than running off to live with your *novio*. No, I forbid it."

Luz felt sorry for her mother's pathetic attempt to shield her from danger. "Joaquin will accompany me. He is to notify Ysidro when the Sky-Bornes arrive."

Trieste snorted. "Joaquin is a good boy, but he is not strong enough to protect you."

Luz stomped her boot, raising a swirl of dust on the ground. "Mama, you are so…old fashioned. Who do I need protection from? It's not as if the Sky-Bornes wish to harm anyone. The piedra de yris, that's what they are after. If anything needs protection, it's your precious stones."

"So? How do you propose to accomplish that?"

Luz knew she had her mother's attention now. They moved to sit on stools. She explained, "The volcano's eruption did scatter more of the stones at lower elevations, but they are fewer and farther between. Only on the high slopes of the mountain does one find huge deposits."

"You and the Brixa found them," said Trieste. "What is to keep the Sky-Bornes from finding them as well?"

Luz had already considered this. "Horses," she said. "We have them. They do not."

Trieste pondered this for a moment. "No, I don't suppose their flying machine would have room for horses. How high on the mountain could their craft land?"

"They need a spot that's fairly flat. Which means the lower slopes, too far for them to hike up," said Luz.

But new questions popped into Trieste's fevered imagination like so many spring weeds. "Suppose that, instead of horses, the Sky-Bornes bring some self-propelled cart that can clamber up the mountain with impunity."

"Anything is possible," admitted Luz, "but they would need a larger flying machine to store it."

"Hmph. Or suppose the flying machine is capable of landing on steep terrain after all."

"I doubt that." But in the same breath, Luz recalled what Keltyn had told her, that only a gear malfunction had prevented the plane from landing on the slope of Erebus last time. Best not to voice this, though.

Trieste seemed to find new objections as fast as Luz could dispel them. "And what will you do, once you have gathered all these scattered stones? Have you thought this through? How do you plan to shield your great treasure from the Sky-Bornes?"

Her mother was right. There was no way that Luz and Joaquin could shield all of the great shiny blocks that graced the steep upper slopes of the mountain. At least they were hidden from view below by other rock formations. Their best strategy was to camouflage what they found on the lower slopes.

Luz huffed, "I'm sure there will be a way, even if we have to bury them."

Trieste cackled, "We? I hope you do not expect poor Joaquin to dig holes for you. No, it will take your sweat to accomplish the deed."

"Then so be it." Enough arguing. Luz turned her back on her mother and started to walk away.

"You will need your own tent and provisions."

This was music to Luz's ears, her mother's grudging consent. Luz turned back and hugged her. "Thank you, Mama. You will not regret it. I will save all the piedra de yris for you."

"Mind you do. Now come help me load the yurt." Her mother led the way behind their house.

The most important question weighing upon Luz had been left unresolved for weeks. Now she decided to push her luck. "What about Ian, Mama?"

"Yes, your novio. I have pondered this question as well. In fact, it may interest you to know that I sought counsel from your grandparents."

This stopped Luz short. Her abelas were both deceased. Her mother must have indulged in Venga. The revelation surprised her, but she was glad that Trieste had enough confidence in Joaquin to patronize him.

"I see. And how did they respond?"

"They both advised, and I agree, that I meet Ian's parents at the Rendezvous. You can introduce us."

Luz gulped. Given the ages of their children, what were the chances that all three parents would consent to a match? By taking this step, she and Ian would give any one of the three the power to veto the marriage. Better to elope.

On the other hand, how could she refuse such a reasonable request? Trieste made it sound like she simply wanted to meet them. Luz wished Ian was around to talk this over with, but then, he had not the guile for such plots. She decided to respond reasonably and hope for the best. If the parents proved recalcitrant, she and Ian could still elope.

"Of course," said Luz, flashing a smile. "With pleasure."

***

By the next day, even half full, the cart already seemed overburdened. Both the wagon and Cozuel the mule, who would soon be hauling it, appeared too fragile for the task.

Luz watched as Trieste, panting from her effort, pulled her stool over to the shade and let water slide from a canteen down her throat.

How many more seasons could her mother sustain this mobile lifestyle? Besides carrying the yurt, the cart had to hold all the necessities of living eight months on the road. Luz did a mental inventory: Trieste's jewelry, pieces ready for sale, plus raw gemstones and tools she used to work them. Pots and pans, dishes, mugs, blankets, cots, a few throw rugs to pad the bare dirt, soap, clothing and a couple of stools. Their food had to keep — beans, salt, maté, crystallized honey, a few herbs, dried chilies, cheese and jerky. Between Nomidar and the Rendezvous, the only things Trieste could count on to buy were fresh meat and occasionally milk from the gauchos and tortillas from Char.

A camp follower needed every bit as rugged a constitution as a gaucho, and clearly this routine was not sustainable for her mother. Then it hit her. What Trieste needed was a way to sell her creations to other tribes without the physical toil of traveling long distances. She obviously savored the camaraderie of her fellow artisans at the Rendezvous, but Luz suspected that, given the choice, she would rather remain in the friendly confines of her studio and let someone else market her joya.

And why limit her sales to Onwei tribeswomen? Could not her market expand to distant lands, places like where Keltyn and Orfea Del Campo came from? Would the Brixa approve of this idea? Better the piedra de yris be used to fashion jewelry than coat the sides of great flying machines.

Luz almost jumped with excitement at her brainstorm. She stilled herself with effort. Best to approach the matter cautiously. She leaned against the side of the cart. "Mama," she said. "Tell me something."

"What is it, child?" Trieste sat with a whiskbroom to fan herself. Her skirt drooped between her knees.

"Is it true that our ancestors had no one to welcome them when they arrived here?"

"Ha. Not only that, they had no clue if this land would even sustain them. Men had visited Antarctica when it lay clad in ice, but no one ever tried farming or grazing stock until rapid climate change forced the issue."

"What if it hadn't worked?" Luz tried to express the worst scenario she could imagine. "What if the crops or the livestock, or the people, for that matter, if none of them could adjust to the long winter night?"

Trieste stared up at her daughter. "What a morbid imagination you have, Lucita. You must get that from your father. Aldo always was moody. What if, you ask? Simple. None of us would be here today."

"Could not they have turned their ships around and headed back?"

"And faced starvation bravely, holding hands as they chewed their last crust of bread? No, I think not. Coming here was a risk, even a desperate risk, but when you have no choice in the matter, the decision comes easier."

Luz needed to follow this reasoning one step further. "From what Keltyn said, it sounds like her people are soon to face the same predicament as our forebears did."

Trieste fixed her stare once more. "Perhaps so. Would you desire the Onwei to be more sympathetic toward strangers since our own ancestors faced this same plight?"

"I'm just saying…"

Trieste cut her off. "You are just saying that the land is big enough for all of us. Am I right?" She bobbed her head emphatically until Luz found herself nodding in agreement.

"And I am just saying that nothing good will come of it. Have you forgotten all the hostility the Brixa faced? How the gauchos and many of the women artisans treat her still? Well over a year since I welcomed her into my home, and this even as they grudgingly acknowledge her contribution to solve the mystery of the dreaded khokri."

Luz kept quiet, even though her mother misremembered what happened. It was only the threat of Aldo's spirit — to haunt Trieste if she did not take Keltyn in — that convinced her to do so.

Trieste pushed on. "Now imagine hundreds, no, thousands of other Sky-Bornes, flitting downward in their flying machines," she wiggled her fingers, "bringing untold other machines to do their bidding. How would that fare with our people?"

"I…I don't know." Luz slumped.

"Hmph. Not well. That much you can count on." Trieste pushed herself up. "Now let's get on with it. We have but one more night here. Then you and I shall head our separate ways. At least the Brixa will still be around to help me set up the yurt wherever we camp. Where is that girl, anyway?"

Luz stumbled forth, dejected. Her bold idea to reshape her mother's trade and save her health would have to wait. More importantly, her plan to set the piedra de yris' price with the Sky-Bornes would surely rouse her mother's ire. Was the risk worth taking without Trieste's consent, or was she sawing off the very limb on which she sat?

***

The next day they set off, herd and camp followers headed one way, Luz and Joaquin another. Nights and days were now so close in length that the difference could be measured in the time it took to boil a pot of water.

By riding steadily from dawn until dusk, pausing only for water breaks at streams, the two of them managed to bring the distant peak of the volcano into view by the afternoon of the third day. Luz, in the lead, paused to take in their destination.

She hoped that she and Joaquin gave themselves enough time to accomplish what they must. They should have left a week before the herd departed. She blamed Joaquin for not striking a deal with Ysidro sooner but, to be fair, neither had she cleared the air with her mother until the day before.

The lower slopes of Erebus amassed a great deal of territory. How could they possibly cover all that ground? Yet only the area closest to Splat Crater was relatively flat. That was where they must concentrate their energies. Each fall, the herd had to wind its way around the steep base of Erebus to find the fertile valley close to the crater.

The volcano's other approaches were too steep to invite a landing by the flying machine.

Joaquin pulled up behind her and reached for his canteen. "First time I ever come on it from this direction. When the herd heads here from the west, other hills block your view until wham, you're right smack in its shadow."

Luz said nothing. Even after last year's uneventful side trip with Keltyn, scouting for lower-lying stones from the prior eruption, the sight of the mountain still held cold memories for her. Her body flung into the air as a tumbling boulder felled Quintara. Her lower spine crashing into the boulder's edge. Screaming in pain as she slid into a heap at its base. Yelling and waving her arms, yet her legs suddenly inert, as good as severed from her body. Pounding her thighs in desperation, trying to will the feeling, the power, to return. Then, later, losing control of her most intimate bodily functions. The slow realization that she might never be able to stand on her own again, let alone ride a horse. Envisioning the shame of a cripple, dependent upon others for the rest of her life.

Despite the lure of the piedra de yris, the ghost of the mountain's malice refused to dissipate.

She spurred her mount and motioned Joaquin to move along. "Come on. We need to find a place to set up camp. Lots to be done tomorrow." She did not bother to watch Joaquin's reaction. He's probably sticking his tongue out at me. Thinks I'm a killjoy. Well, maybe so. Too bad.

They drew up to the rim of Splat Crater. This rekindled warmer memories for Luz, her first encounter with the Sky-Bornes, along with the startling discovery, forged only in hand signs, that she and Keltyn shared the same passion for the piedra de yris.

Luz slowed to let Joaquin pull abreast of her. He seemed pensive, ruminating, not a bit nostalgic.

"What's the matter?" she asked.

"Oh, just remembering our last confrontation, right there in the middle of the crater."

Luz laughed. "You mean hotheaded Ysidro's posse? That was a joke."

"Yes, but Ysidro wasn't the true villain. That mal hombre Nestor." Joaquin spat out the epithet like a rotten egg. "I saw the whole thing. He was just plain trigger-happy. Keltyn wasn't his only target, just the closest one."

They both paused, and Luz mulled how things would have turned out differently, but for Nestor's aim. A better shot, right through the heart or even close, and Keltyn would have died within minutes. A worse shot, missing or just grazing her, and she would have had to return with her crewmates, to face the wrath of Sir Oscar Bailey.

"Should we camp in the crater?" Joaquin mused. "The terrain is sure flat, so Buck might favor the crater to land in again. That would make us easier to find, and there's plenty of scrub brush for a campfire."

Luz had other ideas. "The crater is too far away from the volcano. The lava flow ended at its lower slopes. We can find a decent spot close to the stones. We should even be able to find one with shade and fresh water."

"As you wish, boss." Joaquin spat that out with the same bile as describing Nestor.

"Don't be silly. I'm not your boss," she said, and spurred her horse forward.

Their shadows from the afternoon sun grew longer as Luz and Joaquin, still single file, plodded on toward Erebus. The wisp of smoke from its peak was unchanged from the first time Luz spotted it years ago and likened it to a sleeping giant. Yet later she learned firsthand how quickly this malevolent mountain god could be aroused from his slumber, spewing forth his full fury by way of rumbling moans, suffocating stink, and molten lava, which wiped out everything in its path. Once was enough. She had no desire to ever climb the high reaches again, no matter how brightly they advertised their treasure.

With the slope beneath their horses' feet rising and the sun nearing the ridge of hills behind them, Luz kept her eyes peeled for a glint or bright flash that might indicate a gemstone in the rough. Whether they spotted any this evening or not, they would soon need to break for camp.

"Up ahead on your left, Luz," Joaquin shouted. "Just at the foot of that scrubby bush."

"I see it."

They detoured to inspect this rock, but as they drew close, Joaquin spotted another a bit farther on. The second was half the size of the first, but still filled her palm. Both gleamed their purple hue at rest, but when rotated seemed to reflect all the colors of the rainbow.

Luz gave both stones a firm squeeze, just to convince herself, then searched around for more. Bright spots were gone; the sun had just dropped below the rim of the hills. A hundred feet ahead stood a grove of evergreens, and she could hear the tinkle of water. "Let's pitch the tents over there," she said. "We can check back here again in the morning, when the light is better."

"Fine with me," said Joaquin. "Betcha there's lots more."

"Bet you're right."

"How are we gonna camouflage every piece, just the two of us?"

Luz herself had wondered that, without having a good idea of how many pieces they would uncover. If this small area was any indication, it would be a big job. "I don't know. I thought you brought along something to track the location of each stone."

Joaquin patted his pack. "Yeah, Ysidro showed me how to make a map, using charcoal on a piece of hide. Finding the ones we bury shouldn't be a problem."

Luz was tired. She wanted only to get off her horse, have supper and settle in for the night. Three long days in the saddle had stripped the glamour from this jaunt. "So, is there a problem?"

Joaquin leaned over his saddle horn. "The problem is, Luz, we're going to find so many stones, it'll wear you out to hide each one."

"Me? I thought you volunteered to help."

Joaquin wiggled his two gimpy paws, left hand and right foot. "Ooh, no. I'm not cut out for digging all day. No, siree. I was sent here by Jeaf Ysidro to be his eyes and ears for when the Sky-Bornes show up."

Luz dropped her jaw. There was no way she could camouflage all the stones they expected to find by herself. It was true. Joaquin had not explicitly agreed to help in the labor. She just assumed. Stupid girl. "What's your bright idea?"

"Don't have one. Not my problem."

"Oh, come on, Joaquin. Quit acting twerpy. We can't just leave them sitting out in the open. That would defeat the whole purpose."

"How's about," Joaquin pointed his finger skyward, "instead of covering up each stone, we gather them all together in one well-hidden spot?"

She pondered that. "You mean dig a giant hole? That would take just as much time."

"Not necessarily dig a hole. Find a hollow, a cave, something already there. Then all you have to do is cover it up good."

"Okay, that'll be your job. Finding a hole."

"What's it worth to you?"

Luz couldn't believe her ears. "Are you kidding me? You expect to get paid?"

"'Quid pro quo,' that's my motto."

"Right. A businessman. Lucky inheritance, and now all of a sudden you're Seir Big Shot."

"Nothing lucky about it. Paid my dues all the way."

Luz thought about all the times she had fed, cleaned and sponge bathed Yoka in the last year, and how Joaquin never seemed to be around when some odious chore needed doing, but she held her tongue. It was true. She needed Joaquin for this plan more than he needed her.

"I'm sure Mother will reward you handsomely, once we deliver whatever stones we can to her."

Joaquin stuck out his lower lip and nodded. "Fair enough."

"Now that you're in on the deal, you'll need to remember where you hide them."

Joaquin patted his pack again.

She grunted. Joaquin was acting entirely too petty about this whole enterprise. By focusing only on what was in it for him, he was missing out on the importance of what they could accomplish for their tribe.

Then a pang of doubt surfaced, and not for the first time. Here were an eighteen-year-old girl and a half-crippled sixteen-year-old boy trying to outwit technologically advanced aliens, who already knew all about them from a prior encounter. How naïve, but it was too late to back out now.

I3

SPACE QUARTET

Helmut Ganz squirmed in his seat. He was uncomfortable in the limelight, yet here he was at a table with a microphone, minutes before a press conference that his boss had scheduled for the big event. Ganz protested to Sir Oscar that he had no flair for media relations. His boss insisted he show up, early no less, to take the temperature of his fellow crew members, particularly Harry Ladou.

The long table sat next to a podium inscribed with the Bailey logo, a sunflower ringed by the caption "The Face of Tomorrow." Various media types slipped into their seats and made small talk, leaving Ganz to study his notes and wish the whole charade would hurry up and be done.

His funk was interrupted by Buck Kranepool, who now dropped into the chair beside him. For most people, the pilot's deep blue eyes and wavy blond hair would evoke a telly star. Yet, for Ganz, the man's leathery tanned face, crisscrossed by wrinkles, instead evoked a dried mud pie.

Buck clapped him on the shoulder with enough force to rock him forward. "How ya doin', Ganz? Blast off bright and early tomorrow."

Ganz pointed his thumb up and forced a smile.

At least he was not the only rookie on this flight. Here came Russell McCoy, shuffling toward his seat, trailing the scent of body odor. The man did his best to conceal his solid build behind a nerdy-looking, absent-minded-professor demeanor. He would look better in a lab coat, decided Ganz. His dialups were adjusted to the thickest lens setting, the black rims doing nothing to soften his acne-pitted sallow cheeks. Every few minutes, he had to nudge the nosepiece back up with his fingertip. His oily thinning black hair was slicked straight back like swamp grass.

Ganz shivered at the thought of being cooped up with McCoy in the back seats of Bailey Voyager. Worse yet was Harry's plan that the two of them should share a tent.

Ladou himself slid into his chair at the far end of the table, closest to the podium. He appeared strangely preoccupied, not bothering to greet any of his fellow crewmates. Arms folded, he gazed vacantly across the hall. McCoy leaned over to whisper something in his ear. Harry made no response. His eyes appeared bloodshot, probably from missing sleep. Ganz had a pretty good idea why that might be: those transoceanic liaisons with Orfea Del Campo.

Well, *arrivederci, Signora*. Furthermore, thanks to Ganz's surveillance tracker, her assignations with Ladou compromised his position in Bailey Enterprises. It just went to show that you couldn't coast; there was always someone nipping at your heels. And yes, Harry Ladou, that's Helmut Ganz tailing right behind you, soon to leave you in the dust.

Despite the hour being at hand and the hall now filled, Sir Oscar, with his flair for the theatrical, had yet to appear. Normally, tardiness on the part of his boss would not worry Ganz. It was just the Chief's way of whipping up the media into a feeding frenzy. Yet, with the plethora of unexplained incidents hitting every corner of the Bailey Empire, Ganz had to wonder if Sir Oscar's delayed appearance signaled another emergency. Body searches at the building entrance, armed guards patrolling the halls, you would think he must be safe. Perhaps the terrorists had just struck somewhere else.

The press began to fidget and consult their timepieces. Where was the boss? At fifteen minutes past the stated hour, just as Ganz was about to summon security, a buzz filled the back of the hall. Sir Oscar Bailey made his way to the front, stopping to greet favored correspondents in the audience. His short, sturdy frame was wrapped in a charcoal neosilk suit, set off by a muted violet cravat. A sunflower logo bronze emblem graced his lapel. The leonine mane of white hair, brushed straight back, tumbled over his neckline. Not a single wrinkle line marred his face.

Sir Oscar had barely to lift his hand and the room hushed. "Here we are, folks, finally ready for Round Two of Bailey Voyager," he began. "I had no delusions that this would be easy. Each of these voyages of discovery builds on what we learned from prior ones. Think of Portuguese seafarers who mapped the coast of Africa in the fifteenth century, inch by inch, culminating in a sea route to the Orient. Think of the NASA space probes of the twentieth century, capped by lunar landings. I envision the same process here."

He turned to his left and held out his hand. "Two of our crew members are veterans from the prior voyage. My second-in-command, the Managing Director of Bailey Enterprises, Harry Ladou, and Buck Kranepool, the savviest pilot I could ever wish for. Please stand, gentlemen." He started a round of applause.

Ganz, watching the two of them, was shocked by the contrast. Kranepool spread both arms in the air, like a victorious athlete, and basked in the ovation. Ladou glared at his boss before grudgingly pushing his chair back. He stood with both hands on the table, as if needing something to anchor himself. He pursed his lips, gave one short nod, and dropped back into his seat. Really? Ladou was turning into a basket case.

"Thank you, Harry and Buck," said Sir Oscar. "We count on your experience to guide us through whatever surprises might await us this time around." He turned back to his audience. "Much as we try to plan for every contingency beforehand, and believe me, we spend weeks in strategy sessions, there are always unknown factors. Steady hands at the helm make all the difference between success and failure.

"Our two novice crew members are each uniquely qualified. Savant Russell McCoy is a Bailey Science Fellow, a world-renowned expert on the geological properties of our quarry, the strategic mineral iridium. He was the mentor of Savant SparrowHawk, who perished in a freak accident on the previous mission, and whose contributions will be sorely missed. However, since Savants McCoy and SparrowHawk were co-developers of the iridium field assay essential to this venture, I am confident that we can smoothly pick up where she left off." Sir Oscar lifted his hand in the direction of McCoy, who in turn stood and raised an arm.

"Last but not least, another highly valued member of the Bailey team, Helmut Ganz. Herr Ganz is Director of Bailey Transnational Operations. His extensive experience in business development and contracts has been invaluable in our rapidly expanding area of European mergers and acquisitions. In addition, he has negotiated licensing agreements with China for cold fusion equipment and other key technologies in which our own progress still lags.

"What does all this have to do with a mission to gather iridium from Antarctica? Perhaps nothing, and if that turns out to be the case, so much the better. Helmut's role will then be akin to an unused insurance policy. But, if we should once again make contact with a tribe of nomadic gauchos, and if said tribe should claim ownership rights to iridium deposits on their land, we shall be prepared.

"You and I might wonder whether a tribe of nomads has any claim to rocks strewn in the general vicinity of a volcano, while they graze their cattle miles away for a few weeks each year…" Sir Oscar paused to mine chuckles from his audience. "In any case, should proprietary questions arise, Herr Ganz will our representative. He has even studied the language of these people, just in case. Helmut, care to give us a sample?"

How typical of Sir Oscar to make his pupil recite some tidbit for a doting audience, but Ganz came prepared. He arose, keeping his posture erect, and bowed at the waist. "*Encantado a conocerte.*" The briefest of applause followed, just enough to make Ganz feel like crawling back into his hole.

"Excellent. Now I shall entertain questions from ladies and gentlemen of the media. Please state your name and affiliation." Sir Oscar scanned the room for hands. "Yes, Ms. McShane," He pointed to an older woman in the second row.

With one hand she alternated placing and removing her dialups, glancing first down at her notes, then up toward the podium. "Thank you, Sir Oscar. Doris McShane, New Economy. The Chinese Presidium in Irkutsk this morning issued a statement, calling this undertaking, quote, another misadventure, end quote, with potential to cause, quote, destabilizing effects, end quote, in relations between China and Canada. Your comment?"

Sir Oscar chuckled. "If memory serves, that verbiage is almost identical to their communiqué on the eve of the previous launch. And my response is unchanged, namely that I do not pretend to speak for Canada about any political implications of this mission."

Ganz smiled to himself. Like most of Oscar's audience, he knew better. Indeed, his own job stemmed from the erosion of democratic governments. Transnationals like Bailey Enterprises deployed quasi-diplomats like himself to forge deals with foreign powers. He liked to think of himself as a peacemaker, for if he failed, Bailey would have to deploy more spies and, if worse came to worse, hungry mercenaries.

"Moving along," said Sir Oscar. "Yes, Mr. Casey?"

A well-worn, red-patterned cravat adorned this man's neck, accentuating a multitude of angry red marks on his face. "Bertram Casey, political affairs, Third Millennium News. I realize that you are trying to keep away from global fallout here, Sir Oscar, but I would like to follow up on the implications of Ms. McShane's question. Do you think that we can expect any changes in Chinese trade policy toward Canada, if these mineral resources do show the technological potential you allude to?"

"Whew, Bert, I'll have to spin that one around." Sir Oscar hesitated. "Let me say this. I believe that iridium may have an impact to rival that of cold fusion technology. The balance of trade, the shape of vehicles, zero emissions, you name it. It's always hard to predict how big a footprint something new will have, but this one has mega potential." He paused again. "That's about as much as I would care to speculate on political import.

Any more questions about the mission itself? Yes, the lady from Zürich?"

"Teodora Chapelle with Edelweiss News, Sir Oscar. Thank you. This question is for your crew chief, Mr. Ladou. I understand your aircraft only holds four people. You must have a wealth of storage space if you plan to bring back such a sizable amount of this strategic mineral."

Ladou opened and closed his mouth several times. He appeared stumped. Sir Oscar stepped closer to the microphone just as Russell McCoy cleared his throat.

"I can take a stab at that," said McCoy. "We are searching for only the high-quality ore, sixty percent grade or more. The lesser stuff we can find in craters here in the northern hemisphere. That was the source of Bailey Voyager's coating, but it's a laborious process to separate the impurities. No efficient means has yet been developed."

He continued in his clipped cadence. "We're traveling light this time, less gear, personal items, et cetera. You may have noticed, the last voyage included two women, while this crew has none. There's a reason for that." He smiled and paused for the mixed chuckles and hoots. "Seriously, though, the reason is to leave room for enough high-grade ore to fill a volume roughly as big as me."

He paused long enough for Teodora Chapelle to interject her follow-up. "And what might such a quantity of this valuable ore be used for?"

McCoy stole a peek at Sir Oscar, who responded with an almost imperceptible nod. Most of the audience might have missed it, thought Ganz. He was constantly impressed at the seeming effortlessness with which the Chief controlled news flow.

"Sufficient to coat a considerably larger craft," said McCoy.

"For future deployment to Antarctica?" speculated Ms. Chapelle.

McCoy pursed his lips and nodded his head this way and that. The correspondent turned to the chief.

"Can you give us further insights on your company's long-term plans to develop Antarctica, Sir Oscar?"

"I won't deny that we've hashed over the options, but nothing has been firmed up. We need to balance geopolitical necessities with the art of the possible. My first priority is getting there and returning safely, for my crew on this voyage and any that follow. No more crash-landings because of equipment failure, or hostile encounters with locals, if either can possibly be avoided."

Nicely punted. More inane questions followed. Ganz stifled a yawn. The inevitable probe — What was Sir Oscar's plan to deal with eco-terrorism? — followed by the inevitable answer: all options were on the table. Someone asked Kranepool what, as the only married man in the group, his wife had to say about him volunteering for another of these risky missions. He drawled that Sally knew the risks when she married a test pilot, and his concussion provided a handy excuse when he forgot their anniversary.

By the time Sir Oscar ushered the media toward refreshments in the back, Ganz felt both relieved and slighted. No one had any questions for him, yet staying below the radar suited him just fine. Would that submersion of ego come back to bite him later? Was he forever fated to be second fiddle? Perhaps it didn't matter, so long as he tethered his career to Bailey Enterprises. The Chief showed no signs of slowing down, nor any interest in handing over the reins of power.

Sir Oscar spotted him and waved him over. He ushered Ganz to a corner. "Take a look at Harry, Ganz. What do make of his behavior?"

Ganz turned to watch Ladou, across the room. Teodora Chapelle stood beside him, holding an iced drink and chattering away. Occasionally, she paused, as if inviting Harry to chime in, but he only nodded vacantly.

"He does appear distracted, sir," said Ganz.

"Exactly," said Sir Oscar. "The man hasn't said a word all day. Big load on his mind."

"Lots of responsibility and all that," ventured Ganz.

"Rubbish. Harry Ladou has thrived on this kind of assignment all the years he's worked for me. That last mission on Bailey Voyager, unknowns much greater than this one, he didn't blink an eye."

The two of them watched as someone offered Harry a soda. He accepted it but then just held it, like a statue.

"The poor sap is caught in a dilemma," said Sir Oscar. "Savant Del Campo has poisoned his thinking, rekindled 'feelings' for this tribe they encountered. We are somehow going to exploit assets that are rightfully theirs, blah blah blah. That kind of mindset, he'll cave at the first sign of resistance."

Ganz nodded, stifling a grin. Exactly the scenario he prepared for.

"Which makes your role all the more important, hear?" Sir Oscar's gimlet eyes probed Ganz. "Harry is still the point person, because these Onwei people know and respect him. But if he wavers, it will be your job to nudge him, remind him of the stakes. I'm sure he grasps that's part of your role, and at some level he will resent it." The Chief paused. "It's a delicate job. What do you say, Ganz?"

"I'll do my best, sir." Without even willing, his heels clicked, on this occasion sending a bracing tingle up his spine.

***

Back in his hotel room, Ganz sat on his bed and pulled out his phone. He wondered if he could reach Zürich on this portable device. On past business trips to northern Alberta, he had put plenty of calls through to the Bailey Europe offices, but always from lines at HQ, and always business. This was different, private. He needed to confide in someone who cared for him just as he was.

He checked his timepiece, did some mental calculation. It would be three twenty A.M. in Zürich. Too bad. He needed to talk now, not in six hours. Even more important, he needed a good night's sleep. As the pilot reminded him, blast off tomorrow, bright and early.

Despite practicing good sleep hygiene, Ganz still found global travel an ordeal, a drain on his constitution. Buck Kranepool assured him that the voyage to Antarctica would tax his circadian rhythms considerably less than a flight from Europe. Overall, it would be no worse than shooting through one of those long alpine tunnels in a train, except there would be only a one-hour stopover to stretch his legs during the whole trip.

Sugar coating or no, Ganz dreaded the voyage. Were the opportunity for career advancement not so dazzling, he would have begged off.

He pulled out his toiletry bag and fished for a sleeping pill, downing it with a swig of water. By the time it kicked in, he would be done with his call. It would not take long. All he really wanted was to hear a sympathetic voice.

A male answered in unshaven tones. "Whazzit?"

"Alain? It's Helmut."

He heard shuffling. "Helmut. What the hell time is it?"

Ganz checked his watch again. "Seven thirty."

"Ha, ha. Very funny. Some nerve." Big yawn. "You need Mama to tuck you into bed the night before your big adventure."

"Something like that." Ganz smiled. Alain could be crude, but he was not callous.

"Yeah? Well, screw you. I volunteered to come to Alberta with you, see you off and all that. We could be wrapped up together right now, snug as a bug in a rug, could've both gotten a good night's sleep, but nooo…"

"Alain, stop it. You know that wouldn't work. There's no time for social life here."

A pause on the other end. "Now's not the time to step out of the closet, is that what you mean? Maybe not, Helmut, but when? Will there ever be a right time for you? It's been four years. I'm tired of living a secret life."

Now Ganz was at a loss for words, a huge lump stuck in his throat. He forced himself to take a deep breath. Alain was simply venting his ire from being so rudely awoken. "Sorry, Alain. I just wanted to hear a familiar voice before they shoot me up into space."

"Scary, huh?"

"Think of all that could go wrong."

"Which I'm sure you have, to the nth degree." Another pause, then Alain continued in a whisper. "You packed your…personal security item?"

Ganz cringed. He used one hand to grope through his bag until he felt the hard bulge. "It's here, but if I end up having to use it, the game will already be lost."

"Now, now. None of that. Think positive."

"I'm trying, Alain. I love you, you know that."

"Aw, you big lug, I love you too. Now go to sleep. When you get back to Zürich, we'll go feed the ducks." Kissing sounds.

Ganz kissed back into the phone and hung up. Yes, feeding the ducks in the pond near their flat would be a welcome diversion, after who knew how many days in the wilderness at the other end of the Earth. He needed that picture to steel him along what was sure to be a bumpy road ahead.

***

As Bailey Voyager approached Chimera Space Station, Ganz was mesmerized. The scene reminded him of one of those molecular stick models, an assortment of nuclei connected by rods sticking out every which way. Once they were ushered inside, though, it was all consoles, screens and railings. Perhaps like an air traffic control tower, he imagined, with one small difference: as soon as you unclasped your seat belt, you joined the other unmoored souls floating across the room like so many balloons. There was no elegant way to steer. You just bounced yourself from railing to railing.

The weightless sensation felt unnerving, tinges of nausea and vertigo pursuing him as he wove his way down a corridor between the main bays. He planned to use his free hour to have a chat with this Huey Lin, to find out whatever more he could about Savant SparrowHawk's Chinese connections. After fifteen awkward minutes and a few missed turns he spied a sign marking the Systems Engineering bay.

Huey, alerted of his arrival beforehand, beckoned him to a recliner with straps, roomier than the cramped seats on Bailey Voyager. The crewcut bespectacled young engineer swiveled from his console to face his guest.

Ganz caught a whiff of garlic. "I offer you beverage, Mr. Ganz, but too messy here. Squirt up nose." He giggled. "How go voyage?"

"So far, so good." Other than this damn weightlessness.

"Excellent. Your first, is right?"

"That it is." Ganz tried to think of something to break the ice. "How long does it take to get used to this state?"

Huey gave a soft laugh. "Zero G, you mean? Months. Is too bad. By time get comfortable, must go back." He pointed to his legs. "Bones get weak."

"I see. But you have had many tours on Chimera."

The man held up seven fingers. "Four months here each time, then two months home. Not bad gig, how you say?"

"You have family?"

"Wife want me home, wish make babies. I tell her plenty time for that later, first make good money here."

Ganz nodded. Enough chitchat. "I understand that you knew one of our crew from last year's voyage, Huey."

He raised his eyes toward the ceiling, as if trying to recall, although Ganz felt sure the man knew exactly whom he was inquiring after.

"Young woman?" ventured Huey.

"Yes. Her name is, or was, Keltyn SparrowHawk."

"You say 'is or was.' What mean?"

"She met an unfortunate accident later on that trip. She may have died. The rest of the crew was forced to leave her in the care of locals in Antarctica."

Huey nodded, pensive. "Spallohawk land in strange place."

Ganz said, "I understand she contacted you while our craft was docked here on the outbound leg."

"Perhaps so." The young engineer crossed his arms and leaned back.

"May I ask the nature of your discussion? I understand she was fluent in your language."

"Ah. Someone hear us talk Chinese, but no understand." Huey bobbed his chin, smiling, mouth agape, soundlessly laughing at his own joke.

Ganz pursed his lips. The man played his hand way close. "Savant SparrowHawk had a mentor from your country, an eminent geology professor, Savant Wan Xiang. Could he have been the subject of your conversation? Perhaps some scientific details he was unable to transmit by normal channels?"

Huey lifted his pointer finger. "Very good, Mr. Ganz."

"Would you be able to share those details? I'm sure Savant Wan would want his student's successor to know as well, and I shall make sure to that he does."

"Ah, but you and I, we not geologists. No understand these things." He picked up a sheet of paper from his desk and flourished it. "I take a note from your Spallohawk, she want send to Wan, is all."

"Did you happen to read it?"

Huey tilted his head to the side, watching Ganz with one eye. "Mostly numbers. How you say? Formulas. Nothing I understand. What so important this note?"

Ganz debated whether sharing more details would earn this man's confidence. Surely, he knew more than he was sharing. He was an engineer; he could read formulas.

"Who can say, but the fact that Savant SparrowHawk went to some length to make sure that Savant Wan received the note suggests it was important. Likely something about soil sampling for iridium, would be my guess."

Huey raised his brows and jutted his lower lip. "Make sense, but if Wan and Spallohawk go such pains to keep secret, must have good reason. If she want her boss know, she tell him. Mr. Ganz, I get feeling you, how you say, on fishing expedition. I think our little chat done." He unstrapped himself and started to rise.

Ganz swallowed, forced a smile and remained seated. "You are so right, Huey. I am fishing for information that may advance scientific discovery."

"Ah, so. And what happen with results of discovery? What benefit to my country?" Huey sat back down and peered over the rim of his dialups.

"Who can predict where new technology will lead us," said Ganz. He gestured around the room. "Perhaps to another joint venture among many nations, like Chimera Space Station."

The man smiled out of one corner of his mouth. "In Antarctica, you mean? China and Canada together? You a dreamer, Mr. Ganz. Chimera launched sixty year ago, when our countries better terms. Is miracle still operating."

He was right, of course. Only a dreamer would propose another joint venture at this date. Still, Ganz sensed that Huey had the heart of a dreamer, one to which he could appeal. "Any detail you can remember from that note might help bring our countries one step closer together."

The corners of Huey's mouth dropped. "Sorry, Mr. Ganz, no details to report. Best you should contact Savant Wan yourself, if these formulas so important." He nodded and arose once more. "Good luck on mission."

And good luck with getting through the censors to Savant Wan Xiang, he might as well have said. Ganz reached across and shook Huey Lin's hand, thanked him for his time, and bounced his way off the walls back to the main bay.

"Formulas" meant some technical details about iridium, from a geologist's point of view. He would need to run this by McCoy and see how important the passing of formulas between nationals of cold war antagonists might be. Specifically, did it constitute a treasonable offense for Ms. SparrowHawk to send this information without revealing it? If not, was there some other, as yet uncovered, correspondence from her addressed to Wan Xiang that contained equal information of similar sensitivity?

The whole question would be moot if she was dead. If not...

14
TEMPTATION

While Luz spent her morning scouting for the iris stone, Joaquin searched for a cache to store them in, someplace safe. Whether it would be for only a few days or for much longer, they had no way to predict.

Every so often, he stole a glance skyward, half-expecting the Sky-Borne flying machine to appear out of the blue. Would it be today, tomorrow, next week? At least the pilot Buck would be able to spot them easily, thanks to the shiny blue tent the Sky-Bornes had gifted him in their hasty departure last year. Joaquin pitched it in plain sight, like a bright blue flag.

As he returned to camp, he checked the sky once more and noticed clouds moving in. A few gusts of wind rustled the high tree branches. He tied up Cisco, sat down ten feet from Luz, and opened his canteen.

Luz stood waiting impatiently for his report, hands on hips. Let her wait. He felt bedraggled. The brush was so rough that he had to trudge through most of the way on foot.

Truth be told, he liked to keep her in suspense. She could be way too demanding. If she had to beg to find out what he had discovered, that would annoy her no end.

"Well?"

Joaquin brightened. "Yep. Found us a great hiding spot."

"Took you long enough."

"Hey. Remember, it's got to be secret so's they can't spot it walking around here, but still clear enough so's we can find it after they gone. Not every little bend fit that bill."

"So? Where is it?"

Joaquin struggled to his feet and pulled a rolled-up piece of hide out of his pack. He spread it out in front of Luz. He had used charcoal to draw a rough map of their surroundings. A large inverted "V" near the top left corner stood for the mountaintop, a wiggly line for the nearby creek and a dense thicket of x's for the forest.

A prominent cross marked a spot beyond the trees. "Right there. I spent the whole morning checking around. No better spot. No sign of no lava nearby, so's they won't be scouting that area. And it's too close to trees for them to land there."

"All right. Just keep your map hidden tight. Better yet, after we're done burying the stones and know the spot inside out, burn the evidence."

Joaquin smiled. "Whatever you say, Luz. You're the boss."

He would just as soon have taken a longer break, but she promptly sent him to scout for more pieces. His clubfoot was beginning to ache after all the plodding this morning.

Luz was a few years older than he, but not as wise as she made out. He called her "boss" to humor her, but her decision-making seemed haphazard at best. He needed to anticipate everything that might befall them. That way, if she came up with some fool impulse, he could gently step in with a better plan, one he had already thought through.

Over the next hour, more clouds rolled in. Less light meant the stones would be harder to find. Plus, the yield diminished the farther they ventured from camp.

Joaquin was relieved when he heard a loud whistle from Luz. "We better call it and get to burying what we have," she said.

Scouting the cache's location should have been the hardest part. Yet when Luz removed the bough covering her temporary cache, Joaquin realized the small natural cave he had found for longer term would be inadequate. He cleared his throat. "Wow, that's a lot of rocks, Luz."

"Yeah. So? You found the perfect spot." She watched him closer. "Right?"

"It's a great spot, but it'll need a bit of digging out to hold this much."

"Go for it. The shovel's in my pack. I'll start loading this up."

Joaquin coughed. "Um, we talked about this last night, Luz. Any digging needs be done, 'fraid that's your gig."

She stared at Joaquin, then heaved the bough aside. "Fine. I'll enlarge the hole while you transport the stash. Lead the way."

They mounted, and Joaquin escorted her to the spot he selected earlier, part of a sandstone ledge just past the far end of the tree line. One of the sides indented into a natural cave, about the length of a man's body, and just high and deep enough to keep that body dry in a storm.

It took ten loads of the huge bag to move all of the piedra de yris. By the time the last heap of stones was emptied into the expanded cave, and the entrance camouflaged with a mixture of boughs and dirt, they both drooped, sweaty and exhausted. They sat with their backs against the ledge and sucked on their canteens. The sky had grown darker. It smelled of rain. Gusts of wind whipped through grasses beyond the tree line.

Luz scanned the horizon. "Surely the Sky-Bornes can forecast the weather. They would be foolish to attempt to land yet today."

"You'd think," agreed Joaquin, "but they been known do stranger things."

Luz pushed herself up. "You sure you want to keep your tent out in the open tonight? Might get blown away. Worse yet, struck by lightning."

Joaquin thought quickly. "Supposin' I leave the tent where it is, so's they can see it, just in case. Throw on a few rocks to keep it anchored. Then how's about I lug my bedroll into your tent, my other tent, that is?"

"Oh great. Now you're kicking me out because both tents belong to you? Forget it, Joaquin."

"Nobody's kicking anybody out. It'll be snug, but there's room for two, and it's just for tonight. Come on, Luz."

Luz squeezed her eyes shut and shook her head rapidly, but Joaquin could see that she had no better plan. Deep down, he also knew that she had long ago adopted him. As stand-ins for siblings neither of them had, they needed to watch out for each other.

When Luz opened her eyes, she said, "I hope you brought some soap. I don't need your aroma in there. Go wash yourself in the creek before the storm hits."

Joaquin gave her a mock salute and hopped to it. Just like Tio Hector told him, women did change their minds. You just had to be patient.

Within two hours, the tempest was upon them. They sat cross-legged, facing each other inside Joaquin's ragged hide tent. Each thunderclap brought an involuntary spasm from one or the other. Every few minutes a flash of lightning lit up their tiny space.

"Did you tie up the horses good? They'll spook and run," said Luz.

He scowled. "I did, so quit worrying." Sheesh.

Luz sulked for a while. "No way any flying machine's going to be able to land in this kind of weather. They'd be crazy."

"Thought we already decided they're crazy to come all this way scouting shiny rocks," said Joaquin.

Luz snorted. "They're going to be awfully upset not to find any."

Joaquin smiled. "No more free pickings. They're going to have to pay the going price."

She straightened up. "Who says we have to sell any? And who's going to set the price? Huh, Seir Beltran?"

"Not my say. That's between the Brixa and Jeaf Ysidro."

"Oh, yeah? And how did either one of them come to own this cache of stones? Seems like it was me and you did all the hard work to herd them up," said Luz.

Joaquin couldn't see her eyes in the dark, but there was just enough light to make out her silhouette, tilting her chin this way and that as she barked. She could get as riled as an untamed filly with the least provocation.

"Well, Luz, you the one's going to get first shot at them, so it's your call. Soon as they show up, I'm off to find Ysidro."

He finished the last of his jerky, took one more swig of water, and lay down flat. The torrent outside had not ceased, but the thunder and lightning were letting up. If new holes in the tent's roof showed up, at least he would not be staring them in the face.

He heard Luz rustle around to lie down as well. After a few minutes of silence, she asked, "Tell me something, Joaquin?"

He waited, silently cursing his suggestion to share a tent.

"Supposing we give the Sky-Bornes a few stones, just enough for them to show off back home." Luz paused.

"Make it sound like we've been scouting here for weeks, and this is all we could find. They don't have horses. How far can they make it on foot? What are they going to do, tie us up and steal our mounts, just to prove us wrong?"

Joaquin stared at the tent ceiling and pondered that. "If it's Harry or Orfea, no way. Buck seemed more ornery, but even him I don't reckon he'd be that cold-blooded."

"Okay," said Luz. "So, they poke around here for a few days, convince themselves there's nothing of value. After a while they're going to give up and go home."

There was a hole in her plan, and Joaquin felt obligated to point it out. "And what you going to do when Ysidro finds out he didn't get his piece of the action?"

"That's where you come in, Joaquin," Luz purred.

"Huh?"

"All you have to do is…nothing. You don't notify Ysidro when the Sky-Bornes land. We both wait here until they leave, then we head back to rejoin the tribe. Tell everyone there that we waited for weeks, but the Sky-Bornes never showed up."

"Sounds like you got it all figured out." Joaquin shook his head in silence.

"Yep. We'll pack out just enough of the stones to use in Mother's joya trade for the rest of this year. I'm sure she will reward you with an ample finder's fee."

"Not going to work, Luz."

"Tell me one reason why not."

Joaquin sensed her shifting to watch him. In the narrow tent, her face was but a foot away.

"The Brixa will figure something's fishy. She knows you and me pretty well by now. She knows them Sky-Bornes even better. If they're on their way, they're going to get here sooner or later. She'd shake the truth out of us. She'd probably force me to send a Venga message to Seira Orfea by way of Tio Hector, find out from her end what really happened."

"Damn." Luz shifted onto her back again. "Maybe we could cut her in on our secret."

"Let's see." Joaquin counted on the fingers of one hand in the dark. "So far there's you, me, your mother, and the Brixa. How long you figure this here secret will stay secret, Luz?"

She sighed. "I guess you're right. Keltyn SparrowHawk wouldn't keep it secret, not if there's something to trade for it."

Joaquin picked up the abrupt change in Luz's tone. "Sounds like you're peeved at her."

"Oh, I'm peeved all right, ever since she sided with my mother about me leaving home to marry Ian."

Joaquin knew better than to venture into that hornet's nest. Ian, when Luz introduced him at the Rendezvous, seemed like a decent fellow, but Joaquin knew that Luz and Trieste had already sparred plenty about her plan to leave. He kept mum.

"Plus, now Mother spends hours at a time teaching the Brixa about the joya trade. I feel like an outsider in my own home. So, I wish Keltyn would just stay put and not try to be some kind of heroine by saving us from the

Sky-Bornes. That goes for you too, Seir Guia Prophet. Don't try to get people all worried about an invasion."

"No?" He felt his blood coming to a boil. In cavalier fashion, Luz had just swept aside all the evidence gleaned from Yoka, Orfea and the Brixa's own Venga journey.

"No! Just let the Sky-Bornes land, snoop around all they want, find nothing and leave. If there's nothing from which to fashion more of their flying machines, they won't return. End of story."

Joaquin wanted to pummel Luz with the facts, but he was tired, and it was late. "Whatever."

"I know we can pull this off," Luz muttered. She turned her body toward the far wall of the tent and pulled her blanket up to cover her head.

The whole idea was dumb, thought Joaquin as he stared up at the tent ceiling, listening to the steady beat of rain. Funny how greed could twist the mind of an otherwise sensible person. Instead of trying to argue sense into Luz, he suspected that the Sky-Bornes' behavior, when they finally landed, would do the job.

***

When Luz awoke the next morning, the rain had tapered off. Joaquin still lay curled up in a ball under his blanket, dead to the world. She debated whether to wake him, but last night's petty squabbles had left a bitter taste in her mouth.

She pulled on her boots and emerged to survey her surroundings, finding everything thoroughly soaked.

The shiny blue tent had gathered a puddle of water in the midst of the large rocks weighing it down, but the hide tarp that protected their food supply was intact. Thank the Spirits, her mother would say.

Still tethered, the horses shook and stamped, moisture steaming off their manes. Luz fished in her pack for a currying brush. She spent twenty minutes giving each a good rubdown before untying them. Cisco and Tinto both wandered off toward the nearby grassy slopes, smelling breakfast.

Luz began to chill. She had worked up a sweat currying the horses, and now the cold dampness was caught under her layers. She flailed her arms and ran in place to generate more heat. Not until a shaft of sunlight peeked through the trees and fell directly on Joaquin's rag tent did she hear any signs of stirring. A good ten minutes later he emerged, yawning and thoroughly disheveled. Hitching up his leggings, he spied Luz, still flapping her arms. A sly grin broke across his mug before he wiggled into his poncho.

"Exercise time, eh?"

"Actually, I'm really craving a bombilla right now."

"Go for it, Luz. I'll join you."

Luz glared at Joaquin. She hoped he would act like a gentleman and see the obvious need for a fire to boil water. Was he really that dense, or just baiting her as usual? "Puhleeze would you build a fire, esteemed Seir?"

Joaquin gaped, trying to act surprised. He placed his right hand across his stomach and executed a deep bow. "It will be my pleasure, Seirita."

With great and unnecessary fanfare, he retrieved from his pack a pouch containing all the essentials: matches, wood shavings and even a small flask of what he would only describe as "spirits." He had a small fire going in no time, just enough to heat the bombilla.

When at last she sampled the maté, it was hot enough to scald her tongue, but so-o-o good, that hardly mattered.

She passed the bombilla to Joaquin. "Thanks. I needed that."

Joaquin took several small sips and studied her before passing it back. "Yeah, you sure did."

She frowned and brushed the hair out of her eyes. "Do I look that bad?"

Joaquin snorted. "You might scare Ian away."

Really? Where was a looking glass when you needed one? Then she spied the smirk on Joaquin's face and snapped, "You're not much to brag about either."

"No, but I'm not the one trying to put on airs."

She fixed him with a cold stare. "What is that supposed to mean?"

"Forget it." He grabbed the bombilla.

Luz stuck her hands on her hips. "That crack was uncalled for. Apologize right now."

"Sorry, Your Highness." Joaquin made a kowtow motion, bowing his head while twirling his hand downward in front of his body.

Luz turned away. Why feed into his baiting game? She spoke without facing him. "They better show up. I guess we're as ready as we can be." Suddenly she felt a pit in her stomach and whirled back toward Joaquin. "What about the cave? We need to make sure the storm didn't damage our excavation."

"Not a chance."

"I hope you're right, but we need to check." She scrambled to her feet.

Joaquin grunted, but pushed himself up and began plodding along. After a short time elbowing his way through the soaking brush, he balked. "Hold up, Luz."

She had already tramped through the woods some distance ahead. Now she turned to check on Joaquin. His face wet and bedraggled, his poncho littered with leaves and twigs, he crouched with hands on his knees, panting for breath. "This is dumb. If you want to check on that cave this morning, only way we're going to get there is hike around edge of trees, and if we have to do that, we might as well round up the horses."

Luz studied the way ahead. She knew she could easily make it by herself through the woods, another ten minutes max. She had a mind to send Joaquin back to camp. When it came to anything involving physical exertion, especially on foot, he would just start crabbing all over again.

She glanced back at Joaquin again and saw pleading in his eyes, like a kid who didn't want to miss out. Beyond that was a knowing look that measured what Luz herself was thinking: out here in the wild, she needed his savvy as much as he needed her strength. Still, it galled her, having to suffer his taunts. Reluctantly, she turned back.

They retraced their steps, rounded up and saddled the mounts. By tracing around the perimeter of the woods, within fifteen more minutes they found their sandstone ledge, or rather, what was left of it. The storm had eroded every bit of dirt and crumbled stone around the top. What had been a clear drop-off of five or six feet was now a shallow incline of twice that length. Even the serpentine border of the ledge was no longer visible, replaced by one long rise, which ended at the border of evergreens.

Surveying the scene from horseback, Luz's heart sank. How could their luck have deserted them overnight? It wasn't fair. It wasn't like she was going to all this trouble for personal gain. One thing after another was conspiring against them. Would they be able to find the exact spot again, and how much digging would it take to do so?

***

Luz turned to Joaquin. "Any bright ideas?" She looked as flustered as a skittish mare.

He patted his hands downward. Managing her moods was becoming his biggest chore. "Not yet, Luz, but here's a big no-no. Don't start dig up everything in sight so's to find the stash. Wait until the Sky-Bornes come and gone. Last thing we want is to pull 'em to our camp with that blue tent, then have 'em nose around and find big piles of dirt. You catch my drift?"

Luz pursed her lips and nodded.

You had to look on the bright side, he thought. They could curse their luck in a week or so, as they sweated to dig up their treasure. For now, their secret was protected better than any way they could have fashioned by themselves.

Back at camp, the weather was still cold and clammy; a thick mist hung over the entire mountainside. How could they dry enough firewood to ward off the coming evening's chill?

Joaquin longed for the gaucho camp. Even after last night's weather, they would have some kind of campfire going where everyone could warm up. Here, today, you couldn't even find a dry place to sit down. They were totally at the mercy of the elements.

What if the Sky-Bornes didn't show up? How long could he put up with Luz while they waited? She still had on her sourpuss face. He felt the least bit guilty about teasing her this morning, but sometimes, like when she put on those self-righteous airs, she was just too sweet a target.

His flattened blue tent was still sopping wet. No way could it be used tonight. He would have to beg to share the other flimsy tent with Luz again. After a cold lunch of jerky, hard-boiled eggs, and dried apple slices, punctuated only by grunts, she retreated to "her" tent, leaving him to sit and flap his hands across his arms in an attempt to keep warm.

He looked skyward again. The cloud ceiling was so low, he doubted that the pilot Buck would be able to spot the patch of blue he had laid out so carefully.

If the weather didn't break soon, they would both catch a chill. He had to get a fire going. Joaquin would just as soon have enlisted Luz to scrounge for more brush, but no sound or movement came from her tent. She must be asleep, still exhausted from last night's storm.

Well, so was he, but he couldn't afford to mope. He sighed and began to sort through the twigs and branches lying around, scrambling for pieces dry enough to feed the few embers that still remained from this morning.

An hour later, he fell back, exhausted. Tiny flames sprung to life now and then, just enough to tease him, then flickered out within seconds. He huffed and puffed for all he was worth, trying to nurture the sparks, but all he had to show for his efforts was a cough and clothing that reeked of smoke. From the damp kindling, a steady cloud of gray curled skyward.

Luz emerged from the tent, rubbing her arms. "What's going on?"

"What does it look like? I'm trying to get us some heat so's we don't freeze our butts tonight."

She circled the perimeter, using her arms to try and keep the smoke at bay. "Looks like you could use some help."

"Go find us some wood that ain't soaking wet, Luz. And while you're at it, say a prayer to your Spirits. If the weather don't break in next hour or so, they're not gonna be able to find us 'fore dark, even if they're on their way now."

"Right." Luz headed off. Joaquin heard her rustle through the brush. Ten minutes later she was back, dragging the ends of several large branches.

He recoiled. "Huh? What makes you think them will burn?"

Luz grasped a small branch and snapped it cleanly. With a self-satisfied look, she proclaimed, "It's all dead wood, Joaquin. Branches felled by last night's storm." She picked out another gnarled piece with small shiny leaves. "Here. Take a whiff of this."

The pungent tarry smell seemed familiar from his two seasons on the cattle drive. "What is it?"

"Creosote bush. It'll work great for kindling." She laughed. "You're not the only one knows about this kind of stuff."

Again, a great deal of smoldering, but after fifteen minutes of close attention, more than he had ever given anything in his life, they were rewarded with the welcome snap and crackle of wood actually burning. Joaquin sat back against a log, more exhausted than ever, but at least now they had something to show for their efforts.

The warmth from the flames soothed him. His head dropped onto his chest and he closed his eyes. A series of quick dreams ensued, in each of which he was awakened by the whooshing sound of a flying machine landing nearby. Each time, he sat up startled, but with no sound except the crackling branches, dropped back to doze off once again. So when, after what seemed like hours, the whooshing sound persisted even after he awoke, he had to pinch himself.

The first thing he noticed was Luz, watching the scene behind him, her mouth agape. He whipped around to witness the Sky-Bornes' wondrous flying machine hover twenty feet off the ground, just up the hillside from where he stood. Its nose pointed straight up and its tail eased toward the ground slowly, gently, like a mother hen about to enthrone herself back onto her nest of eggs.

When, finally, the tail pods made contact with the ground, the whooshing sound ceased, replaced by a whir as the giant bird edged onto her stomach, resting on three wheels. Then she fell silent.

Joaquin felt every bit as awestruck as when first encountering her a year and a half ago, even more so now as she put on her full landing display right in front of him. In that moment, the heavy sensations of bone-chilling cold and fatigue evaporated from his body like so much dew exposed to the morning sun. He felt sure that his efforts to build a fire had somehow guided the giant bird to land safely.

15

TRADE WAR

The scanner on her table beeped. The briefest of messages, from Greta Szabo, the producer of her telly series, urged Fay to: "Check Third Millennium News. Now."

Reluctantly, she clicked the remote. What could possibly be of interest at this stage? Bailey Voyager wasn't equipped for any direct coverage from Antarctica. It would likely be a week before further developments.

Fay watched the whole press conference yesterday, an anticlimax if ever there was one. As if Oscar Bailey gushing his usual platitudes were not enough, there was the sorry sight of her inamorata, Harry Ladou, as stiff as a zombie.

If he didn't snap out of his funk by the time they landed at Erebus, chaos would surely follow any contact with the Onwei. Helmut Ganz's heavy-handed negotiating style would go over like a lead balloon for Act One. Then Buck Kranepool would have to fight it out with Ysidro and his gang of drunken gauchos for Act Two. They would be lucky to return anyone home alive.

It made her queasy trying to sort out her feelings about this whole mission. Of course, she wanted Harry back in one piece, physically and emotionally. Yet, if the price was ushering in a ferry service to Antarctica, she wasn't so sure.

She perched on the edge of her armchair, eyes fixed upon the telly screen. A familiar talking head greeted her, his dialups framed in tortoise-shell. His gaze bored directly into Fay, making her shudder. It was Bertram Casey, TMN's seasoned political commentator, already launched full bore into his nasal drone.

"…during yesterday's press conference marking the sendoff of the second Bailey Voyager flight to Antarctica, Sir Oscar Bailey made predictions…"

Blah, blah, blah. More tensions between Canada and China. Trade war, higher tariffs. A Canadian journalist imprisoned for spying.

Fay went to mix herself a drink. Three minutes later, Casey was still going strong. "…colonization of Antarctica by Canada could be the next step. If conditions there prove to be inhospitable or inadequate to support permanent habitation, expect Bailey to next develop an interplanetary vehicle with iridium as its shell. This is assuming that large deposits of that vital metal are as abundant in Antarctica as geologists predict."

He had Oscar's ambitions right on. It pleased Fay that someone else could read his cunning mind. So enthralled was she to be part of the first mission, she had been blindsided by the truth. Yoka Sutu had parsed his true intentions in no time.

"Political implications aside, the idea of colonizing Antarctica has merit, despite the inevitable denunciations from the Chinese regime if this goes forward, and despite the opposition of Native Peoples United and their eco-terrorist allies. For the wild card in this whole affair is Savant Orfea Del Campo's discovery on the previous mission."

Fay jerked to attention.

"A race of Indigenous humans does indeed live on in Antarctica, having somehow survived global warming without the benefits of modern technology. Recall that landmass and population in the Southern Hemisphere were much lower than the North, well before the Hurricane Belt separated the Earth into two isolated halves. Now we stand on the threshold of an era where those halves may be reunited. What sane observer can doubt that these tribes of impoverished Antarcticans will benefit from contact with the rest of the world?

"My chat line is open for your comments." The florid image faded from view.

Fay flicked off the telly, fuming. Bert Casey, you windbag! Typical media commentator, implying that his opinion was the only sane one. The Onwei, this race of "impoverished Antarcticans," could not help but benefit from contact with the rest of the world! Really?

She needed to set Mr. Casey straight, challenge him to a televised debate. Plenty of programs reveled in this sort of thing. She sent a quick note to Greta.

There was a more urgent matter waiting, however. Consul Teng had again summoned her to the Chinese embassy. She wondered what sort of dressing down awaited her, no doubt again having to do with Sir Oscar Bailey. For better or worse, she had become the messenger between Oscar and the Chinese government.

***

The same protocol — guard at the gate checks ID, young flunkey escorts her to reception room — left Fay once again stranded in the leather armchair. This time, she happened to peek at the ceiling, a huge fresco of brown leaves and branches on a pastel pink backdrop. How had she missed that before? Perhaps it was the hour; now, sunlight filtered through the nearby window to produce a subdued but elegant radiance.

It dawned on her that she was surrounded by the outpost of a five-thousand-year-old civilization, considerably older than either her own European one or the upstart North American one of Sir Oscar Bailey. It would take her best efforts to parse the subtleties of whatever message she was asked to convey.

After the *de rigueur* five-minute wait, the far door opened, and Consul Teng appeared. This time, he did not bow, but rather strode directly to the big teak desk and sat, clasping his hands on the table.

She tensed. If a Chinese diplomat forgot his manners, he must have bad news.

Consul Teng's eyes met Fay's. His face was devoid of expression, his mouth shut as tight as a trap door.

Fay tried to keep her expression noncommittal as well. So far as she knew, none of her actions could have troubled the government of China, yet Consul Teng acted like he expected some kind of apology.

She allowed herself raised brows. Sorry, Zhou Baby, the first move is yours.

After a prolonged silence, during which Teng's sphinxlike stare was not once punctuated by a blink, he took a deep breath and set his hands flat on the desk. "Savant Del Campo. Let us first clear air, as you say. You deliver message from my government to Sir Oscar Bailey? About moratorium on high-grade iridium ore?"

"Yes, of course I did."

"And what his response, may I ask?"

"I'm afraid he did not perceive any advantage to accept a moratorium." Fay bit her lip. Consul Teng might chastise her for failing to convey his government's warning of striking back if Sir Oscar failed to accept the Chinese offer, but that would be grossly unfair. She had no bargaining power; she should not even have accepted the role of messenger in this sorry exchange.

"Hmph." Consul Teng grunted and, finally, blinked. "I not surprised."

"Does that mean your government will retaliate?" Fay took a sharp breath, wondering if she invited such a response simply by asking the question. But if she was to be the courier, she had every right to know.

The straight line of Consul Teng's lips softened into the faintest of smiles, not nearly enough to expose his corn kernel teeth. "We keep options open, but be assured my government not make idle threats."

"I understand fully," said Fay.

"Then please convey same to Sir Oscar Bailey," said Consul Teng. "Also, another matter must hold accountable."

She pulled back. What now?

"One of his underlings, name of Helmut Ganz. Perhaps you know him?"

"Yes, I have met Herr Ganz." Pinballs ricocheted off the inner walls of Fay's skull. What kind of transgression could a straight arrow like Ganz have committed?

"I am sure he act under orders. When Bailey spacecraft dock at space station, he seek out Chinese staff engineer Hunany Lin." Consul Teng stopped to gauge Fay's reaction.

She was still clueless. "Something beyond a get-acquainted chat, I presume."

"Indeed, yes. Herr Ganz try very hard pump information, as you say, from Hunany."

"Oh? May I ask what about?" She had an inkling.

"Have to do with Savant Keltyn SparrowHawk and your dear Savant Wan Xiang."

Fay took a quick breath. Were Keltyn and Wan still in touch? Somehow Fay assumed she was the only conduit, just like her role between Teng and Sir Oscar. "I see," was the only response she could muster. Even if Teng knew more details, he was not about to share them with her.

Teng studied her with his unblinking stare. "Any idea why Herr Ganz so interested in old conversation between Comrade Hunany and Savant SparrowHawk?"

"Perhaps he suspected that she might have engaged in industrial espionage by passing sensitive information on to a Chinese national."

"Ah, very perceptive, Savant Del Campo. Supposing she was, and supposing this proven. What penalty she face?"

Fay strained to recall Canadian legal customs. "I suppose it would depend upon the importance of the secrets passed on."

"Come, come, Savant. Assume worst, for sake of argument."

"Life in prison. Sometimes exile." Bertram Casey's citation of an incident from ten years ago jumped to Fay's mind. "Sometimes nations trade convicted spies."

Consul Teng broke into his yellow-toothed smile.

Fay tilted her head and studied him. What was so funny? Then it struck her. If Keltyn were still alive, and if somehow Ganz could persuade or force her to return to Canada, and if, furthermore, she were convicted of espionage, such a fate might await her. Traded to China for another spy, she could reunite with Savant Wan Xiang. Not too bad a prospect, all things considered. Certainly, it would be a net gain for China.

Fay, too, broke into a slow grin. She nodded to Consul Teng.

He quickly resumed his formal air. "Very well, Savant. You please convey formal complaint to Sir Oscar

Bailey regarding interrogation of Hunany Lin on neutral territory, as well as my government's displeasure with breaking of moratorium." He paused, waiting for her to nod. "If it come to trade war, I assure you and Sir Oscar Bailey, Canada will be loser." He stood, bowed his head, and maintained that position.

Fay, caught off guard by the man's mercurial mood shifts, gathered her things. "I shall do my best to communicate your sentiments, Consul Teng." Even as she exited the room, the corner of her eye caught the man frozen in his deep formal bow.

As she left the consulate, Fay's head spun. This Machiavellian role that had been thrust upon her made her feel at once thrilled and chagrined. Thrilled to be the lens by which the two greatest world powers stared each other down. Chagrined to realize that, if she misinterpreted the nuance of a message — Consul Teng was a master of the oblique — major international repercussions might result.

It was time to fine tune her diplomatic radar.

16

POINTS OF CONTACT

Luz eased closer to Joaquin. "Wow. Isn't that something? We didn't get to watch them land last time."

"From what the Brixa told me, it was a whole lot rougher than this," he said.

The freshly landed flying machine exuded vapors of burnt fuel, heat waves dancing off its skin. A door on its side opened. Out stepped the tall blond pilot. Buck waved and Joaquin waved back, clearly thrilled to see a familiar face again. Luz made no move to greet him, his lewd behavior at their last visit still fresh in her memory.

Next came Harry, who wiggled through the small door awkwardly. He appeared to have gained weight. After straightening his posture and the vision aids on his nose, he gazed around vacantly. When he spotted Joaquin and Luz, he nodded. Stumbling toward each of them, with a slight bow, Harry grasped their hands in both of his. They felt cold and stiff. His usual good cheer had deserted him.

Luz watched over Harry's shoulder to see who would disembark next. A tall, hawk-nosed, lantern-jawed younger man preceded a shorter, broad-shouldered but slouched older man with thick vision aids. Both of them grimaced as they surveyed their alien surroundings.

Seira Orfea was nowhere to be seen. Something felt quite awry. Luz and Joaquin exchanged worried glances. Among the previous group of Sky-Bornes, Orfea had been the most adept in smoothing the rough edges, defusing tensions. Without Orfea, that task should fall to Harry, but his wan excuse for a greeting signaled he was not up to it. Luz wondered if she herself might have to step forward.

She studied the tall, gaunt man, barely emerged from the plane, his eyes jumping to and fro. To Luz, those eyes radiated unease, contempt and even fear, as he tried to fathom his alien surroundings with nobody but these two youngsters here to greet him.

Nor did the older man pay Luz and Joaquin any mind. As soon as he stepped off the plane, he surveyed the ground, kicking and tapping with the toe of his boot. Neither he nor the tall man made any attempt to act sociable.

Luz stuck her hands on her hips. This was going nowhere. Nervous as she was, she was about to ask Joaquin to pull out his language decoder when Harry, at last, seemed to remember his own role. He held up his palm toward Luz, then said something to the tall man, who loped back to the flying machine and returned shortly with the same kind of translating box that Fay had gifted to Joaquin. Luz exhaled.

The tall man pulled several earpads out of his pocket and passed them around. "Testing, one, two, three," he intoned while watching Luz. "Can you understand me?"

"Yes, perfectly, seir," answered Luz. She recalled that it took Orfea days of intense trial and error, as Yoka prattled on about every subject under the sun, to achieve the correct settings. No doubt this man had taken some training beforehand, perhaps even from Orfea herself. Who else among their people had any inkling of the Onwei tongue?

Harry beamed. He turned to the tall man and nodded sagely. "Good work, Ganz." He summoned Buck and the other man closer, then took a labored breath. "Let's do introductions. Luz and Joaquin, bless both of you." He clasped his hands as he spoke, yet the faint flicker of a smile disappeared as soon as he finished greeting them.

He seemed lost, no questions to ask of them, though she had expected plenty. How had she and Joaquin managed to predict another voyage from the Sky-Bornes? How did they place themselves right in the landing zone?

Luz felt suddenly wary. At her previous encounter with Harry, he had gone out of his way to act sociable, even making an ill-advised attempt to fit in at the gauchos' barbecue, overindulging in pulce beer to the point of a nasty hangover. Now he was just going through the motions. Indeed, the simple act of greeting seemed to sap all his energy. He stumbled through a wooden attempt to reintroduce himself to the two of them. She cocked her head back. Why such formal behavior?

Harry lifted his chin. "We are also anxious to determine the fate of Keltyn SparrowHawk, and, if she is still alive, to return her to Canada."

To Luz, Harry's little speech sounded rehearsed. She blinked several times. Keltyn had sworn them not to reveal her whereabouts. Luz was not a good liar, and had urged Joaquin to be their spokesman, at least for this matter. Despite being younger, he had lived by his wits so long that he knew all the tricks to make a story believable.

Harry eyed them both, awaiting a response. Luz bit her lip, trying to stay mum, waiting for Joaquin to take the lead. He remained silent as a block of wood, seemingly unfazed. Her palms began to sweat.

She watched the tall gaunt man join Harry, fixing stares on both her and Joaquin. The silence felt like torture, and Luz prepared to clear her throat to get his attention. Surely, he had rehearsed some story about Keltyn.

Then, out of the corner of her eye, Luz noticed the laconic smile on the face of the pilot. Of course. This staring pose of Harry and the tall, gaunt man was a bluff, and Buck was amusing himself by watching it play out. She peeked at Joaquin and noticed the hint of a smile. He had already detected the bluff. No need to spin a tall story about Keltyn.

After several more tense moments, Harry shrugged and pressed on with his introductions. "Of course, you remember our pilot, Buck Kranepool."

The tall, rugged, blond man stood with his thumbs dangling from his belt. He raised his right hand to shield his eye in a mock salute. "Great to see you kids again. How's every little thing?"

His eyes caressed the length of Luz's body, in the same way she found so offensive on their prior meeting. Even with another year and a half of maturity under her belt, she fought to keep her composure.

Buck's boldness persisted, as if testing her. "Miz Luz, I'd be mighty jealous of whoever manages to round you up," he drawled.

She felt a blush come on.

Having scored his point, Buck next studied Joaquin. "Looks like you've been doing some growing, son." He patted his stomach. "Put some meat on them bones. That's a good thing."

Joaquin grinned but said nothing.

"Used your noggin, too, building a big fire. Your smoke signals wafted up through the cloud cover, good as a runway beacon. Otherwise, we would have had to take our chances and try to land on the steep side of the mountain." Buck reached out toward Joaquin with his palm raised. After seconds of puzzled hesitation, Joaquin reached up to slap it. "Attaboy," said Buck.

Harry cleared his throat and gestured at the short, broad-shouldered man to step forward. "This is Savant Russell McCoy. He is a geologist like Keltyn, a specialist in your iris stone. In fact, he was Keltyn's teacher."

Luz studied this man, his rumpled clothes, his thick, black-rimmed vision aids that needed to be pushed up his nose, his greasy, disheveled and thinning black hair, his wan pockmarked complexion. His gaze had come unpeeled from the ground and now favored Luz. He certainly did not go out of his way to make any kind of impression on strangers, but then Luz recalled how reticent and disinterested Keltyn had been at their first meeting. That all changed as soon as Luz showed her a sample of the piedra de yris. Perhaps this man likewise had no passion beyond these rocks. In any case, he barely nodded, even after Harry's introduction.

"Luz should be able to fill you in later on what's available where. You must have been back to scout the area since we left, eh, Luz?"

She tried to give a noncommittal shrug. Much as she had rehearsed her answers, she was not prepared to encounter another expert on the iris stone. Could Keltyn conceive of her former mentor joining this expedition? How would that alter the negotiations that Harry and Ysidro both envisioned?

Harry introduced Ganz, eyeing his compatriot with his head tilted, as if inspecting him for the first time. From their stiff body language, Luz had the impression that the two were not close.

"Herr Ganz is a master of negotiating business deals for our boss back home, Sir Oscar Bailey," Harry said.

To Luz's untrained ear, Harry's comment seemed laced with sarcasm, or was she reading too much into this? His open palm invited Ganz to say a few words, but the man only forced another tight smile and remained silent.

"Herr Ganz will lead the talks with your new jeaf to arrive at a fair bargain for the iris stone." Harry flashed a quizzical glance at Luz and Joaquin. "When last we met, your jeaf had just died. May I ask who has taken the lead now?"

Luz and Joaquin exchanged glances.

"Ysidro Correon," said Joaquin.

Harry and Buck both frowned, no doubt recalling their last encounter with the rogue gaucho leader. But Ysidro had learned his lesson, or so she hoped.

She was about to ask the question that had bothered her since the door of the plane opened, but Joaquin beat her to it.

"Where is Seira Orfea?"

Harry raised his chin and glanced knowingly at Ganz. "I should have explained earlier. Savant Del Campo has a difference of opinion with Sir Oscar about our mission, and she was not invited to join." He stopped abruptly and opened his palms.

Harry was apologizing for omitting details of their plans; Luz was sure of it. She couldn't tell whether he did not want to disclose more in the company of the rest of his crew, or whether they really planned to play the whole thing by ear. She would have to stifle her curiosity for now, but so far, the Sky-Bornes seemed as ill prepared for their second mission as for the first.

She watched in dismay as the four men scanned their surroundings, trying to decide where to set up camp. They seemed so lost, and again it struck her that, without Orfea, if anyone was going to extend a welcome it would need to be her.

"Gentlemen," she called out, "would you care for some maté after your long journey?"

Harry and Buck brightened, while Ganz and McCoy stared at her vacantly.

"Why not?" said Buck. "You brewing?"

Luz pointed toward Joaquin. "He is the fire starter." Joaquin stood still, frowning, until Luz lifted her chin. "Get on with it. Enough for six."

She busied herself gathering blankets to sit on, but a few moments later, among the vast assortment of gear the four men unloaded from the plane, four of their folding stools appeared.

Shortly, Joaquin brought the bombilla of maté, ready to pass around. Perceiving that the beverage was meant to be sipped through a communal metal straw, Ganz cast a doleful look and hurried back to retrieve cups for himself and his mates. The ensuing awkward moment of sampling this strange drink ended only when Buck broke open a package of biscuits to pass around. Another creature comfort, thought Luz. She could get used to this.

McCoy surprised Luz by offering her his chair with a gallant gesture. She shook her head, but he planted himself firmly on her blanket, sitting cross-legged as if used to living outdoors, which she found hard to believe. Nonetheless, she acquiesced to his repeated hand gestures to park on his seat, and thus found herself several feet above his eye level. She nodded her thanks, amazed that the flimsy-looking contraption took her weight without slipping an inch.

McCoy sucked his steaming brew and winced. "Strong stuff," he said. "Bracing."

"It is meant to be sipped slowly, seir," said Luz.

"Naturally." He eyed Ganz, sitting some distance away. He put up one hand next to his mouth to confide to Luz, "I'd be fine with your metal straw, miss, but Herr Ganz is a bit of a prig, if you haven't already guessed. Hygiene and all that rot." He chuckled under his breath.

Luz smiled. McCoy was trying to curry her favor by painting himself as a regular guy. Why?

The answer came in no time. "So, I gather that you are a fellow — what would you call it — enthusiast of this remarkable stone. What is your name for it, by the way?"

"We call it the piedra de yris, seir."

"Piedra de yris. A sweet sound. And your mother turns it into jewelry? I'd love to see her work sometime."

Should she show this man? His interest seemed sincere. Luz fumbled inside the front of her tunic and retrieved the small teardrop-shaped pendant that Trieste had finished a few months ago. She dangled it in front of McCoy.

He drew a breath and held out his hand. "Oh. May I?"

Luz pulled the chain off her neck and passed him the ornament. A flush of pride swelled within her, along with the notion that the Sky-Bornes might covet such jewelry.

McCoy rolled it in his hand and held it up to the fading light. "Exquisite. This miracle mineral — yet another function."

As the pendant swung before his nose, Luz watched his reaction closely. The thick vision aids distorted the expression of his eyes, but she picked up a twitch around the corner of his mouth, along with the feral scent of greed.

The joya had cast its spell upon him. From years of watching her mother sell her wares at the Rendezvous, Luz knew the lure of a finished, mounted gemstone was altogether different from that of bright ore on the mountainside, or from the gleaming shell of the Sky-Bornes' flying machine.

After more clumsy fondling, McCoy handed the pendant back, never taking his eyes off the gem until Luz had tucked it inside her tunic. Then a sigh escaped him. "Forgive my crude manners, Luz. You must think that I have developed some kind of fetish. It's almost to that point, I admit. For the past ten years, iridium has become my mistress, I guess you could say. Since shortly after Keltyn first showed up at my laboratory, as a matter of fact." He paused. "It sounds like the two of you became close."

"Yes, we did," said Luz, taking a measured breath. She gulped, praying he would probe no further. She really didn't wish to force a half-baked lie about Keltyn's demise.

Instead, McCoy turned dreamy-eyed, and recounted his role in launching Keltyn's prodigious career. "I set out to develop a field assay — test the stuff out here, you know — but it wasn't until Keltyn returned as my graduate student five years ago that we actually pulled it together. When it comes to field work, she's a natural. Best student I've ever had." He paused and studied Luz.

She nodded once, still worried how much she would unwillingly reveal if push came to shove.

Thankfully, McCoy seemed too caught up in his own musings. He continued to scrutinize her. "You seem like a bright girl, Luz. How's about tomorrow you and I spend a little time together, swap what we each know about your piedra de yris? You probably have some idea where to search for it around here." He turned his head to scan the sloping rock face behind them. "Somewhere within hiking distance, I hope. These old knees aren't what they used to be." He slapped them.

Perfect. Luz raised her brows and nodded. She knew the terrain; this man did not. She could lead him every which way until he was ready to give up on the piedra de yris.

"Meanwhile, I brought along a couple of gadgets that might help too. The field assay, of course, to tell us the ore grade. Also, another little gismo that I just put together recently." McCoy flashed a grin. "This one — wait 'til you see it work — it picks up signals from iridium ore buried up to five feet below the surface. Hoo hah."

Luz's skin tingled. She would need to keep him far away from their buried stash. She tried to act nonchalant as she arose and signaled Joaquin. "It will be a pleasure to scout for the piedra de yris with you tomorrow, seir. For now," she waved to each of the four Sky-Bornes, "we will leave you to set up your camp before it gets dark. Until morning, then."

***

Meanwhile, Joaquin, knowing full well the weight of the secret entrusted to him, was left with Harry. He needed to get some answers from the Sky-Borne jeaf, so he could report accurately to his own jeaf Ysidro. That's what "eyes and ears" was all about.

Despite Harry's obvious unease during introductions, he did his best to come clean. "Joaquin, you've got to understand the situation I'm in. Things have changed a whole lot since the last time." Harry eyed Russell McCoy chatting up Luz. "I hope you will share what I'm about to tell you with Luz." He leaned forward, his voice low-pitched, almost a whisper.

"Of course, seir." Joaquin couched forward as well.

Just then, the tall, thin Ganz approached them, holding out his mug of maté. "This is quite a stimulant, Joaquin. I feel revived already, after that long flight cramped in the back seat." He cast a cold smile at Harry. "Mind if I join you?"

Joaquin nodded, but Harry directed an icy stare at Ganz that froze him in his tracks.

"We're catching up on old times. You'd be bored, Ganz. How about setting up the tent? Buck will help you." Harry lifted his chin. To Joaquin, it was like shooing away an uninvited guest. The tension between the two men was palpable.

Ganz spun on his heel and stormed away. Harry watched until the man was well out of earshot, then turned back to study Joaquin. "I think you understand where I'm coming from, don't you?"

Joaquin's glanced back and forth between Harry and Ganz's retreating angular figure. "I think so, seir. You don't trust this fellow?"

Harry's lips tightened. "It's a sad thing. We work for the same boss, the man who sent us here."

"Sir Oscar Bailey," Joaquin recited the syllables.

He had only met the Sky-Borne lord once, or rather met his image on a screen, and for only a few minutes, yet the force of Bailey's personality left a lasting impression. Joaquin felt like a branded cow, and if the man bade him again at some future time, he knew he would be unable to refuse Bailey's call. It made perfect sense that Ganz and Harry, both summoned by the same master, were thrown into this mission together, despite the obvious scorn between them.

"You do get the picture, Joaquin. But there is more." Harry peeked sideways again to make sure Ganz was still out of earshot. "Before I explain it to you, I need you to promise you will keep this part to yourself, just you and Luz."

"You can trust me, seir."

"I know I can, Joaquin. You showed your mettle last time, and I'm sure you have had to deal with a lot since then, eh?"

Joaquin blinked once but kept silent.

"Okay, not my intention to pry, but I'd like to hear more about it sometime. Anyway, what you need to know is that Savant Del Campo has made it her mission to open my eyes."

Joaquin blinked again. "Open your eyes? How is that, seir?"

Harry pursed his lips. "Educate me, to her point of view, about peoples like your Onwei tribe, and how my company's activities, like mining your iris stone, might endanger them." He studied Joaquin. "Does that make sense?"

Joaquin tried to suppress a laugh.

"What's so funny?"

"Sorry, seir. It's just that, well, since the last time when you were here and my boss, Ysidro, made a fool of himself by trying to frighten you all to death…"

"That he did." The corner of Harry's mouth raised in a half smile.

"Well, now Ysidro has changed his tactics. He sent me here to welcome you, and then report back to him when you have landed, that he may come here to bargain with you in person."

"Bargain? For the rights to the stone, I assume."

"Exactly," said Joaquin.

Harry now sprouted a full smile. "How weird is that? Me, the chief of Bailey's mission to procure the stone, and now I have grave misgivings about the whole enterprise. Meanwhile, the chief of your tribe, whose land my boss is hell-bent to exploit, has decided he wants to make a deal."

Joaquin nodded slowly. "Indeed strange."

Harry put his mug down and clapped his hands. "This should get very interesting. Especially since Ganz," he stole a peek over his shoulder once more, "will do the negotiating for us, and he is quite the deal maker too."

Joaquin studied the tall thin figure again. He seemed all thumbs, as Buck tried to direct him in setting up the tent. How could someone so awkward and gangly win anyone's respect? Ysidro would laugh at him.

Luz arose from her chat with McCoy and eyed Joaquin, as if ready to leave. Harry took this in. "We have much more to talk about later. Tell me just one thing before you go." He searched Joaquin's eyes.

Joaquin stared back at him. He knew what was coming next. What he didn't know, despite weeks of rehearsal, was how to answer it in a way that would both maintain his self-respect and protect Keltyn. Yet Harry engendered trust by confessing his own thorny situation. Joaquin made a hasty decision. "She is alive."

Harry let out a deep breath. Before he could ask any more questions, Joaquin stood, retrieved the bombilla, and caught up with Luz.

"Did you tell him?" Luz whispered.

"Yes."

Luz frowned. "We were all counting on you to keep them off the scent."

"There's more to it," said Joaquin. "A lot more. C'mon, let's pep up our fire and I'll fill you in."

***

In the fading light, Ganz watched the girl and boy retreat to the edge of the woods, beside a nondescript hide tent. The girl planted herself on a log while the boy kneeled. Within a few minutes, a plume of smoke rose, followed by the crackle of burning branches and flames licking upward.

They clearly knew more than they shared. If Savant SparrowHawk died from her wounds last year, there would be no reason to keep a secret. It might be hard for them to tell the whole story, sure, but a year and a half should be plenty of time to get over the worst of their trauma.

No, SparrowHawk had survived. She was around, somewhere. Had she become so embedded with this tribe, so valuable to them that they insisted upon shielding her? More likely, she knew there was a price on her head and must rely upon her friends to protect her. If so, she was naïve about human nature. Anytime an outsider intrudes upon a group, someone in that group will feel threatened. His own job was to find that someone who was not her friend, someone who would talk.

He turned back to his own camp, set up beside the plane. Buck had hung a lantern, and now stirred a pot of some kind of stew. The stove had an amazing little heater. The size of a fingernail, it was powered by a tiny cold fusion battery no thicker than a pencil lead. Ganz was proud to have closed the deal to import them from the Chinese manufacturer for the Western market; it was all he could do to keep from pointing this out, but gloating wouldn't do in present company.

He parked his angular frame on a folding cloth chair next to Harry. The chief stayed hunched forward, a mug of cocoa between his hands, not even bothering to acknowledge Ganz's presence.

With Harry Ladou's compromised position, could his judgment still be trusted? Ganz decided to test the waters. "Well, Harry, what do you think so far? Were you surprised by the welcome committee?"

Harry raised his head but continued gazing forward. "Not particularly. Joaquin confirmed what I suspected the moment I first spotted the two of them." He paused and continued in a monotone. "Fay Del Campo knew the launch date. She and Joaquin have this common ancestor to channel each other. Don't ask me any details. I wouldn't believe it either if someone else tried to explain it." He let out a soft snort.

Ganz sneered, too. Every primitive tribe had its own brand of magic. "Sounds like you and the boy had a good chat," he said.

"Mostly catching up."

The subject of Keltyn must have entered that conversation somewhere along the line. If Harry did not volunteer what he learned, Ganz was prepared to ask him point blank. One skill he had mastered: he could sniff out a lie in no time.

Harry leaned forward and stared into his cocoa. "Joaquin did let on that their new chief, Ysidro, is very interested in negotiating for rights to the ore. In fact, Joaquin's job right now is scouting for Ysidro, waiting for us to show up."

"Then what? They don't have any kind of radio." Ganz peered into the dark. "Or does everyone channel messages around here?"

"Ha." Harry's expression softened a bit. "No, they use the Pony Express. Joaquin has to go find Ysidro and bring him back. He'll head out in the morning. He figured three days before they return."

The smell of rubbed beef, simmered carrots and onions wafted over to Ganz. He began to salivate.

Russ McCoy pulled his camp chair closer to Buck's stewpot. "Well, that should give me plenty of time to find however much of the good stuff is around here. Then we can decide if it's worth bargaining for."

Ganz stiffened. He didn't like where this was going.

Harry said, "Absolutely. The Onwei are involved beyond just the rights to mine the stone."

Ganz flared his nostrils. "Am I missing something? What are the other issues?"

"There has been talk of Bailey Enterprises transporting Canadian farmers to colonize Antarctica," said Harry.

"News to me," said Ganz.

He noticed the slightest uplift at the corners of Harry's lips. "Really?" he said. "Why else would Sir Oscar need this big stash of iridium?"

"I'm told it has many potential uses." Ganz shifted his weight. "This whole idea of colonizing seems fanciful, almost delusional. I'm sure I would have heard if…"

Buck looked up from his stewpot. "Poor Ganz. Always out of the loop."

He flushed. "What are you insinuating? I've been briefed at least as thoroughly as any of you."

Buck snorted. "You think? Official briefing is one thing. Keeping your ears open for scuttlebutt is something else. That'd be pretty hard for a guy who spends most of his time in Europe."

Ganz flared again. He gazed down at Harry. "Where did you hear this rumor?"

"Gossip has been flying," said the chief. Avoiding eye contact, he stood up and moved toward the stewpot. "The idea of colonizing makes sense. What with hotter climate and rising sea levels, Canada can't feed her people anymore. Antarctica may be the only viable outlet, on this planet, anyway."

Russell McCoy, cradling his dish of stew, looked up. "You can dispense with the righteous shocked expression, Ganz. No one is going to get out of here unsoiled. Now be a good lad and eat your stew. I'll need all of you in good shape to do some digging in the next few days."

Ganz reluctantly moved his chair closer to the stewpot. It was obvious that Sir Oscar had thrown a number of big egos together for this mission, presumably with the idea of seeing who would rise to the top of the pecking order. As far as Ganz was concerned, his main obstacle was Harry Ladou.

He had only one sentiment for the mission leader at this moment, neither loyal nor charitable. Whatever qualities had propelled the man to the penultimate position of the world's largest corporation were now sadly missing. Whether this lapse was temporary — a function of his meteoric diversion to Signora Del Campo's orbit — or irreversible, that was beside the point. They were on a mission with a limited time frame, and Ganz would be damned if he would let a lackadaisical performance from Harry Ladou sabotage their goals.

Sir Oscar Bailey would expect no less of him.

17

PATHFINDER

Joaquin was off at first light, fully expecting to run into the gaucho camp within a day and a half's ride at the most. As promised, Ysidro had drilled him on directions.

Yet, knowing the general course was one thing, while traversing the barren wasteland was another. When Joaquin questioned Ysidro on what to expect, the jeaf was evasive. "No one knows, boy. You shall be the first." Not much comfort there.

The signs when departing the Erebus region were subtle and easily missed by the untrained eye. Just follow the direction of the sun, Ysidro said, and he would find the herd in due course.

Painful memories of Aldo washed over Joaquin, how different a path his life might have taken had Aldo not perished prematurely. Would that be a better life than learning the Venga trade at Yoka's feet? No way to tell. Try as he might, over the past year and a half, since that single week when everything changed, Joaquin had not been able to shake off the worthless habit of second-guessing what might have been.

Now here he was again, in the midst of another round of what could only be described as trouble, again sparked by the Sky-Bornes and their greed for the shiny purple rock. A reflexive kick with his boots made Cisco jump.

Joaquin glanced over his shoulder and noted that the peak of Erebus had receded behind a lesser range. From here on, Ysidro cautioned him, there would be no distinct landmarks. Cisco, the poor pony that he was fast outgrowing, would have to haul him through more than a day's worth of scrub brush and rocky footing before they encountered the grassy plain marking the herd's springtime route. He was not looking forward to camping in this stretch of no-man's land alone tonight.

The range of hills to his left, those that he had paralleled below, gradually leveled out as he gained altitude, until he ascended to a vast plateau that stretched endlessly in three directions.

There was no sign of water anywhere, neither standing nor running. Not even a bit of shade, and it was warming up fast. Under his breath, he cursed Ysidro for sending him on this mission through hell.

He dismounted, sucked from his canteen, and removed his sweater. Cisco, his head slumped, turned to watch Joaquin. He had naively counted on finding water somewhere and had brought only a hemp feedbag full of sweetgrass for his pony. He fought to suppress his panic, while slipping the rancid feedbag over Cisco's mouth, the straps over his ears, then carefully decanting water around the inner edge of the bag, keeping up a low flow in time with Cisco slurping it up. When he had emptied half the canteen, he stopped, even though his pony appeared far from sated.

"Sorry, boy. Got to save some for later, in case we don't find water tonight."

He removed the feedbag and wrung out the few drops left in the damp fabric into the pony's open mouth.

By mid-afternoon, Joaquin had to admit that he was seriously lost, finding nothing to focus on in any direction. He could no longer see the spot where he had emerged from the range of hills. Nothing but chaparral and rocks, none of the rocks even big enough to provide shade from the sun, still inching ruthlessly across the blue heavens. Two corpses, his and Cisco's, would slowly bake in solitude amidst this vast plain, bereft of buzzards or even flies. Their vital juices would evaporate in due course, leaving no scent, nothing but bones and leathery hides to mark the route for some future pilgrim, equally cursed.

He might just as well wait until dark when it was cooler. There would be a half moon tonight, more than enough to guide him. Yet in the meantime, they had not a bit of shade, let alone any sign of fresh water. He shook his canteen. If they did not stumble upon some creek or spring soon…

Was it his imagination, or did the distant horizon now appear lumpy? An irregular horizon meant hills, and hills meant spots of shade, and shade might mean plant life and water. Or was it just as likely a mirage, one of those tricks the desert sun plays on a person's mind? At this point, he felt numb, beyond either hope or fear.

Cisco plodded onward, ever slower, until Joaquin was forced to dismount and lead his pony on foot. Tio Hector was long overdue. He should have shown his doggedly smiling mug by now, attempting to cheer Joaquin onward with optimistic platitudes. Was his sly uncle busy elsewhere — perhaps engaged with Orfea — or did he aim to purposely let Joaquin find his own way out of this mess? He stuck out his parched tongue. Curse you, Tio Hector. Go stuff your hocus-pocus. He tried to spit, but nothing escaped his mouth, now as arid as this godforsaken desert.

The sun moved slowly downward until it shone full in his face. Just below it was indeed the silhouette of hills. The ground beneath Joaquin's feet also roughened, making him stumble more than once. Finally, he noticed tiny tufts of grass and, after a while, mesquite bushes, only a foot high, but patches of green nonetheless. He wanted to jump for joy but had not the strength. Instead, he turned and patted Cisco's muzzle. The end of their ordeal was in sight.

He kept his eyes peeled until spotting a prickly pear cactus. Perfect. He knelt down and sliced it off at the base, then skinned the spiny parts with his knife until only the pulp was left. He chewed a slice with gusto. Not exactly juicy, but good flavor, and it would stretch his dwindling water supply. He held a piece in front of Cisco's nose. The pony nipped it out of his hand and munched on it solemnly.

Up ahead, Joaquin could make out shadows among the hills, and even clumps of green. Was he anywhere close to his intended course? Darkness would fall in another hour. He would need to wait until morning to find if the hills led to grasslands beyond.

***

"Up there, Brixita." Efrain pointed toward a spot halfway up the hill to their left.

I tried to make it out. I spotted a small-framed rider on a short mount. Joaquin! He'd found us. His arrival must mean Bailey Voyager had landed. My stomach knotted.

I clenched Efrain's arm, watching Joaquin plod down the slope toward the two of us. Both the boy and his pony appeared exhausted. I ran to him as he pulled up. He tried to dismount, stumbling as he set foot on the ground.

"Whoa, Scout." I encircled his shoulder. "Efrain, help him."

Efrain eased the boy onto a stool, then loped off. I squatted next to him, hunched forward and silent, watching closely. Joaquin's haggard face was caked with dust, his eyes bleary and bloodshot. He smelled like a stale turd.

Efrain returned a few moments later with a bombilla of steaming mate. He held the vessel as Joaquin drew on the straw. Finally, he glanced up and made eye contact.

"Tell me," I said.

"A day and a half through hell to get here," Joaquin spat out. He stole a peek around to see if anyone else stood within earshot. "Ysidro don't know what he's talking about. No one in their right mind's come that way before, for good reason." He stuck his tongue out and grunted.

I blurted, "What about the Sky-Bornes, Joaquin? Did they show up?"

"Hold your horses. I'm gettin' to that part. Can't a fella bitch and moan a bit? I 'bout died so's you'd get the news."

I clamped my lips and stewed while he took another long draw of maté.

Finally, he allowed, "Yep, they're here. Four of 'em. Harry and Buck and two new fellas."

Two new ones? Both men? That was a surprise. "No Fay?"

Joaquin shook his head. "She and your boss Sir Oscar had a falling out, sounds like."

"Really? How do you know?" I was not all that surprised.

"Harry took me aside. Said Seira Orfea had opened his eyes about Oscar's naughty plans, like."

I tried to imagine Fay taking Harry into her confidence. Perhaps credible, especially if she turned on the charm, something she was perfectly capable of doing. But if Harry was no longer acting as Oscar's agent, why come at all? I took a deep breath. Keeping myself out of circulation might soon become impossible. I needed to talk to Harry and see where he really stood.

But, meantime: "Who are those two new fellows you mentioned, Joaquin?"

"One of 'em's named Gans or Gants. He's tall and skinny and eagle-eyed. Acts real formal like. I wouldn't trust him far as I could throw him."

I'd never heard of someone matching that description. "Why did he come along? Any idea?"

Joaquin smiled. "He's the deal maker, Harry said. He'll be the one to negotiate with Ysidro about the stone."

Efrain and I exchanged glances. "Ysidro will need to be on his 'A' game to get fair trade from a professional," I said. I had some idea of how these dealings would proceed. "All the more reason for me to accompany Ysidro."

Efrain frowned. "No, Brixita, you mustn't. It's much too dangerous." He angled his head over his shoulder. "Besides, you needn't be concerned about Ysidro. He is an astute dealmaker in his own right, as are all the Correons." He flashed a confident smile.

I considered this. "Maybe you're right. As far as the crew is concerned, I died last year. No reason to dispel that notion."

Joaquin grimaced.

"What?" I felt a sudden chill. "You didn't tell them! You promised."

"Harry asked me point blank, practically pleaded for you to be alive. I couldn't lie to his face."

I hung my head. "No, I guess you couldn't." I reached behind for Efrain's hand, resting on my shoulder. I gazed into his weather-beaten face. "I should be okay."

Efrain nodded and rested his other hand on mine. "Yes, you will. I shall be there to make sure."

That would be some comfort, though I suspected Efrain would bring his rifle as a show of strength. Who knew how that might end?

There was something else to clear up, though. I turned back to Joaquin. "Who is the fourth person?"

The boy met my gaze with an enigmatic smile. "Someone you should know. Says he was your teacher."

I gasped. "McCoy? Not Russell McCoy?" I clapped a hand over my mouth as soon as the name escaped.

"That's him."

The chill spread, rushing down my back. My legs wobbled, but Efrain grabbed me under the armpits and eased me onto a stool. He squatted beside me, rubbed my back. "What is it, Brixita? Why does that one's name trouble you so?"

Hands covering my face, I moaned, soft and fast. A voice within slowed my breathing and forced me to stay in control. I thought I had long since buried the awful memories of McCoy's sexual predation. Now, thanks to Oscar Bailey, they were alive and well again. I began to shiver. Efrain rubbed my arms and made soothing sounds, but he was powerless to stop the tide of cold recall that enveloped me, as if it were yesterday.

McCoy opens the door. "Keltyn. So glad you could make it. Come in, come in, my dear." He holds one arm wide. He sports a Hawaiian shirt, knee-length shorts, floppy sandals. The shirt print motif is a palm-lined white sandy beach with an azure ocean background, speckled by small sailboats. I've never seen McCoy without his lab coat before, but then, I've never visited his home.

"You've brought that field assay manuscript? Good. What kind of deadline did Stone give you for the rewrite?"

"Next week."

"I love deadlines. Nothing focuses the mind better."

I step past him in the doorway and note the scent of aftershave, something I've never detected on him in the ten years we've known each other. The aroma signals something that his attire hasn't, kindling a trickle of sweat at the base of my spine.

I gaze at the walls, lined with woven hangings, depicting raven, owl, bear, leaping fish, tall conifers surrounding deep blue lakes, all of them in the same primary-color-laden Cree motif.

"You are a sight for sore eyes, my dear. I've mixed up some Daiquiris. Care for one?"

"Uh, sure."

He pours two drinks into long-stemmed glasses and offers one to me. He settles himself on the couch beside me and holds up his glass. "To you, my dear. Once this gets published, you'll be able to write your own ticket."

We clink glasses. He quaffs his draught like a man who has taken many, while I try only a sip. The taste of lime is the perfect thirst quencher for a hot summer's day. I sip again.

"Now, then," says McCoy. "Let's see what you've got."

Somewhat reluctantly, I put the drink down and open my device to find the document.

McCoy scrolls through it. "Good, good. Mm-hm. Mm-hm. Yes, this draft should satisfy them." He picks up his glass and we toast again. "All this will be worth it very shortly. You'll see."

I take another swallow, this one larger. He's right. A drink is what I need. "I'm sure you're correct. It's just that..."

"What?" He leans closer.

I meet his eyes, those deep penetrating black orbs magnified even further by the thick dialup lenses. "I've never been involved in anything so complex before. The field studies, the engineering design, the machine fabrication, the data collection, the cross-validation, the statistics, the writing and rewriting..." A touch of frenzy creeps into my voice.

McCoy reaches out to put a finger on my lips. "Hush, hush, my dear. You mustn't beat yourself up over this. You are on the verge of completing work that many scientists in the prime of their careers only dream about. If the applications of iridium pan out half as well as their potential, there may be a Nobel in chemistry awaiting you someday."

I search those deep eyes once again. The suspicious side of my nature disparages such fanciful talk, while the dreamer part laps it up. "Don't go dangling the moon in front of me," I say. "It's hard enough to concentrate as is."

"Au contraire, my dear Keltyn." McCoy removes his dialups and sets them on the coffee table. "One thing I have

observed about you is that you tend to concentrate too hard. You never take a break, which is why I suggested that we meet away from the lab. Someplace undisturbed."

Uh, oh. I try to straighten up, but this only pushes my shoulders right into McCoy's waiting arm. He keeps the arm firmly in place.

"Well." I clear my throat. "Thanks for going over the draft, Savant McCoy. I better go back and put the final touches on it, so's I can get it posted tomorrow." I try to get up, but the firm pressure of his hand says otherwise. "Please," I intone. It comes out much too passive.

"Now, my dear. As I said, I think it's terribly important for you to have a little rest from the lab ever so often."

My heart pounds. I vaguely know a few self-defense tricks, but I've never tried them out before. The bag I carry between my room and the lab has a bottle of deterrent spray. Where is that when I need it? "I really would like to leave," is all I can think of to say.

"It's your choice," says McCoy. His eyes turn cold and his lower lip juts out. He releases his grip on my shoulder and crosses his hands behind his head. "But this is a two-way street. Do you seriously think Stone will touch your two-bit paper with a ten-foot pole if it doesn't have my name as co-author?"

I gasp. "You wouldn't."

McCoy smirks. "Wouldn't I? Try me."

The room blurs. I slump back in my seat. For several minutes I stare at the image of a fish jumping out of water on the opposite wall. Then I reach for the remainder of my Daiquiri and down it.

McCoy chuckles. "That's the spirit. Have another?"

I swallowed my pride and let Savant Russell McCoy have his way with me. Not once, but at least half a dozen times over the next six months. At first, I told myself that I would have the leverage to break it off after the paper in Stone was published. With stunning naiveté, I later realized, I expected this would catapult me to instant fame, being able to "write your own ticket," in McCoy's phrase. The ticket turned out to be a seat on the first Bailey Voyager.

Now here I was, being comforted by Efrain, while my mind stared into a deep, dark void. All of my preparations to keep Bailey's crew off the scent of the stone had been for naught. Of all the scenarios I had pondered on how to deal with their return, none had included Russell McCoy.

There were many reasons why I might now wish to return to my homeland, and but a single reason why I loathed the idea: in order to save my career, I would once again need his support. When it came time to face those charges of espionage, likely the only way out was if McCoy interceded on my behalf. And I would have to pay his price.

Ysidro's booming voice made me jerk upright.

"Well, boy, I see you made it back."

Joaquin grunted, not bothering to engage the jeaf.

"What, you had a tough ride through the desert? Well, I'm sorry, my little friend. If there was an easier route from there to here, I would have sent you that way instead. Now, what news?"

Joaquin met the jeaf's piercing gaze with a sullen expression. "Just as you predicted. They wish to negotiate for the rights to the stone."

Ysidro rubbed his hands together. "Excellent. Good work, boy. Don't worry. You will be justly rewarded when this business is finished." Only now did he stop to scrutinize Joaquin. "After you have cleaned up and fed your face, you can use my yurt to rest in. I'll need you to guide me back, first thing in the morning."

I clenched my teeth. Russell McCoy or no, I could no longer stay in the background. "I must join you."

The jeaf's eyes narrowed. "Are you sure? Did we not decide before, that would be too dangerous in your position?"

"With respect," I lowered my chin, "you will be better off to have me along to advise you, especially since the Sky-Bornes brought someone new just for this purpose, someone very skilled. They may well try to trick you."

Ysidro appeared dubious. "They will have their eye on you, try to capture you and force you to return with them. Is that what you want?"

"Of course not."

"Then why provoke them? Let them think you perished a year and a half ago."

Joaquin cleared his throat.

Ysidro glared at the boy. "Surely you did not mention the Brixa to them."

"Harry, their leader, knows."

Ysidro turned away in disgust. "Oh, great."

Efrain chimed in. "Do not worry, tio. I will accompany you and protect the Brixa from any danger."

Ysidro took a deep breath. "I am afraid I cannot spare you away from the herd, nephew. You are the only one I can trust here in an emergency." He viewed the gathering clouds. "Bad weather, for instance. No one else can command the respect of all the charros."

I bit my lip. I could hardly trust Ysidro to watch out for my safety. After all, only last year he and his nephews kidnapped me to use as bait for their attack on my crewmates. Ysidro might just as easily wash his hands of me if it meant getting a better deal on the iris stone. No, only I could watch out for myself, and that meant taking certain precautions.

Efrain cast me an anxious look, but I forced myself to smile and squeeze his hand.

***

Darkness fell. Efrain and I sat bootless and cross-legged in his yurt. It was spacious. Like Efrain's rifle and his house, it formerly belonged to his uncle Aldo. A single candle perched on a stand overlooking the door.

I pulled a cord to cinch my saddlebag tight. It was stuffed with a few essentials — rain poncho, sweater, a single change of underwear and socks. I anticipated the trip to last no more than four or five days. Pushing the bag aside, I accepted the mug of pulce beer that Efrain offered me. Though still plagued by doubts, I needed to convince him that I could manage for my own safety.

Our mugs clinked, and I forced down a swallow with a grimace. The stuff was too sour, but Ysidro permitted nothing stronger than beer on the trail. The only real celebrating that he allowed his charros was a few days at the summer Rendezvous and the season-ending feast in Nomidar, hosted by the extended Correon family.

I focused on Efrain's glum face in the candlelight. "Hey," I said. "We have a deal. No bad vibes."

"I can't help it, Brixita. You'll be in harm's way, and I'll be stuck here instead of by your side."

"Cheer up, dude. It's only for a few days."

"A few days is more than enough time for the Sky-Bornes to capture or cajole you back to their side."

"Oh, quit it with the cajole. There is absolutely nothing they could say to make me wish to return to Canada. It might be different if I left friends behind, but I've always been a loner. As for family, there's no one but my mother, and last I saw her, she was pretty far gone." I tipped the mug toward my lips. Whenever I thought about my mother's losing battle with the bottle, the same urge struck me.

Efrain said, "If push comes to shove, my noble uncle would think nothing of giving you up to strike a better deal. That's just the kind of hombre he is."

"The same thought occurred to me," I said. "I need some kind of weapon for self-defense. And don't bother with that big rifle of Aldo's. I've never shot even a little stun gun like Buck's, let alone your mega-sucker."

Efrain put down his mug and sorted through his bags. He produced a hunting knife with a three-fingered grip and an eight-inch blade, then held it out to me, handle first.

My eyes bounced between the knife and Efrain. "You're kidding."

"Go ahead. Try it."

I reached for the handle. The knife was surprisingly lightweight and well balanced for its size. I practiced slicing and stabbing feints.

"Guess I could take it along, but I can't have it sticking out of my belt. I'm no pirate." I raised the knife and grimaced my scariest toothy smile.

Efrain held his hands up in mock fright. "You need not display it. Just slide it into your boot."

I stood and did as instructed. My boot was the right length to conceal the blade, tucked snugly beside the back of my calf. The haft was too thick to fit into the boot, but by pulling the cuff of my breeches over the handle, no bulge stuck out. I pulled down the cuff over the other boot and turned to and fro for Efrain to inspect. "What do you think? Too obvious?"

"Perfect. No one will suspect you are a lethal weapon." He held up one finger. "Just to test you, I shall attack, so you may practice your self-defense skills. Ready?" He stood.

"Bring it on."

Efrain lunged toward me. I deftly sidestepped him, yet when I attempted to reach for the knife, my hands fumbled in pulling up my pant leg, giving Efrain plenty of time to regroup and pin my arms behind me.

"You'll need to practice that move, Brixita."

"Try it again." Surging adrenaline rushed blood to my ears: kwoosh, kwoosh.

Efrain released me and backed off. "Ready?"

I nodded. Same lunge, same sidestep. This time, I managed to retrieve the knife from my boot. I whirled around to confront my attacker. Efrain feinted a grab at the wrist of my knife hand. I pulled the knife away, pointing it overhead, but Efrain easily clenched my wrist with his other hand, so tight I immediately dropped the knife. In a moment, he deftly had my arms pinned behind once again.

With a low growl, I stomped the heel of my boot on Efrain's unshod foot. He yelped in pain and released me, then sat down and massaged his toes.

"Ow. What did you do that for?"

"Self-defense, remember? Just having a knife tucked in my boot isn't going to be enough, as you just proved."

Efrain continued to rub his toes and frowned.

The adrenaline receded and I moved closer. "Did poor little Brixita hurt big macho charro? Let's have a peek."

I pulled off his sock and was surprised to find several toes discolored. The big toe shone particularly angry, red and blue and swollen. Both of us grimaced at the sight.

I was the first to recover my wits. "I'll go fetch a bucket of cold water." I bit at my lip.

Foot soaking and several more draughts of pulce seemed to take the edge off Efrain's pain. Lying flat on the sheepskin rug that served as his bed, he appeared to finally relax. I could only tell this because his meaty paw finally loosened its ironclad grip on my hand. I lay my head on his chest, and his arm drew me closer.

"I'm glad you're on my side, big guy," I said. "Hate to think what would have happened if you hadn't stuck up for us last year."

"Don't press your luck, Brixita. For one thing, I wouldn't be nursing three broken toes right now."

"Let's see if I can take your mind off your owie." I untoggled the clasps of his tunic.

"No rough stuff. I can't move without pain."

"You don't have to move an inch." I unbuttoned his breeches and reached inside. His flaccid member needed but a moment of fondling to wake up.

I slipped easily out of my own tunic and breeches. By the time I knelt astride him, naked in the light of a single candle, Efrain's spirits appeared considerably lifted. He pulled me down for a kiss, and our probing tongues intertwined.

"You're right," he mumbled. "I feel better already."

"Good," I whispered. "Let's go for a ride."

With shudders of pleasure, we merged into one. Each push seemed to carry me to a higher plane of consciousness, like springing through layers of clouds piled one atop another. As I came to climax, I felt weightless.

Afterward, still lying atop Efrain, I placed my ear over his heart. Though I had scant idea what lay ahead, the big hunting knife in my boot would remind me of its owner's strength and spirit. These would guide me through thick and thin, and with that, I felt comforted.

18

ROCK TALK

The thick damp haze of early morning had already lifted, and the sun was out full force. This past hour, Luz had led Russell McCoy well beyond the flying machine. He would have every reason to expect they would find the iris stone scattered hither and yon. She was equally intent on shielding from him as many of the stones as possible. She needed to keep them hidden, at least until Ysidro, with his greater authority and experience, returned with Joaquin.

In one hand, McCoy carried a little red metal box with a dial on the front. In the other, he held a pointed wand tethered to the box by winding coil. He pointed the wand to and fro like a child with a toy sword, thrusting and jabbing it at every small bright rock in sight, in an effort to get some action on his dial.

"Nothing around here that looks like your iris stone, Luz. Funny."

"What's that, seir?" Luz licked her lips.

McCoy turned to face her with a mirthless smile. "Call me Russell, my dear. 'Seir' sounds so formal."

Luz tried out the sound. "Russ-ell." It felt softer than "McCoy," less formal. She was okay with that.

Russell surveyed their surroundings. "That eruption, when you and Keltyn were trapped on the mountain, was just last year."

Luz shut her eyes and nodded.

"I'd have bet that we would find your stones scattered on these slopes. Check this out." He bent down and picked up a shiny, jagged black rock and held his hand out for her to examine it. "You must know what that is."

"Hardened lava, no?"

"Right. We call it obsidian," said Russell. "Only one place that comes from." He pointed toward the peak of Erebus several miles away, then lifted his floppy hat and scratched his balding pate. "I don't get why we haven't run into any iridium ore." He tried to fix his stare at Luz, but she quickly shook her head and shrugged.

Clearly, she and Joaquin had done too good a job. Best to have left a few small pieces around in plain sight. As it was, she would have to lead Russell a considerable distance up the slopes of the mountain to find any they missed. She could only hope he fatigued before they got that far.

Sure enough, after another fifteen minutes heading uphill, McCoy put up his arm to signal a break. He set his meter on the ground and remained bent over, hands on knees, breathing labored.

Gazing around where they stood, Luz spotted a few gleaming multi-hued stones nearby. She hurried over and brought them for Russell to examine. He brightened and reached for the meter. The dial bounced immediately.

"Good work, Luz." He sat down and glanced around. "Too bad it's this far away from camp. Can we come back later with your horse to collect more?"

Luz cringed, remembering the last time she came down the mountain with her mare's pack full of the iris stone. The volcano erupted, and Quintara was fatally wounded in an avalanche. "I am afraid, Russell. What if the mountain blows again?"

He studied her. "You're that worried, eh? Guess I can see why. What if I told you that an eruption like that happens only once every hundred years?"

Luz made a face and eyed him back. He was Keltyn's teacher and an authority on this sort of thing. On the other hand, nasty greed might bias his judgment. She caught his mouth twitching again.

"The footing for horses is poor on this bare rock, Russell."

"Hmm." He squinted at her a moment, then opened his backpack, deposited the samples in one pocket, and rummaged around until he found some sandwiches. He held one up for Luz. She thumbed it open. Cheese.

She sat down and pulled out her canteen, eyeing the ground while she ate, trying to make sense of Russell's extraordinary claims. When she gazed up, she found him studying her over the rims of his vision aids.

"Have I confused you enough, young lady?"

"No. Well, actually, yes you have." Blood rushed to her cheeks.

"It gets even more fantastic." He waited, watched her.

Luz straightened up. "Try me."

"How long has your mother made her fine jewelry from the iris stone?"

"She devised a way to smelt the ore when I was but a small child."

"And yet you and Keltyn discovered the rich deposits on the mountainside only last year. Where did she procure the stone before that?"

"She traded for it. The trader would never disclose his source."

"You think somehow he knew it was scattered on the mountainside?"

Luz had considered that before. "He was an older man. I doubt he would have had the stamina to scale the mountain. But there are other deposits as well. Before Keltyn and I climbed Erebus, I found a vein of ore on the side of a nearby crater."

"Ah," said Russell. "You must show me this place. A crater, you say. Have you any idea what made this crater?"

"Some say a great ball of fire fell from the heavens."

He grunted. "A great ball of very hard rock. So far as we know, there is plenty of your iris stone in the universe, just very little on the earth's surface. All that we find here comes from either outer space" — he pointed heavenward — "or from the Earth's core." He fingered the plume rising from the volcano.

Luz's eyes widened. Wait until her mother heard about this. Even if Russell was spinning tall tales, Trieste was shrewd enough to incorporate them into her pitch. Truth or fantasy, these stories would only add to the allure of the piedra de yris.

Minutes later, as they headed back down the hill, he was at it again. "You know, there was an ice sheet a quarter mile thick, right here where we're walking, only three hundred years ago."

"I have heard that too." Luz kept up her brisk stride.

Russell had to pick up his pace to match hers. "Your people know about that, but there are no written records, correct?"

"No writing," muttered Luz. "Just stories."

"Well, here's something I doubt you have any stories about. Did you know that, long before there was any ice here, Antarctica had much the same mild climate it has now?"

Luz slowed down to watch Russell out of the corner of her eye. She couldn't tell if he was toying with her now, seeing how much she would swallow.

He chuckled, nodding for emphasis. "It's true. What's more, long, long before that, your land was located on a different part of the earth. Every day throughout the year had days and nights of equal length."

Luz picked up her pace again. The more she encouraged him, the more outlandish his tale. Then again, let him exhaust himself by reciting arcane facts. So much the better to keep him off the scent of the stone.

Russell's words came in harsh breaths as he half-stumbled down the rocky slope. "Still, I have to think it's more fitting the way Antarctica is now. Long days in summer, long nights in winter. Especially the nights. You know, the name 'Erebus' comes from a god in ancient Greece."

Before she could even ask about ancient Greece, Russell plunged onward, as if impelled to share all he knew. "Erebus was a primitive god, representing darkness. In Canada, where I live, we have long winters too, but during that season we spend most of our time indoors, where everything is well lit. It's hard for me to picture how your people spend those long months of perpetual night."

She glanced back at him, wary. He was inviting her to share her story. That fact alone made his own stories more credible, she had to admit. Yet, if what he had told her in the last twenty minutes was true, it meant that her universe had just exploded beyond comprehension. The thought at once frightened and sobered her.

"Your stories are fascinating, Russell," said Luz, and she meant it. If he was trying to beguile her, he was succeeding.

"Let's stop at my tent when we get back," he said. "I want to show you something."

"All right." Much to her surprise, Luz felt her attitude softening, exactly as Russell seemed to wish. Though

Keltyn had labeled him a lecher, the man clearly had some redeeming qualities.

Certainly, Keltyn would not begrudge her for exhibiting intellectual curiosity, like what had launched the Brixa's own career. And if she did not approve? Too bad. Luz no longer felt beholden to ask Keltyn's permission for her dealings with the Sky-Bornes.

***

Russell pulled out a stool and placed it beside the tent, then retrieved what he called a "book" and offered it to Luz. It smelled musty, like old wooden furniture. She leafed through its paper contents, joined together at one end to keep them ordered in a certain sequence. The "pages" included both pictures and an indecipherable text of characters. She tried to imagine how these characters, if she could decode the sounds they represented, might unlock the secrets in this book. She tried to envision an entire calling built on learning these secrets. The idea seemed at once daunting and fanciful.

Nonetheless, the pictures kept her turning the pages. Scant surprise. The illustrations were of different rocks: round and pointy, smooth and jagged, bright and dull, gold and black and red and green and everything in between. Line drawings accompanied crisp illustrations of landscapes where the rocks might be found, Luz presumed. The pages devoted to the piedra de yris showed a panorama that included a volcano and a crater.

Without taking her eyes off the pages, she said, "Your book is beautiful." Leaving it open, she picked it up and held it close to her chest. Her eyes swept over the real landscape in front of her, the same as depicted on these pages. How did the artist know what to draw if she had never been here?

Russell smiled. "I would be honored if you would accept this as a gift."

Luz quickly let the book drop onto her lap, closed it, and tried to hand it back to him. "Oh no, seir. Thank you, but I couldn't."

"Please, Luz. I have many more like these, back home." He made no move to take it.

She eyed him closely. The smile on his lips was set off by a faint line of sadness in his eyes, as if already prepared for her to reject the offer.

She withdrew her extended arm and viewed the book again. The scene on the cover reminded her of Splat Crater's rim: slabs of different rock piled neatly one layer atop another, a thick one of dark brown under a thinner one of gray, then a thin vein of the violet piedra de yris, a thicker layer of burnt orange, all sandwiched between multiple others. It was as if some child god assembled layers in a giant cake. Yet the lines were tangential instead of horizontal, as if the cake sagged to one side.

"All right," said Luz, gazing at Russell once more, "only you will need to explain it to me."

"With pleasure."

Good. The longer she could keep him distracted from searching for the iris stone, the more time for Ysidro to return with Joaquin.

The rest of that day, and most of the next, Russell McCoy used the pictures in the book to tutor Luz in the basics of recognizing different types of rocks, or, as he termed them, "minerals." Often, in making his points, he could not find enough to elaborate on them in his book and made notes to himself.

Every few hours, he summoned Luz to stretch their legs and take a stroll around the site. He kept his eyes peeled and, as like as not, would find an example of what the book failed to illustrate, say a rock with multiple types of minerals melded within.

By the end of the second day, he had covered a good selection of the stones in the book. Luz felt doubly proud. She had managed to kill time that Russell would otherwise have used to sniff out the whereabouts of the iris stone. Equally important, she had learned many facts about all different stones, and who knew when they might come into play?

Luz went over to her tent and tucked the book in her pack. When she returned, Russell had moved to the camp circle to join the other men. Harry stoked the fire and Buck stirred the stewpot. Ganz sat by himself, fiddling with a small gadget on his lap.

She moved to sit next to Russell. This seemed like second nature now. The man was a walking font of knowledge, and Luz intended to soak up as much she could in the few days that he would be here. This idea that Russell embodied, being an expert in a single field of knowledge, appealed to her for reasons she could not yet grasp.

Harry dropped into a stool on Luz's other side. Russell leaned over and said to him, "She's a fine girl. Good head on her shoulders. She's a natural when it comes to ID'ing rocks. Could be a first-rate geologist if she had a mind to." He winked at Luz.

She blushed and ducked her head.

Russell continued. "Luz, tell me. How many days were you and your friend Joaquin here before we arrived?"

Something about the question made her wary. "Two, seir."

"Surely you must have scouted the whole area for your precious stone."

"We did, seir."

She heard Harry shift in his seat beside her. Ganz glanced up from his private amusement, cocking his head toward them.

Russell McCoy continued. "What a shame you found none. I predicted this spot would be so thick with iridium ore that we would trip over piles of it. When we spied your smoke signals from the plane, I practically jumped out of my seat. So, imagine my surprise when we came up empty-handed."

Luz's throat felt parched.

"What, may I ask, made you and Joaquin decide to camp at this spot in the first place?" Russell's tone turned pointed.

Luz tried to choose her words carefully. Four pairs of eyes and ears followed her every action, but she found it impossible to meet any of them. "It…it seemed like the ideal place. An open spot for Joaquin to pitch his tent to signal you, next to a grove of trees to shelter us in a storm. Which there was, a bad one, the night after we arrived." She nodded repeatedly for emphasis, but no one nodded in return, their critical gazes still fixed on her.

Ganz broke the strained silence. "Two days. Plenty of time to gather whatever stones lay around and hide them elsewhere."

Luz took a breath, ready to issue a denial, but Russell McCoy cut in smoothly. "Now, Herr Ganz, are you suggesting that this young lady might be…?"

Ganz nodded, pointing an accusing finger. "Exactly. She's holding something back. Look at her."

Luz felt herself clamming up and shaking, on the verge of tears. She had known from the start that she would be unable to survive an interrogation. Desperate, she glanced at Harry. He responded with the tiniest shrug and blink, imperceptible to all but Luz.

Russell's arm slipped around her shoulder, patting gently. "Now, now, my dear, take it easy. No one here means to hurt you, but if you have something more to tell us, please do so."

Luz hunched forward on her stool, hands clasped around her knees. Should she reveal her and Joaquin's secret, what the two of them had spent a full day of strenuous labor to keep hidden? Keltyn would be chagrined, perhaps angered, but then, she was not the one on the spot here.

On top of that, the storm buried their cache so deep that she and Joaquin might never be able to locate it again, let alone dig it out. Then what use would the stones be to anyone?

Buck straightened up from stirring the stewpot. "Enough, you guys, give the poor girl a break. C'mon, grab a plate. Dinner's ready."

Luz smiled her thanks at the pilot for this short respite to sort her thoughts. The four men all deferred to her in line. Buck ladled out an assortment of beef chunks, potatoes, carrots and onions, all of it swimming in a thick brown sauce. She sat back down and thrust a forkful in her mouth. Delicious. It tasted as good as her mother's cooking, though, so far as she could tell, Buck had simply dumped the contents from a packet and added water.

As she ate, Luz peeked around the circle, sizing up these four men once more. Buck was fully engaged in his dish, while Harry sent his compliments to the chef. Russell glanced at Luz, nodded with eyebrows raised, pointed to his dish and flashed a thumb's up.

Only Ganz continued his icy stare, causing Luz to avert her eyes. She knew he would not let the subject drop. As soon as dinner was over, he would resume his grilling.

Why continue this cat and mouse game? In the first place, she was a lousy liar. In the second place... A plan began to take shape as she finished her meal. She would use Russell McCoy's iridium detector to pinpoint the stash, and the labor of these four men to uncover it. Its contents were more than what would fit in the cargo space of their flying machine, leaving an ample amount for Luz to supply her mother for years to come.

She put her dish down and waited until she had caught everyone's eye before making her announcement. "We hid the stones."

Russell lifted his chin. "Ah. Now, doesn't that feel better?"

Yes, as a matter of fact, but half-measures would not suffice. "They are buried, not far from here."

Buck chimed in. "Four grown men should be able to dig them out from a hole in the ground."

Luz gazed around at these four sets of eyes. "You don't understand. A great storm battered our camp the very night after we hid the stones. When we returned to the site the next morning, the spot was unrecognizable. All of the terrain has shifted."

Russell appeared unfazed. "T'will be a good test for my iridium detector. What say you, gentlemen? Should we go check it out?"

Ganz jumped up, ready to march over, but Harry and Buck both checked for Luz's reaction.

She covered her mouth to hide a snicker. Ganz's boyish eagerness was foolhardy. "I advise you to wait until morning, when you are fresh. Even if your machine locates the spot readily, it will take hours of digging to unearth. How many shovels did you bring?"

Buck frowned. "Just one. The girl's right, best wait till *mañana*."

Ganz clenched his fists. "We need to dig it up before the boy returns with their chief." He cast his eyes around the circle, daring anyone to contradict him.

Luz did the mental calculation and lifted her finger. "You will have until at least tomorrow evening."

Ready nods among three of them, Ganz more reluctantly. Eyes moved back to the dancing flames.

Luz hugged her knees and savored the distraction of a crackling blaze. She had confessed in order to take the pressure off. Could she justify her action to Joaquin? To the Brixa? The die was cast, but instead of feeling at peace, second thoughts swirled within her. Should she try to keep the Sky-Bornes off the scent somehow? Lead them around in circles, claim she didn't remember the spot? Yet Luz had already proven to herself and everyone else that she was a poor liar, and they would see right through another attempted subterfuge.

No, best to take this bull by the horns. Her reasons for sharing the stash of stones with the Sky-Bornes were just as valid as whatever reason Joaquin or the Brixa might have to hide it.

19

HIGH STAKES

I'd never felt so exhausted. Despite Ysidro's self-professed knowledge of the terrain, and Joaquin's best efforts to retrace his route from two days prior, our party of three lost several hours in trying to find the flat plateau's exit into the hill-lined gullies that led to the base of Mt. Erebus. Only my rudimentary pocket compass kept us from veering further off course, as we searched in vain around the rim of flat upland.

Eventually we stumbled upon the route, mostly thanks to more distinct shadows cast by the late afternoon sun. The shadows played on the sides of hills and gullies, pointing the way as clear as could any marker. Here, finally, was the way out of this merciless desert scrub.

Still, it was well through the evening when the three of us stumbled into camp on the slopes of Erebus. I felt ill-prepared to face, let alone bargain with, my former crewmates and this Ganz toady of Oscar's. It would fall on me to smooth whatever hard feelings Buck and Harry might still have for Ysidro.

Even worse was the thought of facing my former mentor, who had blackmailed me into becoming his sex toy.

The glowing orange coals of a campfire greeted us. I recognized Harry and Buck as the lone night owls, their stools huddled close and conferring in low tones, until stirred by hoof beats and loud horse breaths. I dismounted and strode toward my former mates.

I could barely make out Harry Ladou's face in the dark. He sounded genuinely choked with emotion as he reached out and hugged me. "Ma chère, ma chère. You are alive. *Dieu merci.*"

It felt like nothing short of a miracle, and I found myself shedding tears as well. Not a soul besides Efrain had hugged me in the past eighteen months, and he only when I sorely needed comforting. It was not the Onwei custom, and I thought I had become used to their stoic patterns, until a moment like this.

When Harry finally disengaged himself, Buck Kranepool stood next in line to greet me. He held my head between his large hands and intoned, "Well, Missy, if this don't beat all. Never dreamt I would see you alive and well again. Not after the sorry shape we left you in."

I closed my eyes to try and stanch the tears, reaching up to grasp Buck's wrists.

Harry broke in. "Pay him no heed, ma chère. With all due respect to whoever nursed you back to health, if it wasn't for Buck's mastery of first aid, you would have been a goner."

I pulled Buck's hands down from my head and squeezed them. "I know. I owe you my life, all of you." I glanced around and noticed Ysidro's burly figure standing beyond the rim of firelight. "Come join us, jeaf."

Ysidro shook his head and remained where he was. "You do not need me now. This is your moment, Brixa. You have long awaited this reunion with your mates."

I waved him closer. "No, stand among us. I wish it to be known by all here that you desire to come to terms with the Sky-Bornes. Is that correct?"

"Certainly. Let bygones be bygones." Ysidro took a step forward, then seemed to think better of it. "But perhaps your former mates think otherwise."

Buck's chin stuck out as he regarded Ysidro. Their eyes locked for several seconds.

Now, boys. I stood tall, reached out for Ysidro's hand and linked it to Buck's, then brought Harry into the mix as well. "I, as the person most endangered by the hostility between Onwei and Sky-Bornes, do commend all of us to respect each other." I placed my hand on top of the other three and glanced around. "Where are the others?"

"Already tucked away for the night," said Harry.

I debated whether to rouse them for this historic moment. Best not to shock them, especially that new fellow, the dealmaker. We would need a proper introduction first. I gazed at Harry, Buck, and Ysidro, still linked by arms extended toward the midst of a circle. I shook my arm up and down, in turn causing each of theirs to shake. "*Amijos.*"

"Amijos," rumbled three male voices.

To seal our newfound friendship, Ysidro pulled a flask out of his pocket, took a deep swallow and passed it around. I was the last to partake. I shook my head at the burning taste in my throat, yet greatly relieved that this first hurdle had been conquered.

***

I awoke with a hangover and winced. What a fool I was to partake of so much hooch last night. After innumerable toasts among four amijos, Joaquin — the only one remaining sober — took my uncertain hand and led me to Luz's tent, into which I stumbled gratefully and immediately fell asleep without removing so much as my boots.

I turned now to look for Luz. No sign: she must have tiptoed out earlier. I stuck my head outside, which was promptly bonked by a falling pinecone. Was it just my hangover, or had a mild tremor arisen during the night?

The morning was crisp and clear, and I heard voices coming from where my former mates were parked.

A time for reckoning was afoot, and I needed my wits about me. I spotted Luz's canteen and doused my face with water, then used my fingers to straighten tangled hair. A sour taste remained in my parched mouth, and my breath reeked, but it was time to face the music.

Joaquin huddled by the fire, sipping on a bombilla of fresh maté. Loud snores arose from inside his tent. Ysidro must be sleeping it off. Softer noises drifted over from a red tent closer to the plane. I could make out two sets of snores, not quite in unison. Must be Harry and Buck.

I moved closer to the campfire and rubbed my hands together. Joaquin offered me the bombilla. I grasped the warm cup between my hands. "Just you and me, scout? Where's Luz?"

"Gone. Left half an hour ago."

I cast a glance around. "Gone? Where?"

"Went to help Russell McCoy sort through the stash of piedra de yris."

I gasped and lowered my voice. "I thought you said the two of you hid it away safely."

Joaquin gave a soft laugh. "Luz said that Seir McCoy started probing what she knew. Didn't take much for her to spill the beans, I guess. She figured she would need their help to retrieve it anyway, as the hiding place was buried so deep by the storm."

"So, they dug it up?" I scowled.

"Yesterday. She said it took the four men all morning." He smiled.

This didn't sound at all like the plan that Luz, Joaquin and I had agreed upon before departing Nomidar. How could Luz have caved in so utterly? "Where are Luz and McCoy now?"

"At his tent. She said he moved it closer to the stash of stones to study each of them. Easier to move the tent than lug all the stones."

"Oh." I slumped. What was that girl thinking? She had given away the whole enterprise. What would be left to bargain for with Ysidro? Then I remembered the new man, the one who was to do the bargaining. "What about that Ganz fellow?"

"He hasn't shown up yet. I think he's sharing the tent with Seir McCoy."

"Maybe I'll wander over there, take a peek at this mighty stash. Can you point me, or will I get lost if I search on my own?"

"It's a ways, other side of this woods. I'll show you, but you sure you want to rush over there right now? You still look pretty wiped out, Brixa." Joaquin reached down and opened a small box of pastry.

My mouth watered as I grabbed a sticky caramel roll. "Hey. Where'd you get these?"

"Your Sky-Borne mates brought them. Lying right here."

I frowned. "Good for them, but remember, not my 'mates' anymore."

Joaquin nodded and winked. "I get it." He grabbed a roll and took a big chomp. After chewing for a few minutes, he eyed what was left of the roll and declared, "They can be my mates." He smiled at me, then immediately lost his grin as he eyed something behind me.

I turned abruptly. A tall, thin man in his late thirties ambled toward us with long strides. Freshly scrubbed and sporting a pressed khaki wardrobe, he appeared out of place amongst this scruffy crowd. Something about the man's air of importance obliged me to stand.

He stopped in front of the fire, clasped his hands behind his back, and faced Joaquin. "Ah. A hot stimulant. Don't mind if I do."

Joaquin offered him the bombilla, but the man winced and held up his hand. "Wait. Let me grab a cup." He turned and fished in the side pocket of a nearby pack.

While the man's back was turned, Joaquin frowned and eyed the bombilla with its metal straw in his own outstretched hand. He threw me a questioning look, as if to say, "What's he worried about?"

The man produced a plastic mug, which he allowed Joaquin to fill with maté. The boy offered him a roll from the box, but the man shut his eyes and shook his head sharply. "I don't do sugar."

He pulled out a biscuit from his pocket and unwrapped it. He took a bite, another sip of maté, and turned to me. "Savant SparrowHawk, I presume. Forgive my rudeness. Helmut Ganz." He made a small bow.

"Howdy," I said. It was all I could summon at the moment. Ganz's hooded eyes, his beaked nose, even the way he pecked at his biscuit, craning his neck forward in jagged swipes, all evoked in my mind a certain image. A raptor, or perhaps more to the point, a vulture, a carrion-eater.

A shiver threatened as he stared at me, but I managed to quell it and hold his gaze. My rawhide jacket, hemp leggings and roughshod boots must scream "I don't care what you think," which was true. He might judge me, but it mattered not one iota. He had no power over me, had nothing that I remotely wanted or needed. Just in case, though, I flexed my ankle for the comforting feel of Efrain's hunting knife, still tucked in my boot.

Ganz finished his biscuit and patted the crumbs from his fingers. "So. Everyone tells me it's a miracle that you survived."

I shrugged and sat back down. "I must have a guardian angel."

Ganz checked around, but seeing no other stools, remained standing. "Let's hope she still keeps watch over you."

That sounded like a veiled threat. "Does she need to?"

"Now, now. I'm just saying…" A gust of wind swirled through, and he hunched his shoulders. "Must be a rough life down here." He studied me again. "Don't tell me you haven't considered returning home if the opportunity arose. I would hardly believe that."

My eyes snapped wide open. "Is that why Sir Oscar sent you along? To lure me back?"

Ganz jerked his head, as if I'd slapped him. "Oh, please. My job is to negotiate with this tribe, to obtain rights for iridium ore mining."

That was a done deal, but this guy didn't know it yet. How would he have taken to Ysidro's whisky, each toast a profession of eternal friendship? I had watched Harry shudder with each swallow, but he managed to soldier on in the name of diplomacy. Ganz's lips, puckered as they were now, would have put a damper on the whole party.

"Glad to hear it." I started to rise.

"Of course, now that we know you're alive and well, we're all curious to hear your plans."

I sat back down. "Plans? As in, return to Canada with you guys?"

"That is an option, you know. Bailey Voyager has been outfitted with a fold-down fifth seat."

"How handy. Someone went to a lot of trouble on my account."

In response, Ganz spread his palms and fleshed out his lower lip.

He was taking pains to make this sound like an invitation rather than a threat, but I knew Oscar Bailey better than that. I flexed my ankle again. "Why does your boss want me back? He recruited my teacher, someone much more experienced than me."

"Your resume includes other valuable skills, Savant SparrowHawk."

I blinked several times. What was he getting at? I could think of only one thing. "China?"

Ganz nodded.

"Last time I checked, that was a liability," I said. What had altered among the great powers in the past eighteen months? I, the hapless pawn, must have some new value in this game.

"Times change," said Ganz. "Now China appears to have joined in the race to develop iridium technology. They see the handwriting on the wall, just like Sir Oscar predicted several years ago."

"What about me? The last conversation I had with Harry on the subject, I was going to be prosecuted on charges of spying for China."

Ganz issued a thin-lipped smile. "As I said, times change."

Oh, really? "Let me get this straight. If I cooperate with Sir Oscar, he'll get that espionage charge dropped?"

Ganz fluttered his fingers as if anything was possible.

Wow! I gaped. "What kind of services does he think I can provide?"

"As I understand, you were still in contact with a Chinese iridium expert."

"Savant Wan Xiang. We remained in touch."

"That alone might prove valuable."

My heart raced. This was turning into a high-stakes game, stakes I never knew existed, let alone that I was already part of.

Before I could respond, I heard the sound of a zipper behind me. I turned to find Harry crawling out of the red tent.

He stood, one hand cupping his forehead, gazing around vacantly. "Damn, whatever's in Ysidro's hooch packs a helluva punch. I haven't felt this hungover in years."

He staggered toward the campfire, where Joaquin offered him a freshly brewed bombilla. He took a long sip and flapped his elbows hard upon his ribs. "That's the stuff." He seemed to notice Ganz for the first time, hovering over my seated figure. "I take it you two have introduced yourselves."

Without taking his eyes off me, Ganz responded, "Yes. We were just discussing what Savant SparrowHawk might have waiting for her, if she chose to return home."

Harry looked around for a stool. Seeing none, he lowered himself onto a log and faced me. "How does all that sound to you, ma chère?"

I shrugged. "Better than it sounded last time we had this chat." I took a deep breath. "Still, it's not just my future we're talking about here."

Ganz furrowed his brow, but Harry leapt in. "Of course not. The whole Onwei people are affected by whatever we do, especially if Sir Oscar procures enough iridium to build transport airships."

I slowly shook my head.

Ganz frowned and said, "I take it you don't approve of the idea, Savant."

"Damn straight I don't. It's a surefire recipe for conflict. You don't need to be First Peoples to figure that out."

Ganz broke into one of his thin-lipped smiles. "But then, it's really not your call, is it?"

"True enough. Why don't you run the idea by the Onwei chief?" I turned to check if Ysidro still snored in the tent. "I'm sure he'll be thrilled with the prospect: hordes of Sky-Bornes farming his prime grazing pastures."

Ganz turned to check his crewmates before gazing back at me. "We only desire to strike a win-win bargain."

"Hmph, I'll bet," I said. "Joaquin, why don't you go see if your jeaf is coming around yet."

Joaquin loped off to his tent. Ganz stood waiting with his arms crossed.

My hungover brain tried to sort through my options. The truth of the matter was — and not the first time the thought occurred to me — most everyone would be better off if Nestor's aim had been cleaner.

Had I taken a bullet straight through the heart, my witnessed demise would have weighed heavily upon Sir Oscar Bailey, perhaps even aborting any plans for a second mission.

Likewise, if Efrain had not stuck his neck out to help the Sky-Bornes, if he had done the simple thing and followed Ysidro's lead, it would have been all over. There was no way my mates could have prevailed, armed only with Buck's stun gun. Ysidro might not necessarily have ordered all of us killed, but he would have driven home the lesson to forget our precious ore and never return.

Lots of "ifs," worth nothing now.

Ysidro groused in the tent, angry at being awoken. My fervent hope was that, roused from his drunken stupor at this relatively early midmorning hour, the jeaf would exhibit his naturally surly side and make demands that the Sky-Bornes could not possibly meet.

But what if Ysidro's newfound neighborliness extended to welcoming Canadian colonists? He might think he could profit by bartering with them, or charge them some kind of land tax, or who knows what? He had seen only a few Sky-Bornes at a time. He had no clue how many thousands of them could end up here.

Somehow, I had to convey to Ysidro that giving his consent carte-blanche was a bad idea.

20

THE ART OF THE DEAL

Ganz stewed as he waited for the man he was supposed to negotiate with. The wind sweeping down this barren hillside sent a chill through him, easily penetrating his neo-down vest. Trying to gain a bit of warmth, he moved closer to the campfire, but the green wood produced an excess of smoke that followed him like a magnet, no matter where he shifted.

He gathered there'd been a celebration last night. He might be the least bit jealous of missing the fun if the rest of them didn't sport such pathetic hangovers. Harry had retreated to silence, slumped on his log, face resting in his hands, probably praying for deliverance. Buck staggered out of his tent just now, plodding with a sailor's broad-based gait to keep his balance.

Ganz was pretty sure they hadn't stayed sober long enough to work out any details. What bothered him was the disadvantage they left him in; Ysidro, Harry, and Buck had become drinking buddies and felt they could trust each other. Not least because of their shared history from last year, they had become almost blood brothers from that shootout. Ganz, on the other hand, was the newbie, and from what he heard about Ysidro, the man distrusted newbies.

Meanwhile, he needed to keep his eye on SparrowHawk. What would it take to reel her in? He brought all kinds of material lures to secure Ysidro's favor. Yet the young geology savant showed no signs of being tempted by gifts, fame, career, or power, and she had no family to tug on her heartstrings.

He toyed with the idea of abducting her forcibly, and he was pretty sure such a step would be sanctioned after the fact, once they put her on trial back in Canada. Yet he had never discussed the idea with Harry or Buck, and for certain, he could not carry it off alone. No, somehow, he needed to make it worth her while to return of her own volition. But how?

He eyed Joaquin, waiting patiently at the door of his tent for Ysidro to appear. The boy was wise enough to bring a mug of maté. After several minutes of mutters and curses, the chief finally emerged.

Ganz stifled a gasp. What had he expected, some kind of telly star? Ysidro could hardly be mistaken for a warrior this morning. Was it the disheveled bushy graying curls? No, the impression of unpreparedness lingered even after he slapped on a rough wool beret to beat the mess down. The U-shaped whiskers spoke to a hint of vanity, as did the reddish-brown leather vest and matching boots.

More than anything else, Ysidro's eyes marked him as unready for prime time, as red and puffy as the others who partook of last night's binge. Ysidro spotted the maté and grabbed it like a lifeline. As he sipped on the brew through a metal straw, he cast his gaze around the group and settled upon Ganz, the only one he'd not met.

Ganz flinched under the scrutiny. No one offered to make an introduction. Just as he was about to suck it up, walk toward this oaf, and extend his hand in a gesture of civility, Buck arrived and dumped his load of firewood. He glanced around as he brushed off his clothes, then quickly stepped between the two men.

"Looks like you fellas haven't met yet. Ganz, this is Ysidro. Correon, did I get that right?" He turned to Ysidro for confirmation. The chief nodded sagely.

Ganz extended his hand. Ysidro grasped it with mighty force but, seeing his victim wince, softened his grip, grunted, and patted Ganz on the shoulder. The high-octane alcohol on his breath was mixed with stale tobacco.

Ganz's lips clenched as he fought off the urge to rub his hand. He sensed that, with Ysidro asserting his role as alpha male, now was an auspicious time to begin their business. He offered Ysidro a fresh set of earpads.

The chief regarded them briefly, wrinkled his nose and shook his head. He pointed at Keltyn and said something.

Appearing surprised, she said, "Ysidro wants me to translate. Thinks the earpads will miss something important."

An unease crept over Ganz. He tried out his best reassuring smile on Keltyn, but her expression remained wooden. That was the nature of those First Peoples, taciturn. He needn't read anything into that.

Puffy clouds moved in to block the sun. The strong breeze off the mountain kept them chilled enough to stay huddled around the campfire, despite the smoke. Ganz turned to Harry, who was supposed to convene this get-together, but the crew chief appeared still in a daze, eyes fluttering aimlessly. After Harry's similar belly flop at the press conference, Ganz had anticipated something like this and prepared accordingly.

He tried out his Onwei phrasing. "Thank you, Ysidro and Keltyn both, for agreeing to meet with us peaceably." He noted their surprised reaction with satisfaction. "Let me say, first of all, that we do come in peace. The conversation we are now having is the first step in what I am convinced will become a lasting trade partnership and, hopefully beyond that, a lasting friendship between your people and mine." He paused to see if Ysidro had gotten the gist of that. He was pretty sure his grammar on this part was okay; he had memorized the phrases.

Ysidro nodded and stuck his lip out.

Ganz addressed him. "I guess you know why we came back."

Keltyn translated this, and Ysidro pointed at her. She squirmed in her seat and said, "He thinks you came back to find me."

It was Ganz's turn to shift his weight. "Of course, that's important, but it's not the only reason."

"Not even the main reason, is it?" Keltyn stared at him. "Don't worry. If I was dealing with the same odds that your mates were, I wouldn't have come back either, not unless something much more important was at stake."

Without waiting for his response, she turned to explain Ganz's comment to Ysidro. Then she delivered his reply. "He understands that your lord still lusts after the piedra de yris." As she translated, Ysidro held out his hand and ran his thumb across his fingers, from pinky to pointer, several times.

Keltyn smiled and said, "You catch that?"

Ganz laughed softly. "He says, 'Forget the speeches. Get down to brass tacks. What do you have to offer?' Well, as a matter of fact, we did bring a number of items that might interest your jeaf."

He arose and retrieved a large duffel bag, pulled out a bright red raincoat with all the bells and whistles, and carried it over for Ysidro to inspect. The chief stuck his arms through the sleeves and pulled the sides snug around his torso. He adjusted the drawstrings top and bottom, pulled up the hood, raised his arms above his head, and twisted right and left. Yet, when finished, he merely tossed it aside without comment.

Ganz turned to Keltyn. "Tell him that the same lightweight, water-resistant fabric is available for their other all-weather needs." He pointed toward Joaquin's tent, the one Ysidro had slept in last night. The chief granted the tiniest lift of his bushy eyebrows.

Ganz clicked his tongue. Was the man genuinely unimpressed? More likely just playing hard to get. He found a pair of dialups and fished them out: a black-rimmed pair he guessed would suit the macho, no-nonsense personality of a gaucho chief. "Does the jeaf sometimes have trouble focusing on small objects, threading a needle, for instance? Many of us, not blessed with Buck's perfect vision, find ourselves squinting as we age. May I?"

With some trepidation, he approached Ysidro, placed the black dialups gently upon his nose, and adjusted the earpieces. Ysidro grimaced, but Ganz held up a finger and deftly scrolled a tiny roller in the black rim, which in turn thickened the soft polymer lens in imperceptible gradations until Ysidro raised his hand. Ganz repeated the same procedure with the other lens.

The jeaf made a clown face as he showed off his mug to the group, dialups and all. He moved his head around in small jerks, eyeing each person furtively. He giggled something, which Keltyn translated as "No one will recognize me." He seemed to derive some pleasure from that prospect, yet, finished with his moment of fun, he unceremoniously tossed the dialups atop the raincoat.

Ganz pulled out a bag of sugar, passing it to Ysidro. He mimicked dipping in his finger to taste the white granules. Again, Ysidro merely shrugged.

Cheez. Ganz shook his head slowly as he dug for a mixture of herbs and spices. After hearing about Del

Campo's offer of a meat rub on their last visit, he'd enlisted the advice of his partner Alain, who happened to be the executive chef at Zürich's finest grill. His blend was in the packet Ganz now anxiously passed to Ysidro for inspection.

The jeaf did as Ganz bid and stuck his bulbous nose in the bag. He closed his eyes and inhaled deeply. A smile of contentment crossed his weather-beaten face.

Ganz breathed a sigh of relief.

SparrowHawk's features pinched as she translated Ysidro's pronouncement. "When our business here is done, you will fly your machine to my camp. We shall have a great feast, and my charros will use this exotic mixture to season the asado." He held the bag high.

This was a surprise. Ganz elbowed Harry to get his attention. "Hear that, Harry? The chief wants to seal the bargain with a barbecue at their camp."

"We'll see if we can swing that," said Harry, still fluttering his eyes vacantly.

A definite maybe. He checked around to see how others responded to Ysidro's invitation. The boy Joaquin seemed thrilled, but Savant SparrowHawk looked like she just swallowed poison. Her eyes bugged out, her copper skin suddenly blanched, her mouth hung open. Something about Ysidro's spur-of-the-moment offer made her distinctly uneasy. *Hmm.* Why might that be?

Ganz rummaged through the supply bag for what was left: antibiotic and opiate patches and other pharmaceuticals. Dangling the packs of nondescript discs in front of Ysidro, Ganz tried to explain their value, but his command of Onwei fell short, and the chief sat impassively. His mind was elsewhere, likely on the big party he had decided to throw.

Ganz dropped the packets in Keltyn's lap and threw up his hands. He had no more gifts. His mind raced through what other enticements he might have brought, but again, it occurred to him that Ysidro was merely stringing him along. He tilted his head for a one-eyed stare at the vulgar cowboy.

Surprisingly, Ysidro smiled, grasped his hand with his meaty paw and squeezed it, this time hard enough so that Ganz yelped, sure something was about to crack.

The chief mouthed a phrase that Keltyn translated as, "Happy, Seir Ganz? You wished to make a deal."

Never had Ganz felt such an exquisite mixture of joy and pain as at this moment.

Buck laughed. "We didn't get the handshake treatment last year. Only some choice words of unwelcome, and later a war party after our scalps."

Ganz rubbed his knuckles, but Buck's comment gave him an idea. "You big boys should try hand wrestling." He went through the motion.

Ysidro seemed puzzled, while Buck frowned. "I don't know that we want to make a game of it, Ganz."

"Nonsense. A game is just what we need now."

Buck eyed the big jeaf and smiled. Ganz knew that his competitive juices were aroused, but that was not what he had in mind. He pulled Buck aside.

"This guy is playing hard to get. Turned up his nose at most all the gifts I brought."

"Yeah. I noticed that. So?"

"So, I want you to give him his money's worth, but in the end, you know…"

"What? Throw the match?" Buck gaped, a twinkle in his eye.

Ganz kept his mouth shut, waiting for Buck to catch on.

"Oh, I get it. Make him feel superior, so he'll be in a better mood to deal."

"Something like that." Ganz patted Buck's arm.

"Oh, the sacrifices we make." Buck shook his head slowly. "Ganz, you owe me for this." He pawed about and found a wooden crate among the supplies. He upended its contents of dried food packages, placed it on its side to make a small table, and set up stools on each side.

Ganz beckoned Ysidro to sit, while Buck demonstrated how to perform hand wrestling. The big oaf laughed. Perhaps he knew the game.

Buck stuck his own large hand, fingers spread, elbow resting on the crate, and Ysidro joined it at the starting position. The pilot glowered at Ganz. "Quit caressing yourself and start us off."

Within seconds, a flash of teeth and red-faced grunts bore witness to the ferocity of their bout. For a few moments, it appeared an even match. Buck even forced Ysidro's forearm backward. Then, with graceful restraint, he allowed the chief to regain the momentum. Finally, without the faintest sound, the back of his hand touched the crate. He frowned at Ysidro, a look that seemed genuinely puzzled. It was the chief's turn to pat the big pilot on the back. Buck forced a smile and shrugged.

Raw strength might be an old-fashioned attribute, but it still mattered. If it ever regrettably came down to real fighting, the Onwei would be no match for Sir Oscar Bailey's elite goon squad.

Now the jeaf arose, sauntered over to Joaquin's tent, and returned shortly with his flask. He held it up for all to see, uncorked it, took a hearty swallow, and tried to pass it to his fellow chief. Harry shook his head violently. Ysidro frowned and extended the flask to Ganz, who tried to act nonchalant in his demurral. It was much too early in the day to imbibe, and besides, the last thing he needed was a hangover like the others were still nursing.

Ysidro appeared forlorn until returning his gaze to the pilot, still squeezing his right hand with his left. "Buck, mi amijo," he shouted, holding the flask up high.

Buck took in the pile of gifts by Ysidro's stool and addressed Harry. "How come you guys don't want to help the jeaf celebrate his good fortune?"

"You'll have to represent us in doing the honors. Ganz and I don't seem up to the task," groused Harry.

"It's a little early for me too, but hey, someone's got to bite the bullet." Buck waved Ysidro hither and took a polite mouthful from the flask.

The chief sat on a rock and patted one nearby for his newfound friend. They took each other's measure for a few minutes. Then Ysidro raised his free hand and made a motion of cocking his pointer finger with his thumb pointing up.

Buck seemed flummoxed. He turned to see if anyone else understood. "I hope this isn't what I'm thinking."

Ysidro's gesture seemed to wake Harry, who said, "He wants to see your stun gun, Buck. He remembers from last year. You stopped a bull about to charge the big crowd at Aldo's funeral, knocked him cold. Same with Soriante the yodeler a few days later. He wouldn't forget something like that."

"I dunno, chief."

"You can keep the safety on, can't you?"

"Sure, but…"

"Just humor him for a few minutes. Let him handle it as a special treat, some kind of jewel. You stand really close. We want to keep him satisfied, right, Ganz?"

"That we do," said Ganz, although, like Buck, he had qualms.

Buck shrugged, held up his finger to Ysidro, and went to retrieve the stun gun from his pack. He returned and checked the safety.

The jeaf's eyes brightened when he laid eyes on the small, sleek, steel-gray weapon in Buck's palm. He glanced at the pilot's face, picked it up gingerly and tested its heft in his own hand, then enclosed three fingers around the butt and aimed at a rock, carefully exerting pressure on the trigger with his pointer finger. Realizing it was locked, he smiled, cocked his wrist a few times to savor the gun's heft, then gently handed it back to Buck. The smile faded slowly.

"Uh, oh," said Buck. "Methinks I detect a note of desire. Beat me in arm wrestling, now he's getting greedy."

Ysidro cast his gaze on Keltyn, but she seemed lost in her funk. He summoned Joaquin, who was watching the sequence with a bemused expression. Ysidro uttered some phrases while pointing at the weapon in Buck's hand.

Joaquin adjusted his earpad and cleared his throat. "The jeaf says that, as a sign of trust between your people and ours, he wishes you to include Seir Buck's weapon among the gifts."

The pilot let out a soft laugh. "Boy, if that don't beat all. What's he gonna want next, fly the plane?"

Ganz frowned. He considered himself an astute judge of character. At this moment, he could not believe that Ysidro's bold request had any motive other than achieving the enhanced status conferred by a new toy. "I don't think it would hurt anything, Harry," he said.

Harry's only response was to check Ganz's reaction, then back at the grinning Ysidro, and finally at Buck. The pilot still held the gun in his open palm. Harry said nothing else, but Ganz detected the smallest of shrugs before he averted his gaze.

Ganz leapt into the opening and turned toward Joaquin. "Please advise the chief that the weapon will be included as a gift, upon our departure."

The boy did so. Ysidro grinned, stuck up both thumbs and wiggled them like worms dangling from a fishing line.

Buck glowered at Ganz. He summoned Joaquin close to translate, then pointed out the stun gun's key features. The jeaf nodded sagely.

What malevolent genie have I unleashed, wondered Ganz? If this guy changes his mind about us, we'll be totally defenseless. He probably already has a rifle stashed in his pack somewhere. Suppose we attend this feast of his. Harry had succumbed to an invitation from the tribe's previous chief on the last voyage, but that did nothing to prevent a shootout later. If Ysidro wanted to send a crude, bloody message to Sir Oscar Bailey…

Ganz's gut told him the wisest course was to gather the stones, make some excuse, and be gone. The challenge would be how to pull this off without offending Ysidro. They would need his cooperation next time around too, and despite the inevitable outcome if it came to a shooting war, Sir Oscar did not need any more blood on his hands.

21

POLES APART

"One minute until airtime." A chirpy voice sounded overhead. Fay patted her curls into place as she waited in the wings of the telly studio. She mumbled silent thanks for the savvy of Greta Szabo, who, within hours of her request, had managed not only to land her a prime time talk show slot, but also to reel in Bertram Casey. Fay's job tonight was to make sure the show's confidence was justified, and meantime to knock some sense into Casey.

She watched the seated moderator, a forty-something square-jawed stud named Rex Bolton, engage in chit-chat with the pert little blonde who hovered over his face. The makeup artist applied final touches of powder to his nose and scampered off. The off-camera director faced him, counting down the last ten seconds with his fingers.

"Good evening," beamed Bolton. "Welcome back to Insight for Thursday, September 24, 2316. Tonight's program is a last-minute addition to our schedule, featuring two eloquent guests familiar to our viewers, though, I am told, who have never met, until now.

"That in itself should ensure some fireworks. Yet the topic of their debate is even hotter: the settlement of uncharted territories. What better a time to argue those merits, with the crew of Bailey Voyager encamped somewhere in Antarctica at this very moment?

"Our first guest is well known from her previous appearances here, most recently on behalf of her advocacy group, Native Peoples United. Savant Orfea Del Campo." Bolton arose and turned to welcome Fay.

She strode confidently across the stage. They grasped hands and she gave him a peck on the cheek, taking in his verbena aftershave. Same as Oscar Bailey's. Ding. She smoothed her dress as she sat in the armchair he offered her.

"Our other guest needs no introduction, period. He has provided political news commentary for three decades via Third Millennium News, during which time his name has become literally a household word. You know you have achieved iconic status when Disney molds a character after you." Bolton reached onto the coffee table and held up a six-inch doll for the camera to zoom in on. It featured the oversized head of a man, his mouth gaping open, his hand raised to make his point. The speckled dialups, the red cravat, and the blotchy red face left no doubt of the doll's identity, but just in case, its base was labeled "Boiling Bert." The doll's stunted rubber body rocked back and forth on the base.

"Please welcome Mr. Bertram Casey." Bolton extended his hand toward the opposite wing. Casey emerged with a canny smile, one hand raised toward the presumed studio audience. So far as Fay could tell, behind the strobe lights hovered only technicians and the show's producer, well out of camera range. Why was the man playing to his fan base, she wondered? He must be trying to get pumped. She sat tall and crossed her legs.

Casey shook Bolton's hand, then bowed stiffly in Fay's direction before taking his seat on the moderator's other side.

Bolton listed ground rules for the debate before proceeding to read excerpts from Casey's comments several nights previously. He turned toward Fay. "Savant, I believe it was your camp that called for this discussion. Presumably you wish to respond to these remarks. Please." He extended his hand.

"Thank you, Rex, thanks to Insight for sponsoring this debate, and especially thank you, Mr. Casey, for agreeing to it."

Casey nodded. "Not at all, Savant. The world would be a duller place if everyone took the rants of us pundits at face value."

"And even duller with no rants at all," Fay ventured.

He chuckled and relaxed into his armchair.

She, too, leaned back. "I do appreciate your bringing the topic of colonizing Antarctica into the limelight. Sir Oscar Bailey, the powerhouse behind this second mission down under, has been disarmingly coy about his global intentions, beyond the obvious goal of obtaining a steady supply of iridium ore."

"You've noticed, too," said Casey. "Yes, the man plays his cards close to the vest. Of course, he has every right to do so when it comes to industrial trade secrets, but now he verges on socio-political initiatives with transnational implications."

Fay eased forward. "How would you advise him to proceed at this point?"

"'Make a clean breast of your intentions, Sir Oscar,' I would tell him. 'Folks will need some time to get used to the idea of moving to the other side of the world, especially conservative Canadian farmers who have tilled this soil for centuries.'" Casey spread his beet-red palms, as if his advice was self-evident.

Fay's smile broadened. She had worried needlessly that Casey would hedge his views on colonization. "So, you're in favor of this policy, so long as it all proceeds transparently?"

Casey sat up straighter and stared at her. "Absolutely. Now, I suppose you wish to weigh in on behalf of the poor Antarcticans who might be displaced." He wagged his head to and fro with an effect much like his namesake doll.

Fay willed herself to stay calm. "No argument needed, Mr. Casey." She turned to face the camera. "Native Peoples United's website speaks for itself. I invite our viewers to avail themselves of all the facts and figures. What I really wish to bring up is the question of Sir Oscar Bailey's integrity."

She paused to gauge the shocked look on the faces of Bolton and Casey. She couldn't see the faces out of camera range but expected that they were equally surprised at this attack upon the most powerful person in the free world. If they perceived she was trying to use the debate forum as a platform for a personal vendetta, they were darn close.

Rex Bolton jumped in. "With all due respect, Savant, I'm not sure we want to use this forum to attack a person not here to defend himself."

Fay tried to suppress a sneer. "Sir Oscar Bailey has no shortage of ways and means to respond, should he so choose. What he lacks is conscience, or anyone powerful enough to hold his feet to the fire."

"You make it sound like he has committed some sort of crime." The lines on Casey's face were deeply drawn.

"Nothing that obvious. No broken laws, just broken promises." Fay pondered whether she should disclose Oscar's promised moratorium on iridium exploration, in return for her calling off a boycott. Too risky. The details, including his hush money donations to NPU, would surface in no time.

Yet now, both Bolton and Casey favored her with questioning looks. She needed to toss some red meat to sate this feeding frenzy. "I can assure you that his present strategy will result in international repercussions."

"You obviously allude to China," said Casey, craning his wattled chin forward. "Is this prediction just an educated guess, or might Savant Del Campo perhaps be privy to some details she would care to share?"

She arched her brows. "I have it from a well-placed source that China is prepared to tap their own domestic iridium reserves, despite the cost, if Bailey proceeds on his present course."

Bolton's eyes, darting hither and yon, suggested her comment had lost him, but Casey's smile showed he had grasped the point immediately. "Ah, glorious. Another tipping point for East-West conflict."

Lips clamped, she nodded and plunged onward. "Not only that. They may well retaliate economically."

"I see." Casey sat back, clasped his hands, and began rolling his thumbs. "Some kind of embargo, like cold fusion technology. We are certainly vulnerable to that sort of leverage." He cocked his head. "Tell me, Savant, if you don't mind my asking. How do you happen to come by such detailed information?"

"Living in a cosmopolitan hub like Zürich does carry certain perks, Mr. Casey."

"Aha. So, having been alerted, via certain diplomatic channels, of China's intentions, you have made it your mission to be their spokesperson."

"I wouldn't put it like that." A flush blanketed her face.

"No?" Casey leaned forward in his chair and pointed a finger at her. "You don't feel like you've been duped, Savant? You have already alluded to Oscar Bailey's broken promises. What sort of inducements has the Chinese government made to you? Or is it simply your hope to add their weight to your proposed boycott of Bailey products? Oh, and let us not forget your overzealous eco-terrorist colleagues."

"You are speaking way out of turn, sir." Fay heard the shrillness in her voice and knew she was losing control of this debate, fast. She fought to stay in check.

Bolton spread his hands in a patting motion, trying to signal both parties to calm down, but Casey was in full rant mode and in no mood to back off.

"Am I? I've been at this game since you were playing hopscotch, Savant. I have witnessed way too many unfortunate saps like yourself get sucked into a role they later regretted. Advocacy is one thing, diplomacy something altogether different. You had best leave the latter to the pros, lest you get chewed into tiny pieces and spit out unceremoniously."

Fay floundered, her mouth opening and shutting wordlessly, unable to summon a rebuttal.

Casey thundered on. "Tonight, in this forum, would be an excellent time, Savant, to publicly repudiate any ties between your organization and those cowardly murderous thugs who are trying to bring down Sir Oscar Bailey." He glared at her.

"How dare you assert that any such ties exist, sir?" It was the only possible response, one that could not be rebutted, so far as she knew. Yet the media were already rife with the same speculation.

Casey held up his hands, as if his charge was common knowledge.

"...good time to take a commercial break," came the voice of Rex Bolton, penetrating the thick fog engulfing Fay. "We'll be right back." The red camera light went blank.

Cold sweat dripped down Fay's spine. Trembling, she reached for a glass of water. Bolton engaged Casey, all the while nervously glancing around at her. Relaxed in his chair, Casey nodded slowly, his hands again clasped, but eyes likewise trained on Fay. A lopsided smile graced his fat lips.

Seeing Fay more composed, Bolton leaned her way. "Savant, I was just suggesting to Mr. Casey that we lower the wattage for the rest of the debate, keep the discussion to verifiable facts. You okay with that?"

"Absolutely," said Fay, though she knew the damage had already been done. Deep down, she also knew that, despite the justice of her position and the millions of potential allies to her cause, when it came to a debate, all that the audience cared about were winners and losers. The telly viewers had already formed an opinion. The only way she might possibly alter that would be to go on the attack, a strategy she had just precluded. Truth be told, at the moment she had not the stomach to fight back.

Next time she debated Bertram Casey, if there was a next time, she would need to prepare much better. At the very least, she would need a debate coach and someone to stand in for her opponent, hitting her with the same ferocity as this man had. For better or worse, she was now playing in the big leagues.

22

OUT OF MY HANDS

I watched in despair as Ysidro and Buck made buddy-buddy with the jeaf's hooch. The Onwei leader's behavior in the past hour was disgusting, caving with no more willpower than a small child to all the material temptations waved in his face. Buck managed to get the jeaf to try an earpad. Now they were trading jokes, crude ones, by the sound of their chortling laughter. The "negotiations" had dissolved into a macho pal fest. If anyone were going to resist Sir Oscar's plans, it must needs be me.

The mild tremors I noted this morning had picked up. Not enough to alarm anyone else, or were they simply too soused to tell? I flashed back to the Venga session where I had encountered the volcano's soul. These shakes from the mountain, was it trying to tell me something?

I set my jaw and summoned Joaquin, all the while feeling a hard pit in my stomach. "You were going to point me toward McCoy's tent."

Joaquin glanced around. "No one will miss me for awhile," he said. "I'll come with you. We'll bring them some maté."

I fidgeted, waiting for the boy to brew a fresh batch and pour it into a thermos from the Sky-Bornes' gear. He stuffed it in his shoulder pack.

"It's a bit of a hike, but too rocky for the horses. We skirt the edge of these woods." Joaquin leaned his head in the direction we needed to take, then set off at a brisk pace on a course that took us uphill before turning back into the pine-scented forest.

Following behind, watching only the ground before me, I nursed my rage. My best-laid hopes and plans were quickly unraveling.

Who was I angry at? This sly Ganz character? No, he was just a minion of Oscar Bailey. Ysidro, then. Who knew that he would change his stripes so easily? I rued Aldo's untimely death. The world held too many Ysidros and too few Aldos. Yet this was the jeaf I was stuck with. We were on the same side, for better or worse.

That left Russell McCoy. As if his past sins were not indictment enough, he had chosen to compound them by succumbing to Oscar Bailey's flattery. It was a slap in my face, no two ways about it. His very presence made him the lightning rod for my wrath. I reached down and patted Efrain's knife, tucked in my boot. I knew what had to be done, and I was damned if I would let McCoy deter me.

"Almost there," said Joaquin. He stopped and turned abruptly. "Did you feel that?"

"The tremor? Ha. The ground has been shaking since I got up this morning. Keep going." Yet, the next moment, another shock sent me sprawling. Joaquin's face mirrored worry, but I bounced up, quickly dusted myself off, and brushed him onward. We skirted between pine branches toward a clearing ahead.

"How did you find this place? And why here?" I was annoyed, not by the tremors, but at having to traipse all the way to a remote site. Whatever its advantages for secrecy, it would be a pain, come time to remove the stash.

"Ow." A needled branch snapped in Joaquin's face. He pushed it away. "I told you 'bout the storm. Then Seir McCoy coaxed the secret out of Luz while I was gone."

"Hmph," I said. Might as well wrap ribbons while we were at it. Shiny gifts for our honored guests, lest they return empty-handed.

The trees parted, and the two of us stood in the clearing, a deep "U" wash, bounded on both sides by dense conifers. The eroded banks marched directly up to the tree trunks, leaving roots exposed like so many tendrils. Pine needles, branches and sandy mud lay mixed at the base.

On the far bank, near the apex of the "U," I saw a depression and signs of recent digging near the tree line. Farther down the wash, past the open end of the "U" where the ground solidified with more rocks and scant trees, I spied the yellow tent McCoy shared with Ganz.

As Joaquin and I walked toward it, I heard McCoy's gruff tones. He uttered what sounded like an "aha." Luz responded with an "ayee." I exchanged a worried glance with Joaquin. Was Luz in danger? She was every bit as tall as McCoy, but, even well into middle- aged, with his broad build he could overpower her if he set his mind to it. I hurried toward the tent.

A great pile of stones, of various hues and sizes and apparently unsorted, lay beside the doorway. I stepped around the pile and peered inside. McCoy and Luz stood with their backs to me. McCoy held a plain-appearing specimen up to the light shining through the far wall of the tent. He pointed to a spot on the stone. Luz, leaning close to him, tried to make out the detail.

"It must be this seam here that makes it read so high." McCoy sounded peeved. "Still, all the shaking, I don't trust these numbers. We're going to have to redo them all again, later, when it quits."

On a folding table beside him sat the fabled meter. It produced the purity data that comprised the heart of the assay. The rest was math. A computer tablet sat next to the meter.

I willed myself to calm down. Luz's shriek must have echoed McCoy's excitement; he had found such potent ore in a stone that, at first blush, appeared insignificant.

That was a big deal, very big.

Joaquin interrupted my musings and edged through the tent door beside me. "What's all the excitement?"

McCoy and Luz turned to discover that they had guests. I watched McCoy's face as he recognized me. It was a mask, really, not a single emotion betrayed. I imagined what raced through his mind: protégé for over ten years, concubine toy, left for almost certain death at the other end of the world, now not only very much alive, but also gone over to the locals in rough hemp threads and vaquero boots. Yet he showed not the slightest hint of joy or shock or relief.

It was all I could do to keep from snarling, just to see if *that* would rouse him.

"Keltyn, my dear. Delighted," he said, bowing his head ever so slightly.

I returned the nod. "Savant McCoy."

Our gaze held for another few seconds. Behind that mask, I knew he was trying to take my measure. Not just how much I had changed, but what leverage he might still have over me. I met his gaze unflinchingly.

A slight twitch of McCoy's lip signaled that his mind was settled on that score. Now he held up the specimen in his hand and lapsed into his default mode of communication, an explanation. I recognized the instinct; I too retreated to expounding known facts when under stress. "The stones have surprised us," he intoned. "Iridium concentration of the ore seems to have very little correlation with appearance. This modest little piece, for instance, came in as seventy-three percent pure."

I noticed the small pile sitting in a box beside the table, presumably those that had already been assayed. "Looks like you've got your work cut out for you." I tilted my head toward the pile outside the door.

"Indeed, I do," said McCoy. "I am so thankful that Luz and Joaquin went to all the trouble of collecting the samples for me before we arrived." The slightest hint of a smirk.

Joaquin, out of McCoy's line of sight, crinkled his nose, while Luz registered a smile.

I glared at her before turning back to McCoy. "You can't possibly expect to carry all of these rocks back on Bailey Voyager," I barked.

McCoy pulled his head back. "Of course not, my dear. That's the whole point of this exercise. Just the purest, just enough to get the job done."

"And that job is…?" I had a strong suspicion, but I needed to confirm it, from the horse's mouth.

McCoy studied me, his head slightly cocked. "I should think you must be quite aware of the answer, dear Keltyn." He paused, then rambled on. "The way Oscar Bailey tells the story, Orfea Del Campo, clued by your local shaman, first floated the grandiose idea of Canadians colonizing Antarctica, using a transport vessel from Bailey Enterprises coated with iridium alloy. Orfea accused Sir Oscar of hatching this idea in secret. Though he had never considered it before, he parsed it and decided: why not? Eventually he recruited me, and here we are." He spread his hands. "I'm sure, once we sort out the best pieces and transport them back to Canada, we'll be able to forge enough alloy to coat a good-sized transport."

I clenched my lips. That sealed it. Bailey had come clean. The only way to stop this sequence of events was at its source, right here. I straightened. "Looks like you have made some improvements on the original design, Savant McCoy." I pointed to an array of dials. How different from the original, the one I brought on the first mission, the strange yellow metal box from Savant Wan's lab, the one that had aroused Buck's suspicion that I was a spy.

"Why, yes, I have been doing some tinkering in your absence, incorporating new sensor diodes and such. Unfortunately, the field tests have been lagging, insufficient sample size and all." He held up a specimen. "That should all be corrected shortly." He nodded toward his tablet. "I really am glad you made an appearance, my dear. Might you like to help me analyze the data?"

I puffed my cheeks, parsing his motive. Then, even as my heart ripped, I forced a tight-lipped smile. "A pleasure."

McCoy seemed surprised. "Really? I can't imagine you've had much opportunity for any sort of geology research during your stay here."

I broadened my smile. One thing working with McCoy taught me was how to flatter a man's ego, even if, deep down, I despised him. "Not to worry. It's still up here." I pointed at my temple. "I had a good teacher."

His lips quivered as he struggled to gauge the sincerity of my complement. "Excellent," was what finally emerged. He rubbed his hands. "Now we have four people to share the labor. Let me think." His eyes darted around, but he seemed at a loss.

Joaquin held up the thermos. "I brought some maté, seir."

"Bless you, Joaquin." McCoy dropped into a squat, cradling a cup in both hands, as he waited for the boy to pour the steaming drink. He snuck a peek at me and scowled. "If I were a superstitious man, I would attribute our current seismic conditions to your arrival, my dear."

You're on to something there, mister. I shrugged and squatted likewise. Joaquin and Luz followed my lead.

McCoy took a draught and passed the cup to me. As it made its rounds, he checked his watch and said, "Three hours Luz and I have been at this. Even with two more of you helping, we'll need another day to sort through this pile." Luz and Joaquin said nothing, but I nodded. My plan required avoiding any air of reluctance.

The cup came around to McCoy again. He took another draught and arose. "Fine. Here's my suggestion. Reading this meter continuously gets tiresome. We never envisioned having to assay so many samples at one time, eh, Keltyn?"

"Not in a million years. What a find." I tried to appear upbeat.

"So. I've already showed Luz how to enter the data on the tablet. This girl has a natural aptitude for numbers. Has anyone ever told you that, Luz?"

"Thank you, Russell." A blush crept across the girl's face.

Russell!? My heart skipped a beat. The signs were all there: familiarity, adoring gaze, trusting body language. In these few short days, Luz had become an eager pupil of Russell McCoy.

McCoy rambled on. "Keltyn can take over the meter readings, while Joaquin helps me pick through the unsorted stones outside. I want to group them based on brightness and sheen, then see if that correlates at all with purity in the assay. It's discouraging to think that outward appearance has no predictive value."

Joaquin and I eyed each other as McCoy exited the tent. I made a pushing motion with my hand at arm's length: he must try to distract McCoy away from the immediate surrounding of the tent.

"Joaquin, it's time to fess up about your other stash," I said loudly.

The boy stared blankly at me. My eyes widened, and my hands made an uplifting motion. Luz stood agape.

McCoy stuck his head back in, fingering his earpad. "Did I hear right? There's more? You've got to be kidding. Four grown men spent most of yesterday digging up this much."

Joaquin gulped. "Best to hide some at a different spot, just in case, seir."

McCoy's puzzled face swiveled back and forth between Joaquin and Luz. Then he broke into a laugh. "Trying to conceal some from Luz, eh? Oh, a sly one you are." He poked his head outside the tent to contemplate the pile at hand once again, then turned back to his assistants. "How big is your other stash compared to this, my boy?" He pulled the tent door flap wide for Joaquin to get a good look.

Joaquin pursed his lips. "Perhaps half as large, seir."

McCoy eyed me. "What say you, my dear? One additional day's worth of assaying?"

I shrugged. "Why not?" His greed was pathetic. I struggled to hide a smirk.

"Right ho," he said, patting a small gauge clipped to his breeches. "Here is the detector." He reached by the side of the tent and hoisted a shovel. "Lead the way, m'boy."

Luz waited until McCoy was out of earshot. Hands on hips, she turned toward me. "What are you trying to pull? There is no other stash."

"No, but I needed to get McCoy out of here, and that was the only way I could think of." I was already surveying the tent's contents. A sudden tremor, greater in magnitude and lasting a full five seconds, sent us both sprawling and scattered the neatly bundled ore samples.

Luz stayed kneeling. "What is so secret you don't want Russell to know about it?"

I whirled. "Don't call that devil 'Russell' around me."

"Sorry." The girl bit her lip.

My gaze darted around, searching for some kind of small tool. How long could Joaquin distract McCoy? Fifteen minutes max, less if the shakes worsened. No need for them to dig if the detector found no sign of iridium buried nearby. McCoy would soon tire of the hunt and head back.

"What are you going to do?" Luz spread her hands on her hips.

"I need to throw this gizmo off, preferably without McCoy realizing it's been tampered with." I kept scanning the tent, but when my eyes came back to Luz, the girl's mouth had twisted.

"Hey, I'm allowed to do this, Luz." I flashed a rictus smile. "Remember, I designed it."

Back to my frantic search. McCoy must have machine repair tools somewhere. I knew that he kept a small gadget containing multiple flip-outs; that might be all he needed for minor adjustments to the meter. Unfortunately, that gadget must be parked in his pocket. I stomped my boot in frustration, then felt the blade of cold steel wiggle behind my ankle. I stood, mesmerized.

"What is it?" said Luz.

I dug inside and extracted Efrain's knife. Not the perfect instrument, but I needed to act now.

I checked Luz. The girl drew back, fearful.

I glowered. "Don't be a wimp. We talked this through long ago. It's the only answer and you know it."

"Are you sure? Russell will take this the wrong way…"

"Shut up with 'Russell.' He's sweet-talked you into believing he's Mr. Nice Guy. Don't you remember that lecher I described when we were stranded up on the mountain, the one who had his way with me again and again. It's the same guy, honey." I tilted my head to search Luz's face. Was she even listening, or had McCoy's attentions brainwashed her?

No response; the girl lowered her head and sulked.

My voice rose. "Luz, I need your help. Stand guard outside the tent."

The girl said nothing and turned away.

"Oh, hell." I took a deep breath and razored my lips. One thing I knew: unlike Luz, McCoy would not just sit by and let me demolish the instrument. He had spent too much time perfecting it. Despite my bragging to Luz, I could no longer claim exclusive rights to destroy it, if ever such a right existed.

I picked up the meter and weighed it in my hands. A novice might take it outside and try smashing it on rocks, but I had designed the shell of sturdy Cro-Moly steel to withstand the hardest beating. My only chance to disable it was to rip it open and remove the guts.

Using the knife's hard steel tip, I worked to pry off the thick glass faceplate. A good foot square, the glass was attached by a dozen small titanium screws, way too securely for easy dismantling. I recalled that my original design included only four screws, for ease of internal repairs. McCoy insisted on a dozen: more protection if you dropped and lost some out in the field, and so much the harder for unauthorized access. Like now.

Yet a dozen small screws were no match for the leverage exerted by the tip of Efrain's hefty hunting knife. Mindful of the next tremor, I knelt and wedged the box between my knees. After five minutes of frenzied stabbing and twisting, a snapping sound signaled the top edge of the faceplate giving way.

Breathing hard, I paused to gauge Luz. No longer sulking, the girl sat on a stool across the tent, her face half buried in her hands. I picked up my ears. From some distance away came the sound of McCoy's voice. My pulse quickened. Might he and Joaquin be returning already?

I ran over to stick my head outside the door flap. No sight of them yet through the trees, but now I could hear

Joaquin's softer voice as well. From his tones, it sounded like he might be offering an apology.

I rushed back in and grabbed the meter. Standing with one foot on top to steady it, I forced the tip of the blade through the loosened edge of the faceplate, as far as I could push it. With all the strength I could muster, I wrenched the hilt of the knife forward. A loud snap ensued as the entire glass panel cracked into pieces. It felt like the chains binding my own body had just burst apart.

In the next instant, another quake, the biggest one yet, knocked the box out of my grasp, as I fell on my face.

I scurried over to inspect the remains. Now its guts were indeed vulnerable. I held the meter up to eye level, the better to see what to grab, but the innards were as black as the metal alloy housing. The tent was too dark inside to make out small objects. I needed a torch, now. McCoy and Joaquin were fast approaching.

I heard McCoy console the boy. "All these tremors must be distracting. Plus, that severe storm yesterday, it's no wonder you lost your bearings, young man. My detector barely picked up Luz's much larger cache yesterday. Maybe we'll scout for yours again after sorting what we've got already."

How to get more light. I dared not take the meter outside. I turned once more to Luz, still seated, slumped forward. "Honey, please. We've got less than a minute."

Luz raised her face, now blissfully blank.

"Just stand by the tent door and hold the flap open." I used the knife to point toward the entryway.

The girl took a deep breath and finally rose to obey. With the flap pulled aside, a beam of bright sunlight pierced the dim interior of the tent. I held up the meter once more. Now I could discern all the components, the dials and diodes, the chips and wires, the battery and light display.

I lunged my hand inside, grabbed as much as I could with my small fist, and yanked with all my might. Snapping sounds as a few connections gave way, but the guts remained intact. The side of my pointer finger was bleeding as I pulled my hand out. "Shit!"

I clutched the knife, stabbing and twisting the weapon inside. This time, the tip had enough purchase so that the blade itself could cut instead of just prying.

Another shake muffled McCoy's approach. I didn't hear him until he was inside the tent. His voice boomed. "What? Are you crazy? Put that down. Now!"

He dove toward me. I jerked away from him, shielding the meter with my body, using my right hand to twist the knife ever deeper. I had to make sure it would Never. Work. Again.

From behind, he seized my left arm and yanked it away from my body. With the meter now visible, he gripped its sides with both hands and pulled. The knife, still in my clench grip, dislodged free from the box's innards.

If the guts were still in one piece, he might be able to repair them. No! No! No! My knife slashed forward, erratic strokes aimed at my foe's hands, trying to loosen his grip.

"Ayee." He wailed and dropped the box, slapping the gash in his left wrist, squirting blood. He gaped at the limb, wild-eyed. I froze.

McCoy shot me the same berserk stare and lunged. I clenched the knife with both hands at waist height and pointed it at him. His right arm clamped onto my shoulder just as the knife pierced his abdomen. His weight pushed me down as he collapsed. I almost tried to spin away, but that meant releasing my grip on the knife. No! The blade had found its targets, both of them. The machine was mortally wounded. Let the only person who might be able to fix it meet the same fate.

Another mega-tremor, the most violent yet, sent the two of us, still entwined, to our knees. Ore samples bounced in every direction, like so many billiard balls.

McCoy's black dialups dropped off his nose. His features contorted in a spasm of pain. "Keltyn," he gasped. "Why?" He made a last, futile reach for the hilt of the weapon sucking the life out of him.

I gave the blade one last twist and yanked it out. Blood gushed from the gaping wound, a dark stain oozing across McCoy's khaki tunic. He tried to clutch the hole, even as his face turned a pale gray. His eyes, barely able to focus, still beseeched mine for an answer.

"I had no choice," I spat out. McCoy's body teetered toward me. I barely managed to scoot aside as he plunged forward, face first.

Still clutching the hilt with both hands, I stared at the bloody blade. I began to shake violently. I wanted to drop it, jump up and run away, but knew I could not. I had used this terrible weapon, not just to take a man's life, but to destroy the object — perfect in form but flawed in purpose — that he and I had jointly created. I must bear witness to the deed.

From the moment Joaquin informed me of McCoy's presence on this mission, I knew he must have brought a meter, and, just as surely, knew I would have to find it and destroy it. Nothing less than the future of the Onwei people was at stake. It was the worst of fortune that McCoy caught me in the act, but what was done was done, and I felt nothing but relief at the sight of his inert body lying on the ground.

I looked up at my friends and co-witnesses. Luz stood frozen, both hands over her mouth, eyes once again widened by fear. Joaquin, his face a blank mask and his arms locked like a strait jacket across his chest, remained, motionless, at the door of the tent. No one so much as blinked. No sound except for the terminal gasps of a dying man. Even the tremors had ceased, as if McCoy's death had accomplished their intended purpose.

Flies broke the silence, drawn by the blood. Heat from the midday sun beat down upon the tent, diffusing the suffocating stench of death. Bodies both alive and dying felt the chilled pall of mortality creep in. The chill froze each of us in place, waiting for the curtain to fall.

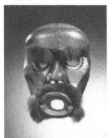

23

SHOCK AND AWE

Luz's world lay shattered at her feet. This man, whom she had just begun to consider a mentor, dead. This woman, who had saved her life last year, a killer.

The overpowering stench of blood and guts appalled her, and her first instinct was to flee the scene. Yet, of the two sane people left in the tent, she was the more responsible. The next move must fall to her.

She stepped toward Keltyn, slowly and carefully so as not to spook her. Her shaken friend still knelt, clutching the hilt of the bloody knife with both hands. Her face was contorted by a mix of rage and anguish. Who knew what her next frightful move might be? Clearly, the weapon in her hand had to go.

Trying not to draw her attention, Luz gestured to summon Joaquin, still locked in a trance by the door of the tent. She tilted her head in Keltyn's direction. He needed to approach stealthily from behind, and together they would try to disarm her. Though both Luz and Joaquin were larger than Keltyn, their superior numbers and size could not match the eight-inch length of crimson-stained steel still firmly in her grip.

"Keltyn." Luz patted the air. "Drop the knife. Please. It's over."

The Brixa glanced down at the weapon in her hands, then up into Luz's face and on to Joaquin's. Only when her fierce gaze returned to the knife did she seem to grasp the enormity of what she had done. Her fists sprung open, and the blade fell to the ground. She held both bloodstained hands in front of her face and shook her head slowly, back and forth, unbelieving.

Luz dropped to her knees in front of Keltyn and grasped her in a bear hug. She caught Joaquin's eye and motioned with her head for him to remove the weapon.

Encircled by Luz's arms, Keltyn began sobbing.

Luz felt awkward. Her friend had never unburdened herself like this before. When Luz lay paralyzed last year and her mare dying, the tables were turned. Then it was Keltyn comforting her. Now, the circumstances were just as dire.

Joaquin squatted beside them. "What are we going to do?"

"I don't know." Luz brushed away a fly trying to settle on Keltyn's bloodstained elbow.

Her mind spun as she tried to think of a story to explain what had happened, something plausible, something that would get Keltyn off the hook. The only idea she could think of was to claim that Russell attacked her, or Keltyn, or even Joaquin. Keltyn used the only weapon available to deter him, and things got out of hand.

But how dumb would it be for Russell to try attacking one of them when two friends stood nearby, even if he was a sex fiend like Keltyn claimed? She found Keltyn's lurid story increasingly hard to believe. Russell had behaved toward Luz like a *cavalero*, a gentleman. From him, she learned more about the study of rocks in four days than she had from Keltyn in a year and a half.

What a waste. It was bad enough that Keltyn killed this generous, nurturing teacher, but it was no less awful to destroy this miraculous machine that could read the composition of each stone. Why could Keltyn not just have run off and hidden it in the woods? Luz would have even helped her escape, set her on the way back to the gaucho camp with her precious meter. Ysidro would be angry that his greedy deal might come to naught, but could that be half as bad as this?

Luz drew her head back to search Keltyn's face. Her friend still sobbed, but quieter now. The convulsions that rocked her pint-sized body had ceased.

"We need to get you cleaned up and then back to our camp. You okay with that?"

Keltyn nodded with her eyes closed. She seemed pale now, about to faint. No way was she going to be able to make the half-mile trek on foot.

Luz turned to Joaquin. "You'll have to fetch the horses from camp."

The boy frowned. "But, the footing's bad enough already, and with these tremors…"

She listened. The shakes had ceased, as soon as McCoy had fallen dead. She shook her head slowly. "The mountain seems to have settled. Anyway, your pony can make it. He's very nimble. Her mare will make it too, if you lead her."

"But can the mare carry the both of you back?"

"I'll walk and lead the mare if need be. Now go. And don't say anything about what happened. Just that Keltyn has sprained her ankle." She waved him off.

Luz led Keltyn over to sit on a stool. Her friend slumped forward, clutching her arms, her body rocking, biting her lower lip. She stole a cringing peek at the now-still corpse.

Luz found a blanket, but it was not long enough to cover the length of Russell's body, only the head and torso. She searched his pack for a cloth, moistened it, and painstakingly washed the congealed blood from Keltyn's hands. There was no way to remove the bloodstains from her clothes, but why bother?

She put one hand behind her friend's head and began cleaning her puffy, blood-spattered face. Her eyes remained shut.

Enough! Luz slapped her. "Look at me."

The Brixa opened one eye, rimmed with tears.

"What are you going to tell them?" Luz demanded.

A whispered mumble. "Dunno." Her eyes remained half closed and inert, even as Luz used a vigorous scrubbing motion on her facial skin.

After several minutes of this futility, Luz unfurled the bloodstained cloth and snapped at a fly, then flung it aside and huffed. She and Joaquin might arrange a plan, but if the Brixa did not have enough fight left to even contemplate her escape, all of Luz's pep talk would be pointless. Somehow, she needed to rekindle the spirit of the woman whose valiant efforts had saved her own life.

***

It was an hour before Joaquin returned with his pony and Keltyn's mare. He found Luz with her arm around Keltyn, sitting side by side on folding stools outside the tent.

"It took you long enough," spat Luz. She seemed glum.

"Yo. Buck, the pilot, knows first aid. Wanted to come along to examine the Brixa himself, bring wrappings and such. Claimed he could ride your stallion, grew up on a ranch and all that." Joaquin grinned. "Was all I could do to promise we'd be careful with Keltyn, bring her right back."

"Did anyone ask about Russell?"

"Not really. Just how his sorting is coming. I got the feeling Ysidro and Buck are keen to wrap things up here in next day or so, fly everyone to the big feast."

"Feast?"

"Oh, forgot to tell you," said Joaquin. "Those two are thick as thieves now. Ysidro is so happy with all the gifts the Sky-Bornes brought, he invited 'em to party at the gaucho camp, to seal the deal."

Luz nodded toward the body in the tent. "So much the harder when they find out about this."

Joaquin cleared his throat. "Listen, Luz. I got a plan. I threw some snacks and water and blankets in my pack. I can guide the Brixa back to the gaucho camp directly from here. She'll be safe from the Sky-Bornes there. You can explain what happened to Ysidro, and I'm sure he'll disinvite them. They don't have no horses, won't be able to track her down."

The plan came to him as he walked the horses back through the rocky underbrush and gave him the bracing rush of an upcoming adventure. They would have to do some bushwhacking in order to bypass the Sky-Borne camp, and they would have to hole up somewhere overnight, probably at the start of that arid plateau. This time, they could head across it early in the morning and beat the worst of the heat.

He expected Keltyn to still be exhausted, but no matter. All she had to do was ride her horse. Joaquin would take care of the rest. He took for granted that Luz would approve and support his bold plan, that she, too, wanted to shelter and protect the Brixa in her time of trial. He looked to Luz for confirmation.

Instead, she shook her head vehemently.

He scowled at her. "What's wrong? Why not?" Probably nixing his idea just to show him who was boss. "You got a better plan?"

"I already thought of this same scheme, but it has a fatal flaw." Luz frowned as she nodded at Keltyn. "Your lady in distress here doesn't wish to be rescued."

Both Joaquin and Luz stared at the Brixa, but all she could do was shake her slumped head slowly.

Luz nudged her. "Honey, do you understand? Joaquin and I are both sure you could get out of here safely. All you have to do is sit on your horse. We'll help you get on, and Joaquin will lead you the whole way, right?" She stole a glance at him.

"Right." Joaquin nodded. "I will take good care of you, Brixa."

Keltyn gave a wan smile at her nickname. "Thanks, guys, but it's no use." She swallowed hard. "I've got to face the music. Just lead me back to the Sky-Borne camp."

Joaquin scowled. Even if she were smart enough to keep her mouth shut, as soon as they found McCoy's body, they would take her prisoner for sure. When Ganz stumbled back here later, it would be all over. Joaquin needed to level with Ysidro as soon as they got back — assuming the jeaf wasn't too drunk to pay attention — and hope that he would step in to protect the stubborn Brixa. If the Sky-Bornes wanted access to the piedra de yris, they knew he was the key.

Then it dawned on Joaquin. "What about the ore samples sorted out in the tent? Are we just gonna let those guys keep 'em? You and I was the ones who salvaged 'em, Luz."

She considered that and checked Keltyn, whose blank expression gave no clue. "You're right, Joaquin. Russell's death is going to put a damper on the whole trade deal. What do we do?" She gazed at the pile of gleaming stones piled up in front of the tent.

"I'll tell you what we do. We bury the whole pile somewhere else nearby. Bury that other meter too, so they can't find the stash anymore."

"We'll need to move fast," said Luz. "They're going to smell something fishy if we don't get Keltyn back soon. They'll think we need help moving her and send someone else."

"Guess I better head back with her then," said Joaquin.

"And leave me here with the shovel," Luz said with a pout.

"Love to help if it wasn't for this darn gimpy hand." Joaquin held up his floppy wrist.

"I'll bet."

***

Ganz consulted his watch. It was two in the afternoon. No word from McCoy. Nothing alarming there; the guy spends the prime years of his career mapping the whereabouts of an elusive but valuable mineral, and all of a sudden, he unearths the biggest pile ever found. It was like those old tales of pirates digging up buried treasure. McCoy had every right to gloat.

What bothered Ganz was their exit strategy, or lack thereof. Seir Big Jeaf insisted they fly Bailey Voyager to the gaucho camp and feast with the tribe to prove they were all buddies.

The more he thought about it, the worse this plan smelled. It might be a trap. More likely, it was an invitation to chaos. The crew would be lucky to get out in one piece.

Ganz shared his reservations with Harry, but the chief seemed blithely serene about their prospects. "I would much rather be on Ysidro's good side, Ganz. We experienced the ugly side last year. Believe me, you don't want to go there."

"Whatever," muttered Ganz. He would not burden Harry with all the petty phobias that bothered him about this new plan. He had a vivid picture of those dust-caked vulgar gauchos climbing all over Bailey Voyager. He had already been treated to the revolting spectacle of Buck and Ysidro turning into bosom buddies, *mano a mano.* Buck even let the jeaf take a turn in the pilot seat. How about that for a breach of protocol?

The more pressing problem was how to deal with SparrowHawk, if she resisted his overtures to return of her own volition. That was supposed to be Harry's call, but the chief displayed a surprising degree of apathy about the whole business, as if problems were supposed to fix themselves. The way Ganz heard the story, that attitude had almost gotten the crew massacred by Ysidro's gang last time. Far safer to anticipate problems and have an action plan ready.

Ganz had an action plan. He patted the pocket of his breeches. The reassuring hard lump was still there. Buck Kranepool was not the only one with a gun. Buck's gun, however, aimed only to paralyze a foe temporarily. Ganz's gun was equally small, but it was designed for lethal effect.

The whole idea of stepping unarmed into danger, meeting savages on the other side of the world, appalled him. Yet here he was. Still, the weapon was only there for peace of mind or, God forbid, as a last resort.

The clip-clop of slow hoof beats roused him. The mounted figures of Joaquin and Keltyn rode somberly into camp. Ganz expected Keltyn's foot to be wrapped up, yet she had both boots on. Her face told the story, incredibly drawn, though not from physical pain. Something had happened, something much worse than a sprained ankle.

Then he noticed the bloodstains on her tunic. He jumped up, but felt dizzy immediately and had to ease himself back down. A sinking feeling pervaded him, a sudden awareness that, for this turn of events, his action plan needed drastic revision.

24

PLAIN SIGHT

Sensing the peril ahead, I tried to sit up straighter in the saddle as Joaquin and I approached camp. My gut told me the danger now was higher than the risk from attacking Russell McCoy's meter. Yet the hazard of doing nothing superseded all. My only hope was to own up to my deed and cast my plight upon whatever fate might await me in Canada. I could not live the rest of my life as an outlaw.

I stopped in the middle of camp and dismounted. Four men might now judge me. I watched the expressions of each.

Ysidro sat on the ground, propped up by a tree trunk. He seemed altogether too mellow, likely still inebriated. Forget him. He was of no help in this state, and even less if sober. I should never have confided in him.

Buck crouched close by Ysidro, his wary eyes taking in my sorry appearance. He knew.

The stunned expression on Ganz's face meant that he, too, suspected something awful. He seemed focused on my clothing. I glanced at my tunic and, for the first time, realized what a sight I must appear.

Harry was the only sober one who did not appear shocked. The chief's manner revealed nothing. He arose and approached with the saddest face I had ever seen on him. He reached out to me, but doing so seemed to pain him.

I let myself be enfolded. If I held any more tears, this would be a safe place to shed them, but I had done all my crying earlier, in Luz's arms. Now I was ready to get on with business, to enter one last and crucial negotiation.

Harry whispered in my ear, "It's Russell McCoy, isn't it, ma chère?"

I nodded.

"Is he still alive?"

"No," I whispered back.

"You must tell the others." He stepped back.

I studied the three of them: Ysidro, sitting up straighter now, but his eyes still glazed; Buck, standing with front leg partly bent, back one straight, as if frozen in motion, like a statue; Ganz, ramrod stiff at attention, his formal posture signaling a silent rebuke.

"I killed Russell McCoy," I said. It came out easier than I expected. Once you owned a truth — or a lie, I supposed — it was not that hard to assert it, no matter the implications of it being known.

Buck's mouth dropped open, but he remained uncharacteristically speechless. Ysidro's gaze jumped from face to face. He could tell something was up, but, perhaps not trusting his earpad, summoned Joaquin to explain.

Ganz seemed unfazed, his expression neither angered nor sympathetic. "I take it this had something to do with the stones," he said.

"Yes, it did," I said, holding myself erect in front of him. "With his assay meter, as a matter of fact."

Ganz held his chin up, awaiting the rest of the story.

I plunged on. "I felt I needed to disable the meter. I had no tools available with which to pry it open, other than a hunting knife. He found me in the act, tried to stop me and I...I stabbed him." Even that admission vented with but a second's hesitation.

"You phrase it as some kind of accident, but it sounds to me like premeditation." Ganz's haughty demeanor bordered on mocking.

"I intended to complete the task of destroying the meter while Savant McCoy was absent. His early return forced the issue."

"Hmph." Ganz watched Harry, waiting, I supposed, for some kind of assent from the chief to take me into custody.

I stepped forward. "I fully understand the ramifications of my actions. I am prepared to surrender myself to your authority." I held out both wrists.

Harry and Ganz glanced at each other. "Handcuffs won't be necessary, Keltyn," said Harry. "Perhaps we can just hobble your horse. Buck, you have some experience with that sort of thing."

Buck snapped straight. "Sure. No problem." He made to lead my mare away.

"Wait. Hang on a minute, Buck." Harry turned to Joaquin. "Where is Luz?"

"Uh, still back with the body of Seir McCoy."

"Well, we better go fetch the corpse, hadn't we? Buck, how about you take charge of that operation?"

"Right." Buck caught Joaquin's eye. "Can you guide me there, son?"

"Of course, seir," said Joaquin.

I sat on the ground cross-legged, relieved to have freedom of movement, at least for the time being. I watched Joaquin and Buck saddle up Luz's stallion and head off, leading my own mount. Tinto, the well-bred mare from Campbell Stables, had served me well.

Would I ever ride a horse again? The wisp of a tear clouded my vision at the prospect of being separated, perhaps forever, from Tinto. And what about Efrain? I couldn't bear to think of that, not now. I bowed my head and drew the back of my hand across my eyes.

Ganz pulled Harry aside and murmured some kind of plea. He pointed to the plane. I had a pretty good idea of what he was demanding, and it was a big reason I had willingly given myself up. Harry shook his head. When Ganz showed no sign of dropping it, Harry abruptly turned away and wandered off toward his tent.

Ganz grimaced, then marched over and squatted down in front of me, balancing lithely on the balls of both feet. "I know what game you are up to, Savant SparrowHawk, but it won't work."

I forced myself not to smile. Mustn't give him the impression that what I did was cold-blooded. "What game is that?"

"You know perfectly well. You planned this whole thing, from the time you found out that Russell McCoy was here and had brought another one of those lovely meters. You couldn't stand the prospect of someone else, even your trusted mentor, completing the assays and upstaging your importance to this enterprise."

"Hmm," I said. "Interesting theory. You think I killed him out of jealousy."

"Sure. That, and he got in the way of your attempted sabotage. Funny, isn't it?"

"What is?"

"Sabotage. That is exactly the conclusion Sir Oscar drew, when Harry described how you tried to make everyone believe the stone was radioactive last year. You discovered what you imagined was some grandiose plan to ferry Canadian farmers to Antarctica on transport ships and figured you could nix the whole scheme at step one." He paused. "Go ahead. Deny it."

"I don't deny it." I withered under his eagle gaze and turned away.

"Well, I've got news for you, young lady. We're going to take the best stones back with us, rich enough in iridium to coat at least one transport ship."

I shook my head quickly, like a shiver that left me cold.

"You don't think so? Wait and see." Ganz stood, spun on his heel and sauntered away.

I grabbed my arms, rocking back and forth. He must have pitched to Harry that I would need to be the odd person out if they needed more space. Harry would stick up for me if it came to that, but Ganz had no intention to leave me be. Why?

Then it struck me. It was Oscar's doing. Ganz was under orders. Bring me back alive or get rid of me.

I shivered again. Harry must not be privy to this secret deal between Oscar and Ganz, or Ganz wouldn't be trying to convince him now.

My heart skipped a beat. Did Ganz have a weapon? How else could he act so cocksure?

He would need a pretext to shoot me. Harry, Ysidro, Joaquin, Luz, not even Buck, much as he liked to taunt me, none of them would stand by for an execution, even if Ganz was bold enough to attempt it. He seemed plenty ruthless, and his bravado suggested deep-rooted insecurity. A potentially lethal combination.

I hugged my knees. How could I possibly monitor Ganz's every movement? Harry was still here, thank God. Soon Luz, Joaquin and Buck would return. Ganz might be armed, but everyone else would also suspect his motivations. For now, I just needed to stay put.

***

Ganz clambered to his feet as soon as he heard the horses nearing, as did Harry and even lethargic Ysidro. The only one to stay put was stoic Savant SparrowHawk, still sitting on the ground, pathetically curled up like an insignificant little ball.

To hell with her. He would deal with her later.

Joaquin led the party of three, four if you counted the corpse. Buck had him stuffed in a sleeping bag. Ganz had already decided there was no way he would again sleep in the tent that he and McCoy had shared. Now, with the body wrapped so snugly that no one need see the dead man's face, Ganz had another idea. He watched as Buck hefted the bundle off the horse and laid it on the ground.

"What now, chief?" Buck asked Harry.

Harry sighed. "We need to get McCoy's body back home before it putrefies."

"Right," said Buck. "That means leaving tomorrow morning at the latest. I'd say leave now, but after today's party" — he took in Ysidro, slumped against a tree nearby — "I'm gonna need some shuteye."

Ganz couldn't believe his ears. "Wait a minute, all of you. Don't tell me we're going home without the stones, just on account of a corpse. Sir Oscar is not going to be very happy when he hears that we found a big cache of iridium — enough to coat a bunch of transport ships — and decided to leave it all behind." He checked for a reaction, but the blank faces greeting him said more than words ever could; to them, he was barking up the wrong tree.

He felt his face redden, finally sputtering, "This is all going to be thoroughly documented, Harry."

The chief checked his watch and smiled. "You've still got three hours of daylight, Ganz."

"Oh, I get it. If I want the stones so bad, I can carry them back myself."

"Buck needs to stay and help me with the body. I need to take pictures of the stab wound for evidence. Did you collect the weapon, Buck?"

"All wrapped up as I found it, chief."

"Good. I'll need a formal statement from Keltyn, and Luz's witness account as well." Harry signaled Buck to unzip the sleeping bag.

Ganz moved away from the scene. He had no desire to glimpse the bloody corpse. He felt tricked, outmaneuvered. The only way to set things right was to gather enough iridium to prove the trip a success. Now, among all this chaos, he had only a few hours of daylight to do a job for which he had absolutely no background, nor training, nor, truth be told, any interest. Nor did he have the one tool that his learned colleague relied upon to separate the wheat from the chaff. It was smashed to smithereens, thanks to the wretched little figure that sat curled up in a ball like a wounded waif.

His eyes fixed on the boy. "You. Joaquin. You're going to lead me there."

***

Joaquin had not dismounted since leading Buck and Luz back around the bottom of the steep slope bordering the edge of the woods.

Now this irritable man Ganz demanded to be led to the piedra de yris, no doubt to plunder it. Joaquin knew that sabotaging this task would be risky, but he needed to try, if for no other reason than to knock this scoundrel off his perch.

If someone wondered whether deceit came easily to him, Joaquin could not have denied the charge. He was getting plenty of practice lately.

He gathered Luz's mount, to carry however much of the ore Ganz could find, then watched the man awkwardly hoist himself into the saddle of Keltyn's mare. Like Harry, gold-rimmed vision aids adorned his face, but unlike Harry, they made Ganz look like a bird of prey.

Last year, Harry had tried gamely to observe Aldo stitch the wound of a horse gored by a bull, only to be sickened by the sight of blood and gore. Ganz appeared even more out of his depth now than Harry had been.

Not bothering to check with Joaquin, Ganz thrust his chin forward. "Let's go!"

Another bossy type. Joaquin scrunched his nose. He was getting sick of them. He set off at a measured pace, trailing the stallion behind him. This would be his sixth trip from the main camp to where he and Luz had buried the stones, and he had a pretty good idea of how fast he could safely lead the mounts.

The deliberate pace did not seem to satisfy Ganz. "Come on, boy. Speed it up. I made the trip faster this morning, on foot."

"Not wise to push the horses on this steep rocky ground, seir."

"Let's see about that." Ganz dug his heels into Tinto's flanks. The mare lurched forward. Her hooves clattered on the rock face and she stumbled, almost losing her balance. Ganz yanked the reins, frightening the mare more. She began bucking her front quarters back and forth.

"Dammit," Ganz fumed, pulling wildly from side to side.

Joaquin jumped off his pony and hurried over to grab Tinto's bridle. Slowly she calmed as he stroked her cheek.

He spoke not a word as he remounted Cisco. To his relief, neither did Ganz, suddenly contrite. For the next fifteen minutes they walked the horses in silence until reaching the site.

Ganz slid off to appraise the small nest of stones piled beside the door of the tent. He stuck his head inside but for a moment. His long face livid, he demanded, "Where are the rest of them?"

"The stones? I don't know, seir." Joaquin anticipated this moment and knew he needed to keep a straight face.

"Liar," barked Ganz. "Someone hid them. Recently. You can't fool me, boy. I was here yesterday, sweating bullets with the rest of the crew. We dug up a huge stash. You and your pal Luz buried it so well that you couldn't locate it after a big storm. That's the only reason she allowed McCoy to use his finder." He swung around, poking beside and underneath the edges of the tent. "Where is that shovel?"

Joaquin feigned to join in the search, fervently hoping Luz had left no trace of her handiwork. He started up the wash, peering here and there. Out of the corner of his eye, he saw that Ganz was still preoccupied with hunting for the tool near the tent, pushing aside brush in his quest. Joaquin hurried on. The shovel lay in plain sight a bit farther on. Luz must have panicked when he and Buck drew near. Now Joaquin retrieved it and brought it to Ganz.

"Ah, she dropped it up there," said Ganz. "All right. Let's take it back where you found it and you can start digging."

"I...I'm no good at that sort of thing," said Joaquin, holding up his bum paw.

"Crap," huffed Ganz. He rolled up his sleeves and grabbed the shovel from Joaquin's hand. "Let's get one thing straight, boy. You may not have re-buried the rest of the stones yourself, but you know where they are." He nodded for emphasis.

"I really don't, sir. Luz must have found a spot while I went to fetch the horses."

"How convenient. You know damn well we don't have enough daylight left to bring her back here."

Joaquin tried to keep mum, expressionless. The odds seemed to have shifted in his favor. Yet some hint of self-satisfaction must have shown on his face, because the next thing he knew, Ganz drew a weapon out of his pocket. Joaquin gaped at the sight. Just like that, the odds shifted back.

The gun was almost the same shape and size as Buck's stun gun. Ganz held the weapon awkwardly, twisting it around in his hand.

"Uh-huh," smirked Ganz. "A jolt of recollection kicking in, is it? That's good, because we don't have time for near misses. Now lead the way to where you found the shovel. It had better be the right spot."

Joaquin trudged on. Every few seconds, he turned back to see if Ganz still brandished the weapon. He would have to put it away when he started digging. Then what? Joaquin could never outrun him, and they were too far away from the horses to attempt an escape.

Would Ganz really use the gun if he was unable to locate Luz's new cache? Somehow, Joaquin needed to take advantage of the fading afternoon light and stall a bit longer. Then Ganz would have to be satisfied with the lesser stones left in and around the tent.

Intentionally passing the spot where he found the shovel a few moments before, he tried to lure Ganz off the scent.

No such luck. "Whoa, whoa. What have we here?" The man stuffed the handgun back in his pocket, knelt down at the side of the wash, and patted the soil. "It's been tamped down. Feels soft. Your Luz must have been in a hurry." He jumped up, grabbed the shovel with both hands, and began a staccato sequence of spading, spooning and heaving the soft dirt.

Sure enough, within moments came the clang sound of metal striking rock. Ganz tossed the shovel aside and knelt once again, pushing his hands apart to spread the earth. He stopped abruptly, then slowly, reverently, lifted a good-sized rock out of the hole. As Ganz brushed it off and held it up to the light, Joaquin's heart dropped.

Ganz turned to him with an icy smile. "This is the good stuff, isn't it?"

Joaquin shrugged.

"No, you needn't say a word. It's crystal clear what happened. Your Luz was helping McCoy since early this morning. She saw which stones showed the highest purity, and I'm guessing McCoy had assayed most of this stash by the time Savant SparrowHawk showed up. After McCoy's murder, Luz rushed to bury the purest ones, leaving the junk to try and decoy whoever came back later. Who's to say that she, or you for that matter, weren't all in on this together?" Ganz raised his eyebrows, waiting, supposed Joaquin, to be congratulated on his brilliant deductions.

Best to say nothing, kick this ogre in the groin, grab his gun while he was down, and shoot him. But that desperate impulse faded as quickly as it arose.

"Be a good boy now," said Ganz. "Go fetch the big horse. You're going to help me load."

In short order, they filled both the stallion's saddle packs and the extra loose tie-on sacks they had brought along. Ganz ducked into the tent and returned with his sleeping bag. He unzipped it halfway and held it open.

"Your turn," he said. "Stuff the rest of them in here, and no funny business."

Joaquin did as he was told, gimpy hand and all. The remaining rocks filled the sleeping bag to its open mouth.

Ganz staggered under its weight. "C'mon, boy. Grab that end. On three. One, two, threeee."

With a mighty heave, the two of them managed to deposit the fortune's worth of piedra de yris stone onto the stallion's flank. The horse barely sidestepped to catch its footing, but otherwise registered no complaint.

Ganz pulled a kerchief out of his pocket and wiped his brow. He led the loaded mount back toward the tent, found his water pouch, and took a long, hard swallow. One last look inside the tent, as he pulled his few remaining personal possessions. "If we must depart at first light, that means leaving this tent behind. Another one for you, boy." He rubbed his thumb across his fingers. "Should be worth something in trade."

Watching the man sneer, Joaquin felt his own blood boil. He took aim and spat at his self-righteous mug.

Ganz used his left hand to wipe spittle off his cheek. With the back of the same hand, and with the other still aiming the gun, he thrashed Joaquin across the face, sending him sprawling.

He stumbled to his knees and checked his nose. A few drops of blood. He glared at Ganz.

"I could shoot you right here, you little rat, and easily claim self-defense. Now move."

They headed off, single file. This time Ganz, seemingly energized by his find and by having fended off Joaquin's pathetic attack, whistled a squeaky tune and took charge of trailing the overloaded stallion.

Joaquin slumped in the saddle, every few minutes wiping blood from his nose. He had failed at every turn. Yet as they plodded back to camp, he slowly took heart.

He knew the Brixa and Ganz's crewmates all despised the man. Even if Ganz was blind to the obvious truth, Joaquin knew there was no way the Sky-Bornes could load this huge stash of ore onto their flying machine, not with a corpse and a fifth passenger to boot.

By the time Harry and Buck set him straight, Ganz would have but one more option. It would involve that itty-bitty gun and he, Joaquin, would be in a unique position to thwart it.

***

With the fading light and the overburdened stallion, the footing was even iffier on the way back. Ganz no longer felt the need to hurry and allowed the boy to lead as slowly as he wished.

By the time they returned, the campfire was alight, and Ysidro knelt over the coals, turning a couple of carcasses on a spit. Drops of grease hissed into the fire every few seconds. He must have sobered up long enough to bag some small game.

Harry and Buck came to inspect the haul as Ganz slid off his mount. Buck gave an admiring whistle as he untied the sleeping bag. He tried to pull it down by himself, then grunted and stopped abruptly. "You've got to be kidding."

Ganz took the comment as admiration, but Buck's pained expression said otherwise. The pilot patted down the great horse's overstuffed saddlebags and turned around. "No way we can fit all this on board. The ship won't lift off."

He glowered. "What are you talking about? We'll make room."

"It's not the space, Ganz, it's the weight," explained Buck, in that same patient monotone that Ganz himself would use to explain a basic legal or finance concept to someone who didn't get it. "You've got probably three hundred pounds here. Like having another couple of passengers, and we're already returning with one more than we came with."

Harry stepped in. "Surely we can accommodate a portion."

Buck's lower lip stuck out as he calculated. "Half. Max."

Ganz patiently raised his finger "There is another option, gentlemen." The fire-lit profiles of Harry and Buck watched him. He pointed to the other sleeping bag, the stiff bundle lying on the ground, and addressed the mission chief. "McCoy. We can bury him right here."

The two men took each other's measure. "I don't think so," said Harry.

"Why not?" Ganz searched for SparrowHawk. She was some distance away, a dark passive ball, hands clasped around her knees, sitting on the same spot of open ground she had staked out for herself hours ago.

Ganz addressed her. "Does Savant McCoy even have any family?"

She shook her head.

"There. You see," said Ganz. He felt himself heating up. "If Sir Oscar wants to have a memorial service for Russell McCoy, fine. What's the point of having a mangled, stinking corpse to prove your point?"

Harry stared at him. "I can't believe my ears, Ganz. You don't just abandon a body, not if you have a choice."

Ganz thumbed toward SparrowHawk. "You abandoned her last year, and she was still alive."

"I lost a lot of sleep over that decision, let me tell you," said Harry. "We didn't find out until the other night that she had come through her ordeal intact." He paused. "I'm sorry, Ganz. We're taking the body back, first thing tomorrow."

Damn. All that guile and sweat to retrieve the best ore samples. He had surely hauled enough to provide the coating on a full-sized transport ship, and now they wouldn't let him load but half of it. Sir Oscar would side with him to bury McCoy here, but Sir Oscar was not around.

Wordlessly, Ganz helped Buck unload the stallion, then went and splashed some water on his face. Suddenly, it came to him. There was yet a final option.

He turned back to eye the small inert form of Keltyn SparrowHawk, still sitting hunched forward in the gathering darkness. No way she could perch there all night, and when she moved, he would be ready. The key was to make it look like she was trying to escape justice.

She had made her new home here in Antarctica. There would be absolutely no reason to return her corpse to Canada.

***

Joaquin removed the saddles and poured out water for the three horses. As they foraged on scattered clumps of grass nearby, he leaned on a tree and tried to anticipate Ganz's next move. Thanks to his own earpad, it was clear the man was unhappy with being barred from loading the entire great stash he had plundered. His body language — shoulders hunched, jerky head movements, wandering gaze — all betrayed desperation.

Joaquin's pulse amped up. From the awkward way Ganz brandished that little gun before, he clearly had little, if any, practice in using it. Good chance he packed it unbeknownst to Harry and Buck, just for whatever measure of protection he hoped it might gain him. If Ganz had any ideas about forcing Buck and Harry to load all the stones, he would have already done so. Likely Buck would have laughed off such a bluff anyway.

For Joaquin, it was crystal clear that Ganz had set one target and one target only: the Brixa. He would need to shadow both Ganz and Keltyn during the upcoming night.

He moved to get a better view of the Brixa. She summoned Luz toward her, and they wandered off into the bushes together. Joaquin stole a peek at Ganz, who had parked himself on the wing of the flying machine for a good view of the whole campsite. The man followed Keltyn's every movement, but otherwise did not budge.

When the women returned, Luz tried but failed to persuade Keltyn to share a log with her around the campfire.

For now, the hearty scent of roasting meat trumped all caution. Ysidro pulled the spit off the flame and used his hunting knife to slice portions of rabbit flesh into waiting plates. Luz urged Ysidro for extra and took her dish over to feed Keltyn. The Brixa still sat curled up on the ground, as if staging some kind of protest.

Should he warn her of Ganz's threat? But what if his own estimation was off base? Why punish her with a threat that might not exist? Best to simply shadow her. Finished with his thigh meat, Joaquin sat on a log in the growing darkness, on the perimeter of the firelight, and gnawed on the bones.

Only the crackling of burning logs broke the after-dinner silence. In due course, Ysidro nodded to Buck, his co-conspirator, and pulled out another flask of whisky. After the third swallow, he began singing lewd verses in an undertone, perhaps in feigned deference to female company. Though Joaquin could understand only the outlines, they were enough to make him blush.

Luz, too, seemed uncomfortable. Ysidro was clearly making up verses as he went along, and his word choice left little to the imagination. Soon Luz arose, excused herself, and headed toward her tent. Keltyn stayed put, seemingly tuned only to her inner turmoil.

Sooner or later the Brixa would withdraw to Luz's tent as well. Joaquin slipped away to find a concealed spot at the edge of the trees. Here he could observe the movements of both Keltyn and Ganz without himself being seen. He leaned against a trunk and waited.

One by one, the others wandered off to their tents: first Harry, then Buck, finally the staggering Ysidro. Soon Keltyn was the only one left by the flickering coals. She remained unmoving, hunched over, for at least twenty minutes. Joaquin began to shiver in his spot, and he at least had a coat. The Brixa had still not changed out of her bloodstained tunic.

Finally, she arose and gazed around. The overcast sky showed no moon or stars. It seemed to take her some minutes to adjust to the darkness before heading off toward the trees.

Joaquin moved stealthily to position himself close to her path, but not too close. He watched her silhouette slide past into the brush, heading in the same direction where she had relieved herself earlier.

About twenty seconds later, Joaquin heard more rustling on the path. He tensed. The tall, thin blackness of Ganz's form materialized. One arm stuck out in front of him, and Joaquin sensed more than saw the tip of the gun, that pathetic little excuse for a weapon.

Ganz tiptoed on, now with Joaquin fifteen paces behind, into the darkness of the trees. After another twenty paces, the rustling of leaves ceased. Joaquin craned to listen. Somewhere up ahead came the higher-pitched sound of water dropping on leaves. Then that stopped, and the rustling of footfalls resumed, more audible with each light step.

Joaquin inched closer. As he approached, the silhouette of Ganz's extended arm clearly showed a pointy object at the end.

The Brixa's form drew near, unsuspecting in the pitch black. She advanced to within ten feet of Ganz before stopping. "Who's there?" Her words emerged in a whisper.

"Duck," shouted Joaquin, and, in the same breath, threw all his weight toward Ganz's shooting arm.

The shot was barely audible, as was the dull squish when the bullet struck a nearby tree. Despite the meager force of Joaquin's weight, the surprise of his attack caused Ganz's grip to loosen. He dropped the weapon.

"Let go, damn kid." Ganz used his other hand to try to extricate himself from Joaquin's grasp.

"Brixa," shouted Joaquin. "Grab the gun."

After a moment's stunned hesitation, Keltyn stooped and pawed on the ground until she found it. She picked it up and, holding the tiny thing with both of her small hands, aimed it squarely at Ganz.

Ganz gave up his flailing and stared at Keltyn, as if weighing whether to take a chance and rush her. After watching her unwavering grip on the gun and knowing that she had already slain one man today, he apparently thought better of the idea and raised his hands.

Joaquin led them back, all smiles in the dark. What would he tell Harry? No need: the hidden gun was evidence enough. The chief would confiscate it, and Ganz's goose would be cooked.

25

RESTLESS FAREWELL

Joaquin slipped out of his tent before dawn, anxious as much to distance himself from Ysidro's snoring as to spend a last few moments with the Brixa before they hustled her away.

The first person he spied was Ganz, the silhouette of his tall angular figure strutting back and forth across the length of the campsite. He seemed thoroughly disheveled, arms flailing at his sides, as if trying to shake off some evil spirit. Yet, it occurred to Joaquin, Ganz was the evil spirit.

After Joaquin turned the disarmed villain over to Harry last night, the chief threw a blanket at Ganz and told him to bunk on the ground. He seemed not to notice Joaquin now. In the man's present agitated state, that was just as well.

Joaquin found Keltyn staring into the remains of the fire. From her haggard look, he guessed that she was too shaken to sleep after Ganz's attempt on her life. She likely spent the whole night sitting on a log, staring into the flames.

He set about brewing some maté, glancing at the Brixa every few minutes. Only the offer of a steaming mug seemed to rouse her from her trance.

"Thanks, Scout." She took a sip. "Don't know what I'm going to do without you around."

"Oh, you'll manage," said Joaquin. "I don't suppose you gave any more thought to escaping." He glanced around. "There's still time. Nobody else up yet, except that toady Ganz."

She smiled ruefully. "Forget it."

"Figured you'd say that." Joaquin reached into his pocket and produced half a dozen Venga nuggets. "Got a farewell present for you. Might come in handy when you're feeling 'specially lonely, all cooped up."

Keltyn stared at the nuggets, as if she had never seen Venga before. Then a slow grin appeared as she pocketed them. "That's sweet of you, Joaquin." She leaned over and kissed him on the cheek. "Come to think of it, I have a present for you, too." A twinkle appeared in her eye.

"What?" He was mystified, as the Brixa had nothing left on her person save her still-bloodstained tunic.

By now, there was enough light that he could see where she pointed, in the direction of the tethered horses. "I want you to have Tinto. You've long outgrown that poor pony of yours."

The shock was every bit as much as when Yoka designated him as her heir. This gift, however, touched the depths of his being. Joaquin could find no words to convey his gratitude. The best he could come up with was: "I'll take good care of her until you return."

Reflected in the Brixa's eyes was the same mixture of hope and fear that he himself felt at this moment. "You're an optimist to think that I'll ever make it back here."

"Hey, you been through worse scrapes than this. Just remember, when you're way down in the dumps," he pointed toward the Venga in her pocket, "unleash the power. It's there for you."

The Brixa reached over and tousled his hair. "What a sales pitch. You're a natural, Scout." She sipped on her maté and studied him. "So, you float with the herd until the Rendezvous. Then what?"

Joaquin brightened. "Trieste promised to line me up with some of her customers." He rubbed his hands together. "They try Venga and like the results. After that, it's all word of mouth."

***

Luz woke shortly after first light, but Keltyn had already left the tent. Or had she even come in last night? No way to tell; the bedroll looked untouched. If she was still in her passive state, she might well have spent the whole night staring into the campfire's flames.

As Luz slipped into her breeches, she decided to try once more and shake some fight into the Brixa. She and Joaquin had failed in that attempt yesterday, but there was still time, before Keltyn could be whisked away to whatever sordid fate awaited her back home.

Luz found her hunched forward in front of the fire to ward off the morning cold. Joaquin huddled on the log next to her, both of them sipping maté. Harry and Buck were taking down their tent. One sleeping bag, containing Russell McCoy's body, and another one, half full with piedra de yris, along with the rest of the camp gear, all awaited loading into the flying machine. Luz could tell it would be a tight squeeze.

Ganz shot Luz a sullen glance, just long enough to send a chill racing through her, before resuming his chin-up swagger. The chill remained. His whole demeanor was radically different since yesterday, as if he were lost in his own tortuous world.

She poured a cup of maté and moved to sit on Keltyn's other side. The bags under her friend's eyes testified to lack of sleep. That explained the untouched bedding. Joaquin was smiling but looked equally haggard.

"Did I miss something last night? You guys stay up late for a farewell party?"

The Brixa gave a rueful grin but remained silent.

Joaquin said, "The only thing you missed was another killing."

Luz bugged her eyes, clapped her hand over her mouth, and swung around to count heads. The only one absent was Ysidro. "The jeaf?"

"No." Joaquin laughed. "He's too ornery to die. Actually, no one died, but that creepy Sky-Borne," he nodded in Ganz's direction, "had a little gun, and he tried to use it on the Brixa when no one was looking."

Keltyn hugged Joaquin's shoulder while addressing Luz. "My guardian angel was there to foil it." She put her cup down and pulled Luz closer with her other arm. "I'm really going to miss both you guys. Who's going to root for me when they throw me in the slammer?"

Luz couldn't think of how to respond. She still felt betrayed by the way the Brixa had sided with Trieste about Ian. Then, when she killed Russell McCoy yesterday, Luz had felt the knife twist in her own belly. Not that she harbored any illusions. Russell was no saint, but did anyone deserve so wretched a fate?

Still, Keltyn was family now, always would be, even if they never crossed paths again. For the first time in what seemed ages, she was smiling. Luz reached to embrace her. If ever there was a chance she would listen to sense, it was now. She whispered, "There's still time. Joaquin and I can get you out of here."

The Brixa patted her on the shoulder, then moved to arm's length and looked her straight in the eye. "We already peeked down that rabbit hole, honey. I don't claim to think straight yet, but it looked like a dead end yesterday, and it still does today."

Luz clenched her fists and shook her arms free from Keltyn's grasp. "Then it's up to you to come up with a better plan. Right now, you're just giving up. How pathetic is that, after all these months you've been preaching resistance?" She looked toward Joaquin to confirm her anger.

He seemed reluctant to take sides, finally allowing, "Luz is right, Brixa. You will disappoint a lot our people, taking the first chance to fly back home."

Keltyn stood up and started pacing with her hands clasped behind her back. A moment later, her eye landed on Ganz, in virtually the same posture, and she stopped abruptly. She sat back down and held her head between her hands, face down.

"Sorry, guys. I'm not cut out to be a fugitive. This just feels like the only way, if there is a way, to stop Oscar Bailey, and whomever else he has recruited to colonize your homeland." She looked up and searched each of their faces in turn. "Don't you see? If I flee now, it's like admitting my guilt. Russell McCoy becomes a martyr, whose name Bailey can use as a rallying point for future colonists. And when they come, they will have no qualms in retaliating by killing your people."

Luz tried to imagine this army of Sky-Bornes, arriving in larger numbers, carrying weapons more sophisticated than Buck's little stun gun. The picture left her nauseous, to the point where she clutched her stomach and covered her mouth. She could not bring herself to ask the Brixa more questions.

Joaquin spoke up. "So, what you expect to do when they throw you in jail? Like that's supposed to stop this Oscar Bailey somehow? I don't get it."

The Brixa gazed skyward, as if praying. "I'll get a trial sooner or later, a chance to plead my case. Too many people know about me to keep it under wraps. Orfea, for instance, and I'm sure she has allies."

Joaquin curled his lip at the mention of Orfea, no doubt trying to picture how this gushy woman could possibly be an effective advocate. "You killed someone, and you admit it. What will this trial gain you?"

"There were extenuating circumstances." Her jaw clenched. "You were both there. You saw it all." She whirled to face Luz. "And you gave a full account to Harry."

Luz uncovered her mouth and took a deep breath. "I did my best. I spoke into his machine. He played my voice back so I could listen to my words and made me clarify details."

Keltyn lifted her chin. "I'll be vindicated, sooner or later. I know it. And even while I'm sitting in jail, I will represent you and the rest of the Onwei. The more of my people who know about your people, the better your chances."

"I hope you are right," said Luz, though she herself was not at all convinced. Tears gathered as she once again reached out to hug her friend.

She spied Ysidro. He had just poured maté into one of the Sky-Bornes' mugs and sauntered toward the three of them. She hurried to dab her eyes dry.

"Oh, *chicas* crying. Brixa leaving. Why you spoil my fiesta by killing that man?"

"Sorry, jeaf," said Keltyn. She set her lips tight.

"Was accident, right? Efrain should never give big hunting knife to little Brixa."

Keltyn closed her eyes and nodded. A second later, the eyes snapped open. "Jeaf, you've got to explain to Efrain. He's the one I really let down."

"No worry. I can handle my nephew." Ysidro bent down and lifted her chin with one finger. "Hey. You gonna get through this. I guarantee it. You bravest woman I ever met."

He turned to Joaquin. "Boy, come with me. Make clear to Harry and Buck. I hold them responsible. They don't get Brixa free, don't bother come back next time." He gave a thumbs up sign to Keltyn before heading off.

Keltyn smiled and grabbed Luz's arm. "There you have it, a personal guarantee from the jeaf. He ain't worried, I ain't worried, no reason for you to worry. And you must explain to your mother. All she did for me, took me in, taught me so much about the stone. Promise her I will return."

Now Luz felt a tinge of the same anger and jealousy that had crept upon her back in Nomidar: the Brixa siding with Trieste against her, compounded by her mother teaching Keltyn all the secrets of her joya trade.

"I will take only as much stone as Mother can craft at a time. No use hoarding it. Mother's vision is fading. She was grooming *you* to take over the trade," Luz clenched her eyes and fists, "but now they will take you away, and we'll never see you again."

But Keltyn held her gaze steadfast. Finally, Luz nodded. "I promise." She tried her bravest smile. If worry was contagious, then so could courage be. They exchanged hugs for the last time.

Out of the corner of her eye, Luz could see the jeaf confer with Harry and Buck. Three heads nodded and glanced at the Brixa. Finally, Harry approached her. "It's time, ma chère."

Keltyn stood and eyed Ganz, still pacing like a madman. "Do I have to sit next to him the whole way back?"

Harry peered at her over the rims of his vision aids. "His legs are too long to fit in the jump seat. We need every square foot of cargo space."

"Fine. Put me in the jump seat. You can even stick a load under my feet."

Harry raised his eyebrows and shrugged. He turned and waved, trying to attract Ganz's attention, without success. He marched up and confronted him. Ganz blinked several times, then loped over toward the flying machine.

Buck winced as he picked up one end of the sleeping bag containing Russell McCoy's corpse, the only cargo left unloaded, and dragged it backward toward the hatch. Ganz also flinched as he picked up the other end of the bag, and together they hoisted it onto the wing, then muscled the load into a rear seat and strapped it in.

Luz could barely see the figure of Keltyn, snuggled in the jump seat, contorting her face and trying to lean away from the corpse. Ganz and Harry appeared equally pained.

Buck stood on the wing and laughed. "It won't be so bad once we get going. Thank God for air filters." He turned and waved to Ysidro, Joaquin and Luz.

She raised her arm, more in a salute than a farewell. Minutes later, the flying machine eased up onto its tail. Luz began a slow count, raising her head an inch at a time, trying to follow its path. By the time she reached thirty, it had disappeared from sight.

What now? She felt a great big void inside, like a crater. The flying machine, that malign giant bird that first transported Keltyn here, landed first at Splat Crater, not five miles from the spot where she and Joaquin now stood. The bird departed once, leaving a wounded Keltyn behind. Luz's tribe nursed her back to health and took her in. Now the bird swooped down a second time and sucked the helpless Brixa back into its fold. What power did Luz or her people have over supernatural forces such as this winged menace?

Maybe none, but Luz would be damned if she would roll over and play dead. The Sky-Bornes would be back, even if the Brixa might not. Next time, Luz would be prepared, no longer to be seduced by their books and machines. The fate of her people depended upon it.

26

TAKING THE RAP

"Sit down, Ganz. You make me nervous, standing there like a robot." Sir Oscar Bailey thumbed through Ganz's report.

"Sorry, sir. It's just the way I was brought up, to show respect in the presence of authority." Ganz lowered his frame into the armchair across from Bailey's oversized desk.

"I know, I know. You had a disciplined upbringing, served you well for the past fifteen years. You are one of my brightest stars." He paused and dropped the report back on the desk. His eyes darkened. "Or need I say 'you *were.*' Tell me this."

"Sir?" Ganz knew what was coming next and cringed.

"How could you be so dumb?"

Ganz opened his mouth and closed it immediately. He had prepared a little speech in self-defense, but now it struck him as futile. His lips tightened. Yet, this might well be his only chance to salvage his position. He needed to frame the sordid episode to look like he was only carrying out Sir Oscar's wishes. To the extent he understood those wishes, that was true.

His boss probed once more. "I mean, what were you thinking?"

Ganz felt Bailey's gimlet eyes bore right through to his soul. "I don't know, sir. At the time, I suspected that Savant SparrowHawk was trying to escape under cover of darkness."

"Did you now? I might believe that presumption if I hadn't already been briefed by Harry Ladou."

"Sir, begging your pardon, but what you said before the mission about Harry being under a lot of stress, I'm afraid that did affect his judgment at several crucial turns."

Sir Oscar smiled. "The possibility of biased recall did occur to me, Ganz, so I interviewed Buck Kranepool. His account backs up Harry's in every detail."

Ganz felt trapped. Still, SparrowHawk must have at least considered trying to escape. She would be a fool not to, what with the serious charges awaiting here. "I stand by my story, sir."

"Have you and Harry compared notes, I wonder?"

"Uh, not so much, sir. He became rather standoffish after..."

"After he relieved you of your little firearm, you mean? The one you were untrained in, unlicensed for, and unauthorized to bring along." Bailey shook his head slowly. "It may interest you to know that Harry interviewed the girl who witnessed Savant McCoy's death. It seems that, despite the earnest pleas of her young friends to provide a means for her to escape before the body was discovered, Savant SparrowHawk repeatedly declined the opportunity."

Ganz said nothing. He wanted to swallow, but his mouth felt parched. He was glad to no longer be standing at attention.

Bailey continued. "It's clear, to me at least, that she was willing to let herself be taken into custody in order to claim a certain amount of cargo space that would otherwise be taken up by iridium ore. Could that idea possibly have swayed you after you worked so hard to gather the prize?"

Ganz shivered a quick shake of his head.

"Your quick denial might be more plausible had you not, according to Harry and Buck, already pushed to inter McCoy's body on the spot, rather than bring it back home." Bailey's brow lifted to invite rebuttal of this claim, but Ganz knew he was trapped.

He tried one last gambit, knowing the risk it carried. He still had Sir Oscar's written authorization. "Sir, the fact is, Savant SparrowHawk is a self-confessed killer, who had the motive and opportunity for escape. It was pitch dark when I took the shot. As you say, I have no experience with firearms. I was merely following your directive to neutralize her if necessary. Under these dire circumstances..."

Bailey cut him off abruptly. "Relax, Ganz. I'm not after a scapegoat."

Ganz breathed a sigh of relief. In the few seconds it took for him to remind Sir Oscar of his complicity, his boss changed his tune entirely.

"When the official inquiry comes around, you'll likely get off with a slap on the wrist and a fine for carrying an unauthorized weapon." Sir Oscar shifted in his seat. "Now, on the plus side, it appears that you were successful in swaying the chief to allow iridium mining."

Ganz sat up. "Yes, sir. He seems to have been won over."

"That's a good thing. I'll definitely need more ore if I'm going to build a standard-sized transport ship that can withstand the Hurricane Belt."

"Oh," said Ganz. "I had hoped this would be enough. Would it have made a difference if...?" He needed to phrase this delicately.

Oscar chuckled. "If those two extra bodies were jettisoned, you mean? I don't know, Ganz. The metallurgy boys haven't examined your find yet. I wouldn't lose any sleep over it, though. You paved the way so that future missions won't have to watch their backsides for hostile locals."

Ganz puffed out his chest. "Thank you, sir. If you wish for me to serve on the next mission as well, I'll be ready. I dare say that preparing by learning the local language made the negotiation go smoother, and we must anticipate ongoing contact with these people." He felt on solid ground here.

Bailey closed his eyes and worked his lower lip. "I don't know, Ganz. We'll see." The eyes sprung open. "Before I can even consider another mission, we've got to break this terrorist gang. Some key arrests are imminent, and I'll need your legal expertise to work with the prosecutors. Oh, and another thing."

"Sir?"

"Time to brush up on your Chinese. Their government seems sorely inflamed about our recent Antarctic venture, though I fail to see what all the fuss is about. No one is stopping them if they wish to follow our lead. Instead, they're picking up their marbles and slapping exorbitant tariffs on cold fusion exports. How petty is that, Ganz?"

"Certainly seems that way, sir."

"I'll need you to talk some sense into them. Start with their Zürich consul."

"I...I understood Savant Del Campo was involved in that aspect, sir."

"Savant Del Campo will soon be indisposed, for an indefinite period of time. Confidential for now, got that?"

"Yes, sir. You can count on me, sir." Ganz stood and clicked his heels.

***

Fay eased herself into the soft leather bench seat across from Harry. They were in a booth at Chez Boulay Bistro Boreal. It had been only a few months since their previous meeting here, but Fay felt a distinct change. His voice, when they made the date, did not sound all that reassuring.

First, of course, she needed to test the waters on their budding romance, or at least what had seemed like the start of one before Harry's tailspin. If he was still game, there was much else to catch up on: Keltyn SparrowHawk, the escalating trade war with China, and a certain pesky detail that sat in her handbag.

The waiter took their drink order and left them to page through the all-French menu. Fay only pretended to study it; she was perfectly comfortable to let Monsieur Quebecois suggest the cuisine. Fay had no business reason to be in Quebec this time, no telly appearance, no Native Peoples United meeting. It was just the most convenient spot to meet Harry without attracting attention.

After the waiter had taken their entree orders — Harry suggested the *boeuf flambeau* — they clinked cocktail glasses. Fay wanted to savor the moment and divine meaning out of Harry's unreadable brown eyes. Yet she was unable to make heads or tails of his mood. Instead, she took one sip of her Campari and reached into her handbag, pulling out the laminated ID badge.

"Know anything about these?" She held it up for Harry.

"One of ours. Not a very flattering shot, sorry to say."

"Thanks for your sympathy." Fay turned it over and inspected it. "I get the impression that these can somehow,

I haven't yet figured out how, be used for…surveillance."
She quickly eyed Harry to see if her last word triggered
any reaction.

"Let's have a look," he said. He held it close and
studied the squiggles under Fay's name. Even with the
dim lighting in their booth, she could see the color slowly
drain from his face. "Where did you get this?"

"At the front gate of Bailey Europe HQ, in Zürich.
Why?"

"How long ago?" Harry tried to crumple the badge in
his fist, but the plastic was too tough for attempted
defacing.

"A couple of months. The Chinese consulate recruited
me to pass on a message to Sir Oscar. A hookup from
Bailey Europe seemed like the most expedient way."

Harry waved the badge in front of Fay. "This ID has
a bug embedded."

"Ha." Her suspicion was vindicated. "That explains
several things, but how can you tell?"

"This code, we routinely use it for surveillance when
we want to track a visitor after he or she leaves our facility."

"Like for industrial spying."

Harry nodded. "Was Ganz there that day when you
visited HQ?"

"Why, yes. Should I have been concerned by that?"

"Twenty-twenty hindsight, but no reason to suspect
at the time. Have you been carrying this with you ever
since?"

"Afraid so."

Harry took a deep draught of his drink and set it down. He reached across the table for Fay's hand and kissed it. "Oscar's got the goods on me now. They know all about us."

"No!" Fay slumped in her seat. She had surmised only some vague breach of her privacy. The entrees arrived, but her appetite had suddenly vanished.

"Someone could connect the dots easily enough. Ganz most likely. He had access to my travel log, and he could track your badge. That night in Geneva, for instance."

Fay stared at the little plastic card. "Surely it can't signal GPS coordinates on another continent."

Harry smiled ruefully. "Another innovation for Bailey Enterprises. Don't worry, we haven't figured out how to encode a bug into your DNA. Yet. This is the last spot they're going to be able to link us together. Now don't let your bouef get cold." He signaled for the waiter. "How about a bottle of red? We've got lots to catch up on."

Ten minutes later, just as they were sipping their wine, Fay noted the color in Harry's face suddenly drain once again. His eye had caught something behind her. She turned to see a pencil-mustached mousey man in a leather coat, accompanied by a young, sturdy, uniformed policeman. They strode to Fay's table, and the official flashed his I.D. at her. She caught a puff of cheap men's cologne.

"Madame Orfea Del Campo?"

"Oui?" Her brows shot up.

The man gave a stiff nod. "Inspector Pierre Mournay, Canadian Security Intelligence Service." He reached into his breast pocket and held out a document for her. "I have a warrant for your arrest."

Fay gaped at this piece of paper, uncomprehending. Something had to be terribly wrong.

Harry jumped up and snatched it. "Let me see that." He scanned it quickly and looked at Fay. "You're to be held as leader of an organization suspected of terrorist acts and accomplice before the fact."

"NPU? That's ridiculous."

"I am sorry, Madame. I have my orders. Please let us avoid making a scene." Mournay tried out his best mousey smile and extended his hand. "Come."

"I will not." She gazed up at Harry. "Can't you do something? Call Sir Oscar. Surely he can fix this."

Harry opened his mouth to say something but shut it just as quickly.

Mournay cleared his throat. "Pardon, Madame. You refer to Sir Oscar Bailey?"

"Indeed, I do, and this is Monsieur Harry Ladou, his second-in-command."

Mournay took in Harry and hesitated a moment. "Then it is my sad duty to inform both of you that Sir Oscar Bailey is the person pressing charges against your organization."

Harry now seemed more stunned than Fay. He sputtered, "Pressing charges is one thing, but you need hard evidence to make an arrest."

Mournay frowned. "Please, monsieur, do not lecture me on my job. We have all the evidence we need to issue this warrant."

Harry shook his head slowly, but Fay could tell that her hopes to avoid arrest had just gone up in smoke. She gathered her things. The Bailey ID badge, surely the means by which they tracked her down, she flung at Harry. He glanced at it and returned Fay's gaze with a mixture of fear and puzzlement. Then he shut his eyes, began to sway, and had to clasp the table's edge for support.

Fay stood up, chin held high. "I assume calls are allowed from your jail."

Another formal nod from Mournay. "*Mais oui, Madame.*"

She clenched her lips and strode away between Mournay and the uniform.

So long as she had outside communication, she could fight this. Harry might or might not go to bat for her, though her gut told her not to count on it. Still, she had legal contacts, plus Greta, plus her staff and colleagues at NPU.

What she did not have was any idea who was behind these terrorist attacks. Had anyone else from NPU been arrested? Oscar Bailey was playing hardball and, like it or not, she would need to do the same.

27

GROUNDED

I sat cross-legged on my bed, playing solitaire. Across the room the muted telly broadcast news. Talking heads alternated with footage of ocean waves crashing against twenty-foot-high concrete dikes. A map of Canada beeped red dots to denote recent or imminent flooding on the Arctic perimeter.

Even before my involuntary exile to the other end of the world, I had never paid attention to the news. Yet that was all they allowed me now. I peeked through my fingers at the telly screen. More shots of storms whipping across the prairies of northern Canada.

During the long day's ride back on Bailey Voyager, cramped in the jump-seat between a corpse and great stash of iridium ore, the realization sunk in: I could not afford to remain passive. I had surrendered myself too meekly after killing Russell McCoy. If I wished to regain my freedom, let alone become a voice for my adopted people, I needed to forge a connection with the outside world when I returned to Canada.

A noble agenda. The problem was, I had only the flimsiest of resources to work with. The isolation of this meagerly furnished room, my new home for the past two weeks, had already sapped my resolve. It sat on the edge of the sprawling Bailey HQ campus in northern Alberta, one of an identical row of twenty or so "guest suites" for low-level visitors to HQ, flown in from distant parts of the Bailey empire scattered all over Canada and Europe. I gathered they were handpicked, sent to learn some product or process, enough to make them experts when they returned home.

As far as I could tell from the brief encounters I had with other guests on my outdoor exercise breaks, I was the only one confined here involuntarily. If I needed any proof, I had only to glance down at my ankle bracelet. I felt as cooped as a barnyard chicken.

Yet I wasn't in solitary confinement. There was no reason I might not befriend one of these guest technicians from other Bailey plants. The only barrier was my own will.

Chatting up strangers had never come easy to me, but I had to do something, anything to combat the deep inertia smothering my soul. I had no idea how long I could survive this state of enclosure and isolation. A few more weeks and I would likely cop any plea, confess to any charge they threw at me, just to get the waiting over with.

Minutes that seemed like hours passed before I regained the energy to sit up straight. I arose and splashed water on my face in the tiny bathroom. The overcast, blustery weather had kept me indoors all day, but now I switched off the telly and put on shoes and jacket for a walk outside. Perhaps I would run into the same girl I had spied yesterday, a young woman who, from her complexion and high cheekbones, I figured must also be First Peoples.

The fenced-in courtyard, surrounded by a row of single-story guest units, reminded me of recess at grammar school. Half a dozen other guests, mostly young men and women my age, paced around the perimeter of the yard in ones and twos, hunched forward against the wind. At this hour of the afternoon, they were likely done with the day's instruction but, with no transportation to town and a limited expense account, were stuck in the compound just like me.

I recognized the girl I was after and picked up my pace until drawing abreast. Like me, the girl wore nondescript shirt, jacket and breeches. She smelled of peach-scented soap.

"Mind if I join you? My name's Keltyn SparrowHawk."

"Lavinia Martelle." The girl smiled shyly, glancing at me only briefly before returning her gaze to the space in front of her.

"Where ya from?"

"Sudbury."

My heart skipped a beat. Good karma. "No kidding. Me too. You work at the lab there?"

"Yup. Materials Science."

"Great field. Lots of opportunities."

"I know. I started out as a tech. Now they're paying me to take this QA course. With enough continuing ed, I'll get promoted to scientist." Lavinia seemed brightened by this prospect. She turned to me. "How about you?"

Stay cool. "Geologist."

"Neat. What are you working on?"

"Well, I invented something important, and now I'm taking a break."

The girl seemed puzzled. "So, what are you doing here?"

"Long story." I nodded.

Lavinia raised her brows. "Try me. I'm a good listener."

"Okay. You asked for it." I paused. "I killed a man."

The girl drew back and stopped dead in her tracks. "Really?"

I stopped too. "Really, and not just anyone. My teacher."

Lavinia clasped her hand over her mouth. "But why?"

"Best leave that be."

"Uh, okay. Did you turn yourself in?"

"Yup, and then I had to spend twelve hours on a plane with his festering corpse, stuffed in a sleeping bag, sitting next to me. Enough gory details?"

"I guess so. I mean, no, tell me more."

"Then c'mon, I need to keep walking." I flapped my arms against the chill.

"So, what's going to happen to you?"

"I'll get a trial, but not just for murder. You're looking at someone also charged with, are you ready for this…?"

Lavinia nodded, eyes wide as saucers.

"Industrial espionage, fraud, and treason."

The girl let out a whistle. "I hope you've got a good lawyer."

"Pretty hard to get a good lawyer when you're broke."

"But…you're a geologist. You must have savings."

"All my assets were frozen eighteen months ago. That's how long I've been out of circulation."

"Won't the courts appoint a lawyer for you?"

"Oh, honey. Where have you been?" I was appalled by Lavinia's naiveté. "No counsel for indigents. The system has become way too backlogged. That, and they claim modern forensics is so finely tuned, the chances of wrongful conviction are minute, if you can believe that."

The girl grabbed my hand. "That's awful. What will they do to you?"

"Dunno, though I doubt they'll execute me. You have to do worse than murder these days to warrant the death penalty. Still, I expect some ambitious prosecutor will try to resurrect it for all of my heinous crimes combined. More likely, I'll get years and years in the slammer. End of geology career, back to a lifetime of menial labor."

The girl slumped. "So now you just have to wait, until the system chews you up and spits you out."

I ran my fingers across my eyes. "Not quite ready to throw in the towel yet, honey." I smiled. "Ever heard of Bertram Casey?"

"That old windbag commentator on Third Millennium News?"

"The same. That's all they've let me do since cooping me up here, watch the damn telly and walk around the yard. The other day he was on, ranting his views on a subject he knows very little about, on which I would love to set him straight. And I'm willing to bet that TMN would pay handsomely for the privilege of an interview."

Lavinia clapped her hands silently. "Great. That fee should pay for your lawyer."

"It better. That's the *only* reason I would do it. Bertram Casey will have all kinds of biases about the time I spent with what he calls a 'preliterate tribe.'" I mimicked his biting diction. "'What was your most frustrating experience in communicating with these people, Savant SparrowHawk?'"

Lavinia giggled, "Well, good luck with that."

"There's a catch, though." I glanced around to see if anyone else was within earshot. "Bailey Security has kept my incarceration secret. I've got absolutely no way to get the word to TMN, unless…" I leaned in, "someone was willing to pass them a message on my behalf."

The girl drew back. "Don't look at me. They'd probably fire me if they found out I aided you." She checked to see if others were watching. "Fact is, I probably shouldn't even be talking to you. Don't you have any family?"

My turn to slump. "Just my mother, and she's beyond being able to help me." Suddenly, another thought assailed me. "Listen, Lavinia, when do you return to Sudbury?"

"Tomorrow."

"Can you do me just one little favor?"

"Long as it won't get me into trouble."

"Take my picture now, then look up my mother and show it to her when you get back. You're First Peoples; she'll trust you. She has no idea if I'm dead or alive. If she would ever see me on a telly appearance with no warning, the shock might be too much for her."

Lavinia stopped walking and fished in her pocket. "Sure, but what was that you said about this tribe?"

"Yup, in Antarctica."

The girl froze. "Oh my God, you're one of the crew from Bailey Voyager last year, the one they left for dead." She rushed to get her mobile ready.

I smiled. "That would be me, still alive and kicking." I beamed as Lavinia took the picture, then I keyed in my mother's address. When I looked up, the girl's expression had shifted. A moment ago, it had been suspicious, fearful. Now her eyes resumed their awestruck luster.

"What do you say, girl? All you have to do is phone in an anonymous tip to TMN: 'Keltyn SparrowHawk

wants to set the record straight with Bertram Casey.'
They'll track down my whereabouts; Bailey Security can't
keep me incognito forever, not if I'm facing trial."

Lavinia checked again to see if they were being spied
upon, then raised a pair of crossed fingers, winked at me
and scampered off.

I watched the girl leave and crossed my own fingers,
as a ray of sunshine peeked through the clouds.

THE END

ACKNOWLEDGEMENTS

Catherine Reed: for "SparrowHawk," and for your patience with my obsession.

Adrienne Sinclair: for suggesting the unlikely romance between Keltyn SparrowHawk and gaucho Efrain Correon.

And especially, Loren Oberweger, my editor: for guiding me through multiple re-writes, until these stories became publishable.

IMAGE SOURCES

The following images were used with permission.

Prologue: No-Jang mask — Korean-Arts, www.korean-arts.com.

Chapter 1: Alt. Huichol beaded skull — Photo Juan Pablo Marakame. Artist Sergio Bautista de la Cruz.

Chapter 2: Bulgarian carved wood mask — David J. Rooke, Weird Wood.

Chapter 5: African wooden mask — WorldofBacara, Leawood, KS.

Chapter 6: Terracotta masks, India — Unknown artist, via www.dollsofindia.com.

Chapter 7: Copper alloy Yorùbá mask, Nigeria — Ali Amonikoyi, ca. 1910. Photo © Brooklyn Museum.

Chapter 8: "Beautiful Face," Ghana — A.A. Mohamadu, Novica.

Chapter 9: General Guan Yu, Chinese — Photo by Paul Stanley Noll. Estate of paulnoll.com.

Chapter 10: American Indian Horse Masks — Hawk Hill Press.

Chapter 11: Maya stone princess mask, Mexico, Papier Mache — Morneo, Novica.

Chapter 12: Beaded Luba mask, Congo — Photo by Gary Stern, Nontando.

Chapter 13: Four Chinese opera masks — Betsey's Beauties.

Chapter 14: Akiti Beauty African wood mask — Theophilus Sackey, Novica.

Chapter 15: Hahoetal Bune (concubine), Korea — Emily Overes, HairOfTheFrog.

Chapter 16: Wooden mask (Pwemwe), New Caledonia, Pacific Is. — Kanak culture, early 20th century. Photo © Brooklyn Museum.

Chapter 19: Red devil mask, Guanojuato, MX — Karen Elwell photo.

Chapter 20: Sun and Moon Ceramic, "Nature's Eclipse" — Eufrosia Pantaleon, Novica.

Chapter 22: Bak'was Wild Man mask — John H. Livingston. Photo © Brooklyn Museum.

Chapter 23: Dzunuk'wa Cannibal Woman mask, Vancouver Island, B.C. — © Brooklyn Museum.

Chapter 24: Korean traditional mask used in Yangju Pyeolsandae Nori dance — Robert Ibold, Masks of the World.

Chapter 27: Bété Nyabwa Spider Mask, Liberia — AfricaDirect.com.

End: Topeng old demon mask, Bali — Ages Tribal Arts.

ABOUT THE AUTHOR

Norman Westhoff is a retired physician and geography buff.

He has visited all of the ice-free continents.

He lives in Lawrence, Kansas.

Alamos, Mexico 2018